DISCRETION IS VALOR

A NOVEL OF FACTUAL AND GRIEVOUS HISTORY PERTAINING TO THE CHÍHENNE AND MESCALERO APACHE

BY

J. HOOLIHAN CLAYTON

AUTHOR OF

COMMENDABLE DISCRETION,

WITH GREAT DISCRETION,

SMALL LIGHT OF DISCRETION

*WITH ILLUSTRATIONS AND ENGRAVINGS
FROM HARPERS WEEKLY AND FRANK LESLIE'S
ILLUSTRATED NEWSPAPER*

DOG SOLDIER PRESS

TAOS

Published in July 2024 by
Dog Soldier Press, PO Box 1782,
Ranchos de Taos, NM 87557
dogsoldierpress.com

Graphic Design: book interior and cover
Ananda M. Sundari
visionaryalchemy.art

Library of Congress Control Number: 2024942952

Print ISBN: 979-8-9877380-3-0
ePub ISBN: 979-8-9877380-5-4

*"To die is to be a counterfeit, for he is but the coun-
terfeit of a man who hath not the life of a man; but to
counterfeit dying when a man thereby liveth is to be
no counterfeit, but the true and perfect image of life
indeed. The better part of valour is discretion, in the
which better part I have saved my life."*

Henry IV Part 1, Act V, Scene 4
- William Shakespeare -

*"My Country! When right keep it right;
when wrong, set it right!"*

- Carl Schurz, Secretary of the Interior, 1877-1881

*"The Indian commands respect for his rights only so
long as he inspires terror for his rifle."*

- General George R. Crook -

"These Indians were promised by various Agents of the Indian Department that they were always to remain on the Reservation at Ojo Caliente... and as this promise has been deliberately violated is one reason they are so bitter. Never were Indians in better condition to fight.

"Victorio must either scatter his Indians in small Bands or in all probability we shall kill or capture him."

- Edward Hatch, Colonel Ninth Cavalry, Commanding -

"Victorio is no common foe, and is worthy of the best soldiers steel. He was looked upon with unsparing contempt when he commenced this murderous war. No one can so regard him now. For long weary months he has been reeking with blood and pillage. More than a hundred of our fellow citizens have fallen victims, thousands upon thousands fails to cover the loss of property – and no one has arisen to stay the renegade's murderous hand. It has been one uninterrupted career of murder, and now he sits in his camp rioting on his plunder, and drunken with the blood of the white man. The contempt he feels for his enemies, he is not fastidious in showing. He never misses an opportunity of sending a message of defiance and hate to the foe he so despises. He has spared the lives of prisoners, that he might send them back as a token of his scorn."

- Grant County Herald, March 27, 1880 -

"Forces under Hatch and Grierson are expected to join at the Mescalero Agency on or about April 12th to capture every Indian there, any who may be caught outside or driven in and hold them. Afterward to scout the country to bring in all the women & children and controlling the issue of provisions it will be a short time only before we hope to get them all and place them in such condition (and keep them so) that they will here-after be harmless. This is what I propose and hope to accomplish."

- General John Pope, Commander
Department of the Missouri -

"You are stronger than we. We have fought you as long as we had rifles and powder; but your weapons are better than ours. Give us weapons and turn us loose and we will fight you again; but we are worn out. We have no more heart. We have no provisions, no means to live. Your troops are everywhere... You have driven us from our last and best stronghold and we have no more heart. Do with us as may seem good to you, but do not forget we are men and braves."

- Cadete, Principal chief of the Mescalero Apache -

"Some important move is in progress near the Mescalero Reservation under Hatch's personal supervision. General Sherman telegraphed last night that if possible an end will be put to these annual outbreaks; that Hatch need not regard the boundaries of the departments and must not allow the enemy to claim safe refuge in the Indian reservation. When made captives they will be stripped of arms and horses, and held as prisoners, some to be surrendered to the civil authorities for trial, and others to work in the stone quarries at Fort Leavenworth."

- The Rocky Mountain News, April 15, 1880 -

"I forbear to comment upon such an exhibition of bad faith, such cruel treatment of the innocent for the sins of the guilty."

- Honorable R.E. Trowbridge.
Commissioner of Indian Affairs -

"We want our horses given back to us."

- Nautzilli, Head chief of the Mescalero Apache -

DRAMATIS PERSONÆ

PRINCIPAL AND SUBORDINATE HISTORICAL FIGURES INCLUDED IN THIS BOOK

CARL SCHURZ   Secretary, U.S. Department of the Interior, 1877-1881.

ROWLAND E. TROWBRIDGE   Commissioner of Indian Affairs, 1880-1881.

GRANVILLE STUART AND BROTHERS   Prospectors, homesteaders, founders of Deer Lodge, Montana.

CHARLES ILFELD   Proprietor of one of the largest mercantile establishments in New Mexico Territory.

ALEXANDER GRZELACHOWSKI   Polish Catholic priest and businessman based in Puerto de Luna. Spoke Latin, Polish, Spanish and Greek.

RICHARD DUNN   Business partner of Grzelachowski. A well-educated immigrant from Nova Scotia.

JOHN CHISUM   Cattle baron from Texas and one-time business partner of Charles Goodnight. Beef contractor to the military, political kingpin. Notorious for protecting his own interests.

VICTORIO   Principal chief of the Chíhenne Apache people. Brilliant strategist and accomplished guerilla fighter, repeatedly betrayed and deceived by U.S. government and military.

COLONEL EDWARD HATCH   Commander of 9th Cavalry and District of New Mexico.

ANDREW KELLEY   Sutler, supposed friend to Chíhenne Apache.

JOHN SULLIVAN   Discharged from military in New Mexico. Became merchant, postmaster and farmer in Cañada Alamosa.

ALEMÁN   Spanish translation of English word 'German.'

Bernardo Gruber, a German merchant, fleeing accusations of witchcraft in 1670, died in the desert of Nuevo Mexico. La Jornada del Muerto (Journey of the Dead Man) and Alemán spring and ranch were named for Gruber.

JACK MARTIN Discharged from military in New Mexico. Ventured to vicinity of Alemán spring (a seasonal water source in La Jornada del Muerto) in 1867. By blasting with gunpowder, he established a permanent well and thereby a stage station, hotel and cattle ranch.

JESUS OCHOA Employee of Jack Martin and his widow.

ALBERT JENNINGS FOUNTAIN Discharged from military in New Mexico. Attorney who represented Mexican landowners and a Mescalero Apache chief against the U.S. Army and challenged violent takeover of Texas cattlemen and rustlers. Founded a newspaper and was elected to New Mexico Territorial Legislature. Murdered in 1896 along with his eight-year-old son. Their bodies were never found.

MESILLA SCOUTS Militia, made up of mostly local Mexican men, established to defend town of Mesilla from Indian attack. Albert Fountain was Captain and later Colonel of the Mesilla Scouts, despite cordial relationships with many Mescalero Apache.

ANA FREDERICK Proprietor of the Hotel Union in Tularosa, New Mexico Territory.

PATRICK COGHLAN Known as the "King of Tularosa." Irish immigrant from County Cork, owner of substantial businesses, land and herds of cattle in and around Tularosa. Probably responsible for the illegal eviction of many Mexican landowners and for the paid assassination of the entire Nesmith family. Purchased stolen cattle from rustlers to fulfill military contracts.

JOSEPH BLAZER Owner of sawmill, farmlands and cattle ranch within the boundaries of the Mescalero Apache reservation. Honest businessman, known for fair dealing with Apache people.

ALMER BLAZER Joseph Blazer's son.

AGENT SAMUEL RUSSELL Indian agent for Mescalero Apache. Former agent for Capote Utes and Jicarilla Apache at Abiquiu Agency. Probably the only Indian agent assigned to Mescalero Agency not accused of fraud.

DR. N.J. CARTER Agency physician and friend of Agent Russell.

NAUTZILLI Principal chief of Mescalero Apache, advocate of peace and welfare for his people.

CABALLO/CABALLERO (also CABALLESO) Principal chief of Mescalero Apache, given permission by Agent Russell to contact Victorio and attempt to bring him in. Probably joined Victorio and was killed.

SAN JUAN Principal chief of Mescalero Apache. Given permission to search for Caballero. Joined Victorio and survived to return to Mescalero Agency.

CADETE Principal chief of Mescalero Apache. Spokesman for Mescalero Apache at Bosque Redondo. Known for integrity, intelligence, dedication to peaceful relations with whites and resistance to the sale of whisky to Mescalero people. Murdered after providing testimony against a whisky trader in Mesilla.

LAWRENCE GUSTAVE MURPHY Irish immigrant. Discharged from military in New Mexico. Fort Stanton sutler, dishonest military contractor, bootlegger and whisky trader, member of political machine based in Santa Fe, part owner of bank, saloon and dry goods store in Lincoln.

JAMES DOLAN Irish immigrant. Discharged from military in New Mexico. Business partner of L.G. Murphy. Pivotal in Lincoln County War.

LIEUTENANT GARST Post adjutant, Fort Stanton 1880.

CAPTAIN CHARLES STEELHAMMER Captain of 15th

Infantry. Transferred to Fort Stanton due to health issues. Temporary post commander Fort Stanton April 1880.

MAJOR CLARENCE MAUCK Assigned as post commander for Fort Stanton May to September 1880. Died of tuberculosis 1881.

GEORGE W. MAXWELL Post trader at Fort Stanton and Apache interpreter. Provided eye witness testimony to J.L Mahan, U.S. Indian Inspector, regarding events of April 16, 1880 on Mescalero Apache reservation.

THOMAS HART BENTON ("Old Bullion") U.S. senator 1821-1851. Father-in-law of John Frémont, uncompromising proponent of American expansionism.

JOHN C. FRÉMONT Explorer, opportunist, failed politician and soldier.

GENERAL STEPHEN WATTS KEARNY Commander Army of the West. Military invader of Mexican territory.

WILLIAM WATTS HART DAVIS Served in Mexican-American War and lived in New Mexico Territory from 1853 to 1857. Historian and author of two books pertaining to New Mexico.

LUCIEN BONAPARTE MAXWELL Owned vast tracts of land in New Mexico Territory acquired through marriage and speculation. Scouted for military in campaigns against the Utes. Friend of Frémont and "Kit" Carson.

KEMP G. COOPER Purchased Rocky Mountain News from founder, William Byers.

SANTA FE RING Cadre of corrupt lawyers, shady real estate investors and businessmen, unethical politicians and their minions. Involved in illegal acquisition of Spanish land grants, range wars and the dispossession of Hispanic residents and indigenous tribes. Founded by Thomas B. Catron and Stephen Elkins. Catron eventually became a U.S. senator and Elkins became the U.S. Secretary of War.

Foreword

In May of 1877, the Chíhenne (Red Paint, also known as Warm Springs or Ojo Caliente) Apache, led by Victorio, were forcibly taken from their homelands in New Mexico Territory and marched to the San Carlos reservation, far to the west, in violation of previous negotiations. Nicknamed "Hell's Forty Acres," this infertile land of scorching heat, unknown diseases and antagonism with other Apache bands heightened the people's desolation at being separated from their cherished mountains and grasslands. In the first days of September, Victorio and most of his followers escaped, fleeing back toward their traditional domain.

The unrelenting pursuit of army detachments drove Victorio and his people to surrender at Fort Wingate in early October and they were quickly returned to Ojo Caliente, the agency from which the Chíhenne had been removed and the location they consistently requested as a permanent reservation. Under no circumstances would they agree to return to San Carlos and Victorio made this abundantly manifest. Nevertheless, preparations were initiated to send them back to the hated reservation. In defiance, Victorio and many of his band slipped away and began raiding villages along the Río Grande.

Permission from military commanders and the Indian Bureau was finally given to propose a compromise with the apostate Chíhenne band. They would be settled on the Mescalero Apache reservation near Fort Stanton. After receiving assurances that the Chíhenne would not be transferred back to San Carlos, Victorio, albeit suspicious and reluctant, finally came into the Mescalero agency. One of his first requests was that his people be reunited with their families still in Arizona and Mescalero Agent Samuel Russell made sincere attempts to have their relatives released from San Carlos.

The chief convinced the Indian agent that he genuinely desired tranquility and safety for the approximately 145 Warm Springs Apache under his protection and he would cooperate with the agent in every way possible. Unrest among local white settlers notwithstanding, Agent Russell reported to the Indian Bureau that he did not anticipate problems. Victorio and his people were abiding by all the agent's wishes, especially owing to profound apprehension that they may yet be returned to the dreaded San Carlos reservation.

In August of 1879, a group of white men from Mesilla passed through the agency on a hunting trip. Because they had litigated cases involving the Mescalero in the past, at least two of the men were easily recognized by the Apache as being officers of the law. Rumors were circulating around the reservation that indictments had been issued against Victorio for theft and murder and the chief mistakenly believed they had come to arrest him. Once again fearing exile to San Carlos, he refused to be taken and the Chíhenne fled to the west, back to their strongholds in the San Mateo Mountains and Black Range. Time and time again, the Red Paint Apache had abided by their agreements with the U.S. government to no avail. Never again would Victorio negotiate for peace or relent in his pursuit of unmitigated retribution.

Meanwhile, Colonel Edward Hatch, military commander for the District of New Mexico and commanding officer of the 9th Cavalry, and General John Pope, commander of the Department of the Missouri, had become convinced that the Mescalero Apache were supplying Victorio and his warriors with horses, weapons, ammunition and government-issued provisions. They summarily formulated a plan to thwart any further support for Victorio. In the spring of 1880, Colonel Hatch arrived from the west to the Mescalero reservation with almost one thousand soldiers, accompanied by San Carlos Apache scouts, while Colonel Grierson, with the 10th Cavalry from the Department of Texas, was ordered by General Pope to report to the agency. The intention was to converge on the location with the goal of disarming Mescalero warriors and confiscating all their horses, thereby rendering them unable to lend succor or material assistance to Victorio and his fighting force.

When finally executed, the strategy went terribly awry, resulting in unwarranted slaughter of many Mescalero Apache and accusations of brutality and malfeasance from Indian Agent Russell and, subsequently, from the Commissioner of Indian Affairs. Several of the Mescalero warriors who escaped Hatch and Grierson's soldiers joined up with the Chíhenne as they laid waste to white settlements, mines and ranches, spreading terror throughout the Southwest. As the summer months of 1880 progressed, the Mescalero people and Victorio's warriors would find no respite from military aggression while the troopers of the 9th and 10th cavalry regiments would endure unimaginable hardship in the campaign to capture or annihilate the Chíhenne. Victorio's destruction had become an imperative of the War Department as well as the newspapers, politicians and civilians across the region, determined to rid themselves of an irreconcilable obstacle to progress and expansionism.

And so began the final period of catastrophic violence between military forces and the Red Paint Apache, extending across New Mexico Territory, Texas and south into Mexico. The Chíhenne would never again return to their traditional homelands and the Mescalero would suffer prolonged imprisonment and degradation. But New Mexico would soon be open for economic development, expanded railway transportation, fraudulent land acquisition and extensive political machinations, thereby fulfilling the promises of manifest destiny.

Prologue

The horse was game, responding to a strain of urgency, inspired by the rumble of hooves behind them. His rider was featherweight upon his back and his stamina held, yet he could not pull ahead, even as he nimbly dodged cactus, yucca and creosote. Stalwart fidelity drove the animal's greater ferocity of exertion, detecting peril to the man who was half of him. All was heat and thirst and inchoate dread. A piercing crack, like the breaking of the sky, lightened his load and he abruptly ceased his headlong flight, circling back to sniff the fallen flesh and blood. Then he raised his head and watched the deadly herd advance, his sides heaving, his limbs weighted in lethargy. He was acquiescent. A crucial bond had been brutally severed and instinct told him to comply. He had already learned there was no escape.

WARPATH

1

The black calf slipped to the ground, slick and shiny, and a man knelt to poke its nose with a stem of dried grass to encourage the animal to take a first breath. A small dog sat nearby, observing the procedure. The man stood and leaned backwards to stretch out his back. He was unused to such labors. Pausing a moment to survey the bucolic surroundings, he smiled. One solitary snipe called from a nearby alder and red winged blackbirds sent their distinctive flat-noted song from the thickets along the creek bottom. The air was rich with moist earth, pungent willow bark and fresh spring cow manure.

Turning back to the new arrival, Charles Wolfe Collins wiped his hands on the front of his coat, bending to remove the pulling strings from the animal's front hocks. He snaked the lariat loose from the heifer's neck and stood back as the mother sniffed her baby uncertainly, as if it might be something to be feared. The little animal wobbled to its feet and began punching its muzzle aimlessly at the belly of its mother until it made its way to the udder and attempted to latch onto a teat. The heifer side-stepped and Collins swore under his breath. When he had purchased the modest ranch populated with a few heavy first-calf heifers, he had been unaware of how frustrating and exhausting calving would be.

The brawny bull calf, however, was persistent and pursued his first meal doggedly until the cow relented and he began to suck enthusiastically. Collins sighed with relief. This was one pair he would not have to bring into the calving sheds to mother up. He coiled the rope and tied it to his saddle. His gelding, Ulysses, had turned out to be a questionable cow pony, but Mona, the little mare, was truly gifted and he could rely on her to stand still, holding slack from the lariat when a cow was on the other end. This had been the fourth calf he had been forced to pull and he was grateful there were only two remaining heifers to calve. Lengthy letters of advice and guidance from his friend, Alonzo Hartman, had proven invaluable.

Mounting up, Collins rode through the cow and calf pairs to look them over. All was well, so he headed back to the house with the dog trotting behind. His new home was a simple log affair topped by with a slab lumber second story, a covered porch and an attached shed for tools and sundries. A sturdy barn sat hard by, constructed of log with a board and batten loft. It even had an unassuming cupola. A jack and rail corral and pens enclosed the structure and the calving shed stood off to the side. The buildings had been weathered by hard Montana winters, but had been soundly built to withstand the rigors of time and wear. The original homesteader, one William Watson, had clearly planned to end his days on the ranch, but cholera and the loss of his wife and two boys had driven the man to whisky and foreclosure. Collins had purchased the ranch from the Donnell, Clark, and Larabie Bank in Deer Lodge. The bank had sold the homestead already stocked with simple and sturdy furnishings. C.W. was slightly ambivalent about having profited from Watson's tragedies.

After unsaddling and turning the mare loose and changing his clothing into those suitable for town, Collins went out to catch his draft mule, Joey. He led him into the barn and placed a large collar around the neck of the even-tempered animal and buckled it. He then swung the harness in place, positioning the hames evenly on the collar and set about tightening and securing the hame strap. He slipped the breeching down over the mule's hindquarters, pulled his tail through the crupper, attached the martingale to the quarter strap and fastened the girth. C.W. then bridled the mule and secured the lines to the bit. Throughout the procedure, Joey was steady and patient. His other mules, Molly and Felix, had wandered into the barn and were standing at a nearby hay bunk, picking at some remnants of dried timothy scattered about. Gal, his dog, sat quietly in a patch of sunlight by the door.

Collins ground drove Joey out to the buckboard wagon and backed him between the shafts. He lifted the shafts and slipped them through the tugs and hooked the trace chains to the singletree. Untethering the lines from the harness, he laid them on the seat and climbed up. He called the dog and she bounded up into the wagon and came to sit beside him. C.W. released the brake and slapped the lines lightly. Joey leaned in and they rolled out of the barnyard with Molly and Felix following behind. At the gate of the horse pasture, Collins shooed them back and they wandered away toward where his mare and gelding stood napping in the sun.

It was a good twelve miles to Deer Lodge and, Collins knew, it would take him the better part of three hours to get there. The day was breezy and cool, but rather temperate for Montana Territory in April. He had purchased and relocated to the ranch in March with all that he could carry on two horses and three mules. At that time, the countryside had been mostly snowbound and now he was on his way to retrieve the remainder of his belongings at the Gilmer and Salisbury freight and stage office. There, he could also pick up any mail that might be awaiting him.

The road followed the Deer Lodge River southward, flanked by low mountains to the east and west. To the north and west were substantial mining districts and

C.W. was aware that Granville Stuart and his brothers had settled the area, even laying out the townsite of Deer Lodge City. He never would have been tempted to establish himself in the valley if Granville was yet a resident, but he knew the man had relocated to Helena. His brother James was dead and the other brother, Tom, had a homestead somewhere near the town. They had never met.

The thought of Helena brought memories of Chicago Joe. She had wed a man named Hensley a few years before, but he had heard her new husband was an inveterate gambler and loved his gin. Collins hoped she could find contentment in the financial success for which she was gaining notoriety. He missed the sporadic visits with his erstwhile paramour and was fully engaged in agreeable reminiscences when a small herd of cow elk burst from a boscage of willows along the river and startled Joey the mule. The dog became agitated and leapt precipitously down from the buckboard, exacerbating the animal's alarm.

The jack spooked and jumped sideways, almost overturning the wagon. Collins tugged on the lines and engaged the brake, while calling the dog back. The elk ran off toward the east and the mule calmed down, though his sides were heaving. C.W. let him stand a moment and Gal rejoined him on the wagon seat. It was almost midday and the sun had become rather warm. He took off his coat and then resumed his journey.

About an hour later, Collins rolled into the village of Deer Lodge. He watered his mule at the livery stable after which he headed over to the nearby Scott Hotel for a meal. Since his arrival in the valley, he had learned that hearty and inexpensive fare was available in the hotel restaurant. He took a hitch weight out of the wagon bed and tethered the mule securely. Pressing the dog down on the seat, he told her to stay in the buckboard and entered Mr. Scott's establishment. As it was well beyond the noon hour, most of the patrons had moved on and he encountered no delays in finding a table.

After a satisfactory repast of steak, mashed potatoes and apple fritters, he drove to the stage office. Three large trunks awaited him, filled with the last of his possessions not sold with the farm in California. A single case alone contained his collection of books, which he had grievously missed. One of the Gilmer and Salisbury employees helped him load the cases into the buckboard after which he stopped in at the office to inquire after his mail and post a letter addressed to Fort Walsh, Saskatchewan. Collins was pleased to find a postal order for the remaining balance owed to him for sale of his property. Leaving Joey and Gal where they were and stowing the rest of the assortment of correspondence under the seat of the wagon, he walked to the bank to deposit the money order in his new account.

When he returned to the buckboard, there was a small figure huddled under the wagon box in the dirt of the roadway. Collins knelt down to examine the person and found a slim Chinese man in torn clothing, peering at him with one eye swollen and nearly closed. C.W. gestured for him to exit his refuge and the man crawled out and stood with bowed head before him as if expecting another beating.

"Do you speak English?" C.W. asked.

"I talk Melican."

It took Collins a moment to decipher the meaning. "Oh American... oh yes, well then excellent. Do you wish to see the sheriff? I assume you were attacked."

"No sheriff. Just go." He began to move away.

Collins restrained the man by placing his hand on a shoulder. "Please, let me help you. Get in the wagon and I will take you to your home."

"No home. No more."

"What do you mean?"

"Men came and burned. No more."

C.W. sighed. He was well aware that Chinese immigrants suffered greatly from calumny and violence all over the western reaches. "How came you to be here?"

"Was wanting to find cousin. Gone now. Chased away."

"Do you have any other family here?"

The man shook his head. He wiped his nose with a sleeve. Collins noticed he was wearing American style attire and had no queue.

"Then you may come with me, if you wish."

"No money. No nothing."

"I have a ranch. You can work."

Gal jumped down from the wagon. The Chinese man flinched and stepped back.

"No, please do not be afraid," Collins said and picked up the dog to place her back in the buckboard. "She will not hurt you."

The man stood as if poised to flee. "Not afraid. Go now."

"I need a man to work. I need a man I can trust," Collins told him.

The Celestial looked at him directly for the first time. "I can work. You can trust."

"Well then, it is settled. You are hired. If you would please mount up on the wagon, I have one more stop to make."

The man climbed into the wagon bed, squeezing past the bulky steamer trunks while Gal took her place on the seat. Collins decided to allow the fellow to arrange his accommodations as he pleased and considered that if his invitation to the Chinese fugitive led to problems, he could amend the situation easily enough. At the moment, he could not turn his back on someone who had sought refuge beneath his wagon. He untied Joey, placed the hitch weight into the buckboard and, gathering the lines, drove down the street. The town was never crowded in general and the thoroughfare was currently populated by a mere handful of pedestrians, mostly men. He drove to Murphy, Higgins and Company and pulled up in front of the storefront.

"I need to pick up some supplies," he told his companion, now sitting up just behind the seat. "May I get you something?"

"No."

"Any food you prefer?"

"No."

Collins shrugged and climbed down. He repeated the process of tethering the mule and went into the building. Inside, he gathered his purchases with celerity, including a large sack of rice and a goodly supply of tea. These were the only items he thought might please his new workman. A boy helped him carry the goods out to the buckboard. When he stepped over to load the supplies in the wagon bed, he saw the Chinese man.

"Hey mister, what you doin' with a Chinaman?"

"He works for me," Collins said, placing the rest of the provisions in the wagon.

The lad stared at the man hunched unobtrusively against the front of the wagon box. "You beat him up?"

"No. Someone else did that."

The youngster scratched his head musingly. "These Chinamen been getting' more plentiful, takin' up mines and such. Some folks ain't keen."

"Yes, well thank you for your assistance."

"Sure mister. Be seein' you."

Heading out of town, Collins contemplated the meanness of spirit that seemed to inhabit the average white citizen of many western settlements. Perhaps it was because they were scrambling for a meager foothold themselves that they became intolerant of any other group of people who were attempting to better their own lot. Hostility toward Chinese immigrants was escalating throughout mining communities in the west. It seemed to him that the Chinese people with whom he had been acquainted in San Francisco were industrious and honest. Yet there existed a pervasive antipathy toward them and copious unfounded accusations of committing crimes and causing difficulties for white inhabitants. After travelling some distance from Deer Lodge, he halted the mule and turned to look at his new acquaintance.

"Will you not come sit up here with me?"

Wordlessly, the man climbed up onto the seat. The dog leaned against C.W. and did not relinquish her position. Instead, she stubbornly remained pressed between the two men. The Chinese man reached to pat her head.

"Clever dog."

"Yes she is," Collins said, smiling. He slapped the lines and Joey resumed his steady pace.

"May I have your name?" Collins asked after a while.

"Wú Peng."

"Have you been in Deer Lodge for a while?"

"No. The truth is I purchased a claim near Henderson Gulch last fall. I was quite contented and acquiring a respectable amount of dust until my neighbors desired my claim for their own. They burned my cabin, stole my gold and fearfully assaulted me. That is when I walked to Deer Lodge to find my cousin. Unfortunately, he had attempted to set up a new laundry in a location outside the acceptable area of town and his well was filled with horse manure, his establishment was demolished and he and his family were encouraged to relocate."

Collins found himself thunderstruck by this torrent of information, so eloquently conveyed. "You have been dissembling," he said quietly.

"It is prudent. An educated Chinaman is simply not acceptable to the local populace."

"And you seem to be very well educated."

"My family comes from the Guangdong region of southern China. They immigrated to San Francisco in 1860 and my father became a successful businessman. I was only a boy and he sent me to a mission school to learn English and American manners."

"And yet you chose to leave the city to come to Montana Territory?"

"I had been managing my father's many business interests, but longed for distant horizons, such as a young man has the propensity to do. My cousin invited me to come here and make my fortune. Now I am without means to make any choice but to accept your civility and employment."

"How came you to be concealed beneath my wagon?"

"Two men emerged from the Metropolitan Billiard Room and exhibited an interest in amending the violence to my person. I chose to abscond."

"Prudent."

"Yes... quite. May I inquire as to why you were less inclined to perpetuate a beating upon my poor person?"

"I am Irish and an immigrant. I have endured denigration and exclusion."

"Then it was very fortuitous that I crawled underneath your particular wagon."

"Indeed." Collins pondered an idea a moment. "If I were to loan you the fare, would you prefer to travel back to San Francisco?" he asked at length.

Wú Peng regarded him solemnly. "I believe I will remain here and see how my fortune unfolds itself. *Nì lái shùn shòu.* When adversity comes, receive it favorably."

VIOLENT EXODUS

2

That evening, Wú Peng and Collins sat at the table in the ranch house, having finished a meal of prairie chicken and rice, as prepared by the Chinese gentleman. They drank tea and C.W. smoked his pipe.

"I suppose I must inquire as to wages," Peng said.

"I can pay you sixty dollars per month and found, as long as I am solvent."

"That is generous enough. And what labor will you expect?"

Collins tamped his pipe with a thumb and relit it. "Most everything. You will have to learn about livestock."

The Chinaman nodded. "I learn quickly and wish to be of great use to you."

"There is a bed in the loft. You may have that. And there are some work clothes in a trunk up there as well. The fellow from whom I acquired this ranch left quite a few items. He was slight in build and they may fit well enough."

Peng nodded again. "I am replete with gratitude."

Laying his pipe aside, C.W. said, "There will come the eventuality when I may have to absent myself for employment. I am assuming that you can commit to me for a substantial period of time and not take it into your head to decamp unexpectedly, Mr. Peng?"

"Wú."

"I beg your pardon?"

"In China the surname comes first. Therefore I am Mr. Wú... but please call me Peng."

"Very well... Peng. Will you stay? If not, as previously offered, I will gladly provide you with the fare to return home."

"I will stay."

Turning to the substantial quantity of mail he had found waiting for him in Deer Lodge, Collins sorted through the items, putting aside the Montgomery Ward & Co. catalog for later. There were a couple of auction bills from the bank, a copy of the American Agriculturalist, a letter from a woman in Cañon City, Colorado, that he would read at his leisure, and an article of correspondence postmarked from Washington D.C.

"May I peruse your catalog?" Peng inquired.

"Of course."

C.W. examined the envelope prior to opening it. It bore a blue five cent Zachary Taylor bank note and was made of expensive cream-colored paper, somewhat soiled by handling. The primary postmark was dated a week before and the correspondence had been forwarded from Chicago, having originally been sent care of the Pinkerton National Detective Agency. Distinct printing on the upper right-hand corner stated that it had been sent by the Department of the Interior and pertained to "official business." He used a table knife to carefully slit open the sealed flap.

The letter heading was from the Commissioner of Indian Affairs office. Collins attempted, without success, to recall who had replaced Commissioner Ezra Hayt, recently dismissed in ignominy. He read the signature on the second page and saw it was one Rowland E. Trowbridge. All he knew of the man was that he had been a supporter of Grant and had close personal ties with President Rutherford B. Hayes. Of a sudden, he realized that Peng was staring at the envelope.

"Why would someone in Washington write to you?" the Chinese man asked guardedly.

"I occasionally provide confidential services for eminent men in the federal government. At times, I have been employed by the Pinkertons."

Peng narrowed his one good eye. "We have many times suspected Pinkertons of assassinating several Tong leaders in Chinatown. They are depraved men."

"It is difficult for an Irishman to find work in America. I worked with Allan Pinkerton during the war of the rebellion and so was employed by him after. I have done nothing for him that I found dishonorable and I certainly have not assassinated anyone." He took a sip of tea. "And I seriously doubt I will continue to work for him, given some of the Pinkertons' recent activities." The detective agency had, of late, become entirely too active in its support of industrialists and intolerably aggressive in relation to labor unions and strikebreaking. And Allan Pinkerton had become all too cozy with Phil Sheridan for Collins' liking.

Peng cocked his head and examined him closely. "I suppose I believe you. *Lù yáo zhī mǎ lì, rì jiǔ jiàn rén xīn.* Time will reveal the true nature of a person."

" 'This above all; to thine own self be true.' "

"That is Shakespeare."

"Yes," was all Collins said in reply.

He read the letter from Trowbridge. The Commissioner of Indian Affairs was requesting he investigate an incident on the Mescalero Apache reservation that had taken place under Colonel Hatch and Grierson's 10th Cavalry. Apparently, the Indian agent, a man named Russell, had complained of cruel treatment and unnecessary bloodshed. At a suggestion from the Secretary of the Department of the Interior, Trowbridge was commissioning Collins to inquire into the occurrence and subsequently send a comprehensive report directly to his office. He also informed him of a pending telegram from Secretary Schurz about a related matter.

Back in '72, President Grant had sent him down to the Mescalero agency to investigate the trafficking of whisky to the Indians. It had been a serious issue and one that had never been satisfactorily addressed. In the midst of the whisky imbroglio, an Apache leader he had known from past experience, and a man with whom he had forged a lasting friendship, was brutally murdered under mysterious circumstances. *Cadete*, an Apache chief, had always maintained cordial relations with the whites and had not approved of his people partaking of ardent spirits. It was tragic irony that he had become the victim of mindless and random violence. Collins had always privately suspected the infamous L. G. Murphy and his pal, James Dolan, of complicity in the murder. It was an occurrence that disturbed him still.

Thusly, being not unduly fond of New Mexico Territory nor kindly disposed toward the citizens thereof, C.W. was decidedly reluctant to accept such a commission. Concurrently, he harbored resentment toward Secretary of the Interior Carl Schurz resulting from previous experiences within his employ. Unfortunately, he was sorely in need of funds after the purchase of the new ranch. Although the sale of his farm had proven advantageous, all related expenses of the move, the shipping of his belongings and the sundry requirements for successful operation of his new agricultural endeavor were proving more than costly. Now he had taken on Mr. Wú as an employee, there would be additional expenditures to be met. He sighed deeply.

"You are troubled?" Peng inquired.

"I am indeed. I have been requested to accept employment in New Mexico Territory. I do not wish to accept... yet it will be profitable and circumstances necessitate additional resources." Collins observed his companion for a moment. "I also do not know if I am able to trust you or that you will be able to successfully manage all the duties that would be required in my absence."

Peng shrugged. "*Wànshì kāitóu nán*. All things are difficult at the start. You must instruct me as to mandatory responsibilities and observe how I perform. There will be no answer to your quandary until an empirical assessment has been achieved."

C.W. smiled to himself regarding the Celestial's mildly pedantic manner of expression. "What you say is true."

The next morning, Peng appeared in a pair of Mr. Watson's old waist overalls held aloft by striped galluses over a floral calico shirt. Upon his head he wore a large black wool cap that substantially covered his ears. He carried a bulky coat over his arm. Collins refrained from comment and his companion did not seem even mildly ill at ease regarding his somewhat outlandish costume. They breakfasted on eggs and side meat and afterward proceeded into a late April morning, blustery with stiff breezes and patchwork clouds.

It swiftly became apparent to Collins that Mr. Wú was a diligent and capable pupil. He addressed all assigned chores industriously and appeared to be undeniably interested in all aspects of ranching. Most importantly, the Chinese gentleman exhibited a distinct fondness for all of the animals, speaking to them in his own tongue and taking every opportunity to spend a moment in their company. Even the dog, Gal, seemed to accept his presence more readily than C.W. would have thought.

Most of the pairs had mothered up in the calving sheds, so Peng opened a series of gates and, according to instruction, released the heifers and calves into the big pasture. While this was accomplished, Collins pitched a feed trail from the hay rack pulled by his jack mules, Felix and Joey. Only one heifer and her calf remained in the sheds and Peng lingered in their company without being asked. By the time C.W. was finished feeding all the livestock, the Chinaman had the heifer and her baby quite bonded and ready to turn out with the other pairs.

"And just how did you achieve this small miracle?" Collins asked.

Peng peered out from under the voluminous wool cap

and shrugged expressively. "I conversed with them and explained what a proper outcome would be."

"Do they speak Chinese?"

"All creatures understand the true original language," Peng answered with great dignity.

Gal perched on the saddle in front of him as he rode into town. It had been a mere five days since his last visit to Deer Lodge, but Peng had already become so proficient in all particulars of ranch work, that Collins did not hesitate to absent himself. If he were to accept the employment offered by Indian Commissioner Trowbridge, and possibly Secretary Schurz, it was required that he respond to the letter and to learn whether, indeed, Schurz had sent a telegram requesting his services.

He rode up to the telegraph office, easily recognized by a substantial sign upon the building's false front. C.W. had heard that a mining magnate out of Butte, an Irishman named Largey, owned the branch line and the man's name was notably featured in sizable lettering. He dismounted and told the dog to stay. Inside, a couple of men lounged comfortably beside the telegraph apparatus, sharing the local newspaper and discussing a report of a tornado that had devastated several towns in Missouri.

"Heck of a way to go," one of the fellows was saying. "Getting picked up and tossed about like a rag doll."

Collins cleared his throat.

"Aw hell," the other man said, removing his feet from a neighboring chair and sitting up. "Sorry mister. What can I do for you?"

"Quite alright. My name is Charles Collins. Does there happen to be a telegram here for me?"

"Been here for couple of days at least." The telegrapher stepped over to a cabinet replete with sorting cubbyholes and retrieved a sheet of paper. "Here it is," he said, handing it over.

Washington DC April 18 1880
To C.W. Collins c/o Pinkerton
National Detective Agency
Chicago Ill

In reference to letter from Comm. Trowbridge
Also requesting you find and meet with
Victorio Apache chief Ascertain intentions
and grievances report directly to my office
Substantial remuneration and no restraints
on methods

C. Schurz
Honorable Sec. of the Interior

"Any reply?"
"Yes."
The man handed him a blank and Collins composed a reply in the affirmative. Now that Mr. Wú appeared to be adequate to the task of caring for his ranch, lucrative employment was not only possible but pragmatical. In view of the fact that he had more or less decided to eschew working in the employ of Allan Pinkerton in future, it was compulsory that he accept any other enterprise that would offer financial remuneration.

The telegrapher sat and transmitted the message while his pal sprawled in a nearby chair, reading the newspaper and making small remarks concerning the content. When the procedure was completed, Collins paid a dollar for ten words, as posted at the entrance, and thanked the operator.

"Will you be expecting another message?" the man asked.

"I doubt it."

Leaving his gelding secured to a rail nearby, with the dog comfortably curled up on the saddle as was her wont, he strolled across the street and entered the headquarters of Gilmer, Salisbury and Company. This particular enterprise was a convenient amalgamation of stage line, freight office and carrier of the United States mail. He went up to the window and a young man, titivated by slick hair parted in the middle and a meticulously groomed moustache, came over to serve him. Having already composed his response to Commissioner Trowbridge accepting the proposed assignment, he only required sufficient postage.

The clerk perused the address, brushed gum on a five cent bank note and applied it to the envelope.

"Will that be all?"

"Yes, thank you." Collins suspected that the dandified young man considered himself to be quite a gift to the ladies. He gave the clerk a nickel.

"Too late today. Your letter will go out tomorrow."

Collins exited the office almost colliding into an older gentleman. The man, idiosyncratic with bald pate and voluminous white whiskers and redolent of whisky, let loose with vernacular so colorful as to cause the clerk to come out of the office.

"Good god, Elwood," he chided, "we do not want you around the premises with language such as this."

The younger man shoved the chastened fellow along the front of the building until Elwood toppled to the ground and lay submissively. Forthwith, the old man stoically removed a pint bottle from his coat pocket, uncorked it with the few remaining teeth in his head and proceeded to devote himself to its remaining contents.

"Crazy old coot," the clerk said under his breath, admired himself in the reflection of a window, and went back into the office with alacrity.

Walking over to where the supine drunkard was sprawled in the dirt, C.W. inquired after his well-being.

The man wiped his mouth with a sleeve pensively and said, "Nothing never rectifies... it just gets worse."

Returning to his horse, amply persuaded that the extemporaneous philosopher Elwood was unharmed by rough handling and remained comfortable in his present reclining condition, Collins loosed the reins and led the gelding, with the dog sitting on the saddle, two streets over to the Boot and Shoe Store. The proprietor carried a stock of ready-made work clothing and he intended to outfit Mr. Wú Peng in something other than the unfortunate Mr. Watson's castoffs. Securing Ulysses to an adjacent hitching rail, he turned to find a young urchin staring at him. The boy was quite filthy and had an index finger stuck firmly up his right nostril.

"That dog ride your horse?" he asked in a nasal tone resulting from the digit obstructing his airway.

"Sometimes."

The child removed his finger and examined it closely. He then wiped it on his soiled trousers and wandered away as if Collins and his animals were no longer sufficient to hold his attention. Not particularly fond of children, he shrugged bemusedly, stepped onto the porch and entered the building.

A very rotund, almost perfectly round gentleman, in red suspenders and matching sleeve garters, was napping on a stool, his head resting on his chest. The long narrow room was packed floor to ceiling with every assortment of practical and sturdy clothing and boots and shoes for every age and sex. Collins coughed and the fellow sprang into life.

"Yes sir, of course sir," he said as if joining a conversation already initiated.

Pulling out a small notebook in which he had recorded the required sizes of assorted items of clothing, C.W. provided instructions regarding the articles he wished to purchase. In a short while, he departed the establishment burdened with two bundles composed of denim overalls, wool jumper, leather boots, linsey-woolsey shirt, tweed sac cloth coat and a soft wool short-brimmed hat. He tied the parcels behind the saddle and next proceeded toward the section of Deer Lodge behind the McBurney Hotel wherein the Chinese businesses were situated.

On one corner squatted an oddly assembled structure of board and batten. The front wall displayed a small sign with Chinese characters and below were stacked crates and ramshackle shelving packed with a variety of substances and objects of mysterious purposes. Collins opened the door and entered a dark space pungent with spices and unfamiliar fragrances. His eyes adjusted to the dim interior and he beheld a plethora of wares, again mostly inscrutable within his limited experience. Behind a counter stood a handsome Chinese man wearing traditional costume. His head was shaved except for a lock that was braided into a queue.

"*Nǐ hǎo*," Collins said in his imperfect Mandarin, acquired during a brief interlude in San Francisco.

"How may I serve you?" the man inquired in heavily accented English. "My name is *Zheng Bai* and I am honored by your presence."

Again taking out the notebook, C.W. removed a slip of paper and handed it to the Celestial. Peng had written out his requests in Chinese characters. Zheng Bai nodded and began to gather together a porcelain bowl, a set of chopsticks, a tortoise shell comb, a bone-handled toothbrush, a packet of incense, an ornately decorated tin marked "*Longjing*" tea, numerous enigmatic food stuffs and a box of some type of pills. He carefully wrapped the items in a sheet of brown paper and tied it with string.

"One dollar and two bits," he said.

Collins gave him the exact amount and thanked him. Zheng Bai bowed.

The day seemed very bright after the shadowy confines of the Chinese emporium. He gently secured this last bundle, tightened his cinch and swung clumsily into the saddle over the mound of supplies fastened behind the cantle. Calling the dog, who was stretched comfortably on the leeward side of the building, he slapped his thigh and she jumped onto his lap. It was well past noon and he wanted to make it back to the ranch before nightfall. Urging the gelding into a fast walk, Collins bypassed the main part of town and headed north along the river.

4

As darkness was falling, C.W. dismounted in front of the barn and unloaded all the bundles from his saddle. After a day of negligible activity, Gal bounded around the vicinity, sniffing here and there and chasing invisible quarry. Jaded from travel, Collins unsaddled Ulysses where he stood and rubbed him down perfunctorily with one of the blankets. The mules and mare had come over to inspect the proceedings. When he turned Ulysses loose, they all trotted into the gloom of the pasture.

A shadow emerged from the nearby corrals, startling him. "Jesus, Mary and Joseph!" Collins exclaimed.

"You are home," Peng said.

"Clearly," C.W. said, slightly vexed by his brief discomfiture.

"Allow me to assist you." The Chinaman lifted the largest parcels and headed back toward the house. The dog followed behind.

Picking up the remaining packages, Collins trailed after them, his way soon lit by a lantern suspended from the porch eaves. He could hear Peng speaking to Gal in his own language as he opened the door for her and let her precede him into the dwelling. When Collins stepped onto the porch, Peng met him and relieved him of his burden, making way for him to enter the house and following after.

"Did the last heifer calve?" C.W. asked as he helped himself to a cup of coffee from a pot on the cookstove.

He noticed there was an appealing and pervasive aroma of food about the room.

"Yes and they are doing very well," Peng told him, placing the bundles on a chair and walking over to take Collins' coat. "You must sit down now. All the labor has been completed and there is nothing amiss. I will feed the dog and then I will feed you."

"Not the same food, I hope," C.W. said, regretting his earlier churlishness.

The man's face lit up at this bit of humor. "Perhaps you would care to have some canned milk, old bread and meat scraps?"

Collins sat down at the table. "What else might there be?"

"I have made steamed buns. I did not, however, possess correct ingredients to make them delectable."

"They certainly smell delectable," Collins told him, concealing a grin.

Gal sat politely as Peng placed her dinner on the floor. He then washed his hands in a basin and poured more coffee for C.W. The table was already set and Peng went to bring a Dutch oven from the stove. He positioned it carefully upon a cast iron trivet and lifted the lid. Fragrant steam rose from the vessel and Collins realized he was terrifically hungry, having neglected taking a meal in town. The Chinaman gently lifted three buns and placed them on Collins' plate, then served himself. The chipped but sturdy Brown Betty teapot, a relic from the old country, sat upon the table. C.W. poured a cup of tea for each of them and handed one to Peng.

"You should not attend me. I am your servant." Peng told him, sitting down.

"There are no servants here." He took a bite of a dumpling. "Delicious," he said. "Really very delicious."

The Chinese man bowed slightly from his place across the table. "I am glad you find my efforts satisfactory."

"Quite satisfactory." He took a sip of tea. "I purchased the items you sought."

"*Xiè xiè ni.* Thank you. It is exceptionally benevolent of you to have confidence in me in this way."

Collins had noticed that where a simple word would suffice, Wú Peng preferred a more elaborate mode of expression. Perhaps this was a product of a missionary education, he mused. "What was the tea you requested?" he asked. "The tin is quite decorative."

"It is *Longjing,* also known as Dragon Well tea… imperial tea of the Qing Dynasty. Green tea has many more benefits for health than your English tea." He made a disapproving face. "Chinese people do not drink this blackened concoction."

"You are drinking it now," Collins observed.

Peng smiled and again bowed. "One must make do. And it was profligately generous of you to provide this beverage until a superior one could be acquired."

After finishing his meal, C.W. poured more tea and took out his pipe. "I sincerely hope you will again make your steamed buns," he told his companion.

"I must travel soon to Zheng Bai's establishment and purchase appropriate spices and other ingredients so that I may provide a more auspicious illustration of my gastronomic proficiency."

It took a minute for Collins to suppress his delight at this ostentatious pronouncement. "I anticipate your efforts with enthusiasm," he finally said. "But I propose we should visit the establishment together, as your last visit to town did not end well."

He puffed thoughtfully on his pipe, meditating upon the significance of his new acquaintance and his luck at finding a reliable man. C.W. had been plagued by the challenge of finding a man to caretake the ranch, especially as he had not adequately foreseen the exigencies of hiring someone who could care for the place in his absence. Mining regions were notoriously peopled by transient fortune seekers and ruffians. Therefore, surplus and trustworthy laborers were extraordinarily rare and he had begun to despair of being at liberty to accept employment, should the occasion arise.

"I am glad you are here," he told his companion impulsively. "I hope you will find that this is your home and will prosper here. It is said that *an té chuireas, 'sé bhaineas.* He that sows will reap."

There was a moment of silence. Peng appeared to struggle with his emotions, although his countenance remained phlegmatic. Following the extended pause, he said, "I, too, hope that we may build a pleasant bond that finds endurance. *Yǒuyuán qiānlǐ lái xiānghuì.* Fate brings people together from far apart."

"Indeed." C.W. laid aside his pipe and got up to retrieve the bundle of items from the Chinese market. He placed it on the table in front of Peng.

"Thank you," the Chinaman said. "May I inquire as to the nature of the language you spoke?" he asked, untying the string that secured the package.

"It is the Irish. My native language."

"It seems we have much to teach each other," Peng said, laying the articles before him, one by one.

"According to that presentiment, I was curious about the types of food that are traditional to your region of China. During a brief sojourn in San Francisco, I sampled a variety of dishes that were, I recollect, mostly Cantonese in origin."

"Yes. Most of us are Cantonese in Chinatown."

"Yet you speak Mandarin."

"I learned so as to perform efficient business for my father. I am also a Confucian. One finds his words more readily obtainable in the Mandarin language."

"But otherwise, your cuisine is predominantly Cantonese?"

Handling the bowl and chopsticks with appreciation, Peng said, "Yes, we love our plum sauce and pickled radish and sweet and sour pork."

Smiling appreciatively, Collins said, "Well, I certainly did not hire you on as a cook, but will be most grateful for your culinary endeavors whenever you are so inclined."

"It will be my pleasure to bring you pleasure."

The dog began barking furiously. Both men started and came to their feet. Suddenly there was a loud pounding on the door and Collins fetched his Winchester repeater from a rack on the wall. He told Gal to be quiet and went to the door and opened it, pointing the carbine in the general direction of the intruder without. The dog crouched behind him, growling menacingly.

A large and inebriated man stood before him on the porch. "Heard you gotta coolie heathen," he said in thunderous tones. "We come for him."

Raising the Winchester higher and aiming more directly, Collins said evenly, "You have no business here."

"We shore as hell do. Man in town said you gotta chink out here. We been clearin' 'em out... I tell ya for true, them bastards need cullin'."

Collins could see there were a couple of other men behind the loudmouth drunkard. A shotgun may have been more appropriate to the occasion, he thought to himself. "Sling your hook," he said forcefully.

"Why... what?" It seemed the dimwitted fellow was momentarily nonplussed.

In one swift and vicious stroke, C.W. thumped the butt of the rifle hard against the man's temple and dropped him to his knees, instantly bringing the barrel back to bear on the man's cronies. "Get your pal out of here," he told them quietly. "Come back and I will not palaver. I will merely shoot you down and bury you in the manure pile."

Wordlessly, the other two ruffians caught their comrade under the armpits and dragged him off into the moonless night. Collins stood in the doorway, Winchester at the ready, until he heard muffled voices moving away and horses departing the ranch yard. He turned to see Wú Peng standing off to the side of the door, holding C.W.'s Colt .45 with resolve. Despite this, the hands that held the gun were shaking.

"They are gone," Collins told him.

"Perhaps you will now reconsider my employment," the Chinaman said, lowering the revolver and holding it slackly in one hand.

"Why?" Collins asked. He went over to take the Colt from Peng and put both weapons back where they belonged. "Are you so easily downcast?"

A spark of resentment glittered in Peng's eyes. "I am not. I was only inquiring as to whether you found it inconvenient to retain my contemptible person in your employ."

"I am not as capricious as that," C.W. said, sitting down at the table. "Nor am I easily alarmed."

Peng came over and sat across from him. "It is baffling that one such as you are so accommodating to one such as me. My experiences in Montana Territory have not included acquaintance with any *gwáilóu* of such a quality as yourself."

"Time will reveal the true nature of a person," Collins said, using the man's own words in response. " 'Let every eye negotiate for itself,' " he added, quoting from *Much Ado About Nothing.*

5

"I must leave the dog with you," Collins told Peng sadly. "It will, no doubt, be unbearably hot and unrelentingly rugged where I am going."

The Chinese man was standing nearby, observing him pack his carpetbag and panniers with clothing and supplies for the journey. "I will be very contented to have her pleasant company, but I believe she will be extraordinarily miserable."

"Yes, but more importantly she will be safe." He stopped to consider his companion. "You will keep her very safe, will you not?"

"Upon my honor and my life, I will keep this small person protected," Peng said, reaching down to stroke Gal's head as she sat watching C.W.'s every move.

"I cannot adequately express my gratitude," Collins said. "Not merely for your care of the dog, but also for this place and all the livestock."

Another week had passed since the incident with the hostile local residents. Collins had been loath to depart until he felt they had been adequately discouraged. In the interim, Wú Peng had proven himself astonishingly willing and capable in every aspect of ranch work. He had become more able-bodied with the labor and his skillful handling of the horses and mules was equal to that of someone with far more experience. His most heartening attribute was the steady and abiding affection he exhibited toward all creatures.

Reaching into his saddle bags lying on the bed, Collins pulled out a pouch bulging with gold double eagles. He tossed it to Wú Peng.

"Here are two month's wages and enough surplus for supplies." He regarded Peng a moment. "I will not inquire again whether you will be here when I return."

Returning his gaze steadily, Peng said, " 'It is more shameful to distrust our friends than to be deceived by them.' "

"Confucius?"

Peng nodded.

"Very well. I will trust you." He placed the last of his personal items and clothing in the carpetbag. With only one pack animal, he would be travelling light. "Oh yes," he said, suddenly, "I almost forgot." He retrieved a small packet from the camel back trunk at the foot of the bedstead. Laying it on the bed quilt, he unfolded the oilcloth wrapping and took out a .44 caliber Frontier Bulldog revolver and two boxes of cartridges. "This is for you."

"You are giving me a weapon?" he asked incredulously.

"I want you to be able to defend yourself. I expect you will need practice with it."

Nodding solemnly, Peng said, "I am most honored by this valuable and useful item. It is abundantly splendorous."

"Well I am not sure about its intrinsic beauty, but self-defense does possess alluring qualities," Collins said, smiling.

"And I have something for you." Peng said. He went up into the loft and when he returned, Peng opened a hand and presented Collins with a small articulated silver fish. "This is a very formidable lucky symbol. You must carry the charm with you throughout all eventualities."

"Thank you. I promise to keep it with me at all times."

C.W. placed the token in a vest pocket. "Come, let us carry my belongings onto the porch, after which we will go and catch up Molly and Ulysses."

Gal followed closely as Collins and Peng walked out into the pasture to catch the gelding and mule. A meadowlark sang cheerily from a nearby fence post and a hawk soared overhead. It was warm despite the breeze blowing down from the mountains to the north. Back at the barn, Peng deftly saddled the gelding while C.W. placed the sawbuck on the mule and adjusted the breeching and breast collar. Joey came into the barn and made a nuisance of himself, investigating every aspect of the procedure.

"He behaves more similarly to a dog than a mule," Peng declared.

"True enough," Collins said, pushing the large animal out of his road and leading Molly from the barn.

In short order, the supplies were loaded and secured. Collins felt a twinge of regret at leaving his new home and all its residents, human or otherwise. He swung into the saddle. The dog made an attempt to join him and Peng had to pick her up and confine her in the house.

"Keep her close for the first few days," Collins instructed when Peng returned.

"Yes. She may endeavor to follow you."

"Be careful and watch your back. You may send a telegram to Fort Stanton if necessary. I will receive it eventually."

"*Yī lù shùn fēng.* Pleasant journey."

"Thank you."

Turning Ulysses away from the dwelling, Collins nudged him into a fast walk with Molly lining herself out after them. He could hear Gal barking in distress and desired to put some distance behind him as soon as possible. He turned once in the saddle to wave at Mr. Wú, then proceeded to attend to the journey at hand.

The route to the nearest railhead was easy travelling through mountain valleys, almost due south. Cattle ranged the open grasslands, interspersed with elk, deer and herds of horses. The day was clear and warm and the last of the snow painted patterns on mountain summits that bounded his course on the east and west. The gelding was fidgety for the first few miles, but soon became compliant and sensible. C.W. patted his neck, musing that the animal was gaining maturity and was, therefore, less susceptible to foolishness.

Collins camped the first evening northwest of Butte City, the straggling and smoke-filled town of mineral wealth. Immigrant miners of Italian, Cornish, Irish, Chinese and eastern European ancestry populated the metropolis and its German residents had opened several commercial breweries, no doubt welcomed by their fellow inhabitants. He made an austere bivouac and was back on the road early the next morning, circumventing the city and following the Beaverhead River toward Terminus, the makeshift town erected around the end of the Utah and Northern Railway tracks and the beginning of his journey south by rail car.

After another uneventful day of travel and a rudimentary camp for the night, Collins arrived at the bedlam of canvas-covered wooden structures and multitudinous freight wagons that made up the railroad hub and the transient town that progressed with the laying of rails to the north. He located an improvised livery stable, constructed of pole corrals, slab lumber and several rack bed wagons, and arranged with the proprietor, a bilious, grizzled man, to leave his gear and animals overnight. The fees were exorbitant, but nothing less was to be expected.

Walking through the chaotic environs of the jumbled settlement, C.W. happened upon a rather large building that had apparently been bolted together for swift dismantling and migration. A painted canvas sign was suspended above the premises proclaiming the site as the Valley House, "a hotel of the highest standards." He entered and was greeted by a dapper gentleman in slightly weary, but stylish attire.

"Were you in search of accommodation?" he asked in a fine baritone voice, glancing down at his brocade waistcoat and tugging it straight.

"For the night. I leave aboard the railway tomorrow."

"Of course. That will be three dollars and fifty cents. This also includes a supper and breakfast."

Collins paid the man and was shown to a canvas partitioned recess that contained a single spring bed, clean linens and a washstand with a chipped porcelain pitcher and basin. An oil lamp sat upon a wooden crate beside the bed.

"Does this meet with your approval?" the landlord asked. "Guaranteed you will not have to double up."

"Then it is ideal," Collins told him. "I will return later with my valise and after I have purchased fare on the Utah Northern."

"Excellent. The evening meal begins at five o'clock. Be warned, however... the best bits go to the first who arrive."

Thanking his host, C.W. exited the modest edifice and went in search of the railway depot. He was directed toward a dingy little structure adjacent to a line of railroad tracks. It had been assembled in sections much as the hotel, but was vastly less aligned and seemingly less equipped to withstand the vagaries of weather. Its roof was a droopy affair of dingy canvas. Inside, Collins found the ticket agent absorbed by a game of patience at his small desk. The cards were worn and notably soiled. C.W. coughed loudly.

"What? What is it?" the agent asked, rousing and looking about in alarm.

"I wish to purchase fare to Ogden."

The man came to himself and rubbed his face roughly with both hands. "You betchya... you betchya. To Ogden you say?"

"Yes, to make connections with the Union Pacific and points south... for myself and two equines."

"First class for you?"

Collins nodded.

The agent took a pencil from behind his ear and scribbled on a notepad. "That will be a total of eighteen dollars. Do your animals load easily?"

"Yes. Especially if I am there to lend a hand."

"Very well. The departure time is nine in the morning. I suggest you bring your animals an hour prior in order to get them loaded and situated."

"I will be here with plenty of time to spare."

Reaching into his jacket, Collins took out his pocketbook and removed two Daniel Webster greenbacks. The agent gave him two silver dollars in change and presented him with a ticket. He thanked the man and left the cockeyed railway office to make his way through the muddled labyrinth of wagons and structures back to the livery stable. There he fetched his carpetbag, carbine and revolver and returned to the Valley House just in time for the evening victuals. He stowed his possessions on the bed in his canvas cell and returned to join several men in the process of seating themselves on benches at a long table consisting of sanded boards resting upon wooden bucks.

The proprietor and a youthful companion commenced to bring tureens of meat in gravy, bowls of boiled potatoes and boiled carrots, platters of pork chops and beef cutlets, a dish of steaming pasta and several pies.

The man beside him gave Collins a nudge with his elbow. "What is the deal with the noodles?" he asked disparagingly.

A fellow across from them spoke up. "Them Dagos in Butte. They learned the Mick sappers to eat noodles so they could drink more. Got so's lots of folks eat 'em."

The other man shrugged and began loading his plate with such a copious mound of food that it sloughed off on all sides.

"Mind yourself," Collins said to him quietly. "I do not care to lay my sleeves in your offal."

He shrugged again and scooted down the bench away from C.W., leaving a trail of food scraps behind him. The hotelier swept in with a cloth and wiped the boards clean.

"My apologies. We get all sorts in here."

"No worries," Collins replied. "The food is really first-rate."

"My thanks." The landlord departed to tend to other duties.

While he ate, Collins examined his dining companions. There were eight of them, all men, and clearly of different occupations. He overheard one of the more refined looking gents identify himself as the editor of the *Missoulian* newspaper. The fellow with whom he conversed was an individual named Amos Buck, recently relocated to the Bitter Root Valley. One of the other patrons was a school teacher from Colorado bound for Helena, or so he proclaimed to his neighbor at the board.

Not for the first time, it struck Collins that the western expanses of America were peopled with a remarkably diverse range of characters, many of them migrating from or to questionable circumstances. For some reason, he recalled an ancient Arabic tale told to him as a child by an old sailor. It spoke of a man who sees Death and rides his horse far away to escape. When he reaches another village, he sees Death again. It is then that Death tells him the first meeting was an accident. Ironically, the man had subsequently fled straight to the town where he had always had an appointment with Death. As the French poet Jean de la Fontaine had written, "One meets his destiny often in the road he takes to avoid it." So much for all of us, he thought, as he dished himself a slice of chokecherry pie.

6

The journey by rail was tedious and laborious. Collins spent much of his time looking after his gear and especially his mule and horse, keeping their legs wrapped against injury, exercising them when possible, ensuring they were loaded according to his specifications for safety and welfare and that they received adequate hydration and nourishment. The rest of his travel was made up of reading newspapers and avoiding social intercourse with fellow passengers. Given his emergent misanthropic tendencies, keeping to himself and evading idle conversation ensured a more tolerable expedition.

Four days later, he and his animals disembarked at the new brick depot in Las Vegas, New Mexico Territory. He stowed his saddles and gear on a luggage cart. An elderly Mexican gentleman offered to safeguard his outfit for two bits and he accepted. It was early afternoon, so he walked Ulysses and Molly until they had recovered from their prolonged confinement. When he returned, the fellow was sleeping comfortably upon his pile of belongings.

"*Dondé está el establo más cercano?*" Collins asked loudly, recalling one of the useful phrases he had learned during his previous experiences in the territory.

The man roused himself. "I speak very good English, *Señor*." He came to his feet and wrested Molly's lead from Collins.

"Excellent. What is your name?"

"Santiago Duran."

"*Mucho gusto,* Santiago. My name is Charles Collins. Would it be possible to employ you further this after-noon?"

"*Por supuesto, Carlos.* With pleasure."

"*Gracias.* I must get my animals to a livery stable and then purchase a few items."

The old gentleman removed the tattered woven straw hat from his head and scratched a shiny bald spot that resembled a monastic tonsure. "There is the J.S. Duncan barn very close to here."

They saddled the horse and mule and slung the panniers on the sawbuck. Collins carried his carpetbag and Santiago shouldered the saddlebags. Leading Molly, Santiago began walking in a northerly direction.

"Almost everything east of the river is Anglo," he said, conversationally. "The railroad is making two villages."

"One white and one Mexican?"

A small brown dog trotted over, sniffed Molly's hind leg and dodged when she raised her hoof to kick.

"*Sí.* There is some of *la superposición, pero* the Anglos like to keep their own company."

They arrived at a newly built livery stable and were met by a young man whose hatless forehead was moist with perspiration. "Need to board these animals?" he asked in a noticeable Texas accent.

"Yes. With feed and water. I will be leaving them for perhaps two or three hours, then we shall depart."

"We got plenty of room."

"Might I also leave my belongings and saddles here?"

"Sure. I promise to keep a good watch on everything. If you be wantin' to eat, there is George McKay's place just yonder."

"Thank you."

Santiago assisted Collins in unloading and unsaddling and they made a pile of his possessions in a corner of the barn as directed by the stable hand. C.W. strapped on his holster with the .45 Colt revolver and sequestered his Winchester '73 under the panniers. He bid the boy farewell and headed back into the warming afternoon.

"*Los Tejanos...* so many of them here *ahora*," the old man muttered.

"I will be pleased to pay you now, if you choose," C.W. told Santiago. "Or would you care to accompany me for a meal?"

"I will happily join you for food, *pero* I do not wish to eat at *una cantina.* We should cross the river and I will take you where *la comida es mucho mejor.*"

"I also do not care to dine in a saloon. Please guide me where you will."

They strolled along a road that angled toward the river.

"What is the name of this stream?" Collins asked.

"*El Río Gallina.*"

"And what is the name of that distinctive mountain above the town there?"

"That is *El Pico del Ermitaño.* It was once the home to *un hombre muy religioso.*"

Walking a little behind his guide, Collins was able to study the man. Although seemingly advanced in age, Señor Duran was agile and carried himself with a straight back and dignified bearing. He wore an immaculate button-front white shirt, grey trousers and serviceable kip boots. The only article of attire that exhibited substantial wear was the straw hat perched jauntily upon his head.

When they neared the river, they were forced to wait for a horse-drawn railway car as it turned from another thoroughfare to cross the bridge ahead of them leading into old Las Vegas. The passengers all appeared to be white.

"There seems to be mostly Anglos headed for the old

section of your town," Collins observed.

"*Sí.* Many of the Anglo *turistas* come to visit *la plazuela.*"

"I require a few items. Will I find merchants on this plaza?"

"*Por supuesto que sí!* You will find many *tiendas.* Many fine shops. What do you desire?"

They stepped onto the wooden bridge and walked along the north side. Collins paused a moment to look down at the water. It was swift and swollen with spring snow melt. "I wish to purchase some food items and a map, if possible."

"*Dónde...* where do you go?"

They began to walk again. A small cart, drawn by two diminutive burros and piled high with firewood, passed them by. The boy walking beside it called a greeting to Santiago. He raised a hand in acknowledgement.

"I am bound for the Mescalero Apache reservation," C.W. told his companion.

"*Que bárbaridad!* And you are journeying there *solo...* alone?"

"Yes. Does this cause you concern?"

"*Sí. Mucha preocupación.*"

The plaza opened before them, dusty and parsimonious in verdure and surrounded by structures of brick, wooden siding and adobe. Almost all of the buildings bore some type of porch to provide shade and shelter. A large windmill derrick rose from the center of the square. The area was populated with a variety of individuals, from graceful Mexican women in somber apparel to tourists in city garb, seemingly unsuited to a pugnacious western town. A gang of roughs gathered on the far side, smoking cigarillos and passing around a bottle. Two stylish buggies were parked along the northern margin near to some shops and a yoke of oxen unaccountably lay beside a brick edifice that housed a dentist. The signboard, fashioned in an outline of a molar tooth, reminded C.W. that the notorious Doc Holliday had practiced dentistry and owned a saloon in Las Vegas the previous year, but had been forced to abscond after killing a popular citizen.

A group of grimy boys emerged pell-mell from a lane perpendicular to their passing. Santiago shook a fist and made a false lunge at the rowdy bunch.

"Mala plebe! Abandanar!"

The ragamuffins paused for a brief moment then, entirely undaunted, resumed their tempestuous game, running into the square and escalating their noise.

Santiago turned to shrug at C.W. *"Sin cortesía...* no courtesy. There are new ways now. The children forget their manners."

The old man led Collins into a side alleyway to a one-story adobe building. A domed mud fireplace was situated off to the side. Collins remembered that these were ovens for baking bread, used almost ubiquitously throughout the region. They bent to pass under a low-slung porch interspersed with strings of deep red chile peppers. The door was open and enticing aromas wafted into the open air. The interior was dim, as there was only one window. An attractive young Mexican woman approached them. She was tidy in a high-necked blouse and crisp apron.

"Bienvenidos señores. Cómo les puedo ayudar?"

"Nos gustería comer," Santiago told her.

She guided them to a worn trestle table, carved in the Spanish colonial style with corresponding chairs. The walls were decorated with small Indian weavings and an ornately carved wooden crucifix was displayed prominently over the lone window. On the opposite wall was a small niche in the thick adobe occupied by a beautifully carved and painted Virgin of Guadalupe. Santiago spoke to the woman in Spanish while C.W. was admiring the sundry decorations.

"What are we eating?" Collins asked when the waitress had departed.

"Many good dishes. You will be *muy complacido*."

After a brief interlude, the meal was served by the woman and a young boy. It consisted of venison in a spicy chile sauce, corn tortillas, glasses of white liquid that tasted of cinnamon, chewy corn kernels in broth, bowls of savory beans and a type of crispy fried sweet dough. Collins found it all to be quite palatable. As they ate, he asked Santiago about the apprehension he had expressed regarding the journey south to the Apache reservation.

"It can be *muy peligroso*... dangerous. Even this town is now full of bad men. Since *El Diablo* came, *muchos bandidos* have been arriving to *Nuevo Mexico*. A man alone can be set upon."

"El Diablo?"

"*Sí.* The great snorting beast of a locomotive that came to our village and brought all the Anglos with it. And *los Indios*, they are killing everyone. You must be very careful."

"I am always exceedingly careful. But I thank you for your advice."

"*De nada.*"

They ate in silence for a long moment.

"*Y las ventanas*," the old man said abruptly.

"I beg your pardon?"

"The windows. There were very few windows before the train came. The glass was *muy caro*."

That made sense, of course, Collins thought. Before the railroad, glass would have been particularly difficult to transport intact. He guessed Señor Duran's age to be well past seventy years and, therefore, he would be cognizant of seminal events in recent history.

"Tell me about Kearny and the U.S. Army," Collins requested. "Do you remember what occurred?"

"*Oh sí… recuerdo…* I remember. *Como si hubiera pasado esta mañana.* I had gone out early *por un paseo…* for a walk. *Entiendes…* as a man does. It was then I saw many cannons all pointing toward the town. *Inmediatamente* I rushed to spread the news. Everyone, it seemed, was screaming and crying. None wanted to become *Americano.* We all wanted to remain under the Mexican flag. *Fue muy malo.*"

The old man told Collins many tales of early days of American occupation, the Taos Revolt and its aftermath and, especially, of the ensuing disenfranchisement of Spanish villagers, farmers and ranchers. He was an engaging and passionate raconteur. When they were finished with their meal, they stepped back out into an afternoon that had grown even warmer.

"*Ahora,*" Santiago said. "We will go to Señor Ilfeld's establishment on the plaza. If there is no *mapa*, we will go to another *tienda* that may have one."

They walked back to the sunbaked dirt square and crossed to an impressive three-story brick structure. Large letters painted on its east side advertised the proprietor's name and his wares, including dry goods, groceries and furniture. The interior building was cool and fragrant with tobacco, leather and mingled odors of food, soap, coffee and various other commodities. A lean and angular clerk in white shirt, suspenders and sleeve stockings approached them. Collins provided him with a list of required goods and he proceeded to fill an apple crate with the items.

"Do you happen to have a recent map of New Mexico Territory?" C.W. asked the clerk.

"No sir. Mr. Brunswick, a couple of doors down, he would have one. He caters to prospectors, military personnel and the like."

When all of his acquisitions had been gathered to-gether, Collins paid the man. He carried his goods out of the building, with Santiago preceding him and holding the door open. There was a wrought iron bench in front of the store.

"I will guard your *cosas* and rest *aquí,*" he told Collins, taking the crate from him and perching on the bench with the box on his knees.

"Thank you. I will return as swiftly as possible."

"*No hay prisa.*"

Mr. Brunswick's establishment did, indeed, possess a recent map of New Mexico Territory, published by one H. L. Thayer out of Colorado. Collins purchased the map as well as some extra ammunition for his Winchester repeater and Colt .45. If the territory had become as dangerous as Señor Duran had pronounced, there was wisdom in being fully equipped. When he returned to the Ilfeld storefront where he had left Santiago, the el-derly gentleman was napping, the crate of purchases now placed beside him on the bench. C.W. felt a twinge of guilt at having compelled him to wander all over town. He patted the man's shoulder lightly.

"*Qué sorpresa!*" he exclaimed, sitting upright in alarm.

"So sorry. I only meant to wake you."

"No, no… " Santiago said, grinning in mild embarrass-ment. "*Por favor, dispensame.* Did you find your map?"

"I did indeed," Collins told him, picking up the case of provisions from the bench. "Shall we make our way back to the stables? Or do you wish to stay in this part of town?"

"I will accompany you to the barn."

Collins wondered briefly where his new friend resided and if he had a family to care for him. He had grown quite fond of the old fellow and planned to remunerate him generously for all his assistance. They sauntered together out of the plaza and headed back toward the river in companionable silence.

45

NEW MEXICO

Molly and Ulysses stood, saddled and loaded, at the hitching rail in front of the livery stable. Collins held a hand out to Santiago after having given him a silver eagle for his services, despite vociferous protestations.

"*Muchas gracias* for all your assistance and advice. I am most grateful."

The old gentleman appeared to be slightly at a loss, accepting the handshake loosely. "*De nada, mi amigo.* It has been a pleasure to know you." There was a moment of awkward silence. "Perhaps you may have requirement of *mi ayuda* on your journey south?"

"What of your family? They surely have need of you."

The old man shook his head sadly. "I have no *familia. Mi esposa* died many years ago and my son has left to California."

Distressed by his inability to accept Santiago's offer, due to its impracticality, Collins reclaimed the man's aged hand in both of his. "I am so very sorry, my friend. As much as I would appreciate your help and companionship, my mission shall be long and arbitrary. I simply cannot expose you to the rigors of my journey."

Santiago slipped his hand free of C.W.'s grasp. "*Entiendo...* I understand." His disappointment was palpable.

With nothing left to say, Collins checked his cinch and swung up on the gelding. Before he could reach down to retrieve Molly's lead rope, Santiago had slipped it from the rail and handed it up to him. The old man suddenly appeared quite shrunken and superannuated.

"I will make certain to find you upon my return," Collins told him. "I have greatly enjoyed your society."

Santiago brightened a little. "I will be here and will want to hear of your great *aventuras*."

"*Adios*, then." C.W. nudged Ulysses forward.

"*Hasta más tarde*," Santiago told him, stepping back and removing his hat to raise it above his head in a gesture of farewell.

Riding southeast along the Gallinas River, Collins departed the burgeoning village of Las Vegas. The day was waning, but the sun had not yet retreated behind the Sangre de Cristo Mountains. He felt rather disconsolate at having left the elderly gentleman behind when he so evidently desired to join the expedition. There was no help for it, however, as he could not be responsible for the man's welfare in the midst of unforeseeable eventualities.

Occasionally, Collins could see smoke rising from among the thick growth of cottonwood trees and shrubbery along the river and assumed there were dwellings scattered along the way. He followed a rugged pathway that seemed to track every bend and loop of the watercourse, wending its way through a narrow passage between steep banks. After a mile or so, the trail emerged into open country. Beside a crook in the stream, he came upon an isolated clearing beneath a gnarled juniper tree. He decided to make camp.

The next morning, C.W. took out the Thayer map and perused it thoroughly. His former journeys to the region had been along alternate routes and this placed him at a distinct disadvantage. From what he could reckon, the most expeditious road to Fort Stanton and the Mescalero agency would be along the Gallinas River to its confluence with the Pecos. From there he would be able to follow the stream to the small village of Puerto de Luna and thence south. A path along the Pecos River would inevitably take him through Fort Sumner, a location wherein he had performed an investigation for Grant during the late war. His findings there haunted him still and he was reluctant to pass through its vicinity, but a detour would mean an unnecessary delay.

The arid country, which he would be forced to traverse, dictated that Collins follow waterways. From the Pecos, he could proceed along the Hondo and Bonito rivers to Fort Stanton. From there it was a short distance to the reservation, located on the Río Tularosa. He was fully aware, even prior to Santiago's counsels, that entering Lincoln County could be somewhat perilous due to conflicts between cattle barons, land speculators and their hired gunmen. Most of the violence of recent years had been resolved as a consequence of several assassinations and arrests, but the region remained intrinsically lawless and several gangs still operated criminal enterprises within the county. Certainly, some of the more pernicious outlaws remained at large.

He caught his animals, saddled and loaded them. Although he had brought his dog tent, C.W. was sleeping rough in order to expedite making and breaking camp. Haste and not comfort took precedence. Swinging into the saddle, he turned to follow the west side of the river in its passage to the southeast, taking a much-eroded trail that appeared to have been quite prominent during an earlier period. He pulled some dried meat from a pocket and chewed on it, full of chagrin at having abjured making coffee before embarking on the day's journey.

The land on either side of the river had opened into savanna broken only by the occasional juniper tree. After an hour or so, Collins passed a small village on the other side of the river and, shortly after, noticed a rather large cluster of buildings off to the west. Cattle were scattered over a great expanse, most of them unmistakably longhorn crossbreds. It was then he recalled that the old Goodnight Loving Trail followed the Pecos River from Texas to Fort Sumner. It had been extended toward Las Vegas and on to Denver and Cheyenne back in the 60's and later diverted to an amended route that departed the Pecos and met up with the Canadian River farther east. This had to be the weather-beaten pathway upon which he rode and it would undoubtedly take him all the way south to the Río Hondo. He was grateful that the cattle trail proceeded along a more direct course than the switchbacks and twists taken by the stream.

Several hours of steady travel brought him to the confluence of the Gallinas and Pecos rivers. Stopping to loosen the cinches and water Molly and Ulysses in a deep pool above a natural dam formed by a large sandstone slab, C.W. stretched his back and ate more jerked meat. He allowed the animals to graze awhile before catching them and, after checking for galls and resetting the saddles, he mounted up to continue his way down the trail following the Pecos. It was midafternoon. The sky was clear and a deep turquoise blue that was unique to the southwestern lands of North America.

The road eventually led him to a shallow ford and he crossed easily, despite the river being rather high and muddy from spring overflow. He rode at a ground eating pace until twilight approached and he found a sheltered glade among some stunted cottonwoods. The river was now the only geographic feature of any note in the vast expanse of barren plains. As Collins prepared another austere camp, he reflected upon the fact he had not encountered another human being all day.

In the early dawn, he built a small fire and made coffee, unwilling to forgo this scant luxury another day. He also fried a piece of salt pork. Despite the delay caused by his breakfast, he was back in the saddle as the sun rose above the inhospitable plains to the east. He had traveled a couple of monotonous hours when he heard horses behind him and pulled up to see who approached. Coming up fast from the northwest was a young Indian man riding a slick bay and herding four other horses before him. He rode bareback with his hands free of reins, holding an old Spencer repeating rifle aimed directly at Collins.

The horses made for the Pecos, apparently thirsty after prolonged exertion. They were lathered with sweat. The Indian slipped from his mount and the animal joined the others at the river. He walked over to where Collins sat his gelding, his right hand resting upon the Colt revolver, awaiting the young man's next move. He presumed this was an Apache, given the traditional costume of leggings, tall moccasins with the distinctive turned up toes and a cotton blouse over a full breechclout. His head was wrapped in a wide strip of blue cloth and his thick, unbraided hair reached his shoulders. From past experience, C.W. recognized this preferred style of apparel.

For a long moment the two men examined each other unceremoniously. Then the Indian gestured with his rifle for Collins to get off his horse. C.W. ignored his directive, saying *"da!"* loudly and definitively while he pulled the .45 from its holster. Swiftly cocking the hammer, he aimed it unswervingly at the Apache's forehead. In the brief time since the Indian's arrival, Collins had adequately determined the fellow was alone and he was resolved to not be disadvantaged by the encounter. He held the young man's gaze and raised an eyebrow as if to inquire how he cared to proceed. The Apache unaccountably gave a slight shrug, turned to leap upon his horse and, with a shrill cry to propel the other horses away from the water, drove his small herd past Collins as if he did not exist. Ulysses pranced about, made restless by the horses galloping by. Collins noticed a Bar 4 brand upon the shoulders of two of the animals.

Shaking his head in astonishment and grateful he had remembered the Apache word for "no," he prodded the gelding into a walk and continued his journey. If the young Apache had not been raiding alone, he would probably be lying dead and his beloved gelding and mule would be the property of Apache raiders. Curious, he thought, that the enterprising young warrior would be depredating so far north by himself. He sincerely hoped his good fortune would hold and his scalp would not ultimately decorate an Apache lance. Perhaps Peng's silver fish was bringing him luck. Collins took a drink of water from his canteen and patted his horse on the neck. He recalled a quotation from Shakespeare's King Henry VI. "What Fates impose, that men must needs abide; It boots not to resist both wind and tide." In other words, in for a penny, in for a pound… there was nothing else for it.

8

Puerto de Luna was not nearly as large as Las Vegas, but certainly appeared to be a prosperous village. The countryside surrounding the settlement was extensively cultivated, watered by a network of irrigation ditches. Vast flocks of sheep populated the landscape beyond. Sandstone escarpments and bluffs bounded the river valley on the east and west. As Collins approached the hamlet, he passed a rough looking man riding a gaunt roan horse and leading a seven mule packstring loaded with hides and bales of wool. The man raised a hand in greeting, but said nothing.

Upon riding into the cluster of adobe structures, he noticed an L-shaped building with a metal roof and a covered porch the full length of its east side. There was an extensive orchard nearby and several flower beds were exhibiting new growth of daffodils, tulips and other variegated blooms. Several children were playing in the vicinity of the building and a few men sat on the veranda, smoking cigars and speaking in low voices. A tall man stood and walked over as Collins dismounted. He watched as C.W. tethered Ulysses to one of the porch columns, wrapped Molly's lead rope around the saddle horn and eased the cinches.

"Good afternoon," the man said. "My name is Richard Dunn. My partner and I run this place."

"This is quite an impressive oasis," Collins said, squinting up at him.

"It is undoubtedly the most prominent in this part of the country. Come on up and rest a moment."

Stepping onto the porch, Collins nodded to the three other strangers seated in the shade. He leaned against a column across from the small group as Dunn regained his seat on a Mexican equipale chair. The door to the building was open and a stocky bearded man emerged. He noticed Collins and held out a hand.

"Alexander Grzelachowski at your service," the fellow said in heavily accented English.

"Padre Polaco," one of the men said and chuckled.

"Yes, yes, that is how you call me," Grzelachowski said good-naturedly. "You see, I am from Poland and came as a priest to this country."

"Charles Collins... Pleased to meet you," C.W. said, somewhat bemused to find such a man in this out of the way place. "You are Mr. Dunn's partner?"

"I am indeed. And Mr. Ilfeld of Las Vegas."

"I was just recently a customer of that gentleman's establishment."

"We dab our fingers in just about every venture," Dunn told him.

"*Age quod agis*," the Polish priest said, wagging a finger as if tutoring a school boy.

"Do well what you do," Collins translated.

"Oh how excellent," Grzelachowski said, delightedly. "You speak Latin."

"Some. I never was the recipient of proper schooling. Certainly not as extensive as the education you must have received in a Catholic seminary."

"He also speaks Greek and some passable Spanish," Dunn told him.

"Only a little Latin." Grzelachowski appeared to be discomfited by his partner's apparent embellishments. "Now, now... enough of that. Have you offered Mr. Collins some refreshment?"

"We can offer you tea, buttermilk, coffee or whisky," Dunn told Collins.

"Coffee, if you please."

The priest stepped to the open door. "Secundina, are you there?" he asked in a raised voice.

A rotund woman appeared in the doorway, her ample proportions restrained by a high-waisted dress. A small child trailed along, holding a twist of frock firmly in a tiny fist. Her face was very comely and her countenance agreeable. "*Sí mi esposo*, I am here."

"Would you please get this gentleman a cup of coffee?"

"Of course," she said smiling at Collins. "*Uno momento.*"

"That is my wife," Grzelachowski said proudly.

"*No exactemente*," one of the men sitting beyond Dunn interjected.

"*Mój Boże!*" the priest exclaimed in what C.W. assumed was the Polish language. "*Homo cogitat, Deus judicat.* Man thinks and God judges, my dear Marino," he told the man and looked over at Collins and shrugged. "I am a priest. She is my common-law wife. What else could she be?"

" 'Curse on all laws but those which love has made,' " Collins said.

"Alexander Pope! You know his works?"

"Some. *Eloisa to Abelard* to be certain."

The woman had returned with a blue and white ceramic mug and handed it to Collins. The child still clung to her skirts.

"Thank you, *Señora.*"

"*De nada.*" She gave a shallow curtsy and swept back into the building.

Collins sat upon a nearby ladder back chair and sipped his coffee. It was strong and quite acceptable. Shade from the building spread extensively enough that his animals were not subjected to the hot sun. He found the priest's company enjoyable and intriguing. Soon enough he would have to move on and find a place to camp for the night, but for now he craved more discourse with the cultured gentleman.

The fellow named Marino and his companions bid everyone *adiós* and sauntered off the porch to disappear around the building.

"These men," Grzelachowski said, nodding in their direction. "They can cause trouble and do not like to work."

"Are they your employees?" C.W. asked.

"I hire them on my ranch and then after a few days they quit and come to Puerto de Luna. Later, they again ask for work and I hire them again. It is preferable to them stealing my sheep and cattle."

"Where are you headed?" Dunn asked Collins conversationally.

"Fort Stanton. I have business there."

"And I detect you have a slight accent. Irish?"

"Yes."

"I am from Nova Scotia, myself. *Fanaidh duine sona ri sith, ach bheir duine dona dubh-leum.*"

"Your Gaelic is somewhat different than the Irish. Do you mean that the fortunate man stays and the unfortunate man takes a leap in the dark?"

"That is as close as can be," Dunn said. "I had no choice but to seek my fortune in faraway lands."

"New Mexico Territory is most certainly a fair distance from your home."

"Not as far as Polska," the priest said, smiling. "Or Ireland."

Dunn stood and stretched. "I must warn you that Lincoln County is not always a healthy locale. I recommend you watch your back," he told Collins. "And Mr. Chisum is a tough customer. The *Padre* here has had

56

dealings with him. If it is your intention to do business with the man, be warned. He is not trustworthy."

"Yes," Grzelachowski said, "he owes me over three thousand dollars, but will not pay even though the courts have made the judgement that he is obligated to do so."

Collins finished his coffee and set the cup on a small table nearby. "I thank you for the advice and the coffee. Truth be told, I do not plan to conduct any type of business that will bring me in contact with the infamous Mr. Chisum. I am aware of him and some of the other influential men of Lincoln County and do not plan to interact with any of them if it can be forsworn."

"But you said you had business in Fort Stanton," Dunn said, displaying unmistakable curiosity.

"My business is more in the nature of inquiry than commerce."

"Inquiry?" Grzelachowski asked. "I possess much knowledge regarding the region. Perhaps I may be of assistance?"

"Only if you are acquainted with Victorio, the Apache chief."

The priest crossed himself. "*Deus Meus.* I sincerely hope you are being humorous. There have been many appalling murders on both sides of the border since he broke out from the Mescalero agency."

Not wanting to share details of his commission, Collins dissembled. "Mostly I have queries at the fort and with Agent Russell. It is of no great import."

"I see that you wish to play your hand close to your chest," Grzelachowski said prudently. "We must not be impolite and plumb your depths. Would you care to stay and dine with us? I should warn you that I have nine children and it is frequently disorderly and sometimes chaotic. As a whole, however, they are exceedingly well behaved"

"Sometimes all hell breaks loose," Dunn said, grinning.

C.W. smiled. "I thank you, but there remains enough daylight for me to cover more ground. I plan to camp farther down the Pecos."

"Do you require any supplies?" the Padre inquired.

"I purchased all I require at Mr. Ilfeld's store in Las Vegas, but thank you."

"A moment, if you please," Grzelachowski said, raising a finger and disappearing into the building.

"The Padre is the best of men," Dunn said.

"I sincerely wish I had the leisure to become more acquainted with both of you."

Dunn wandered over to the edge of the veranda. "Perhaps on your return journey. You have some nice animals there."

"Thank you."

"I am not being overly scrupulous, Mr. Collins, when I say you must be cautious while traveling alone in these parts. Especially with such fine stock."

Grzelachowski returned bearing a package wrapped in paper. "These are the finest *tamales* in all of *Nuevo Mexico*," he said, handing the parcel to Collins.

"My thanks to you. I am most grateful." C.W. stepped down to place the bundle in his saddlebags. He adjusted the saddles and tightened the cinches. "Gentlemen, it has been a genuine pleasure to converse with you." He swung onto his horse. "And I will, indeed, be mindful of your counsel, Mr. Dunn."

The Polish priest came over to stand beside the gelding with his head bowed. "*Sancte Michael Archangele, defende nos in proelio, contra nequitiam et insidias diaboli esto praesidium. Imperet illi Deus, supplices deprecamur: tuque, Princeps militiae caelestis, in virtute Dei, in infernum detrude satanam aliosque spiritus malignos, qui ad perditionem animarum pervagantur in mundo. Amen.*" He made the sign of the cross.

"That is the prayer to St. Michael," C.W. said. "My mother must have whispered it a hundred times on the ship voyage from Ireland. Thank you... I appreciate the sentiment."

"Come see us again, Mr. Collins."

"I will endeavor to do so. Farewell gentlemen." C.W. turned his horse and headed south out of the little village with Molly steadfastly trailing behind.

The late afternoon light was taking on a golden rose hue. He could cover a few more miles before night fell, then camp along the river. As he rode, he contemplated Grzelachowski's seemingly conflicting enterprises of business and religious vocation. Perhaps, he thought, the priest's interests were not so irreconcilable. After all, the Vatican in Rome was certainly not impoverished and the Church, throughout the centuries, had possessed most of the wealth and much of the land in Europe. Such is the nature of self-deception. One can justify anything.

TENEMENT

9

He could hear the hobbles clinking on his gelding as the horse grazed desultorily along the riverbank. Collins usually slept well, especially after a long day in the saddle. This night, notwithstanding, he simply could not fall asleep and his mind kept hearkening back to his days as a police constable in New York City. He had many repugnant and disconcerting recollections of his time with the Metropolitan Police Force, but one in particular caused him supreme disquiet whenever it ascended unbidden from the recesses of his memory.

A woman had found Collins and another constable attempting to rouse a drunkard from where he lay in the middle of Kenmare Street. She begged them most stridently to come with her to a nearby tenement building, claiming she had discovered a gruesome crime. The other constable stayed behind with the inebriate and C.W. had followed the malodorous and toothless crone to one of the narrow, wretched and overcrowded apartments of the lower east side of Manhattan.

She had beckoned him to accompany her to the back of the structure, passing by a line of four privies that emanated stench so foul as to make his gorge rise. He was forced to dodge a line of newly washed undergarments and he was struck by the irrelevant thought that they would surely absorb the odors of human excrement as they dried. The old hag had scurried into a back entrance of the tenement where another forceful and abominable odor assaulted his senses. In the pale light from the open door, Collins could see a heap of refuse that almost filled the entire space and tossed upon it was the rag doll corpse of a small child. The woman had pointed to it almost gleefully.

When he had moved closer, C.W. had been able to discern it was the body of a girl. Her size might have implied her age to be at around five or six years, but he was well aware that malnutrition and disease stunted the growth of many of the immigrant children who dwelled in the pesthole warrens of the city. She wore a filthy frock and, despite recent cold weather, was host to seething masses of fly maggots. He turned to vomit and the old woman cackled delightedly. He made a move to strike her and she scuttled clear, departing the room and shrieking epithets as she went. When he had examined the cadaver more closely, he could make out severe bruising around the face, neck and arms where they extended from the clothing, regardless of the blotchy yellowing color of the skin, and the side of the head appeared to be caved in. The body had been discernably gnawed upon by rats and the eye sockets were empty.

Abruptly, one of his animals roused a bird from undergrowth near the river. Collins sat up, his heart pounding and somewhat nauseated by the grisly memory from his past. He covered his face with his hands and sought to exorcise the ghost. There had been no resolution or punishment and he had never been able to locate the little girl's parents. She had been savagely murdered and discarded with the garbage and there had been no promise of justice for the tiny child. It was one of those sepulchral tales recounted by many of his fellow constables in the Metropolitan. He certainly had witnessed far more ghastly scenes during the late war, but the child haunted him still, as if entreating that some solitary soul remember she had lived and died.

Fully awake and restive, he slipped from the bedroll and stepped a few feet away to relieve himself. There was a gauzy halo of light on the eastern horizon, so he yielded to his insomnia and packed up his bedding and kindled a small fire to make coffee. He was perched on a dead tree that lay near camp, grinding coffee beans, when a figure emerged from a neighboring brake of willows. Already edgy from lack of sleep and uncongenial reminiscence, Collins reached for the Winchester that leaned against his packsaddle nearby and stood to meet the stranger.

"What do you want?" he asked unceremoniously.

"*Por favor señor*, I am in a bad way."

The person moved into the firelight and Collins could make out a Mexican boy dressed in tattered rags. His face was grimy and his feet were bare.

"I have come far *señor*. I have much hunger."

Gesturing toward the log, Collins said, "Sit down. I will give you some food."

He placed the rifle on the bedroll near to hand and poured ground coffee into the pot on the fire. He remembered the tamales and went to retrieve the package from his saddlebags. He handed two of them to his guest. The boy stripped back the cornhusk wrappings and devoured the food swiftly. C.W. hunkered down on his haunches and watched the young man pick at the remnants of corn meal on the husks.

"Tell me your story," he said.

The boy belched loudly and wiped his mouth on a sleeve. "*Me llamo* Felipe Ronquillo. I was captured by *los Apaches* many days ago... they surrounded me when I was herding sheep on the hills near Bosquecito. They treated me very badly and left me with *las mujeres* when they hunted. I ran away when there was only one to watch. That is all."

He assumed the boy was telling the truth, given the state of his clothing and feet, but Collins had learned to be cautious. "How many days were you captive?"

"*No sé.* I do not know. I ran away two days ago."

"Do you want some coffee?"

"*Por favor.*" Felipe scratched his head. "What is this river? *Dónde estamos?*"

He handed the boy a tin cup of coffee and poured one for himself. "We are just a few miles south of Puerto de Luna."

Felipe blew on the hot liquid. "I have a *tío* in Los Ojitos. It is a little down the river from here."

"Then you may accompany me. My horse is able to carry both of us."

"*Muchas gracias, señor.* It is very good of you."

Collins put out the fire and packed up his belongings. Felipe helped him saddle and load the animals.

"This mule *es muy bonita,*" the boy said, stroking Molly's jaw. "You must not allow *los Apaches* to steal her."

"No... that would not do." Collins held the gelding's bridle. "Mount up," he told Felipe.

After the boy had clambered onto the horse, C.W, swung up behind him and they moved off along the river, still following the old cattle trail. Dawn was breaking and birds were singing uproariously among the trees and brush that lined the stream.

"Your parents must be very worried about you," Collins said after a while.

"*Mi papa es muerto. Mi madre* has married a man who is very hard. I work for some Anglos with the sheep and they give me a place to sleep and some food. It is not so bad."

"How old are you?"

"*Quince.* Perhaps more... perhaps less. I will be a

man soon and then I will take my mother away to some other place."

Smiling to himself, Collins thought about his own mother, dead now for several years. She had been a fierce and devout Irish woman who had always been a steady harbor in his youth and a wise counselor when he became a man. Despite the fact his father had died when she was quite young, she never considered any of the offers she received from other men. She would say, "*Ba sgaradh sinn fria colainn an sgaradh sin.*" Their parting was as the parting of the head from the body. Instead, she devoted herself to supporting and educating her only child and lending aid to the needy.

Smallpox had taken her during an epidemic that raged throughout Irish tenement housing in New York City. Although they had saved enough to rent a snug apartment above a saloon owned by one of her admirers, and she worked as a maid in a fine house, his mother spent her Sundays nursing the sick in the poorer neighborhoods. Her loss was felt not only by him, but by many of those who relied on her generosity and care. Unwittingly, he let out a long sigh.

"You are sad, *señor?*" Felipe asked.

"I was thinking of my own mother."

"Did she marry *un mal hombre?*"

He laughed. "No, Felipe, she is gone these many years."

"That is unhappy."

"Yes."

He took a piece of jerked meat from his saddlebags and handed it to the boy.

"*Como te llama, señor?*"

"I am called Charles."

"*Muchas gracias,* Charles."

They rode companionably as the early morning

passed. Felipe recounted details of his days with the Apache and Collins came to the conclusion that the boy had been fortunate. He had heard that the Apaches tended to keep younger captives alive, either to replace children who had been slain by soldiers or held in bondage. If kept in servitude, they were eventually accepted into the band and were largely contented to be so. Either way, they had not killed him outright nor been fiercely vigilant in guarding him. As Cervantes had written, "The wheel of fortune turns quicker than a mill wheel."

10

The houses of Los Ojitos were remarkably similar to those of Puerto de Luna, but there were fewer of them. It appeared only a few families populated the settlement. In the heart of the village were a series of clear springs that emptied into the river and small ditches fed humble kitchen gardens beside the adobe dwellings. Flocks of Churro sheep grazed on the riverbanks and in surrounding fields. A woman was stirring something in an iron pot suspended over a fire. Aromatic *piñon* wood smoke perfumed the air downwind.

Collins dismounted and Felipe slid to the ground after him. A man came around the corner of one of the houses accompanied by an enormous dog. The animal began to bark and make lunges at the two of them. Molly spun around and cocked a hind leg in anticipation of attack. The man called for the dog to come back to him.

"Perhaps you should explain why we are here," Collins told Felipe.

The boy walked over and began speaking rapidly. The man nodded and patted Felipe on the shoulder. The woman and two other men arrived and after much discussion, they attempted to guide the youth into a nearby residence. He shook his head and turned to point at Collins. One of the men came over to him.

"*Buenos días, señor.* Will you come and take a meal with us? It was kind of you to help this boy. His *tío* will be very glad to see him."

"The uncle is not here?"

"No, he is out with *los ovejos*... the sheep. He will return this evening."

"I am glad he has family here. Felipe has been very fortunate in his escape and survival. *Muchas gracias,* but I must keep traveling and so cannot accept your kind offer of food."

"*Pero* we would wish you to come to our house. *Verdadamente.*"

C.W. could see all the people, now gathered around the boy, watching him. "No *gracias*. I am very sorry, but I must keep riding." He checked his cinch and mounted up. He waved at Felipe.

The young man came running over. "*Muchas gracias... Muchas gracias* Charles!" he exclaimed.

Reaching down to lay a hand on the boy's shoulder, Collins said, "You are very welcome, Felipe. Take good care of yourself."

"*Vaya con Dios.*"

As he road out of the small village, he thought about Felipe's ordeal with the Indians. They had been harsh and not overly generous with sustenance, but he could have fared much worse. The Apaches had been betrayed and deceived and forced to live in land that was unknown to them, such as San Carlos, an ungodly location of vermin and blazing heat. Many of the military men from the East were hard pressed to endure such conditions when they were assigned for duty on that particular reservation. Apache reprisals for maltreatment were sweeping across the territories of Arizona and New Mexico.

There was plenty of daylight remaining, for the hour was still early. It warmed considerably as he travelled and by the noon hour, Collins was decidedly uncomfortable. Furthermore, the landscape was mortally tedious. He found shelter under the shade of a lone tree on the

Pecos River and dismounted. He eased the cinches and led the animals to water. They drank deeply and afterward, C.W. checked their hooves for stones and adjusted their saddles. He had returned to follow the stock trail after Los Ojitos, but it had led him quite a distance west of the river and he now resolved to remain along the waterway, despite its snaky meanderings. At least there would be intermittent shade and available water.

After filling a canteen, he swung into the saddle and departed the pleasant awning of the cottonwood. The floodplain of the Pecos possessed sparse vegetation and few trees. Grass was scarce due to overgrazing. Collins imagined that many alterations to the flora, fauna and landscape had taken place since the arrival of the Spanish back in the 16th century. He scanned the horizon for signs of life and saw nothing but *cholla* cactus and the occasional juniper tree. Pausing only to water Ulysses and Molly and to relieve himself, Collins rode steadily until early evening, wanting to cover ground and move through the monotonous terrain as swiftly as possible. Sporadically, he had to skirt arroyos and dry creek beds that broke up the riverbank and cut deep scars into the land.

Coming to a sharp bend in the stream with a shallow pool and a few runty alder trees, C.W. decided to make camp. He had had a prickling sensation on the back of his neck for several hours and, after unsaddling and watering his animals, he picketed them among the brush out of sight, feeding them each a good measure of grain from the supply stowed in Molly's packs. He eschewed a fire, not wanting to announce his presence, and ate a cold can of beans. He had filled an extra canteen with coffee from the morning. It would suffice for the next day.

Settling down on top of his bedroll as the evening remained stifling, Collins laid the Winchester close to hand and slid the .45 under his hat beside his head.

Still edgy with an inchoate disquietude, he lay awake for what seemed to him to be half the night. An enthusiastic pack of coyotes, gleefully yipping and wailing, were a further hindrance to slumber. He finally fell asleep from utter exhaustion. Precipitously, without any sense of passing time, he awoke at the slight rustling of underbrush. Reaching for the revolver, his wrist was crushed beneath the weight of a foot. In the light of a waxing moon, he could make out the silhouette of a man bending to retrieve his rifle and handgun. The Indian's attire made Collins to understand beyond a doubt that his life was now in extraordinary danger.

More Apache warriors entered the camp and dug through his packs. The first man yanked Collins up by the hair, punched him forcefully in the face and shoved him down again on the ground, binding his hands together while pinning C.W. with one knee in his abdomen before he could get his wits about him. The warrior then aimed Collins' own Colt .45 at his head to keep him supine. One Apache led Molly and Ulysses into the clearing. The mule was braying in distress and the gelding was clearly terrified, his eyes showing white and his head pulling upward like a stargazer against the weight of the man who gripped his rope. Despite certain knowledge he was probably about to die, C.W.'s heart broke at his animals' anguish. Yanked to his feet, he was lifted savagely by two Indians and thrown face down across a raw-boned nag. They bound his hands to his feet beneath the animal's belly with rawhide strips and ran his lariat around him and the horse several times, lashing him firmly in position. The animal's backbone dug into his gut painfully and he could feel blood running from his nose. He kept twisting his head in an attempt to catch a glimpse of his horse and mule, but dust from the milling Apache horses obscured his view. He guessed he was at the mercy of about nine warriors. He could not comprehend why they were keeping him alive.

With a word from the leader, the Indians mounted up and set off at a dead gallop. Collins could not tell in what direction they were moving and his physical discomfort was such that it was nearly unbearable. The Apaches seemed to be driving a large bunch of horses before them, no doubt plundered from ranches and settlements. He assumed they were moving west back toward the Apache mountain strongholds, but feared they could also be riding south toward Mexico. He had no way of knowing by which band he had been captured. If by the Chiricahua, then Mexico could very well be their destination. If they belonged to the Mescalero Apache, it was possible he might still be able to escape. Old Mexico, on the contrary, would portend small chance for survival.

The day grew hotter and Collins suffered acutely from the sun beating down upon his bowed and elongated back. His ordeal was worsened by the rawhide fetters cutting into his flesh, the horse's serrated spine grinding into his stomach, the choking dust and the sheer discomfort of being trussed in a position where his head snapped back and forth with every jog of the animal's irregular gait. The greatest torment, however, was the trepidation he experienced in regard to the welfare of his beloved horse and mule, as well as his own questionable fate. Again, he strove to lift his head to catch sight of Molly or Ulysses to no avail. The Apaches were riding alongside the horse herd rather than endure the plumes of pulverized dirt raised by their hooves. C.W.'s skeletal pony had been turned loose to trail behind and his mouth and nose filled with chalky grit. He soon ran out of saliva with which to expectorate, as dire thirst increased his abominable misery.

Unbelievably, the hours passed and Collins did not

lose consciousness, even though he truly longed to swoon so as to find respite from his suffering. Instead, mile after mile of open country slipped past at a killing pace, only occasionally punctuated by a trot or walk to allow the horses to blow. Once, the Apaches let the animals water at a shallow spring, sheltered in a defile among some sandstone boulders, while they slaked their own thirst from woven willow containers. They offered him nothing and his own thirst was magnified abysmally. The sun reached its zenith, then began to descend. It slowly came to him, in his seemingly inexhaustible purgatory, that they were, in fact, travelling west. This revelation afforded him a glimmer of hope, but as the afternoon progressed, the horse to which he was tethered began to falter. Soon it began to lag behind. Collins' original captor dropped back to give the nag a lash with a quirt and the animal found a new burst of speed for a while. Finally, it stumbled twice and, mercifully for C.W., halted its progress, crumpling to the ground in a slow and almost gentle stagger. With a pathetic groan, the horse rolled onto its side and gave up its life, pinning Collins' legs beneath its weight.

At first, he thought he might have been forgotten, doomed to die slowly beneath the decomposing carcass of his erstwhile mount, but three warriors summarily appeared and leapt down from their ponies, one of them slicing through Collins' restraints. They rolled the horse's body off him and he crawled a short distance and attempted to stand, his hands still bound in front of him. One of the Indians actually caught his arm and supported him a moment. He thought there was a hint of recognition, but it passed in a flash and another of the Apaches grabbed his hair and brandished a sizeable skinning knife before his eyes, speaking loudly and angrily. An animated discussion took place while Collins considered stratagems for flight, all of which were astoundingly impractical. Instead, he stood docilely, waiting for the blood to fully regain tenure of his legs and contemplating the likelihood of having his scalp lifted then and there. In the moment, he gave no effort to recalling any of the Apache language he had acquired in the past. He was beyond caring.

Finally, the young warrior who had assisted him in standing, dragged Collins to his Indian pony and motioned for him to swing up. C.W. grabbed a handful of mane and leapt feebly onto the horse, grateful it was not more than fifteen hands tall. The Apache sprang nimbly up behind him and they loped after the other warriors and the herd of horses. Unaccountably, Collins glanced back at the dead animal and experienced a tinge of pathos at its sad end. Then he wound his fingers more tightly into the pony's mane as their pace quickened and the countryside swept past. He thought the Indian behind him whispered the word "jackrabbit," but the wind and his debilitated condition made him doubt his own senses.

WARRIORS

11

It was with unspeakable gratitude that he discovered his new mount was to be his own darling mule. When the band of warriors had again halted to allow the horses to rest, he was thrown down from the Apache's pony and another warrior shoved him toward where Molly stood, sides heaving from fatigue. Her head came up as Collins approached. One of the Indians tossed a bosal bridle at him and he slipped it over her nose and ears, speaking softly to her. He had only ever ridden her once and fervently hoped she would permit him to do so again. Jumping onto his belly across her back, he swung a leg around and sat up, realizing the Apaches were observing him as if eager for a scuffle. Molly merely turned her head and sniffed his left leg, then stood patiently. Almost at once, some of the warriors let out ululating cries and rode past him at a gallop, spooking the horse herd into action and causing the mule to tuck her rump and take off after them.

His hands still tied and unused to riding bareback, C.W. squeezed his legs around Molly's sides and took up the *mecate* reins, tying them together so he would not lose one. She had a surprisingly smooth gait and he yielded to the cadence, heartened by having some semblance of dignity back. Despite his limited knowledge of Apache ways and creeds, he knew enough to realize if he continued to mildly accept captivity, his life would be forfeit. Apaches had nothing but contempt for weakness. Now that he could feel his legs again and he was at least upright, it was imperative that he make a show of defiance or attempt escape. He would bide his time and look for an auspicious opportunity. He was certainly angry enough to kill.

Purposefully nudging Molly ahead, he moved up alongside the horse herd and sought a glimpse of his gelding. It was then he perceived that Ulysses was being ridden by one of the warriors just ahead of him. The horse was frothy from exertion and eating up ground in the smooth even gallop that Collins valued greatly. Suddenly overcome by rage, he urged Molly to come abreast of his gelding, letting go of the reins and precipitously reaching out and looping his tethered hands around the Indian's throat before the man realized what was happening. With surprise on his side, he jerked the Apache off the horse and ruthlessly choked him, dangling the Indian from the side of the mule, before hurling the man into the dirt so that he tumbled and rolled into a heap. Reaching out for Ulysses' reins, he turned Molly with his legs and veered away from the running horse herd, making a desperate bid for freedom.

As if his animals knew what was happening, they heightened their stride and increased the distance between them and the Apache warriors. He could hear the Indians yelling and expected to be shot off the mule at any moment. Beyond any plan except that of escape, he rode doggedly into the badlands before him, fixated on a line of low timbered hills ahead. Against all reasoning, he thought perhaps he could make some kind of a stand if he could only make it to cover. Gunfire rang out behind him and he lay low on the mule's neck and spoke words of encouragement to his animals. As he drew nearer the hills before him and his animals tired from their Herculean efforts, he was bracketed by two warriors who took hold of both sets of reins, pulling the horse and mule to a stop. Collins kicked out at the Indians and attempted to swing his clenched fists to strike a blow at the nearest man. In response, the Apache clipped him viciously on the temple with his rifle butt and he dropped to the ground insensible, only dimly registering another impassioned argument. Then he was thrown across Molly's back and again secured with rope and he descended into oblivion.

Night had fallen before he fully regained consciousness. He was lying on his side beneath a cottonwood tree and could hear running water. His hands and feet were bound and he struggled to sit up. The Apaches were gathered around a small fire not far away and C.W. could smell roasting meat. He searched his memory for some word that would be of use.

"*Tú*," he said forcefully, remembering the word for water "*Tú.*"

The Indians looked over. "*Duha guuń'ał da*," one of the men told him.

"*Tú*," he repeated.

The youthful warrior who had cut him loose from the dead horse came over. He motioned for him to open his mouth and tip his head back. Pouring water in a stream from a wicker vessel, the Indian allowed C.W. to drink a good portion. He paused, then gave him more. The Apache whom Collins had knocked off his horse, his face and throat bruised and abraded, walked up. He was about to kick C.W. in the face when he was thwarted by the other man and a brief quarrel ensued. The apparent leader of the group barked a command from his place by the fire and the recalcitrant Indian retreated.

"*Gah'tsu*," the young man with the water said to Collins, slapping his chest. "You are *Washindun'*. I remember."

"Jackrabbit," Collins said, remembering. "Yes you

were a boy. You are Mescalero."

"I have another name now. A warrior name. But you may call me Jackrabbit."

"*'Ixéhe,*" C.W. said, recalling more of the language.

"I will get meat," Gah'tsu said and went back to the fire. He spoke at length to the leader while gesturing with his lower lip in Collins' direction. Then he returned with a generous portion of roasted meat and handed it to Collins.

"*'Ixéhe,*" he said again and tore a bite from the flesh with his teeth. It was half-raw venison and acute hunger rendered it a feast. Jackrabbit squatted on his heels and watched him. The leader left the fire and joined them.

"You speak *Ndé Bizaa'*. Why?"

"I was sent to Mescalero a few years ago to track whisky peddlers."

Gah'tsu was about to say something, but the chief held up a hand.

"You are here now. *Por qué?*" he asked.

"To find out about something. To find out about the killing of Mescalero people and the taking of horses and guns."

The man, lean and dark with clear eyes and obvious intelligence, considered him a moment then walked away.

"He is called *Ch'iguna'ái Huyáá*. Sunrise," Gah'tsu told him.

Finishing his meat, Collins thanked Jackrabbit again and the young man returned to the fire. He was endeavoring to find a comfortable position in the hopes of getting some sleep when the chief, Sunrise, returned and stood over him.

"Some of them want to kill you. Others think you might be useful for trade. Another asks me to trust you."

Sitting up, Collins simply nodded, careful to avoid

prolonged eye contact. "This other man. Is it Gah'tsu?"

"That was his name once. We call him *'Ashí' Huguł'n.*"

"He knew me from before."

"Should we kill you? Why should we trust you?"

"I have been sent by important white men. Agent Russell at Mescalero has been saying the Apache have been ill used. I am supposed to learn the truth."

Sunrise gave a truncated and contemptuous laugh. "The truth? White men want truth?"

"I do," C.W. said quietly.

The Apache was silent, gazing into the darkness. Finally he said, *"'Ashí' Huguł'n* seems to think much of you. I will offer you a choice."

Collins sat quietly, unsure of how to respond.

"Will you accept?" the chief asked.

"How can I answer? If one choice is death, I will accept the other."

"We will speak more," Sunrise said, fading into the night.

All of the other Indians seemed to be bedded down near the dying fire. Collins slumped onto his side and curled up against the growing chill. He wondered briefly where he was, thinking the distinct sound of flowing water could mean they were on the banks of the Río Grande. He was wakeful, pondering his circumstances and apprehensive about what he would encounter in the morrow. Sleep finally embraced him in spite of his anxious musings.

APACHE CAPTIVES

12

Strong hands choked him and he pitched instinctively out of their grasp. The waxing moon was bright and he could see that his attacker was the same warrior he had snatched off his gelding. Collins was wide awake now and aware he was fighting for his life. At a terrible disadvantage with both hands and feet secured, he swept his legs to knock the Indian off balance, then threw his full weight on top of him and began to pound his clenched fists into the man's face over and over. His only advantage was his size and superior mass. The Apache was reaching for something in his belt and, figuring it was a weapon, C.W. rolled off and booted the man as hard as he could in the head. Momentarily stunned, the Indian lay inert and Collins seized the man's knife, pulling it free from its sheath and slashing through the rawhide strips that bound his feet. By this time, his assailant had come back to himself and made a lunge at him. Collins was already on his feet and, bracing for the assault, drove the knife deep into the warrior's shoulder with both hands, dropping the man to the ground.

The other Apaches had come over and were impassively observing the skirmish. Enraged and tired of being their whipping boy, C.W. felt more than inclined to kill the man, but was truly unsure as to whether this would guarantee his survival or seal his fate. The chief jerked the knife from his hand, thereby eliminating the quandary.

"Juanito Luna wants you dead," he said, pointing his lower lip at the man on the ground.

"Clearly."

"Do you want to kill him now?"

The warrior named Juanito Luna was sitting up, holding the knife wound while blood oozed between his fingers.

Collins shrugged involuntarily. "I was defending myself."

"It is shameful to attack an unarmed man who is also helpless."

"I agree. But I am no longer ready to kill him." Collins paused. "I was," he said honestly. "But not now."

Several of the other Indians went back to the fire ring and stirred up the coals. Soon flames were casting a mantle of light across the encampment. Sunrise, the leader, pulled Juanito Luna to his feet. He spoke to him at length in their language, after which the wounded man walked over to the group by the fire.

The chief turned to study C.W. for a long while. This time, Collins returned his gaze defiantly. At last Sunrise narrowed his eyes and said, "We must raid for ammunition. Will you fight?"

"I will fight."

"Will you fight as a *Chihenne* Apache?"

"Yes."

Without another word, Sunrise cut his hands free and strode away. When C.W. walked to the fire, the chief was speaking to the warriors. They glanced up at him, then occupied themselves with roasting more meat. One of them was wearing his hat. Juanito Luna tossed him a half-roasted chunk of venison with his good arm. Collins hunkered down beside him and began to eat it. The man's wound had been dressed with a moistened wad of some type of plant and had stopped bleeding. His face was the color of raw liver where Collins had battered him.

"We have your supplies," Gah'tsu told him. "Will you make coffee?"

"*Au,*" he said, using the Apache word in assent.

Jackrabbit led him over to where his panniers were piled. He dug out his coffeepot, cups, mill and sack of beans, also retrieving a package of sugar. He noticed that most of his provisions remained intact. "Will I get my animals back now?" he asked.

"Perhaps."

They returned to the fire and Collins made coffee. The Indians took turns with his two tin cups, adding sugar and visibly enjoying the beverage. He was included in the sharing of coffee and Collins thought this might be a good sign. The sun was coming up and birds were creating a raucous chorale among the trees. After the coffee was gone, an Apache kicked sand on the fire and they dispersed. C.W. went back to his packs to stow away his belongings. At a loss as to his next move, he wondered where his animals and saddles were. Gah'tsu called his name and he looked up to see the young man holding Molly and Ulysses. The mule wore her halter and sawbuck and the gelding was saddled and bridled. He also handed over Collins' Stetson hat, slightly worse for wear.

Together, they loaded the panniers on the mule. Collins was astonished that all his belongings had been returned, except of course, his Winchester and Colt revolver. Not so long ago, he had been convinced he would die. He tightened the cinches while Jackrabbit went to fetch his own pony. He spent time patting and reassuring his animals, profoundly grateful they were unharmed. His original captor walked up to him and handed over the .45 Colt in its holster and the Winchester.

"*Di'hi,*" he said, pressing his hand against C.W.'s chest. "*Washindun'.*" He turned and strode away.

Gah'tsu returned with his horse and they joined

the others. Sunrise watched indifferently as Collins slid the rifle back into its scabbard and strapped on the holster. They all mounted up and the Apaches headed for the riverbank. Maneuvering at a lope between trees and thickets of willow, they followed the water course north, driving the horse herd before them. Eventually, the Indians slowed to a walk and the chief fell back to ride alongside Collins.

"We will leave the mule here. There are two villages ahead, one on each side of the *rio*. That is where we will raid. There are mines and this means guns and ammunition."

Dismounting, Collins eased the cinch on the packsaddle and tethered Molly to a stout cottonwood, displeased at having to abandon her. The Apaches herded the extra horses into a small clearing nearby and swiftly fashioned a makeshift enclosure of dead brush and branches. C.W. swung back onto his gelding and checked both his rifle and his revolver to ensure they were fully loaded and free of debris. Sunrise maneuvered his pony up beside him again.

"Betray us and you will die," he said simply. "That is your choice. *Entiendes?*"

"I understand."

The Apache leader gave a whoop and rode at breakneck speed up the sandy bank with the other Indians following hard behind. Without much urging, Ulysses caught up with them. They angled out of the riverine floodplain and onto the open plains just to the east, pressing their mounts until they bolted ahead as if airborne. The raiding party entered a small village of adobe dwellings, stone buildings, wooden tipples and coke ovens at a gallop. Mexican women and children scattered while white men in work clothing dove for cover. Riding up to a long stone building, bearing a sign that read "San

Pedro Coal and Coke Company" in bold letters, Sunrise gestured for four of his warriors to dismount and break into the offices. They climbed through open windows and broke through the door and, shortly afterward, C.W. heard yelling and the sound of gunfire.

Shots came from a neighboring building and the Apaches returned fire. A singularly courageous fellow came running around the side of one of the buildings firing a brace of revolvers. Collins pulled his Colt and winged him before he could be killed. The man rolled in the dust and took cover behind a freight wagon. The warriors emerged from the mining office, loaded down with two ammunition crates and several rifles, jostling a pint-sized man, who appeared to be an office clerk, before them. They shoved the clerk down a short embankment and handed the boxes and rifles up to some of their compatriots before leaping back on their horses. One of them turned and fired his carbine at the hapless clerk, now on his feet and running for shelter. He collapsed and the Indians and Collins kicked up their animals, heading due west toward the river. Throughout the raid, the Apaches seemed to have a distinct plan and an understanding of the layout of the village and location of ordnance.

Stopping momentarily to allow the horses to drink, they forded the sluggish river and the scene was repeated in another hamlet. There were more coke ovens and a variety of buildings, including what appeared to be a blockhouse normally used for storing explosives. Encountering very little resistance, one of the Indians produced a rusted bayonet and used it to pry open the hasp on the door of the windowless structure. Five Apaches crowded inside. The Indians reappeared carrying wooden boxes. One was awkwardly handed up to Collins, whose gelding had become unruly from the commotion and gunfire that broke out periodically. The box was heavy and he balanced it unsteadily in front of him while two other crates were managed by Sunrise and Gah□tsu. Turning their horses in the direction of the Río Grande, they slowed their pace and paralleled the waterway, disappearing into the heavy vegetation along its banks.

When the raiding party again forded the river and had returned to the herd of surplus animals, there was a burst of activity as the Indians lashed boxes of ammunition and weapons to several horses. Collins was instructed to add one of the crates of rifles to Molly's load. With Jackrabbit's assistance, he loaded and secured it on the pile of his other gear with a diamond hitch, hoping his mule would not be subjected to a killing pace when they quit the area, as the animal now packed considerable weight. When he was back on his horse and had wrapped Molly's lead rope around the saddle horn in preparation for a swift departure, Collins was surprised to see that the Apaches were sitting their horses waiting for him.

"You will come with us," Sunrise told him. "Then we will see."

Forsaking the river bottom, the Apaches rode southwest at an almost leisurely gait. The wind whipped across the land and gusted fiercely, bringing a sensation of being repeatedly pummeled. To the west was a low ridge of hills and beyond a taller range of chiseled mountains. No villages or ranches were evident as they travelled. It was desolate and arid country and, especially owing to an apparent drought, C.W. was baffled that their route angled farther Vand farther away from the river. Then he remembered that Fort Craig was situated on the Río Grande. From what he had been able to discern, the Indians had kept to a westerly course from where he had been captured on the Pecos. Now they were making their way southwest and if the location of the fort was, indeed, driving the Indians away from the river, he might actually have an idea of where he was. In any event, he had no chance of eluding his captors in the present circumstances and he was certainly moving farther away from Fort Stanton, the Mescalero Agency and any countryside with which he was knowledgeable.

The chief had said they were the *Chihenne*, meaning a band of the Chiricahua, but Collins had no idea to which particular group they belonged. He knew Jackrabbit was Mescalero, but many of the bands tended to intermingle, according to his previous experience, and more were supposedly joining up with Victorio. If these Indians were ultimately bound for Arizona Territory, it would be imperative that he find an opportunity to escape. For the present, he would bide his time and endeavor to hold his own, since that was the most reliable avenue through which he would survive.

INDIAN ATTACK

13

When the sun was nearing its apex, the Apaches stopped to drink and water the horses at a broad arroyo that was fed by a freshet arising from melting snows high in a broad mountain range that loomed before them. Collins remarked that the warriors did not lie on their bellies to drink, but squatted on their heels and scooped water with their hands, constantly surveying the locality. C.W. dismounted and checked on his mule, readjusting the box of rifles and tightening the ropes. Jackrabbit came to stand beside him.

"You shot a damn white man," he said.

"Yes."

"I do not think Juanito Luna will try to kill you any more."

C.W. turned to look at the young man. "Good."

The Indian boy grinned and walked away.

Leading Ulysses and Molly to drink upstream from where the Indians' ponies were churning the water into mud, Collins looked up at the mountains towering above. He despised not being the master of his own fate and wondered briefly what would happen to Peng, his animals and his ranch if he never returned. Perhaps he was not presently in imminent danger, but that could alter swiftly enough. He sighed deeply and leaned his forehead against the gelding's neck. There was a sharp yell and he looked up to see the Apaches mounting up. The chief brusquely gestured for him to get moving.

It was soon evident that their new route would take them into the rugged country to the west. They followed a dry wash that climbed steadily into rocky foothills scattered with juniper trees and the occasional *piñon*. Bunches of golden dried grass were laced with nascent green growth. As the gulch narrowed into a steep canyon of volcanic rock, the Indians climbed onto adjacent upland and tracked a game trail until it rejoined the gully, wide and sandy again and periodically showing moist earth and shallow pools of snowmelt water. Their path took them through a gap between two low timbered mountains as they gained more elevation. Blessedly, the wind had somewhat abated.

Perceptibly acquainted with the region and their pathways through the arduous landscape, the Apaches maintained a steady pace as the group ascended into dispersed yellow pine trees, cured fescue grasses, small patches of dirty snow and pockets of gambel oak. When they, at last, topped out onto what C.W. assumed was the highpoint of the mountainous terrain, they brought their animals to drink at a spring hidden in a redoubt of volcanic rock and sheltered by a few cottonwood trees and thick undergrowth. The day was waning and the chief directed his followers to make camp. Their horses were shiny with sweat and plainly in need of rest. Collins dismounted and promptly began to untie the ropes that held the case of guns on his mule. One of the warriors came over to lend a hand. They lifted the box to the ground and together, they removed the rest of the gear and panniers.

Collins thanked the man in Spanish. The Indian gave a brief nod and went back to assist in unloading the horses that had been carrying the other crates of munitions. Turning to unsaddle both of his animals, Collins found that he was nearly prostrate with fatigue and his body still ached from the punishment of the past couple of days. He made a pile of his tack and trappings, fervently hoping he would be allowed to sleep unfettered and undisturbed. He led his animals to a spring-fed pool away from where the Indians were making camp. He noticed that at least three or four of them were missing and guessed they had gone hunting or were scouting ahead while the others were busy hobbling the horse herd. Juanito Luna's shoulder seemed to be much improved.

Taking one of the saddle blankets, he rubbed down his animals and examined them for injuries, then hobbled his gelding and turned them both loose to graze among the pine trees and brushwood that surrounded the camp. He stepped off to relieve himself and survey the horizon. Climbing to the top of an outcropping of volcanic rock, he could see more mountains to the south and west. There appeared to be a plume of dust rising from the valley floor below. A tantalizing odor of cooking meat drew him back to his companions. The missing Apache warriors had returned and there were several rabbits roasting over nearly smokeless flames. It seemed to C.W. that the Indians did not particularly want their presence known, given their precautions of obscured campsite and surreptitious fire. He admired their ability to camouflage their presence.

Gah'tsu was squatting on his heels, chewing and sucking on something that appeared to be a strip of light brown leather with obvious pleasure. Without a word, he passed a sliver to Collins. He found it to be tough and fibrous, but sweet and delicious to the taste. It took a fair bit of saliva to moisten the substance, but the result was satisfactory. *"Inaada,"* the young man told him, indicating the food. C.W.'s original abductor said something and gesticulated at Jackrabbit, who tossed a piece over to him.

"What is he called?" Collins asked, curious about the fellow who had abused him unrepentantly. He took a seat on a flat rock nearby.

"He is called Tarango. He is angry all the damn time."

The man looked up at the sound of his name, then lost interest almost instantly. Some of the others had broken open one of the wooden boxes from the raid and were distributing rounds of ammunition. Tarango went over and demanded a handful. Sunrise, the leader, was not in evidence. C.W. noticed that none of the other crates had been opened, presumably for ease of transport or because the ordnance was destined for someone else.

"Where are you taking the weapons?" he asked Jackrabbit.

His face lit up. "We are going to meet Victorio."

Momentarily thunderstruck, Collins licked sticky residue from his fingers. He had inadvertently been swept up by a band of Apaches who would effectively compel him to fulfill Schurz' vague commission. Whether he would live long enough to receive remuneration was yet to be revealed.

"Where is he?" he finally asked.

"Duha guuń'ał da!" Sunrise said sharply, coming up behind them.

Gah'tsu sprang to his feet. His manner was subservient. Collins also stood, but adopted an attitude of quiet detachment.

"Why do you ask this?" the Apache chief asked vehemently, coming close to him menacingly. "Why?" he asked again, narrowing his eyes and grasping the handle of a large knife suspended from the belt that encircled his striped cotton shirt.

Standing his ground as impassively as possible, C.W. said, "I was sent to this place for two reasons. The first was to find out what happened on the Mescalero agency when the army took the horses and guns. The other is to meet with the great chief Victorio and try to make peace."

Some of the other warriors were gathering around. Collins felt decidedly unsafe. Sunrise continued to study him in an antagonistic manner. After a long while, his anger seemed to diminish.

"No more questions," he said. "I have not decided if we will kill you, *'indaa',*" he added dismissively and strode away.

"No hay paz con los anglos," one of the other Apaches told him. *"Y cuando no hay paz, debemos luchar por ella."*

"When there is no peace, you must fight for it," Gah'tsu explained.

The sun had disappeared beneath the western horizon. The Indians gathered around the fire and meat was distributed among them. Collins hung back, not sure if he would be welcome. Jackrabbit beckoned him over and, when he glanced at Sunrise, the chief made a motion with his head indicating C.W. was allowed join them. He went to his packs and retrieved a tin of Huntley and Palmers biscuits he had found in Ilfeld's emporium. A warrior tossed a leg quarter of rabbit to him and he opened the tin and handed around wafers. His companions appeared to enjoy them and the container was soon empty.

Without formality, the Apaches lay down by the dying embers and prepared for sleep. Some of them wrapped themselves in blankets or jackets and others eschewed any type of covering. C.W. checked on his horse and mule, went to his pile of belongings and saddles, unrolled his bedding and was summarily asleep, in spite of ongoing doubts about his personal welfare and the physical pain he still suffered. Shortly before dawn, he was awakened by low voices. He sat up and watched as several Indians cast pinches of fine powder toward the east, speaking softly. He had witnessed morning prayers among other tribes and assumed this was a similar practice. Quietly, he packed up his bedroll and went to find Ulysses and Molly.

After a brief search, Collins finally found his stock in a patch of new bunchgrass beside a tiny rivulet that emanated from the spring. Evidently, his animals had shunned the Indian ponies. When he led them back to the camp, the warriors were securing crates to several horses. He sprang into action, rapidly saddling and loading his animals, wanting to be prepared for departure when the others were. The case of rifles that Molly had carried the day before had vanished.

Unceremoniously, the Apaches rode downslope from the spring, pushing the spare horses before them. Disregarded and unremarked, Collins trailed behind. He felt confident if he made a break for it, however, the warriors would certainly come after him and, besides, remaining with his captors would be the most viable avenue through which to meet Victorio. *Eisd le tuile na h-amhna, a's gablhaidh tu breac,* he thought. Listen for the flood of the river and you will catch a trout.

Their route took them steadily along another dry gulch that descended from the pine forest back to junipers, sagebrush and *piñon* trees. It broadened into a wide and superficial canyon and then, abruptly, they broke out into broken country of grasslands that were bounded by the mountains behind them and an undistinguished ridge of timbered hills to their west. A fair amount of smoke was rising in the distance behind the far low range. Given the drought conditions that existed in the area, Collins supposed its provenance must be a forest fire.

The Apaches slowed their pace and bore northward

following a worn track that paralleled a wide wash, damp in places from what moisture a deficient spring runoff had granted. In a short while, the Indians climbed out of the bottom and headed back up toward the mountains. As the horse herd neared the first trees, they were surrounded by other Apache warriors, yelping and whooping. The chief rode out ahead. The rest of the band fell back and surrounded Collins, walking their ponies and moving into a defile of rocks, a thick copse of underbrush and a few cottonwoods. There he saw a substantial camp of brush shelters, small hide covered lodges and several habitations that were constructed of flimsy peaked frames covered in blankets. There seemed to be an inordinate surplus of mules and horses interspersed throughout the stronghold.

Tarango motioned for Collins to dismount. Gah'tsu slipped off his pony and came over to him.

"Show nothing. Be very still," the young man told him.

Women and children gathered around. The overall posture was hostile. C.W. kept his hand well away from his revolver and stood silently and blankly with his arms slack at his sides. Jackrabbit remained beside him and, astonishingly, Juanito Luna walked up and seemed to have adopted a protective stance. A fly pestered his gelding and the animal stamped a front hoof impatiently. After a seeming eternity, Sunrise appeared from out of the camp and walked in their direction, accompanied by a sturdy, athletic warrior of late middle age. He appeared to Collins to possess serene composure and feline poise, despite his apparent maturity, and did not seem to display the antagonism toward him that was evident among the others. He made a sign with his right hand. Tarango, Juanito Luna, Jackrabbit and the other warriors reluctantly departed the area, as did the various bystanders.

The man stopped directly in front of Collins and studied him without any change of expression. He was able to examine the Indian in turn and noted the warrior's simple clothing of a cotton shirt over a buckskin breechclout, an open vest, a floral scarf gathered at his throat by a silver slide, the traditional high moccasins with turned up toes, a dark red head band wrapped around his shoulder-length hair and a wide belt from which hung a knife sheath and a holster for what appeared to be a Hopkins and Allen army revolver. The man bore a fearsome scar upon his face.

Sunrise said something in his language.

"*Ch'iguna'áí Huyáá* has told me you have come to speak with Victorio," the warrior said at last.

"Yes."

"*Por qué?*"

"The big man in charge of the Indian Bureau wants me to find out if an acceptable settlement will end the fighting."

"You work for *Señor* Schurz?"

"Yes." He was taken aback by the man's insightful question.

"What is your name?"

"Collins."

"*Ven conmigo.* Leave your *caballo* here," the Apache told him and turned back toward the camp.

Sunrise and C.W. followed behind him. Not certain whether he was in the presence of Victorio, Collins attempted to ask, but Sunrise made an admonitory gesture and shook his head, forestalling any inquiry. As they walked into the cluster of shelters, he said, *"Nantaą' dé' yaa'n.* He is the greatest Apache."

The encampment was confined to a small area, tucked into the safety of a virtual fortress of vegetation and granite. The man whom Collins now confidently assumed was Victorio took a seat in front of one of the larger brush shelters. Sunrise did the same. C.W. stood until invited with a gesture from Victorio. A comely woman in a cotton dress and draped in a blanket, tied as a sort of cape, brought shallow baskets with roasted mutton and thick corn tortillas. They ate in silence.

When the meal was finished, Victorio said, "The soldiers, the smoked Americans, are hunting us. Hatch and Morrow want to be in on the kill. They are angry they did not catch us at the battle of the *cañon* near *el lugar de arena blanca.*"

"I have heard that there have been many white people killed. Not soldiers, but civilians… settlers."

Victorio shrugged. "*Anglos,* Mexican people… many, many *Ndé.* We have abided by the white laws, we have honored agreements. It did no good. They put our families in the terrible place called San Carlos. We escaped and the soldiers chased us and took many of the people back. *Ahora* we raid and kill and the soldiers keep coming. There are Apache scouts working against us." He paused and a profound melancholia appeared to descend upon him. "May some of the *niños* survive to carry our ways."

"What will end this?" Collins asked.

"All we have ever asked is to be allowed to live here in our traditional lands. My home is here, *mi gente* were born here. General Howard made promises. First they say yes you may stay. Then they say no you must go. *Pero* it seems the great men such as Schurz pay more heed to the whining of *Anglos* and *los Mejicanos.* The village near here called *Cañada Alamosa* trades in whisky and stolen cattle and yet they do not wish to move these people for our sake."

"I heard you were safe on the Mescalero agency. You left."

The man sneered bitterly, momentarily abandoning

his dignified manner. "My people had been obeying the agent Russell and not causing trouble, but he did not want us. *Porque* some of the warriors there wanted to fight, he blamed me. Then white men accused me of stealing their *caballos*. They would sneak onto the agency and look for the brands on Apache horses. The next day, they would come and say 'that is my horse... that is my brand.' Ask *Señor* Blazer. He knows this to be true."

"Yes, I have met Dr. Blazer when I was at Fort Stanton in '72. I will ask him about this."

"*Pronto* I was told men were coming to arrest me. Perhaps even for *la matanza. Por qué esperar?* I knew the agent would give me to them."

"It is possible. There has been much wrong done. But if you keep attacking white men, the soldiers will punish you. If Washington will not give you your land, then you must stop fighting for the sake of the women and children."

"It is always the same. Virtue always for the *los Anglos* and none for the *Ndé*. If we give up, there will be nothing." He struck his chest with the flat of his hand. "We must be allowed to live in our land."

"*Níl aon tinteán mar do thinteán féin.*"

Victorio eyed him curiously. "What are those words?"

"My language. There is no fire as good as your own fire."

The man thought about this and nodded. "*Sí, la verdad.*" He stared off at the western horizon for a long moment. "*Pero*, there is another fire and it is not so good..." he finally said, pensively. "*Es un incendio* that will burn up all the *Chíhenne* people. It makes its noise on the wind and is filled with *la tración* and lies."

14

In the end, C.W. plainly understood that, offered any agreement short of being allowed to remain in peace where they were, Victorio's people would keep fighting. Never much of a diplomat, he was profoundly angry at his own impotence to resolve the situation and at the recalcitrance of the Indian Bureau in its apparently unwarranted insistence that these people return to the brutal environs of San Carlos. His message to Secretary Schurz would be meaningless. There would be no favorable endings here, he feared. He was physically ill at the thought of this small band of people being run to ground in a tragic parody of justified military action. There was to be more blood spilt on both sides.

At his request, Victorio allowed Collins to go and look after his stock. The chief sent Sunrise with him for protection, speaking to the man at length in the Apache language. Glancing around the village, Collins saw women packing belongings and horses being caught. Perhaps Victorio's band was about to relocate, he thought. Probably a necessity with the entire U.S. government seeking to annihilate them.

As they passed out of the encampment, a youthful warrior rushed up and brandished a pistol in C.W.'s face, shouting angry words in Spanish. Sunrise made an abrupt lunge and yanked the gun from the boy's hand, slipping it into his belt. They braced each other a moment and Sunrise spoke forcefully in his language, clearly delivering some type of command. The warrior became submissive and, giving Collins a last wrathful glance, he strode away.

They found Ulysses and Molly where he had left them, being watched over by an older woman. She did not glance up and departed as soon they drew near. The animals were still saddled and all his trappings were intact.

"You should go," Sunrise told him. "Victorio wishes it."

"Is it possible to see Jackrabbit before I leave?"

"No. You are to go now. Many wish to kill you."

Stepping over to the gelding and mule, Collins quickly tightened cinches and mounted up. Sunrise stood vigilant.

"Thank you for my life," C.W. said quietly.

The warrior nodded and they held each other's eyes a moment. Then Collins wheeled his horse to ride down slope, certain he would never see this man again. Picking his way carefully through a rocky wash that angled to the southward, he eventually found his way to another wider arroyo offering a sandy pathway that was less demanding on his stock. He and his animals had endured many privations in the past few days and Collins wanted to make the next phase of his journey as easy as possible. His only present concern was the certainty he was being watched. It was imperative that he travel as far from the Apache camp as daylight would take him.

After riding for an hour or more, following the gentle meanderings of the dry wash, he came to a small pool of snow melt water sheltered beneath an overhang of dirt bank. C.W. dismounted and led Ulysses and Molly to water. While they drank, he pulled the map from his saddlebags and attempted to get his bearings. He located a village called San Pedro along the east side of the Río Grande and assumed this was one of the hamlets they had raided. From what he could surmise, they had subsequently travelled southwest from the river and climbed into and over the San Mateo Mountains. This, then, would place him just a few miles north of the military post of Ojo Caliente. He would be able to find shelter and protection at least. As long as he was circumspect about recent activities, he thought with irony.

Absorbed by his study of the map, concealed by a bend in the wash and the steep undercut, a rider was almost upon him before Collins became aware and yanked the revolver from its holster. Ulysses raised his head and perked his ears. Cautiously, Collins peered out from his refuge and recognized Gah′tsu, who was following his tracks at a fast trot. He pressed back against his animals and searched his memory for a word to hail someone loudly, not wanting to yell out in English so as to avoid being shot.

"*Shu!*"

The young warrior seemingly heard him because he pulled in his pony and skidded to a halt, raising a small cloud of dust.

"*Washindun'?*" the boy called hesitantly.

Stepping out into the open, C.W. holstered his pistol and raised a hand in greeting. Jackrabbit rode over to him and slid down from his mount.

"I found you."

"Yes."

"I am going with you. I think those people are going to *Mehigu.* I do not want to go there."

"Going where?"

"Across the damn border."

"They are going to Mexico?" Collins asked, now comprehending.

"'*Au.* I think the *Chihende* will be in trouble there."

The young man led his horse to the water to drink. Knowing his mule's nature, Collins took Molly's lead rope and pulled her to the side. Sure enough, she attempted to bite the Indian pony on her way by. Ulysses followed and then wandered over to the other side of the wash to tug at a clump of dried rice grass.

"Why go with me?" C.W. asked, dropping Molly's rope and walking over to Jackrabbit.

"You are going to Mescalero. You told Sunrise."

"I am going there, but I am also going to places where there will be soldiers and white people. It will be dangerous."

The Apache youth appeared confused. "I helped you. I know you will keep me safe."

Collins realized this was an unadulterated expression of *quid pro quo*. And a young Apache warrior would probably not fare well travelling alone, given the animosity of local civilians toward Indians.

"You certainly saved my life," he admitted. "I will do my best to keep you safe."

"'*Áxąh!* We can go together," Gah'tsu said, grinning largely.

Gathering the horse and mule, Collins swung aboard his gelding and headed down the arroyo. He was wondering what the reception at Ojo Caliente military post might be when he arrived with his fierce looking companion. Tempers were bound to be short, given recent altercations with Victorio's fighting force. He recalled the small garrison was predominantly manned by soldiers of the 9th Cavalry. These men were colored troopers. Commanded by Colonel Edward Hatch, with whom he had an acquaintance, these army regulars seemed to be just as bellicose toward the Indians they fought as any white soldiers. The 9th Cavalry had been sent to Texas in '67 and had been engaged in confrontations with diverse tribes since.

Jackrabbit rode up beside him on his round-bellied

little roan horse. He seemed to be in high spirits and C.W. hoped this would last.

"We are now going to Ojo Caliente. Have you been there?" he asked the boy.

"No. It is the sacred place of the *Chihende*. Now it is a place of the enemy."

"Yes, well there are negro soldiers there. But this will not make them any different."

The young man laughed. "I know the *t' eeshínde*. They have killed us the same as the damn whites. I will kill them if I can."

Shaking his head, Collins said, "Not today, Jackrabbit. You must be very quiet and behave as if you are a friendly person who is my guide."

The Apache pulled in his horse. "Like a slave?" he asked. "I will not be a damn slave."

Reining in his gelding, Collins shook his head again. "Not a slave, but you must act less than you are. If you cannot do this, then you must go back to Sunrise. I will not be able to keep you from harm."

Swiftly regaining his good nature, the young man urged his pony into a walk. "I can do this," he said. "We can go together."

"I mean it, Gah'tsu," Collins told him sternly, nudging Ulysses forward. "You must be very unimportant."

"I will be like the *dibéhé*. The sheep."

"See that you remember."

MILITARY POST

15

Following the sandy arroyo, they rode in silence for a while. C.W. could not help but be apprehensive about their visit to the post. He had enough to conceal about his commission and recent associations without having a wild young Apache warrior as company. Especially one who was conspicuously armed with a Spencer carbine, cavalry issue Colt .45 and a very sizable knife suspended from his belt in a rattlesnake skin sheath. Perhaps, he thought, there would be a contingent of Apache scouts stationed at Ojo Caliente. This might prove advantageous in that having Jackrabbit along may not seem such a novelty.

The day was growing warmer. Flies began to pester the animals and buzz around his face. C.W. was reminded that spring was well along and he wondered briefly how Peng was progressing and whether his ranch and livestock were safe and intact. With luck, the local population was inclined to leave well enough alone. It occurred to him, not for the first time, that he had come perilously close to dying in recent days. There would have been no way for his Chinese friend to know whether he was coming back or not.

The view of the San Mateo Mountains had been blocked by golden foothills, overspread by a pale green hue from budding grasses and interspersed with juniper trees. It was too dry for the time of year and he imagined that rains would bring an explosion of growth. Signs of drought were everywhere. The faint scent of burning wood and haze in the air no doubt emanated from a distant forest fire. The wind had come up, raising dust devils and thrashing men and animals with grit. Rounding a sharp bend in the now shallow dry wash, the hills promptly bore east and Collins could now see the impressive mountain range looming above them, the southern rampart of which resembled a sleeping buffalo. Below the summit ran a serrated ridgeline that followed a narrow draw, crowned by a distinctive hump of granite.

Jackrabbit suddenly pulled in his pony. Collins began to detect inevitable clamor from the military outpost. The sounds of shouting, indeterminate metal clanking and a variety of other rackets announced the garrison's proximity.

"We must be near Ojo Caliente," he told the boy, tugging on the reins and pausing a moment.

"You will not tell them of Victorio."

"No. We are agreed upon that. Even if scouts are there... Apache scouts... we can trust no one."

Gah'tsu made a disparaging noise in his throat. "I do not trust those who hunt their own people."

"Maybe so," C.W. said as they rode ahead and crossed a shallow stream that flowed into a spectacular rocky cleft, breaking the steep escarpment to their east. "But you cannot show this."

Grinning at Collins, he rode his pony in a circle around Molly and Ulysses and back beside him. "I am a *dibéhé*," he said, then made a bleating sound like a sheep. He dropped back to follow the mule.

The buildings of the small fort rose from a flat plain on the south side of the creek and appeared to be organized in the predictable square of most frontier military posts, with all the structures facing the parade ground. As they approached the northwest corner of the grounds, a couple of young colored privates, who had been loafing in the shade of the nearest building, sauntered over.

"Where in hell did you comc from?" one asked.

Collins reined in his gelding. Jackrabbit remained behind Molly.

"I am looking for the commanding officer," he said, ignoring the question.

"Who you got? A captive?" the other private asked, gesturing toward the Apache youth.

"Who is the commanding officer?"

"Well you are in luck there, friend," the first private told him. "The big man himself has come to our humble diggings."

Collins was cognizant that questionable discipline tended to be typical of remote forts. "Who may that be?" he asked with thinning patience.

"Why Colonel Hatch. God almighty of the 9th Cav.," the private told him with exaggerated deference.

This surprised C.W. "Where might I find him?"

"Right 'round the corner there," the other trooper said. "Probably with his feet up and dining on fine victuals."

Tapping Ulysses lightly with his heels, C.W. rode past the two soldiers without another word and entered the parade grounds, deeply grateful that his companion was mutely coming up beside him. He could see a few soldiers engaged in a range of activities scattered about the post and there seemed to be quite a bit of activity around what appeared to be a blacksmith shop across the way. Distant gunfire announced target practice. He surveyed the locale and noted a significant adobe edifice that ran north and south just to their right. He turned toward the structure and dismounted, wrapping Molly's lead around his saddle horn and handing the reins to Jackrabbit.

"Will you stay here?" he asked.

"Yes," the boy said soberly, slipping from his pony. "I will stay."

"Shout if you need me. I will not be long."

"Yes."

Knocking once on the wooden door set near the middle of the adobe building, Collins stepped inside. The structure had a startling number of glass windows, given the remote location of the post, and the interior was brightly illuminated. There was a narrow corridor that led to a back door and opened into two separate chambers on either side. He heard a faint sound and looked into the room to his left to find a sergeant seated behind a wooden desk, busily writing in a ledger book. The man sat ramrod straight and glanced up from his paperwork.

"I am Sergeant Jordan," he informed C.W. "How may I assist you?"

"My name is Charles Collins. I am looking for Colonel Hatch."

"Mr. Collins, by god," came a voice from the room across the hall.

The colonel came striding in and shook Collins' hand vigorously. "This man did me a good deed up in Colorado last fall," the officer told Sergeant Jordan, who had come briskly to his feet. "By god," the colonel said again, "What a strange eventuality to find you here." He glanced at the sergeant. "Some coffee if you will?"

"Yes sir," came the reply.

Collins thought Hatch appeared enervated, despite his bluff manner, and seemed to have aged several years since their last meeting. "You remain in command of the 9th Cavalry then?"

"Yes... And grateful to be shed of that lamentable situation with the Utes, I can tell you. I am, however, being presently and thoroughly vilified by Arizona and

New Mexico newspapers. But never you mind. Come let us retreat to my quarters and you may tell me how our paths have crossed once more." He guided C.W. across the corridor to a sparsely furnished but comfortable room. "I take up residence here when I am at Ojo Caliente," he explained. "The officer's quarters are full with Captain Hooker and Lieutenant Emmett and another… oh yes, Captain Parker, the Chief of Scouts." The officer slumped into an upholstered high back chair by a table.

Taking a seat on a bench against one of the walls, C.W. asked, "Why are you here, Colonel?"

The man eyed him closely. "I could ask you the same," he said.

Collins smiled wryly. "I only meant it seems an out of the way location from which to be moving your chess pieces."

Producing a deep groan of frustration, the colonel said, "That infernal Victorio is running my troops into the ground. I just arrived here from the field on Friday. My stock is so broken down we can no longer pursue him rapidly."

The sergeant arrived with a coffee pot and two stoneware mugs. He placed everything on the table near Colonel Hatch. "Sugar?" he asked.

They both answered in the negative.

"Thank you, Sergeant. That will be all," Hatch said.

"Yes sir." The man saluted and made a perfectly executed about-face to leave the room.

Here, thought C.W., was a dedicated noncommissioned officer. "The sergeant seems to be a fine example of a professional soldier," he told the colonel. "I ran into a couple of privates outside who could use some prompting."

"Another problem I am currently undergoing. Lack of discipline. Mostly arising from low morale." Hatch poured a mug of coffee for himself and waved Collins over to the table, clearly not intending to relinquish his chair.

"It is understandable, given your circumstances," Collins said, standing up and coming over to pour himself coffee. He retrieved a folding chair near at hand and joined Hatch at the table.

"They are about to get a comeuppance. My horses are worn out, but I am intending to send troopers out on foot to comb the San Mateos. My instincts tell me the old wolf has come back home."

"What makes you so sure?" C.W. asked with concealed trepidation.

"There have been serious depredations of large flocks of sheep near the Black Range west of here. Damnable herders run off at the sound of every yipping coyote... practically invite the Apaches to help themselves." The colonel slurped from his mug loudly and smacked his lips. "Jordan makes good coffee."

"Is there no way to acquire fresh mounts?"

The officer laughed sardonically. "General Pope is doubtless weary of my insistent telegrams begging for more troops and mounts. Deaf ears. And Fort Craig is slow to respond with feed, clothing, boots and other supplies."

Some sort of commotion arose from outside the building, replete with the uproar of men's voices, laughter and the braying of mules. Hatch came to his feet and peered out one of the windows.

"Ah... Here is my Chief of Scouts. I am sending him out with the last of my sound animals. Come." The colonel departed the room precipitously, suddenly imbued with newfound vigor.

Following Hatch from the building, Collins found the immediate area in front of the headquarters crowded with Apache warriors, five pack mules and one uniformed officer shouting directions to Indian scouts who took some while to come to order. A couple of them were off to the side with Gah'tsu, speaking in low tones beneath the din. The boy looked over at him and nodded. The horses and mule were tethered in the shade of the building and there was a bucket of water in front of them.

It seemed to C.W. that the Apache contingent numbered somewhere around fifty individuals. They were attired in a creative array of Anglo and traditional clothing, many of them flamboyant in brightly colored head bands and neck scarves, tweed waistcoats, dress blouses and an impressive array of silver jewelry. Most of them appeared to possess at least two weapons, a revolver and rifle, and all of them had a knife sheath on their belts. Some of them wore uniform jackets, but all wore boot style moccasins. Only a few pairs of footwear lacked the notable upturned toe, particular to the Apache people.

Colonel Hatch had gone to speak with the Chief of Scouts. Collins joined them, curious about the proposed destination of the reconnaissance.

"Go out and kill one or two Indians," Hatch was telling the man. "Try to keep things stirred up until I can get these troops in shape to continue the pursuit."

"We have cooked rations," the young man said in a strong Texas drawl. "The scouts will pack around three days' worth of food and the mules will carry ammunition,"

"Do your best. Head in a southerly direction," the colonel told him. "Morrow should now be somewhere to the southeast of the Río Grande and I will send out troops on foot into the San Mateos. Perhaps we can roust old Vic from his hidey hole."

"Yes sir."

"Dismissed, Parker. Good luck to you."

"Thank you, sir." The officer saluted.

"I believe these scouts are the only way we will bring

Victorio to heel," Hatch told Collins. "Major Morrow does his best, but is forced to pursue the enemy through the most ungodly country. Furthermore, he is an inebriate. I myself have just come in from one hell of an ordeal with nothing to show but sanctimonious and defamatory newspaper articles decrying my incompetence. And Hooker is practically useless. Last September he allowed the Apaches to run off his entire horse herd."

"*Dá fhaid lá, tigeann oidhche.*"

The colonel scowled at him. "What?"

"The longest day has an end."

"The sooner the better."

They watched as Parker gathered the scouts and, with the assistance of an Apache man wearing sergeant stripes on his uniform coat, lined out the pack animals and mounted up on the only horse. The two scouts who had been speaking with Jackrabbit fell in and the disorderly column advanced from the parade grounds to the southwest.

"God speed," Hatch muttered under his breath.

16

"Now, what exactly are you doing here?" Colonel Hatch asked as they returned to his quarters and resumed their seats at the table. The coffee had grown cold, but they refilled their mugs anyway. "And who is that Indian boy tending your animals?"

It was not unexpected that the colonel had finally come to it, thought Collins. From previous acquaintance, he knew Hatch was a keen observer as well as a blunt and perspicacious officer.

"I am here at the behest of Secretary Schurz and Commissioner Trowbridge." C.W. already had formulated a plausible, and mostly truthful, explanation.

"To do what?" the colonel asked, studying him through squinted eyes.

"Fact finding. As always, my mandate is clandestine."

"Clandestine? I am commander of the District of New Mexico."

"I apologize for being obtuse."

"Ah yes... that is your métier is it not? Discretion?" Hatch said, somewhat condescendingly. Then he shrugged. "Well... certainly not astounding that the Indian Bureau would not want to keep me informed. I must suggest, however, that you be decidedly wary. You may lose your scalp and my good will."

"I plan to keep my hair, Colonel," Collins said, smiling. "But thank you for the advice."

"I assume your Apache henchman is insurance against bodily harm?"

" 'Strong reasons make strong actions,' " he replied, quoting Shakespeare.

"Indeed... indeed."

Pausing a moment to collect his thoughts, Collins hesitated, then said, "I am, however, required to ask some questions about the events of April 16 on the Mescalero Agency."

"Ah... That mealy-mouthed agent has been whining to Schurz and Trowbridge. Of course." The colonel sighed and vigorously rubbed the back of his neck. "What have you been told?"

"Frankly, sir, I would prefer to hear it from you in entirety."

"Very well... although if it is Schurz for whom you are inquiring, you should know the plan was spawned by General Pope and the Secretary himself." The officer gazed out a window. "The army was convinced that most of the Mescaleros were giving supplies and succor to Victorio. Secret orders were issued and Grierson's 10th Cavalry began marching from Texas. I informed Agent Russell that a number of soldiers would be arriving around the 12th ultimo, but that was all."

"You did not warn him of their purpose?"

Hatch glanced at him reproachfully. "You said you desired my account of events, did you not?"

"Yes, of course. My apologies."

"The Mescaleros were on the warpath with scarcely an exception and had been from the last of February. The reservation has, for the past year, been a rendezvous for stolen stock sold and bartered by the Indians for anything they required. Especially for money when they could obtain it for the purpose of purchasing arms and ammunition. On arriving at the agency with troops, the Indians were sent for and informed what the government had decided. That their horses and arms were to be given up. There were then about four hundred Indians present at the agency, sixty-four of which were warriors. Grierson had also arrived from Texas with companies of the 10th Cav and the 25th Infantry. The Indians, after objections, agreed to the arrangement and a day was given them to bring in other outside parties whom they said were hiding arms, which they informed me some of the young men had cached. Not only one day was given them but it was extended to two. The Indians were informed and they expressed themselves satisfied that any Indians absent from the agency would be treated as hostiles."

"Had you confiscated any weapons or horses as yet?"

"No. Not as yet."

"May I smoke?" C.W. asked.

"Of course."

Taking out his briar and tobacco pouch, Collins said, "Please continue, Colonel."

"You need to understand that Agent Russell told me he sanctioned the killing of any Indian found absent from the agency by April 15." Hatch turned to look out of the window again. "On the morning of the 15th, Gatewood, of the 6th Cavalry with Indian Scouts, was south of the agency, and later stated he was attacked about daylight. Two Mescaleros were shot and killed. That is when I ordered troops to move in on the Indian flanks. It was at this time that the Indians were also informed that any attempt to escape and run off their stock would prove disastrous to them. Captain Steelhammer with sixty men of the 15th Infantry were deployed in rear of the camp and five companies of Grierson's 10th Cavalry so dispersed that it seemed impossible for the Indians to escape. Lieutenants Maney and Gatewood's scouts were located a mile to the left and rear and Morrow had been sent with his command to the right and rear. Captain Steelhammer's company of infantry, selected for the purpose, was to march into the Indian camps at precisely 2 o'clock p.m."

Colonel Hatch retrieved a bouquet cigar from an inner pocket of his open jacket and struck a phosphorus match on the underside of the table. He smoked broodingly for a few minutes. Collins waited patiently for him to resume his narrative.

"The weather was stormy and threatening, having been unpredictable for the previous two days. The disarming went on until the entire tribe suddenly made a desperate break for the hills," the officer said at last. "To have opened fire upon them would have been to kill many of the women and children. Not until the men had dashed away from them and some of the escaping Indians opened fire, did the command return it, and it is greatly to the credit of the soldiers that but one woman was struck, which was unquestionably an accidental shot. The Indians were, after much trouble, finally corralled in a stockade and disarmed. It was the original intention to have left the confiscated horses under guard near the agency. But the Indians having resisted openly, after pledging themselves to accede to the terms offered them, certainly were not entitled to any consideration except that of being held prisoners."

"What happened to the horses?" Collins strove to restrain all judgement in his tone, in spite of his incredulity.

"The animals were driven into Stanton except such brands as were claimed by owners who were daily applying for them. Excluding a few Comanche ponies, all the stock was stolen largely from Texas and settlements on the Pecos." The colonel's manner became noticeably more defensive. "It is questionable whether one animal of the six hundred taken had been obtained honestly by an Indian of the tribe. They were the accumulations of theft for many years in New Mexico and Texas. And if there was any legal title to the animals mentioned they had forfeited it by their bad faith and by being in open hostility to the government." Hatch flicked ash from the end of his cigar onto the floor. "That rattle-pate agent has accused me of unnecessary cruelty. I am not aware of any acts of unnecessary cruelty perpetrated upon the Indians in question during the time my command was at the Mescalero Agency. On the contrary, they were treated with a consideration not merited by their behavior at the time and prior to the occupancy of the reservation. That there were Indians killed, and many more than the Agent is aware of, was due entirely to themselves. Every effort was made to avoid injury to all non-combatants. I am unable to understand what treatment Agent Russell considers cruel." The officer paused and regarded Collins blandly. "Is it your intention to further calumniate me in this?"

"Certainly not, Colonel. That is not my directive."

"And you are not able to elucidate me as to your directive?"

"No sir."

"Very well," Hatch said, waving his cigar in a dismissive gesture.

"And how are you finding colored troopers in the field against Apache warriors?" Collins asked, prepared to shift the conversation.

"I have no complaints. Usual problems... poor discipline, impertinence, slacking of duties... the same as white soldiers, but all in all there have been some momentous occasions of bravery. One of my black sergeants drove off a surprise attack on Fort Tularosa a mere week ago." He idly fiddled with a penknife, spinning it around on the tabletop. "I certainly do not hold them responsible for our lack of success. They nurse a habituated contempt for the Indians and have endured appalling conditions. This country makes the Modoc lava beds a veritable lawn."

Collins placed his spent pipe in a pocket. "What is the attitude of the white citizens? I was briefly with the Freedman's Bureau. I cannot imagine much has changed."

Hatch shook his head. "Sadly, the same civilians these men are protecting often sling cruel epithets at them. Most of them will not allow the troopers in their towns. And many in the army are unwilling to associate with them. Did you know that Custer refused to command a colored regiment?"

Collins smiled contemptuously. "Not a thunderclap."

"He was worried they would cut and run when faced with a formidable enemy. I can attest to the fact they do not. Except for a few deserters, the men of the 9th can be relied upon to do their utmost."

"And yet they do not harbor sympathy nor exhibit special regard for Indians?"

"Most definitely not. Oddly, I have even heard them refer to the Apache as 'voodoo niggers' or 'prairie niggers.' Of course, the more animosity they have for the enemy, the better it is for the campaign." The colonel paused and thought a moment. "They seem to get along with some of the scouts."

"Cicero wrote, 'Men condemn because they do not understand.' "

"Perhaps… I had forgotten your proclivity for classical quotes," Hatch said, somewhat derisively. "Well now, what can I do to assist you? I harbor no ill will toward you or your mandate."

"I am sufficiently supplied at the moment. I would, however, benefit from the acquisition of a couple of water bags. I am headed into some dry country."

"I will see to it. Anything else?"

"Is it possible to stable my animals for the night and camp somewhere in proximity to the fort without my guide and I being pestered?"

"You would be best served by the post trader's house on the northeast corner of the post. It is empty, now that he has built another, and it is often employed to billet guests."

"Excellent, Colonel. I am in your debt."

Colonel Hatch called to the sergeant who arrived promptly and stood in the doorway awaiting his orders. While the officer issued instructions, C.W. studied Jordan. He was well over six feet in height, muscular and his skin was the color of treacle. The man cut a fine figure and gave the impression of being a steadfast and intelligent soldier and a person of integrity. Collins never could fathom any justification for the vitriolic hatred directed toward colored people, such as that he had witnessed in Atlanta after the war. He recalled a line written by Fielding. "How apt men are to hate those they injure." Perhaps that was the answer. It was disturbing, though, that those who were oppressed would so willingly subjugate others.

Taking his leave of Hatch, who appeared to be almost napping in his chair, and promising to return for mess, Collins followed the sergeant out of the building. He motioned for Jackrabbit, who was sitting on the ground in the lee of the structure. The boy jumped up and gathered the animals to lead them over.

"Is it possible to have my horse and mule seen to by the blacksmith?" he asked Jordan. "We are bound for rocky ground."

"Come this way," the sergeant said and strode toward the blacksmith shop located across the parade grounds. C.W. accepted his gelding's reins from Jackrabbit and they followed behind.

"Did you learn anything from the scouts?" he asked the boy softly.

"Yes. I will tell you."

A few men were loitering around the shed. They scattered at the approach of the sergeant, visibly intimidated by him. The blacksmith was shaping a shoe on an anvil. The banging was deafening and they stood waiting until he had finished.

"What do you want?" the smithy finally asked, as he submerged the shoe in a tub of water, creating a hiss of steam. The beefy man was white, plainly a civilian and had some type of eastern European accent. He wore a heavy leather apron and an odd little cap on his head.

"I would be grateful if you would check the shoes on my horse and mule," Collins told him.

"I am busy," he said defiantly.

"Colonel Hatch has requested it," the sergeant informed him. "You will see to these animals now."

The smith came over and Collins handed Ulysses' reins over to him, pulling Molly's lead rope free of the saddle horn and turning her aside. Gah'tsu faded away with his pony while Jordan and Collins stood and watched the man check all four hooves. He reset the shoes, crimped the ends of the nails and made certain all were secure, then brought the gelding back and reached for the mule, repeating the process with her. He was efficient and thorough, even if not pleased with the task.

"They should hold," he said sullenly when he was finished.

"Thank you."

"*Bazd meg.*"

Sergeant Jordan guided Collins over to the stables, just beyond the smithy's shop. "That man has a well-developed sense of indignation," he said.

Laughing, C.W. agreed, somewhat taken aback by this unexpected show of humor. Together, they unloaded and unsaddled the animals and placed them in a stall, while conversing offhandedly about mules and the weather. Jordan filled the manger with hay and Collins filled a water tub from a pitcher pump. He piled his saddles and belongings in a corner of the spacious pen. The rest of the stables were empty and when they walked back outside, C.W. could see the remaining stock grazing out beyond the building on stunted native grasses, discernibly insufficient due to drought. Two soldiers stood picket on either side of the herd.

"The trader's house is over there," Jordan said, nodding toward a rambling one-story adobe house to the north. "I will have two water bags filled and left with your saddles. Is there anything else you might require?" All informality had vanished.

"No, thank you Sergeant. I greatly appreciate your assistance."

"My pleasure." The man strode purposefully back toward the post headquarters.

Collins went in search of Jackrabbit and found him by the stream that ran east and west along the northern boundary of the garrison. His pony nibbled on grasses beside the waterway, more verdant than the rest.

"Will you sleep in the house?" C.W. asked.

"No. I will sleep nearby in the hills up there." He pointed with his lower lip.

"Do you need food?"

"You can bring me some."

"If you can wait, I will bring something from the officer's mess."

"I can wait. No damn fish. I do not eat fish."

"No fish."

Sitting on the bank, Collins closed his eyes and relished the judicious sun of late afternoon. He could hear the Indian pony behind him, nipping and munching vegetation, occasionally respiring the equivalent of an equine fricative. Basking in the serene interlude, in stark contrast to the fear and physical agony of recent days, he yielded to a brief repose from duty and apprehension, allowing his mind to wander. After a few tranquil minutes, an insistent bee began droning about his face. Grudgingly, he roused. Glancing about, Collins found Jackrabbit stretched out on his back beside him.

"What did the scouts say?" he asked the boy.

Jackrabbit sat up and stretched. "They told me Victorio has been making the soldiers chase him until their horses are no good. He has been putting dead animals in water holes and rolling stones down on them from ambush. He has killed many, many people from towns who are hunting him and others with wagons and those who search for gold. He is a great warrior."

"How long had you been raiding for him before I was captured?"

"I had gone off with Sunrise when he went to visit Blazer. We came raiding to where you were. I wanted to kill *'indaa'*... white men."

"I am grateful you did not kill me."

"No, I would not kill *Washindun'*," Gah'tsu said solemnly.

"Did you know Victorio when he was at Mescalero?"

"Yes. He was peaceful there. He tried to tell that damn agent he would not kill whites if his people could live where they wanted. Then we heard some men were coming to put him in jail. Now he will never stop the killing." The young man shook his head and gestured with his hands. "White people are crazy... crazier than a rat trapped in a tin shithouse."

Having noticed Jackrabbit's partiality for curse words, it was plain to Collins his companion had been learning hyperbolic English from some of the soldiers at Fort Stanton. He laughed in spite of himself. "An accurate statement indeed."

The boy grinned then became serious. "The scouts said they think they know where Victorio will go. I do not understand why they are damn traitors."

"Nor I, my friend. But I have seen it before."

"It is like killing yourself," Gah'tsu said. He came to his feet. "Come. We will go to the place of hot water. Then you can get food."

17

Rio Alamosa was fed by hot springs that flowed from a side canyon into the stream. Riding through the enormous and impressive fissure just to the east of the military post, Collins and Jackrabbit entered an alley of high ramparts of volcanic rock. They picked their way along a narrow trail that wove back and forth across the creek, where track and water crowded together in the restricted gorge. Hemmed in by jagged bulwarks, they rode single file, following the extraordinary twists and turns of the waterway as it snaked drunkenly along its channel. After a few miles, the chasm expanded. Its curves became more judicious and cottonwood trees grew here and there. They were able to ride abreast.

"The post commander told me there is a small village up here," C.W. told Jackrabbit.

"They are damn robbers and sell whisky. But I have heard there is one who is not so bad."

"How is that?"

"I was told he has talked for Victorio. It was *biyeexa...* only a little while ago. *Nantaq' dé' yaa'n* wanted to talk to the head officer but he did not trust him. This man Kelley remained with the warriors while there was a parley. It is the reason the soldiers did not kill him then."

"Did Victorio want to surrender?"

"Hell no. He wanted his people to stay in their home near the *tú siduyá.* That is what he asked for. Later *tuhénde* scouts led soldiers to his camp in a mountain canyon above the white sand. He took his people out of there and the soldiers did no good."

They rode in silence for a while. The ravine widened. Collins could see a butte on the western skyline above them and shortly afterward they rode out onto a broad floodplain of sandy soil. The battle mentioned by Gah'tsu, he thought, must have been the one in Hembrillo Basin of the previous month. Colonel Hatch had described details of the conflict over supper the night before. There had been a defined and carefully laid out strategy for attack, but the troops under Captain Carroll's command from Fort Stanton, marching west across lava country, had come across a poisonous spring. Animals and men had drunk freely of the water and become perilously ill. They had then sought another water source and found it dried up from the drought, forcing them to seek out a spring in the San Andres Mountains where the Apaches were entrenched.

According to Hatch, the Indians pinned down the troopers and they would have been annihilated, had another detachment under Captain McLellan not arrived. The Apaches were driven into the mountains and the colonel thought this had been proof that Victorio had been routed. Collins knew from past experience, however, that the first duty of an Apache leader was to ensure the safety of his people and prevent loss of life among his warriors. After the rescue of Carroll's men, Colonel Hatch, believing the Indians were cornered, rode north to intercept Captain Hooker with the third battalion and send him into the fray. Ultimately, the Indians had faded away and slipped through their grasp.

"Was that the fight at the waterhole?" Collins asked.

"*Au.* Sunrise told me of it. It was night and the damn soldiers were sick. Some other soldiers came and they decided to leave. Later the big chief of the soldiers, the one from the fort, rode north out of there very close to Victorio and his people. They just watched and thought it was humorous. Some of the Mescaleros went back to the agency and that is when Sunrise went there. The other people went south. They used the tracks of cows to cover their trail."

The canyon began to narrow once more. Collins pulled up and dismounted, easing the cinches and allowing Molly and Ulysses to drink. Gah'tsu sprang down from his pony and hunkered down by the stream, scooping water with his hand in the same manner Collins had seen before. Reaching into his saddlebags, C.W. took out a sack of dried meat and shared it with the boy. Again, he found it difficult to believe his captors had not robbed him of all his supplies. Perhaps they had intended to, but when he had joined in the raid on the villages, they decided to leave him his belongings. A bald eagle soared directly above in the sultry air of late afternoon. The sky was a splendid color and it occurred to him that New Mexico Territory must have been an isolated paradise before the Spanish arrived.

After refilling his canteen, Collins tightened all the cinches, checked Molly's packs and mounted up. They rode a few more miles and the gorge snaked sharply back and forth several times, then opened up again where two dry gulches merged with the creek from either side. The sun was descending below the western ridges.

"We should make camp," he told his companion. "I do not want to ride into an unknown village in the dark."

"'Áxąh, this would be better."

They chose a place under some leafy cottonwoods at the bottom of a small canyon that emerged from the high mountain range above them to the northeast. Collins imagined that during normal spring weather, the crevice ran with water, fed by melting snows from the peaks, but the scarcity of moisture, evident everywhere, had left most of the region parched and barren. Rio Alamosa, fostered by numerous springs, created a belt of lush growth and thriving trees.

After they unsaddled their horses and turned them loose to graze, Jackrabbit helped Collins unpack and unsaddle the mule. All his belongings and food supplies in the panniers were in disarray from having been violently knocked about over the past few days, so he took time laying out all the items and fastidiously repacking those not necessary to an evening bivouac.

"Will we eat?" Gah'tsu asked, wandering over to scrutinize the proceedings.

"We will have to make do with bully beef, coffee, hard biscuits and dried apples."

"I can hunt."

"No gunfire. We cannot safely announce our presence."

"I can eat that food," the young man said agreeably. "I will make the fire so there is no smoke," he added and began to gather wood, particular of type and size.

The next morning they were on the trail before the sun rose over the mountains to the east. As the morning progressed and the canyon spread wider, a stout wind began to blow, seemingly gaining momentum through the gap. Two ravens arrived and hovered overhead for a while, performing assorted maneuvers and visibly reveling in the hard breeze that set Collins' teeth on edge and made the horses skittish. Toward noon, there were many more cottonwoods along the creek and intermittent dry arroyos joined the main passage. Sporadic signs of agriculture were visible. They passed what appeared to be an abandoned sawmill on a side hill and, not far away, came upon the head of an irrigation canal drawing water from the stream by way of an earthen dam reinforced by wattles, diverting it more directly toward the settlement ahead.

"Colonel Hatch told me that the people in this Cañada Alamosa trade with the Apache for stolen cattle, horses and army mules," Collins said, yanking his hat down against a gust of wind. "You said they are robbers."

"I have heard that the damn *Mejicanos* there trade whisky. I also heard they are not honest and make very bad trades after the people are full of whisky. Now I hear there are *Anglos* there who do not want to trade but kill people."

"We must be wary. I need supplies, but perhaps you should ride around the village and wait down the valley."

"I do not want to go there. I will go around."

Presently, they entered a substantial floodplain of the Rio Alamosa that was entirely cultivated with numerous crops. New plants were flourishing from sustained irrigation, in sharp contrast with the native vegetation on the slopes above. Collins could identify corn, beans and possibly squash or melon seedlings. As they rode farther south, he could see small flocks of sheep and goats grazing on mostly infertile hillsides. In one field, an old man was working with a grub hoe, encouraging a trickle of water to flow around dirt mounds and rows occupied by young plants. He paused in his labors and stood staring at them in what appeared to be a hostile stance.

"You should probably move into the hills now," C.W. told Jackrabbit. "I will see you south of the town. Watch for me."

"I will be there," the boy said and eased his pony out of the creek bottom and into the eastern uplands above.

Local residents became more numerous as Collins rode closer to the village, tending to animals, working in gardens or washing clothes in the stream. No one made a show of amiability, mostly glancing at him then turn-

ing away. As Collins entered the plaza of Cañada Alamosa, shaded by grand cottonwoods and bounded by a
crumbling adobe wall, he remarked that, as with the Ojo
Caliente military post, there were a remarkable number of glass windows evident in the hamlet. He thought
briefly of Santiago Duran back in Las Vegas. Reining
in his gelding momentarily, he searched for any building that possibly housed the local merchant. Given the
aloof surliness he had already encountered, he was loath
to request directions from any of the few people visible
around the dusty square.

Just diagonal to a well-tended whitewashed church,
there appeared to be a place of commerce. It was a long
narrow adobe building fronted by a generous porch with
plank flooring and double doors. A thick set white man
sat on a bench to the left of the doors, tossing small
rocks at a sizeable grey cat under a nearby tree. A direct
hit incited the animal to bound out of range. The fellow
spit a copious stream of tobacco in its wake.

"Hate those fucking cats," he said as Collins dismounted and secured Ulysses and Molly to one of the
porch supports.

Unsure as to how to respond, Collins said nothing,
loosening the cinches, brushing dust from his clothing
and retrieving his billfold from a saddlebag.

"My name is Kelley," the maligner of felines informed him.

Collins realized this must be the individual to whom
Jackrabbit had alluded. Stepping onto the planking of
the porch, he accepted Kelley's extended hand and shook
it. "Charles. Is this your establishment?"

"Aw hell no. This here belongs to a fella named Sullivan and his two Frenchy chums. I own the store near
the Caliente post down the way."

"Oh, I see," Collins said and moved toward the doors.

"What brings you 'round here? Kinda out of the way."

"Please forgive me, but I require supplies and must proceed."

"Fuck. Suit yourself," Kelley said and spit. "Hey, if you wanna hear 'bout my pal Victorio, the deadly Apache marauder, come on back," he added, swiftly regaining his hearty manner.

Turning around, Collins looked at the man. "Victorio is your pal?"

"Sure as shit. You wanna hear 'bout it?"

"Perhaps," he responded, leaning against the wall near the bench and taking out his pipe and tobacco pouch.

"Well, I will tell you. Last January, just this last one mind, old Victorio sent in for me to talk for him. He always trusted me, see, and wanted to give a word to the commanding officer at Caliente. The C.O. wanted Vic awful bad and promised a safe pass to come in and have a peace talk."

"Victorio wanted to talk peace?" C.W. asked, lighting his pipe and sending puffs of smoke into the breeze.

"Seems so," Kelley said, clearly pleased to have his attention. "Not sure if it would of done good. I can give you information that the Indians have not been treated fair." He aimed a stream of tobacco juice at the cat, which had moved to the side of the porch and was cleaning itself. He missed.

"Do go on."

"Vic would not come in 'til I gave my word that he would be all right. But he said I should stay with his warriors as a hostage until his return. Then he went to the fort and after a long talk, the C.O wanted to put him in irons. Old Vic's warriors would of done for me sure, if the lieutenant who was second in command did not make a strong protest and save my hair. Close thing and that commanding officer was damn cold to me after. Later I beat the shit out of him and it did me a whole lotta good."

"I can well imagine," Collins said. "Well thanks for the story. I must get on now." He went to the edge of the porch and knocked the ashes out of his pipe on the bare dirt, placing it back in his jacket pocket.

"It sure as hell ain't no story. Happened sure as shit."

"Thanks all the same, Mr. Kelley," Collins said and opened one of the doors to enter the building.

Inside, he found an extensive open room bisected by three pillars that supported the roof and were bedecked with multiple articles of harness, head stalls, rope, cinches and whatnot. The floor was made of the same wooden planking as the porch and a long counter took up the entire east side. A wood stove squatted in the middle of the room and the walls were covered in shelving that displayed a myriad of dry goods, hardware, boots and sundry other items. A barrel-chested gentleman in a stylish suit, his pleasant face adorned by a full moustache and bushy goatee beard, stood behind the counter, meticulously dusting bone china cups and saucers and placing them on shelves above him.

"Kelley tells that story at least five times a day," the man said without glancing up.

"Is it true?" Collins felt certain some part of it must have been.

"Heard it was, but there is no telling with Kelley," he said, finally looking up from his task. "I know for sure that some of those Indians seem to trust him. And more than one Apache has tried to kill him. How can I help you?"

18

Having purchased a variety of comestibles and received advice as to the most salutary route to Fort Stanton, Collins rode south out of Cañada Alamosa, following a well-defined track. There were scattered dwellings along the creek and a number of cultivated fields. Before long, the road brought him to another village, much smaller than the previous, but also boasting a tidy, albeit diminutive, Catholic church. A few horses, goats and donkeys wandered freely among unassuming houses and the interspersed deciduous trees were bare of branches within the animals' reach. One cottonwood was occupied by an enterprising goat that had climbed to a lofty and precarious branch. A couple of elderly women were the only discernable human inhabitants, making their laborious way toward the adobe chapel.

In an hour or so, the trail departed all signs of agriculture or tenancy and the Rio Alamosa dwindled to a perfunctory rivulet, having been diminished by persistent irrigation upstream. Cottonwood trees had abandoned the stream bank, giving way to hardier vegetation. The wind increased in intensity, raising minor whirlwinds that skipped frenetically along arid slopes above the creek bottom, then dissipated. There had yet to be a sign of his traveling companion.

As he rode, C.W. found himself pondering the sheer barbarity of European colonization and the aggressive forces that had originally combined to decimate Indian

populations. Fanatical abolition of all aboriginal spiritu-
al beliefs and a maniacal quest for riches accompanied
the Spanish throughout the New World, even as merciless conceit led to mass atrocities and the destruction
of entire cities by slaughter and disease. In 1494, a
mere two years subsequent to Christopher Columbus'
arrival, Pope Alexander VI created a line of demarcation
running north and south, dividing newly claimed territories between Spain and Portugal, the only European
empires, as yet, to have established a hold in the Amer-
icas. Thusly, all native peoples were rapidly disenfran-
chised through the machinations of arrogant and mighty
men who gave no consideration to abundant evidence of
indigenous intellect, architectural skills and advanced
civilizations. This plague of antagonistic procurement
had spread expeditiously north, much to the ruin of indigenous populations along the Río Grande.

Following the incursion of U.S. troops in '46, the entire territory became inundated with eastern white settlers searching for acreage or gold or both, many of them
recently discharged from the ranks of the military. John
Sullivan, proprietor of Cañada Alamosa's commercial lo-
cus, had told him a bit of his own history. Mustered
out of the 15th Infantry, having been stationed at the
old Fort McRae on the banks of the Río Grande, Sullivan established himself as a rancher and farmer in the
mostly Spanish village. He married the sister of French
immigrants, Alphonse and Aristide Bourguet, and had
subsequently gone into the mercantile business with
the two brothers. In antagonism to Kelley's oft-repeat-
ed tale, the storekeeper had adamantly expressed his
opposition to local trade or friendly dealings with the
Apaches. Sullivan had made it clear to Collins that he
and his brothers-in-law would put a halt to any such
transactions, saying, "We have made up our minds that

the cottonwoods in this vicinity shall bear fruit if there are any midnight meetings between Victorio's men and some of the persons of this town." C.W. wondered why so many white men were entirely convinced of their own rectitude. Self-doubt was never a shortcoming.

Suddenly, a flock of quail exploded out of some underbrush, spooking Ulysses and forcing Collins out of his reverie. Gah'tsu emerged from the mouth of a small arroyo.

"Da'anzho," he said, offering his engaging grin. He dangled four juvenile cottontail rabbits from a fist. "No gunfire."

"Splendid," C.W. said, smiling. "I also acquired food with no gunfire."

The boy tied the rabbits to his horse's mane, the animal all the while evincing an aversion to the procedure. They fell in together, riding abreast along the trail. The creek bottom had opened up into a sandy valley and was steadily losing elevation, eventually breaking out into desert terrain bestrewed with sotol yucca plants, saltbush, prickly-pear cacti and patches of fluffgrass. The sun was fierce and there were no clouds. They were now headed due east and Collins assumed they would be converging with the Río Grande before nightfall.

"Will we go to the hot water?" Jackrabbit asked after they had ridden in silence for quite some time.

"What is that?" Collins asked, having been deep in thought once more.

"The *tú siduyá,* another hot water place. I have heard of it. It is on the big river ahead. "

"I do not think so. We will camp on the river when we meet it, then cross and head south to Fort Selden on the road through the desert. I spoke to a man in the village. He said if we follow the river, there is quicksand."

"The other way... that is a bad way. *Nii naguyeesgq.*

There is no damn water there."

"A white man built a well there, so we will have water."

"I do not want him to shoot me."

"I will prevent this from happening," C.W. reassured the young man, smiling to himself.

Toward nightfall, they came upon the Río Grande and camped among a grove of trees where there was ample grazing for the animals. Gah'tsu skinned and roasted the rabbits while Collins made coffee and biscuits. After they ate, Collins smoked his pipe and Jackrabbit worked at putting new soles on his moccasins.

"Do you have a woman?" the boy asked, pausing a moment to stretch.

"No. Are you promised to someone?"

"There is a girl. A *zhannuuch'į...* someone who has lost a man. There are those who think she is bad luck."

Pouring himself more coffee, Collins leaned back, resting against his bedroll, and studied his friend curiously. "What will you do?"

Having completed his task with one moccasin, Jackrabbit considered his work and appeared to be satisfied. He picked up the other and resumed his repairs. "I must do more to prove my worth as a warrior. Maybe then I will be able to choose this woman."

"You have a warrior name. Sunrise told me. You must have earned it."

"Yes. I killed some white men. Some bad men. And saved another warrior from death."

"Well then, this was not enough to prove yourself?"

"I did this when I was with the *Chihende* warriors. I must prove myself to my own people and be given a new name with them."

"Is this why you wish to return home?"

"It is a reason."

There was rustling in nearby undergrowth and they

both reached for their rifles. A stray longhorn cow wandered into the outer reach of the fire's glow and ambled past the camp as if it was beneath notice.

"We could have the meat," Gah'tsu said eagerly.

"Best not." C.W. told him, knocking the ashes from his pipe. "We do not want trouble."

The next morning they arose and began packing up camp before dawn. Collins knelt by the river's edge and refilled the canvas water bags, acquired from Colonel Hatch, in preparation for their passage across a long stretch of inhospitable desert. It would take them two days of hard riding to traverse. John Sullivan had told him the Spanish called the route *Jornada del Muerto*, meaning Journey of the Dead Man. They would follow the old road, established by conquistadors in 1598 for travel from Mexico to an Indian pueblo on the northern reaches of the Río Grande. Fortunately, according to Sullivan, back in '68, an ex-soldier had used gun powder to break through rock and reach water at the site of an old seasonal spring. The place was called Aleman Ranch and was currently the location of a stage station, in spite of sustained Apache raids in the area. They would be able to water their animals there and rest for the night.

They crossed the river where it spread wide into shallows and allowed the horses and mule to drink deeply. They rode southeast away from the Río Grande, leaving trees and most vegetation behind. Creosote bush now dominated the terrain, only interposed by an occasional bunch of grama grass, scattered mesquite and an oddly shaped broad-leafed plant with white and purple flowers. The inhospitable landscape stretched monotonously to each horizon, barely broken by distant and hazy ridges of low mountains and what appeared to be a rocky butte to the south. A few delicate clouds hovered over the western skyline, too thin and unsubstantial to promise rain. As the sun climbed higher, the temperature rose to harsh intensity.

The day wore on and Collins and Gah'tsu spoke very little. They drank sparingly and stopped to give water to the animals a couple of times. Once, a light tan dust pillar rose in the vastness, thin and towering to a great height. It traveled an exceptional distance and almost seemed to pursue them. As they proceeded southeast, the desert also became populated by another type of mesquite and occasional tall, spindly cacti, some of which displayed red flowers at their tips. C.W. was astonished to see hummingbirds flitting among the blooms, given the scorching heat. In addition, there were low shrubs with yellow flowers among intermittent clumps of sallow green grasses, striving to exist in the arid land.

"That is good for stopping blood," Jackrabbit said, pointing at a gangling cactus with his lower lip.

"I will keep that in mind. Have you been on this road before?"

"*Da*. But I know some good plants for helping cure things."

"That will be useful if we become injured or take sick."

The day was nearing its peak and a stiff wind had begun to blow when they perceived a great plume of dust ahead on the road, propelled by the breeze in a sweep to the east across a lengthy escarpment of naked volcanic rock. Collins reined in his gelding. "That has to be wagons or livestock," he said.

"Or soldiers."

"Or soldiers," Collins agreed, removing his Stetson and wiping his brow with his scarf. He dampened the cloth with water from his canteen and retied it loosely about his neck.

"I will not run. There is no damn place to hide."

"You stay with me. No one will pester you." C.W.

reached down to loosen the Colt in its holster.

They rode ahead and the soaring chalky cloud drew nearer. Finally they could hear the tramping sound of hooves and lowing of cattle and Collins relaxed his guard. Soon they saw a chuck wagon coming up the road, headed north, then the first of the herd, flanked by two cowboys. They turned off the trail about a hundred feet and swung to face the throng of longhorns. Gah'tsu prudently drew his pony in behind Molly to become less obtrusive. The cook waved from his seat on the wagon and continued along the way. One of the cow men turned off and came over to where they sat their horses.

"Hidy," he said. The fellow was long and lanky with an abundant red and gray moustache that concealed his mouth. His clothing, stovepipe chaps and hat were coated with a tan residue of powdered earth. "Interestin' chum you got there." His restless bay horse reached his nose toward Molly and she nipped at it.

"None of us are overly fond of inquisitive strangers," Collins said quietly.

The man put up his hands in mock surrender. "Whoa pal, just bein' friendly. Know this country much?"

"First time in the vicinity."

"It can be right hostile. Just keep to the road and water up at the Martin place. It'll cost, but better than chokin' out. 'Magine your comrade there knows it."

"This your outfit?" C.W. asked, nodding at the surly animals lumbering by. Occasionally one would attempt to intimidate a neighbor with a toss of its daunting horns.

"Naw. Just an ol' ramrod, workin' for a fella down in Mesilla. Name's Hal." He touched the brim of his hat lightly. "These beeves are bound for Fort Craig." He glanced over his shoulder to see that the last of the cattle were straggling past, followed by a middling horse herd. Trailing behind the entire procession rode a young boy in an imposing hat and wearing a generous scarf tied across his face. "That'll be the cavvy and Ramon, our wrangler. Best be gettin' on." The cowboy gave a two fingered salute. "Aydiōse." He spun his horse offhandedly and loped away, returning to the front of the herd and keeping to the upwind side of the horses and cattle.

"Son-of-a-bitch," Jackrabbit said.

19

The Aleman Ranch, built by John "Jack" Martin, now deceased according to Sullivan in Cañada Alamosa, consisted of a collection of adobe buildings. Aside from the multiple water tanks, supplied by the celebrated well and windmill, there was a rambling ranch house, small two-story hotel, stage station, stables, corrals and several outbuildings. Craggy ridges of an inhospitable mountain range traced the eastern horizon. Collins and Jackrabbit rode into the settlement, wary of any show of animosity toward them. An elderly man attired in baggy cotton trousers, white blouse, suspenders and dilapidated felt hat approached them.

"*Buenas tardes, señor. Me llamo Tadeo.* How may I assist?"

"We would like to water our horses and perhaps rest for the night."

You may water your *caballos* at that tank," he said. "*Cuesta* two bits per horse. And we have a very nice hotel *para descansar.*"

Tadeo was apparently undaunted by the presence of a young Apache warrior.

"Thank you," Collins said. "But we prefer to make our own camp. May we do so?"

"*Sí señor.* There are those trees over there. Two bits *por dos.*"

"Do I give the money to you?"

"To me," said a slim white man walking toward them.

He had a heavy Texas accent. Tadeo removed his hat deferentially and shambled away, seemingly in trepidation.

"Very well," C.W. said. "I believe it was two bits per animal for water and two bits for making camp in those trees?"

"You can water your animals, but there ain't no setting up camp for you and your ameego." The Texan wore a wide holster for a Smith and Wesson .44 as well as a belt of ammunition above it. He clearly displayed the mannerisms of a bully.

"Very well. We will water our horses and move along. Is it possible to fill our water bags?"

"Right there at the windmill."

A small detachment of colored soldiers rode in, raising dust that dissipated quickly in the late afternoon wind. They dismounted near the biggest water tank and led their horses to drink. The Texan sauntered toward the troopers, joined by another Anglo.

"We should not stay here," C.W. told Jackrabbit.

"No. We should get water and go."

They rode over to a smaller trough. "Will you take care of the animals?" Collins asked, swinging down out of the saddle and waiting for his legs to adjust. "I will return soon."

"*'Au.*"

"Be alert."

"*'Au.*"

He shouldered the water bags, Gah'tsu's wicker container and his canteens. Walking over to where the Texan and the other man stood watching the black cavalrymen care for their horses, Collins sorted through a handful of coins and picked out three liberty quarters. The men turned to glare at him when he approached.

"Got quite an amount of gall coming in here with that rascal," the Texan said, raising an eyebrow.

"He is a hired guide. No more. Here is the fee for water." Collins held out his hand holding the quarters.

"Tom!" shouted a smartly dressed man coming from the direction of the hotel. "Get back to work and do not interfere with these people. Mrs. Martin is coming up from Mesilla tomorrow. I will report to her."

The Texan strolled nonchalantly toward the stables, as if he had decided to move on and had not been ordered to do so.

"My apologies," the new arrival said to Collins. "This man is always causing trouble." He spoke with a refined Spanish accent.

"Do I pay you for watering my three animals?"

"Yes. Thank you."

"I also wished to fill these," C.W said, indicating the containers suspended from his shoulder.

"Oh yes... well then that will include an extra quarter."

Collins paid him. "Your hireling said I could not camp here with my Apache guide."

"He was correct in that. It would make our other visitors most discomfited and a stage is due in this evening. Perhaps you may send him down the trail and remain as a guest in our hostelry? It is quite comfortable and the meals are excellent."

The soldiers had remounted and departed the compound at a trot, heading north.

"Thank you for the suggestion, but I prefer to remain in company with my scout. You do not charge the army for water?"

"They are always welcome here." the gentleman told Collins. "When we request a military presence, a troop of soldiers is posted at the ranch. Two years ago, we had some horses stolen from our corrals and a detachment of the 9th Cavalry assisted me in retrieving them. One animal was an Andalusian stallion of which I am inordinately fond."

C.W. thought the man was peculiarly turned out for the middle of a desert. He was wearing immaculate tan waist overalls with tall brown leather boots reaching up to the knees, a waistcoat, string tie, a dark brown cut away jacket and a straw planter's hat. In truth, he most especially resembled a plantation overseer.

"Forgive me," the fellow said, as if suddenly aware of Collins' scrutiny. "My name is Jesus Ochoa. I run the Alemán Ranch for Mrs. Martin. Come, I will show you where to fill your vessels."

Ochoa escorted Collins to a tall cast iron hand pump that extended above one of the smaller water tanks. "This is very clean and cool water from deep in the ground." He began to pump vigorously and they proceeded to fill the bags and bottles.

While thus engaged, Collins asked, "Where did the name Aleman come from? I was told this ranch was established by a man named Martin."

"It is actually Alemán, after the Spanish word for German." Ochoa was slightly breathless from his exertions.

"How did that come about?" C.W. asked, stoppering one of the canvas bags and lifting another under the steady flow of water.

"Many years ago, in the late 17th century to be precise," he said, pausing in his efforts, "this road was the passage from Mexico to all of the territory in the north. A German merchant named Gruber was traveling through, supposedly running away from persecution as a witch. It was very dry and he died of thirst. His remains were eventually discovered and buried. Someone placed a cross in his memory near here and from then on this area became known as *La Cruz de Alemán*."

"So Martin merely kept the name."

"Yes. It was already a very famous landmark."

They finished their task and Ochoa gestured for Tadeo, loafing by the corrals, to come and assist Collins in carrying the water. The three of them walked back to where Gah'tsu waited with the stock.

"This drought is so terrible. It has been two years since a general rain has been had. Apaches come here at night to water their horses. They are never charged and we do not disrupt them, but the soldiers do not know this," Jesus Ochoa said as Collins and Tadeo loaded the heavy canvas bags on Molly. "I am very sorry I cannot allow you to stay," he said directly to Jackrabbit.

The boy shrugged, but said nothing.

"Is there a location south of here where we may camp undisturbed?" C.W. asked.

"*Sí señor,*" Tadeo said. "*Con permiso?*" he asked Ochoa.

"Yes, of course," the foreman answered impatiently.

"There is some black *piedras* to the south and an *arroyo* away from the road. There is shelter and you will not be seen. *No está lejos.*"

"It is not far," Ochoa said. "Just head south and a little east. You will find it." He spoke in Spanish to Tadeo. The old man nodded farewell to Collins and ambled toward the house.

A broad-shouldered white man walked over to them, briefly narrowing his eyes at Jackrabbit in disapproval. "I have news," he told Ochoa. C.W. recognized him as the individual who had joined the Texan and the soldiers earlier.

"This is Harley Gregg," the foreman said to Collins. "He is the station keeper and blacksmith for the National Mail and Transportation Company."

"Not for much longer," Gregg said grimly. "The railroad will be headed through and no more stage line."

"Perhaps, Harley, but then there will be other employment. We will certainly remain."

"I suppose."

Evening sunlight, distilled through a veil of wispy clouds along the skyline in the west, cast saffron and rose light across the outpost. Collins readjusted the saddles and tightened the cinches on Molly and Ulysses.

"What is your news?" Ochoa asked.

"Victoria and his redskins got pummeled up in the Black Range. Them nigger boys told me."

Turning quickly to look at Gah'tsu, whose face was dark with rage and anguish, Collins shook his head in an attempt to dissuade him from any rash response.

"Did they tell you any more than that?" Collins asked indifferently.

"Couple of days ago a fella named Parker, head of a bunch of Injun scouts, stumbled onto the old scoundrel's camp in a canyon on the Palomas River. He sent sharpshooters 'round the position at night and let 'em have it at first light. Bottled 'em up and slaughtered a good forty or so. Some of the dead ones was Comanche, so it proves a growing army of savages."

"And Victorio?" C.W. asked, stressing the "o."

"Apache scout claimed to have shot him in the leg. Guess the soldiers ain't so sure about that, but the story goes when the scouts hollered to the squaws to give up, one old harridan yelled back that if their chief died, they'd eat him rather than let a white man see his corpse."

"Are they all captured now?" Ochoa asked.

"Naw, that fiddle-headed Hatch failed to send reinforcements and they melted out of there that night. Betcha all them agency critters will skedaddle back home now."

Swinging into the saddle, Collins said, "We must be on our way. Good luck to you."

Jackrabbit kicked up his pony and bolted down the trail.

"That buck you got there," Gregg said. "No gaging for why you took him on, but do not turn your back on the bastard. Red devils live to maim and kill.”

About to ride after his companion, Collins paused a moment. “ ‘Nothing blackens like the ink of fools,’ ” he said contemptuously, quoting Alexander Pope.

“Look there Harley,” Ochoa said curtly. “The stage is coming.”

Gregg scowled at Collins menacingly for an instant. “Suit yourself, you lunk. Your carcass will festoon the badlands.” He departed their company for the stage station.

“I do not share such sentiments,” the foreman said, looking up in distress at C.W. “I am marooned among the benighted.”

Laughing, Collins said, “I frequently find myself thus. Thank you for your hospitality, Señor Ochoa. It has been a pleasure.” He wheeled Ulysses and, wrapping Molly’s lead rope around the saddle horn, rode south to search for Jackrabbit.

APACHE SCOUTS

20

About three miles to the southeast of the Alemán Ranch, Collins found the rocks and secluded coulee to which Tadeo had directed him. The sun was now setting behind distant hills and he decided to make camp, even though there was no sign of Gah'tsu. He unloaded and unsaddled his animals, then grained and hobbled them and turned them loose to graze on the sparse grama grass scattered among creosote bush and cacti. He was unsure whether he would see his young friend again, thinking perhaps the young warrior had deserted him in order to seek an opportunity to fight, given the news they had received at the ranch.

The evening was swiftly turning chilly. Collins gathered dried cow manure and dead brush to build a small fire. While the limited fuel lasted, he made a pot of coffee and heated a can of beans. Before long, all heat and light were expended and he was enveloped by near darkness. He fumbled about, finishing his meager repast, unfurling his bedroll and organizing gear until a waning but fulsome moon rose in the east, spreading welcome light across his surroundings. He found Molly and Ulysses on a bank of the arroyo several yards away and led them back to camp, wanting to secure them for the night against theft and harm. When he returned to camp, Jackrabbit was sitting on his pony nearby, waiting.

"Anglos are worthless damn dogs," the boy said matter-of-factly.

"Most of them, to be truthful, are shit sacks. Glad to see you."

Slinging a leg over and leaping off his horse, the Apache pulled a simple hackamore from its head and turned it loose. "You are not a shit sack," he said.

"Thank you."

Jackrabbit spent time gathering more dried sticks of mesquite and creosote bush and built up the fire again. C.W. opened another can of beans and placed it near the low flames to heat. The boy did not wait long to eat the food, plainly hungry.

"More?" Collins asked when Gah'tsu was finished scooping the last bits from the can.

"*Da.*"

Lying on his bedding and leaning against the pack-saddle as a backrest, Collins smoked his pipe and sipped coffee, now grown cold. He watched as Jackrabbit sharpened his knife on a small stone. After a while, he asked, "Were you at the agency when the troops came in last month?"

The boy scowled. "When the soldiers stole our horses and took our guns?"

"Yes. I want to know about that. Will you tell me?"

"It was bad. I am still damn angry."

"Will you tell me?" Collins asked again.

Jackrabbit was silent a while, his strong, earnest face lit by dying embers. "*Au.* I will tell you." He slipped the knife back into its sheath on his belt and stared into the distance of the night, as if summoning images from his memory.

"That agent man named Russell with the long damn beard, went around seeing people in their camps. He said the army was coming, but not to harm us... not to harm the people who had not done wrong. I did not trust this. I had heard of soldiers killing some people at

Shake Hand Spring not long before. I left my mother's camp and went into the woods to hide and watch. Also I thought I would hunt some. After two days, many, many soldiers came. I heard them coming and followed to *kįyá...* the agency buildings. That is when all the people there ran away. We all thought they had come to take us to that place of hunger and snakes. *Saangáadayá.*"

"San Carlos?"

"San Carlos. Then the agent found *Nautzilli* who has always worked for peace. He told him he should speak to the soldiers so the chief and his father went to speak for the people. After this talk, Nautzilli went around with the head men Roman Chiquito and Griego to bring many of the people back to the agency. I stayed to watch but told my mother to go away and hide."

"Did she?"

"The camp went up to *taje bitu'* and stayed away. But many of the people came back near the agency after the head men asked them to. Then after much friendly talk from the agent, the soldiers shot two men who had been herding run-away horses back to the agency like the damn agent wanted. One of the men shot was the father of Nautzilli. The agent came to the main camp for more talk, but that is when some people left again. After they left, the agent told the rest of the people they must give up their guns and horses. He said there was trouble because the people had been helping the *Chihende* and their chief Victorio, but when the trouble ended, they could get their horses and guns again."

"You heard this?" Collins asked.

"I was in among the people. I wanted to know why this was happening. More people left then because they would not let their horses and guns be taken. That is when I rode my pony out of the way again. I saw a head soldier, like the one you saw at the fort near the hot water place, take out his gun and fire three times. The people became very afraid and ran for the trees. Most of the soldiers had been somewhere else and they came when the shots were heard. They fired their guns at the people running and killed a few. Many got away. Nautzilli got away, but many were taken back to the agency and the soldiers put their hands on them and took away all the guns and knives and other things. Most of the people who got caught were old men and old women and children. Not many warriors. They also took all the horses away. Many many horses were taken away. I think they took them to the damn fort."

"Fort Stanton?"

"Yes, I think so."

"Was it over then?" Collins asked. "Did the soldiers allow everyone to leave?" It was certain that the story he was hearing now was substantially different from Colonel Hatch's version.

"*Da.* They could not leave. The soldiers pointed guns and pushed the people into the corral where the cows are put for killing."

"How many people?" C.W. had allowed his pipe to go out and he put it on the ground beside him.

"More than *naakidntu'* I think. More than two hundred. They made them stay many days and the soldiers were always there to make them stay. They were pushed together and they had no place to go do what they had to and they got sick. I went away then and that is when I found Sunrise on his way to talk to Blazer. I told him what happened. After that Sunrise took me to raid up to *ch'ila'énde* country. That is when I wanted to kill white people. That is when some others left to find Victorio and fight."

"It is a shameful story," Collins said, shaking his head. "I hope your family is safe."

"Yes, I saw my mother's camp before I left."

The boy precipitously lay down beside the dead fire, covered himself with a blanket and closed his eyes. Collins slipped inside his bedroll and found he could not sleep. His restless thoughts begat a memory he had long forgotten. Back when he had still been a young police constable, he partook of the occasional pint at McSorley's Old Ale House down in the Five Points neighborhood of the city. One night a coal heaver, originally from Belfast, had entered the establishment with intentions of antagonizing Catholic patrons. Patently inebriated, the massively built Ulsterman bully had proceeded to beleaguer a diminutive fellow who worked as a clerk in Tammany Hall. Collins had intervened and the beating that followed was of epic proportions. It had taken him weeks to recover and he suffered greatly from terrible pain as well as the loss of wages. C.W. had been told much later that the Dead Rabbits pursued the man and his body was never found. At the time, he had wished he could have killed the man in vengeance and understood Jackrabbit's desire for retribution. Lying awake in the deserts of New Mexico Territory, Collins frowned at the viridity of his younger self and contemplated the unending round of antagonism between disparate religions, races and kingdoms. After much effort, he managed at last to still his mind and he drifted into a restless slumber.

Back on the main road in early dawn light, they covered as many miles as possible while the day was still cool. A small bunch of antelope shadowed them for a while, then moved off toward the San Andres Mountains to the east. By mid-morning, they came upon an impressive rim of lava rock, rising above the trail. Beneath, the old royal road of the Spanish carved a wide depression into the fragile soil, exhibiting the passage of thousands of hooves and wheels. Stopping to rest the animals and give them water, they ate some dried meat and biscuits and shared lukewarm coffee from one of Collins' canteens.

"That is a nice little horse," C.W. said, nodding at Jackrabbit's pony. "Have you had him a long time?"

"My mother's brother gave him to me. I call him *Xe*. It means lard."

"I wanted to say… well I was sorry to hear of the battle on the Palomas River," C.W. said, not having mentioned it the night before. He took out his pipe and packed it with tobacco methodically. "I hope Sunrise was unharmed."

"Fuck the bastards."

No doubt this was more descriptive terminology picked up from the troopers at Fort Stanton, Collins thought, amused. He smoked his pipe quietly a moment and his reflections sobered. "I know you must be very angry. Will you still return to the agency?"

"I want to kill white men, but I also want to live. It is difficult," the boy said, allowing a handful of sand to drift from between his fingers, dispersed by a rising breeze.

"I think you should return to the agency. You can protect your family there."

"Yes. That is important."

"And there is a woman."

"Yes."

Finishing his smoke and stowing away his briar, Collins took the map from a pocket and scanned their route. "We will be at Fort Selden by nightfall. I wonder if you should go there."

"I do not want to go to another fort. I know of a way to *kiyá* through the mountains and along the place of white sand. I can see you again when you come to our country."

"Will you be able to avoid the soldiers and Anglos all

the way?" Collins stood up from his seat on a boulder and stretched.

"I can be like a coyote, fading into the dirt and rocks. But you must be watchful of the shit sacks."

Rubbing his mouth to conceal a grin, C.W. said, "Then I will find you at the agency. Do you need food?"

"No," the young man said, gesturing at a pouch suspended from his belt. "And there are places where food has been hidden all over." He nimbly sprang onto the back of his pony. "Aydiōse," Jackrabbit said, mimicking the drover from the day before, and pressed his heels into the horse's sides.

Turning to readjust saddles and snug cinches, taking time to scratch and offer words of affection to his Molly and Ulysses, Collins found he was melancholic. The oppressive heat of the day, the stiff wind, the barren landscape and the departure of his young companion all converged to darken his mood.

OLD FORT SELDEN

21

The day was waning when Collins rode into Fort Selden and was dumbstruck by what he encountered. The post lay in ruins. Most of the adobe buildings no longer had roofs and the walls were crumbling from neglect. Skeletons of dead trees scraped and creaked eerily in a strong breeze. Certain that John Sullivan in Cañada Alamosa had directed him to the fort as a way station, he could not decide whether this had been an elaborate prank or the man just did not know that the site had been abandoned by the army. Regretting he had encouraged Gah'tsu to go on alone, C.W. departed the ghostly environs and rode west toward the Río Grande.

In a dense grove of trees, Collins found abundant grazing for Molly and Ulysses. He made camp and ate a meal of beans, dried apples and hard biscuits, washed down with strong coffee. In the nascent morning, he refilled all the water containers and rode along the old military road his map showed would lead him through the San Augustín Pass and along a series of springs to the Río Tularosa. The air was chilly and he donned a coat he had not worn for days, having been stowed deep in a pannier. In an inside pocket he found the silver fish given to him by Peng and a small stone from Ladder Creek in Kansas. The keepsakes made him smile.

It was frustrating to have to travel a circuitous route to Fort Stanton, but from the post at Ojo Caliente, there had been a choice of circumnavigating the Sierra Oscura

Mountains and protracted lava fields or heading south around the bottom end of the San Andres Mountains, and a blazing hot and waterless expanse of white sands, by following the old army trail built in 1855. His capture by Apache raiders had taken him far afield from his original destination. Small enough price to pay, he thought, for remaining alive.

Bypassing a small settlement just beyond the old fort and another negligible farming village a little beyond, Collins reached the cutoff that angled to the northeast. The terrain was flat, except for a ragged palisade of windswept ridges ahead, and the countryside was mostly gravel and sand with scant vegetation. The military road seemed to be aiming itself directly at a notable fang-shaped pinnacle of naked rock and was steadily gaining in elevation. As the day advanced, the wind was resuscitated and the temperature soared. Collins shed his coat and jacket but remained disagreeably warm. By noonday, he was climbing the western slopes of an austere crest of sandstone, grateful now for the robust breeze cooling his abundant perspiration.

Near the summit of the scorched backbone of rock and sand, Collins halted to rest his animals and give them water. Rifling through his packs, he retrieved a collapsible canvas bucket and filled it with the contents of one of the water bags. Abruptly, Ulysses lifted his head and whinnied, startling Collins. He jerked his .45 from its holster and gathered the gelding's reins and Molly's halter rope, scanning the ridgeline above him. A tight group of riders precipitously appeared against the cloudless sky and headed in his direction. They pulled up a few feet away. C.W. counted five of them, all heavily armed. He made certain they could perceive the revolver in his hand.

"Hello there," one of the men said cheerily. He was a

pleasant looking fellow of middle age and seemed to be the only Anglo in the bunch. The rest appeared to be of Mexican descent. One of them rode a horse that was disturbingly notable.

"Hello," Collins said without inflection.

"I am Albert Fountain of Mesilla," the man said, dismounting and walking over to offer his hand. "Captain of the Mesilla Scouts."

Slipping his Colt back in its holster, Collins diffidently accepted the hand in greeting. "Charles Collins."

"You are either a most courageous individual or foolhardy," Fountain said, smiling engagingly from beneath a generous and well-groomed moustache.

"Neither, I would expect."

"I regret to say the Apaches are at present murdering every unprotected soul on this frontier. Traveling alone is imprudent." The man removed his hat and wiped perspiration from his balding head with a sleeve.

"As may be, Mr. Fountain, but my imprudence should be a matter of indifference to you." Collins gestured at one of the mounted men. "I know that roan horse. Where did you get it?"

The deeply tanned Mexican was fingering his pistol and eyeing him closely.

"Miguel's filly collapsed on our way back from Tularosa," Fountain answered. "Fortunately, we came upon a gentleman at one of the springs who sold him this little stud. I doubt you could possibly recognize it."

"Nevertheless," C.W. said. There was a sick sensation in the pit of his stomach. "Run into any Indians on your way back from Tularosa?"

"Nary a one. We have been patrolling for several days. It is believed that Victorio and his warriors are headed to old Mexico. We will soon be able to develop this land into a prosperous Eden. Especially now the railroad is coming."

"Perhaps," Collins said noncommittally. "Well... if the Apaches have left the country, then I suppose I am quite safe to travel alone."

Fountain shrugged. "There are other Apaches about, Mr. Collins. And Comanches." He walked to his horse and mounted. "Good luck to you."

"And you."

The Mesilla Scouts walked their horses past Collins and his animals. Captain Fountain touched the brim of his hat in farewell and a couple of his men nodded as they rode by. The man on the roan pony kept his distance and made no eye contact. When they were downslope about a hundred yards, they kicked up their horses and galloped away toward the west.

After Molly and Ulysses had drunk their fill, Collins repacked the bucket and empty water bag in a pannier, removed his field glasses from the saddle bags and swung onto his horse. He had most certainly recognized Jackrabbit's pony and was plagued with foreboding. Reaching the top of San Augustín Pass, he paused to survey the vast landscape spread out before him, but there was no indication of human activity anywhere. On a rise off to his left, a herd of desert bighorn sheep regarded him suspiciously and retreated a few yards when he nudged Ulysses back into a walk. To his right rose an implausible rampart of batholithic spines slicing into a cloudless cerulean sky.

Along about midafternoon, Collins came to a spring where a dirt tank had been excavated to collect a substantial pool of water. As he approached, a number of insects and rodents abandoned the surroundings, proclaiming him a dangerous intruder with their trepidation. A rattlesnake buzzed a warning from the shade of a mesquite bush and a shiny, darkling raven scolded from its vantage point on a yucca stalk. Dismounting at a distance from the snake, C.W. led the mule and horse to drink. The water was clear and he walked around to the other side of the pool and knelt to refill the canvas bag and an empty canteen. He noticed a smooth white shape on the sand nearby. When he picked it up, he realized it looked like one of the shell earrings Gah'tsu always wore.

Coming to his feet, Collins perused the area for any sign of his friend in the vicinity. Spoor of animals of various species was evident in every direction. He found several boot prints, probably made by Fountain and his Mesilla Scouts that morning, and some that could have been made the day before. After a few minutes of searching, he discovered fresh moccasin imprints a few feet away from the water hole and surmised they probably belonged to Gah'tsu. Unshod horse tracks were also visible nearby, but he could find no clue as to how the pony had gotten away from the young man or where he had gone. By following the horse's hoofmarks, Collins found the animal had moved away from the well-used army road and proceeded into the uninhabited territory to the east. He was not a skilled enough tracker to decipher whether the Indian boy rode him or not. A short distance away, other tracks, made by more than one shod horse, departed the spring and appeared to shadow the Indian pony's course.

Loading the water containers on his mule, he checked cinches and mounted up. Collins decided to follow the path as best he could, knowing he had plenty of water and could easily find his way back to the road, given the flat, open terrain. As he vigilantly searched for signs along the trail, it seemed manifest to him, from the spacing and shape of the hoofmarks, that the pace of all the horses had steadily increased into an outright chase, with the pony keeping well ahead of its pursuers. It was nearing dusk when he paused and raised his field glasses to scan the country ahead. He noticed a considerable wake of turkey vultures gathered on the ground about a quarter mile away. As he drew near, the smell of carrion reached him and some of the birds took flight, revealing a human form reduced to mostly skeletal remains.

The discovery bespoke a tragedy, no matter the identity of the poor soul now corrupted into bones and scraps of flesh and gristle. The corpse was twisted ignominiously by the grappling and tugging of scavengers. Collins dismounted several feet away and secured his gelding by wrapping reins around a shrub. Molly stood well back behind Ulysses and both animals were uneasy. He patted them and spoke reassuringly, then hesitantly approached the grisly scene, waving his arms to chase off the remaining buzzards. A snarled wad of black hair was visible near the skull and ripped and bloodied tatters of a cotton breechclout and blouse fluttered in the wind, snared by a patch of prickly-pear cactus. A leg bone had been yanked free and lay close by, still encased in a tall, distinctive moccasin.

Awash with guilt and grief, C.W. bent down to examine the skull, traced by remnants of gory tissue, and discerned a bullet hole in the back of the cranium made by a large caliber gun. The fatal wound had come from behind, so his friend had probably been shot from his pony. Horse and boot tracks were present all around the scene. There was no sign of the pistol, knife or rifle. Something caught his eye a few paces away and he walked over to find the grey wool U.S. army blanket the boy had always carried with him. Pulling it loose from where it was entangled on a dead yucca, Collins took it back to the body, snapping it sharply to frighten a persistent vulture that had returned to the scene.

As the sun was setting, he used one of his tin plates as a shovel to dig through gravelly loam and burrow out a grave. Not normally squeamish, given the carnage and putrefying flesh to which he had been exposed throughout his years with the Metropolitan Police and during the war of the rebellion, Collins faltered at handling the wretched, flayed cadaver of the Apache boy. He wrapped all the bones, fragments, hair and scraps of clothing in the blanket and gently lowered them into the trench. Mutely weeping as he scraped earth over the pitiable woolen mound, nestled in its truncated hollow, he patted the soil firmly into place, pressing the boy's shell earring into the dirt. He removed his hat and knelt a moment by the grave with both hands resting upon it.

"I am so sorry," he said softly. "I broke my word and did not keep you safe. I am so sorry."

Standing up, he retrieved his Stetson, wiped the tears from his face and walked to his mule and horse. He wrapped Molly's lead rope around the saddle horn and, pulling the reins free, led his animals west toward the military road, shambling dejectedly across the desert through the feeble light of a waning gibbous moon.

MILITIA

22

Exhaustion drove him to make camp in the early morning hours. After unloading and unsaddling the horse and mule, he grained and watered them. Concerned about their welfare, Collins picketed the animals close together and rolled out his bedding nearby, his Winchester and revolver close at hand. He did not slumber, but lay on his back and grappled with the overwhelming anguish that threatened to devour him. From previous encounters with uninterred remains, he could judge about how long the buzzards had been at the body. The young man must have been killed the day they had separated. A direct route along Apache trails through the San Andres Mountains would have brought the boy to the spring around nightfall. He must have been ambushed there and made a desperate run. It was heartrending to ponder the shock of a bullet smashing into his head and flinging him violently from his pony, driven solely by avarice and odium. The contemplation did Collins no good. He knew too well that such were the customary deeds of belligerent ascendancy.

Sleep never came and, as the first halo of light traced the eastern horizon, C.W. drank the remaining cold coffee from a canteen and chewed on a shred of jerky and a hard biscuit while the animals wandered close by, grazing on clumps of fluffgrass. He was already headed down the trail when the sun appeared on the skyline. The day grew steadily warmer and by noon he began to see traces of white sand blown across the road from the gypsum beds to the west. He came at last to the next natural spring on his map. A great iron tank had been sunk into the ground to capture the slow trickle of water. Collins assumed this was the work of the army. He drank a handful of water and found it mildly saline, but he filled all the containers and then allowed Ulysses and Molly to drink.

The road was hot, dry and dusty. A revived incessant wind blew grit in his eyes and rivulets of perspiration seeped from under the brim of his Stetson. The land was intolerably dull. Collins found it difficult to stay awake and fought to remain alert. He was in dangerous country and could not afford to drop his guard. His thoughts turned unremittingly round and round the fate of the Apache boy and his remorse was profound and agonizing. They should have stayed together. Honor and the value of his word were at the very core of who he considered himself to be. He was shaken and distraught and off his axis.

The afternoon dragged interminably in both physical and emotional distress. His map displayed the location of one more water source before reaching Tularosa and C.W. hoped to make it to the site before day's end. Distant mountains now showed in the east and he knew these to be part of the Sacramento range. To the west lay low ridges of snow white, the borders of the expansive, bleached barrens. Near sundown, he came at last to another artesian spring that fed a rather substantial excavated pond. Birds and butterflies populated the vicinity in abundance, creating a lovely scene. Nature's steadfast beauty, the cooling of the evening air and his own unconquerable temperament all worked to put him back in equilibrium, in spite if his enduring penitence.

After watering his stock and drinking his fill, Collins

washed and shaved. Molly and Ulysses picked at the minimal grass that grew around the pool. Moving off about a half mile, he then made another rough camp, but allowed himself a small fire with which to make coffee and fry up slices of canned corned beef. Hot coffee and hot food, followed by a can of peaches and a smoke, further uplifted his mood and when Collins lay down on his bedroll, his animals and weapons close to hand, he drifted rapidly into slumber. Rising early the next morning and returning to the spring to water animals and replenish his canteens, he came upon a supine form of a person, entirely concealed by an army blanket and sheltered under one of the stunted mesquite trees that grew on the edge of the spring-fed pond. He watched as a rather large tan scorpion traversed the blanket lengthwise. Subsequent to filling all containers, attending to Ulysses and Molly and readying to depart, C.W. went over to see if the individual was alive or dead, poking the blanket lightly with the toe of a boot. A colored man threw off the covering and jumped to his feet.

"What the hell... who the fuck are you?" the fellow shouted.

Collins noted that the man wore the miscellanies of an army uniform, the blue sack coat hanging open over a civilian blouse. His trousers showed the yellow stripe of the cavalry, tucked into iconic boots worn by same, and the holster slung from a cartridge belt showed the butt of a Remington army revolver. His hat was missing. The soldier was resting his hand on the pistol and glowering pugnaciously.

"I apologize for startling you. Have you lost your detachment?"

"Not your fuckin' concern."

"Most definitely not." Collins turned to tighten cinches, loop Molly's lead around the saddle horn and prepare to leave.

"That there is an army mule," the erstwhile soldier observed slyly.

"And mine now."

"Except it has an army brand. And I have need of a mount."

Collins placed a foot in the stirrup and swung aboard Ulysses. "As you said, that is not my fucking concern." When the man moved toward him, he slipped the Winchester from its scabbard and aimed it loosely in his direction. "I believe you are a deserter and therefore have forfeited any right to army property... not to mention *my* property," he said quietly. "Make a move and you will die here."

"I meant you no harm," the man said in a wheedling tone.

" 'A staff is quickly found to beat a dog,' " C.W. said, quoting Shakespeare.

"You callin' me a dog?"

"Perhaps."

"You just gonna leave me here?"

"Most assuredly," Collins said, restoring the rifle to its sheath. He prodded his gelding into a walk, giving the deserter a wide berth.

"I ain't no fuckin' deserter, just so's you know," the man called after him. "Got separated from my company."

Returning to the road, Collins headed north. The deserter continued to yawp behind him, slinging colorful epithets. With nothing but disdain for the man and uncaring about his fate, he thought about the negro soldiers who deserted during the war. Almost all of them had had excellent reasons to abscond, including draconian discipline, menial and grueling labor and criminally low wages that allowed their families to starve. Many of them found army life to be disturbingly similar to their recent enslavement. In spite of this, the 9th and

10th Cavalry and 24th and 25th Infantry Regiments had proven equal to any white troops throughout ensuing years. The fellow at the waterhole, however, displayed Pecksniffian conduct that bespoke cowardice and guile. He was near enough to Tularosa that he need not perish in isolated wastelands nor on an Apache lance. It was entirely up to him.

It was midday when Collins began to see stands of verdant trees in the distance. In short order, he entered the village of Tularosa, a viridescent island wedged between the Sacramento Mountains and the desert, watered by a network of irrigation channels that extended like arteries from the Río Tularosa. Cottonwood trees shaded the dirt streets and several fruit tree orchards spread out on either side of the main road. Herds of cattle and flocks of sheep inhabited pastures in all directions and farm fields were arrayed in rows of burgeoning crop plants.

A couple of Mexican boys were playing hoop and stick along a sandy thoroughfare. C.W. paused to inquire as to the location of the stables. The boys stopped their game and one squinted up at Collins as if he were not to be trusted.

"It is *adelante, señor,*" he said. "Just there," The boy waved his stick at a long structure a few yards away.

"*Gracias,*" Collins said and tossed him an Indian Head penny.

"*Gracias, señor.*"

He rode through two substantial wooden gates and a stable hand came out of a nearby pen. The worker was also Mexican, but grown into maturity.

"Do you require boarding?" he asked.

"Yes. Only overnight. My animals need rest and good feed. Do you have pasture or only hay?"

"There is a small pasture of ryegrass, clover and fescue. They can be by themselves. We have had few patrons for many days because of Indians."

Collins dismounted. "Do you have some clean grain as well? I do not want any moldy feed."

The laborer nodded. "Very clean. Mr. Coghlan provides the best of everything."

"Then I wish to purchase a quantity to take with me as well. Is there a place where I may store my packs and saddles?"

"Yes, follow me. My name is Maximo. I will help you."

"Excellent."

After being assured of his animals' care and welfare, Collins retrieved his carpetbag and rifle and walked across the road to the two-story Hotel Union. This, according to Maximo, was one of the few enterprises in Tularosa not operated by the same man who owned the stable and wagon yard, a general merchandise store and a local saloon. The hotel was constructed of adobe, as were most of the buildings in the hamlet, and possessed a long wooden porch running along its front. This created a balcony for the second story where it also supported another roof sheltering separate entrances for each room. A small, narrow wooden sign suspended above the front door declared the name of the lodging house. Collins stepped into a cool, whitewashed lobby and walked to a wooden counter, carved in Spanish colonial style, backed by shelving and a row of cubbyholes recessed into the adobe. There were colorful Indian blankets displayed on two walls. He could detect the odor of roasting meat seasoned with red chile. His appetite was instantly honed.

Given the absence of a bell, he leaned his rifle against the counter and knocked loudly on the top of the wooden surface. After a few minutes, a woman emerged from an adjoining portion of the building. For an instant, C.W.

was taken aback. She was attired in a simple green chambray dress, but her deportment and lovely visage seemed out of place in the remote and primitive setting of New Mexico Territory. She wore a buff-colored scarf tied loosely around her shoulders and her raven hair was gathered in a mass on her head, framing an arresting tawny face, tinged with rose from heat or exertion. The woman moved behind the worktop.

"Did you wish a room?" she inquired abstractedly.

It seemed to Collins that she evinced a wistfully cheerless mien. He removed the Stetson and ran a hand through his unruly mane. "Yes. For just one night."

"That will be one dollar. I have had to cut my rates. Many of the local ranchers have departed for Las Cruces or Santa Fe and travelers, even prospectors, are giving us pass." She examined him as if she expected him to speak.

"Indian raids?"

She nodded. "And the drought. I expect it will improve soon."

"Are meals available here or shall I search elsewhere?"

"There are meals. An extra two bits, for supper and a breakfast."

Extracting his coin purse from a vest pocket, he handed the woman two Morgan silver dollars. "Please keep the full amount. I may request some provisions for the trail."

The woman regarded him, her face absent of discernable expression. "Very well." She placed the coins in a lock box, returning it to a shelf behind her, then slid a leather-bound register book toward him.

"May I inquire as to your name?" Collins asked.

Handing him a stylographic fountain pen, she said, "Ana Frederick. I am the proprietress of the Hotel Union."

He entered his name on the line indicated by her and

picked up his satchel and rifle.

"Come, I will show you to your room," she told him and came out from behind the desk, preceding him toward a staircase that went up four or five steps then angled perpendicular to the left and ascended behind the counter and along the back wall of the hotel lobby. A windowless door opened onto one end of the balcony. The woman showed him to the second door along the gallery.

"This one is the nicest. When you desire a meal, come down to the *cocina.*"

"Is it Miss or Mrs.?" Collins asked impulsively and was promptly ashamed of his unfortunate caprice. "Pardon me. I did not mean to be discourteous." The woman was having a ruinous effect on him. Her unblemished beauty, poise and absolute dearth of sentiment was unsettling.

"It is Mrs. Frederick. I am a widow." Again, there was a vacancy of emotive nuance. "I hope you will find the room to your liking," she said and withdrew.

23

The rustic wooden table on one side of the kitchen was spread with assorted dishes of meat marinated in chile and fragrant vegetables. Mrs. Frederick sat at the opposite end from Collins and did not eat.

"Before the Indian raids, my dining room was full in the evenings," she said, nodding toward a darkened room through an archway. The woman was perceptibly of Spanish decent, yet she spoke without a trace of accent.

"I have heard that Victorio and his warriors have gone to Mexico." He took a bite of dark greens sautéed with beans. "What is this dish called?" he asked.

"*Quelites.*"

"It is very good."

"Thank you."

There was negligible conversation as Collins finished his repast. Inspiring the woman to speak was arduous and he wanted to enjoy the excellent meal. It had been many days since he had eaten proper food. Through the back door, open to allow heat from the massive cookstove to dissipate, he could see blue shades of twilight. Mrs. Frederick cleared dishes when he had eaten his fill and poured coffee for them both.

"May I smoke my pipe?" C.W. asked.

"If you wish."

As he prepared his briar, the woman sat quietly, scarcely moving. Collins found her stoic tranquility to be disconcerting but admirable. He had only ever known his friend Arbuckles to be so self-possessed. He lit his pipe and met her steady gaze.

"May I inquire whether you are from this part of the country?" he asked.

"I am from San Antonio. I was born Ana Marcela Flores." There was neither a hint of pride nor shame in the statement.

"And how came you to Tularosa?"

"When I was very young, there was violence in San Antonio toward those who were neutral in the Mexican War. My father, Tranquilino Flores, was killed by the Americans because he only desired to be left alone. He was an educated man and did not wish to join the barbaric conflict."

Mrs. Frederick arose to pour more coffee. Smoking his pipe silently, Collins waited for her to continue her tale.

After resuming her seat and contemplating the contents of her china cup for several minutes, she said, "My mother found it difficult to cope and placed me with the Ursuline nuns until I reached twelve years. I did not see her again."

"Siblings?"

"Yes, there were eight. The little ones died during and after the war and my older brothers were killed fighting on the side of the Americans. Their sacrifice did not save my father." She looked down and turned a silver ring on her right hand around and around. It was the first display of emotion Collins had observed.

"And then?" he asked after she had remained taciturn for long minutes. His pipe was spent and he put it away.

She glanced up at him. "At twelve, an aunt in Santa Fe sent for me. She had arranged a marriage with an older, very wealthy gentleman. He directed servants and a carriage to convey me to him. The journey was long and I did not care to marry this old man. When we reached Fort Craig, I had determined to run away. Instead I met a Captain Frederick in the New Mexico Volunteers. Unlike most of the others, he was a German immigrant. I married him and we lived at the fort until after the rebellion when he was discharged. We had very little money but he had an idea to build a hotel and we came to Tularosa. He died of consumption and I remained as you see."

"You have done well."

"I was forced to borrow money and have toiled diligently. My husband was neither clever nor kind."

This last statement seemed to close the door on her willingness to relate any further details of her life. Mrs. Frederick removed the coffee cups and summarily carried them to a long stand with sink and basins. With the impression of having been dismissed, C.W. thanked her and retired to his room.

She came to him that night. With none of the reserve that seemed to define her earlier temperament, she disrobed and slipped into his bed. Nearly asleep, he roused and gave in to the woman's sensual captivations that clearly arose from previous and wide-ranging knowledge of male delectation. In turn, Collins devoted his preceding and plentiful acquaintanceship with women to rewarding her bountiful generosity, summoning forth cries of delight. Neither was rushed nor impulsive and when the prolonged exchange of gratification was concluded, he fully expected an interlude of conversation. Instead, Mrs. Frederick wordlessly left his bed, donned the voluminous dressing gown she had previously shed and glided softly from his room, leaving Collins mildly thunderstruck at the woman's inscrutable conduct.

Long after she had departed, the scent of lemon oil and bergamot lingered. He lay awake, contemplating women and their finer qualities. The woman's munificence had eased his misery in regard to the loss of his Apache friend, for he certainly felt a hint more blithesome than previously. Mrs. Frederick was a quite a conundrum, however, and Collins suspected she had suffered greatly from unrecounted tragedies. She might bear her mutilations internally, but they seemed to be manifested in her reserve and cautious self-restraint.

When he entered the snug dining room the following morning, one of its five tables was occupied by a pair of Anglo men. One was attired in a suit and the other in the rough clothing of a cow hand. C.W. sat across the room, uninterested in social intercourse of any kind. Ana Frederick arrived with a bone china coffeepot and cup and saucer, setting the items on his table without greeting or catching his eye. She promptly whisked back through to the kitchen. While filling his cup, Collins casually studied the men at the other table. The one in the suit had an air of complacency that spoke of being in command. He had grey hair but peculiarly affected a dark beard resembling that of an Elizabethan rake and had not bothered to remove his Coke hat. Collins took this as evidence the man felt assured of his own privilege. The other wore a plain white shirt and tan pants with suspenders. A black felt, planter-style hat was placed on a vacant chair. The men had finished their meal and spoke together in low tones.

While awaiting the return of Mrs. Frederick, Collins removed the map from an inner pocket of his jacket and spread it before him. The old military road followed the Rio Tularosa up to the Mescalero Agency. Once there, he would be in territory with which he was conversant. Back in '72, President Grant had commissioned him to go to Fort Stanton, then agency headquarters, in order to reconnoiter issues with whisky peddling and the Mescalero Apache people. Agent Andrew Jackson Curtis, a Unitarian, had been contending that L.G. Murphy, post trader and erstwhile post commander at Fort Stanton, was making illegal liquor in the vicinity and selling it to the Indians. According to Curtis, both Mexicans and Anglos in Lincoln, Tularosa and La Luz had also been supplying illegitimate whisky to the Apaches.

Mrs. Frederick returned with a plate of eggs, side meat and sourdough biscuits. She placed the food on the table and produced a jar of homemade jam from a pocket of her apron.

"Do you care for anything further?" she asked evenly, meeting his gaze only fleetingly.

"No thank you... this will do very nicely."

She paused at the other table to clear some dishes, then left the room.

"And what brings you to our fair village, friend?" the man in the suit asked on a sudden. He had a strong Irish accent proclaiming his genesis in County Cork.

Glancing up from his breakfast, Collins swallowed a mouthful of biscuit and narrowed his eyes quizzically. "I did not inquire as to your particular business," he said, beckoning his own notable Irish inflection. "What is your interest in mine?"

"See here, pal," the other man at the table said, shifting his chair to brace C.W. "Mr. Coghlan was only at being hospitable. Mind your manners."

"*Tarruing do laimh comh reidh a's thig leat as bèul a mhadaidh,*" Collins said quietly and with menace.

The cowboy sprang to his feet. "What? What was that?"

"Sit down, Tom," the Irishman directed. "You are out of your league."

Tom sat back down deferentially. "But what the hell did he say?"

The Irishman appeared amused at his companion's disquiet. "It is the Irish. He warned you to ease your hand out of the dog's mouth. Good advice by the look of him."

"He ain't no threat," Tom said petulantly.

"Never you mind," his boss told him.

As he finished his meal, Collins ignored the men, who once again were speaking privately. After a brief interlude, he rose from the table, stowed his map in a pocket, picked up his carpetbag and Winchester and made to leave.

"*Is fearr lùbadh nà briseadh,*" the Irishman said as C.W. strode past.

"And who are you to advise this?" Collins asked, pausing at the door to the lobby.

"His name is Mr. Pat Coghlan," Tom informed him, obsequiously.

"I see. And who intends to break me and for what particular reason?" he asked Coghlan, disregarding his toady.

"Merely some kindly advice," Coghlan said, shrugging. "Will you be remaining in Tularosa for a spell?"

"No."

"Safe journey to you, then. Safe journey." The Irishman smiled and there was a palpable warning behind his expression.

Holding Coghlan's eyes for a long moment with a stony aspect, Collins said, " 'Courage mounteth with occasion.' "

"Let us pray that Shakespeare was correct in that," Coghlan called after him as he left the dining room.

24

The woman was absent from the kitchen and lobby and he left the hotel without seeing her again. It had been a singular encounter. He was reminded of another quote: "Love sought is good, but given unsought is better." Perhaps not precisely what Shakespeare had meant, but the spirit was unerring.

C.W. crossed the roadway and entered the gates into Coghlan's stable and wagon yard. A young Mexican lad was seated on a crate oiling an assemblage of harness.

"I have come to pay my bill and collect my livestock and belongings," Collins told him, walking over.

The boy jumped up and ran into the barn. In a moment, Maximo emerged. "Ah hello, sir. This is my son Porfirio," he said, nodding at the boy who returned to his seat in the sun and resumed his task. "Your horse and mule are in a stall in readiness as you requested. I will assist you."

In the gloom of the barn, Collins perceived that both animals had already been saddled and his panniers and other possessions were neatly piled just outside the pen. Maximo led Molly and Ulysses into the alleyway. Together, Collins and the stable hand tightened cinches and loaded the packsaddle with panniers and the rest of his outfit, skillfully tying down the load. When all was in preparation, they led the horse and mule out of the stables.

"How much is owed?" Collins asked, taking out his

coin purse.

"Four bits."

He paid Maximo, tipping him another quarter for the excellent service.

"Many thanks to you," the Mexican said, bowing slightly.

After greeting Ulysses and Molly and offering them each a biscuit purloined from his breakfast, C.W. mounted up, rode through the wooden gates onto the street and headed east to rejoin the army road that followed the Río Tularosa. The trail began to ascend out of the desert basin as it followed the course of the river. The land remained arid beyond the riparian swath of the waterway, but he could soon see the foothills of the Sierra Blanca and ridges of the Sacramento Mountains ahead. He thought about Ana Frederick and her family. Much like hers, countless lives were lost or dictated by the requirements of others, most of whom had more money or power and influence.

Having survived *An Gorta Mór*, The Great Hunger, in his home country, Collins was fully aware that the avarice and colonial prerogative of Anglo Protestant landlords caused the death and migration of thousands of Irish peasants. Not far from his home in Sligo, one Major Mahon had inherited an estate encumbered with substantial debts. In an attempt to rid himself of over a thousand tenant farmers, who had lost their ancestral rights to the land through British imperialism, he evicted them or coerced them to emigrate on one of the notorious coffin ships. These ships were destined, through negligence or willful purpose, to sink long before reaching any proposed terminus and thusly many of Major Mahon's tenants perished by drowning.

In neighboring Ballykilcline townlands, combined forces of cavalry, police and infantry cruelly evicted Irish peasants and destroyed their meager cottages, confiscating all belongings and auctioning them off for pittance as rents. As a boy, it had not been uncommon for him to roam the countryside and come upon entire families huddled in a ditch, sheltered beneath a few sticks for cover. His mother had done her best to feed as many of the outcasts as she could, but in the end, economic strife and the threat of starvation compelled both of them to take passage to America. Such was his own course permanently altered by the oppression of privileged liege lords.

It was not a leap to compare the pitiless displacement of his own people from their ancient lands and kinships to the marginalization of Spanish descendants and Indian peoples in New Mexico Territory by Anglo usurpers. The alacrity with which settlements and vast ranches were established, and previous inhabitants were dislodged or subjugated, bore witness to the determined preeminence that defined the colonization of American soil. As Alexis de Tocqueville had so eloquently written, "They go to inhabit new deserts, where the importunate whites will not permit them to remain ten years in tranquility. In this manner do the Americans obtain, at a very low price, whole provinces, which the richest sovereigns in Europe could not purchase."

He rode for two or more hours, then Collins dismounted and led Ulysses and Molly down an incline to water in an exposed bend of the stream. His whereabouts were unintentionally obscured by undergrowth that created a dense screen. By chance, he glanced upward at the sandstone crag that had served as a landmark for some distance along the way. Two men happened to be passing above him and one was easily identified as Tom, crony of Pat Coghlan. Instantly on his guard, C.W. guided his animals into the cover of a willow thicket and waited for a good while before swinging into the saddle and climbing back up the embankment to the road.

The trail ahead was empty, but he was vigilant to possible ambush. Coghlan's unsolicited counsel, in the Irish language, of bending rather than breaking, had been portentous and less than cordial, probably inspired by his lack of obeisance to someone accustomed to deference. The presence of the man's sycophant upon his track, Collins reckoned, was cause for prudence. He proceeded along his way and eventually espied a tendril of dust rising from the road ahead. Riding onto the river bottom, he slipped to the ground, eased Molly's cinch and secured her in a sheltered grove of young cottonwoods. Back in the saddle, Collins loped warily along the road until he again caught sight of a chalky wisp signifying the passage of riders. Reining his gelding onto the grassy riverine floodplain that paralleled the north side of the trail, he progressed almost silently and came abreast of the men. Wrapping the reins around the saddle horn, C.W. pulled the Winchester free, chambered a round and, passing the rifle to his left hand, yanked his revolver from its holster and prodded Ulysses precipitously onto the road, coming up just behind them.

"Hold there," he commanded, catching the men by surprise. One of the horses reared in alarm and almost unseated its rider. They reined in their mounts and sat uneasily.

"What is this now?" Tom asked, his mouth forming a disagreeable sneer.

"I merely wish to know if you were dogging me."

"Why would we do that?"

"At the behest of your master."

"Not sure what you mean, pal," Tom said.

"I sincerely doubt that." Collins cocked the revolver pointedly. "I suggest you return to Tularosa, having no compunctions whatsoever about shooting you and your companion merely as a matter of insurance."

"Well that just ain't friendly," the other men said with a flagrant Texas accent.

"No, it is not. But this is rather lawless country and I feel certain I will be able to manage a skillful getaway."

In truth, Collins was not as *sang froid* as he appeared. If, in fact, the confrontation evolved to where he was obliged to shoot these men, there was a certainty that some representative of law would respond and complications could arise. He was, however, no stranger to the art of deception and his bluff held. The men looked at each other.

"It ain't worth it," the Texan said. "Not for just one horse."

"I agree," C.W. said and pulled the hammer back on the rifle with his left thumb. "And in all fairness, I must inform you that I am perfectly capable of taking you both at the same time."

"To hell with this," said the man from Texas and kicked up his horse, riding past Collins at a dead gallop in the direction of town.

"Mr. Coghlan may have something to say about this," Tom said maliciously.

"I wonder what he will say about my getting the drop on you."

"Motherless bastard."

"Get moving." C.W. motioned toward the west with the barrel of his Colt.

Tom rode tentatively past Collins, who kept both guns aimed at him and directed the gelding with his knees to keep the man in his sights. When down the road a good distance, the coward spurred his mount and disappeared around a bend.

Securing his weapons and riding back along the floodplain, Collins kicked Ulysses into a lope and made for the place where he had left his mule. He found her safe and sound and apparently content, for she had stripped leaves from every tree branch within her reach. Tethering his horse beside Molly, he cautiously edged toward the road in order to survey his back trail. He hunkered down and watched for a long while, pestered incessantly by a large and tenacious horse fly. When assured that the men had, indeed, retreated back to Tularosa, C.W. returned to his animals, led them to water, tightened cinches and climbed into the saddle.

The day had warmed significantly and Collins judged by the sun it was well beyond the noon hour. Chafing at the unwarranted delay, he drank deeply from his canteen and eased his gelding into a ground eating walk. Before long, he noticed a rider coming toward him at a canter along the road. Savvy to the slightest indication of belligerence, he rested his hand upon the butt of the Colt. The man's horse was lathered with sweat and two bulky sacks were lashed down behind the cantle of his saddle, distinguishing him as a mail carrier. Passing by without altering his pace, the fellow gave a fleeting nod and Collins responded with a transitory salute.

The afternoon wore on and the surrounding countryside became more mountainous, defined by tan foothills punctuated with juniper trees and higher summits cloaked in the dark green of conifers. By now, he surmised he had entered the Mescalero reservation and he thought of his young Apache friend once more, saddened they would not be reuniting after all. Given the horse thieving inference of the Texan's proclamation, he wondered whether a member of Coghlan's crew had been responsible for Jackrabbit's profligate demise. If he could definitively identify the boy's murderer, he would not hesitate to gun him down.

It was toward sunset when Collins first detected the

sounds of human activity. He recognized the area now, having visited some of the Mescalero camps back in 1872 and met with Dr. Joseph Blazer, an early Anglo settler and trader in Mescalero Apache territory. He recalled that, having first arrived in the region as a freighter for the army, Blazer had purchased an old sawmill, originally built by the Spanish. The mill had supplied much of the lumber for nascent building ventures in Tularosa. Blazer had quickly become known among Indians, Mexicans and whites as an honest and fair-minded man. He became a successful entrepreneur, postmaster, local commissioner, juror and frequent adviser to the Mescalero people and several agents. Collins knew he would be an excellent source of intelligence regarding recent events.

He rode into an expanse of ground where thick trees and undergrowth along the Río Tularosa had been cleared for farm fields. Ahead, he could see the multiple buildings and sawmill of the Blazer operation. A tremendous cacophony was spawned by the machinery of the mill. A few men could be seen moving about, occupied by different tasks, and he unexpectedly came upon a young lad of adolescent years attempting to pull a milk cow free of a mudflat along the stream. The boy had no horse, wore layers of muck up to the knees of his trousers and was definitely not abetted by the ceaseless barking of a robust canine, running up and down the bank.

"Might I lend a hand?" Collins asked, riding over.

"I would be most obliged," the young man told him, relinquishing his struggles and allowing slack in the rope that was secured to the cow's halter.

"Hold my mule, if you will, and I will see what I can do."

Exchanging Molly's lead rope for that of the cow and stepping back a few feet, the boy waited expectantly. The dog turned its attentions to Molly, yapping and lunging, and she grazed its muzzle with a glancing blow from a hind foot. The animal yelped and made for a two-story house, situated a short distance away. Collins dallied the rope around the saddle horn, turned Ulysses to head away from the cow and eased the gelding forward. In no time, the animal was pulled free of the quagmire, albeit exhausted and coated with sludge.

"I am most grateful to you, sir," the young man said, handing Molly's rope up to C.W. and accepting that of the bovine. "Poor old Lupita was wearing out. All the horses are either lent, on a mail run or out skidding logs." He grinned sheepishly. "And Plato was making quite a nuisance."

"I apologize for my mule. I hope she did not injure him." Collins dismounted and walked with the boy toward a barn and set of corrals, leading his animals behind alongside Lupita the milk cow. The sun was setting and evening was sketching shadows across the valley. The many workers previously visible about the grounds had withdrawn to the bunkhouse or elsewhere and the din of the sawmill had ceased.

"If she did, he might learn a valuable lesson. By the by, my name is Almer Blazer. I suppose you are here to see father?"

"I am Charles Collins." They reached toward each other for a brief handshake. "Yes, as a matter of fact, I was hoping to speak with Dr. Blazer, if he is indeed your father."

"I believe he went up to the agency buildings for some business or other. He should return soon."

At the barn, Almer led the cow into a stall, gave her a bucket of water and pitched in a mound of grass hay from a full crib along one wall. "You can put your horse and mule out back in the small pen, if you wish," he told C.W. "There is a water trough and some hay in the bunk. Then we can go up to the house. The cook will have coffee on. And there is plenty of room for you to spend the night."

"Thank you."

Together they quartered Molly and Ulysses, hauling saddles, panniers and other gear into the barn. As they were headed for the house, someone called a greeting behind them. Turning to look, Collins could see a tall figure striding toward them along a path from the river.

"It is father," Almer said and they paused to wait.

LOGGING

25

"As I recall, Mr. Collins, you had some connection with the government," Joseph Blazer said.

They were sitting at a sturdy table in the kitchen of the Blazer house, several oil lamps illuminating the interior. Demetrio, an aged Mexican man who was employed as cook, had served them steaming cups of coffee, tureens brimming with venison stew and mounds of fresh flour tortillas. As they ate and conversed, the cook busied himself with various duties within his domain among pots and pans, chile ristras, a variety of dried herbs suspended in bunches from the ceiling, and a collection of *retablos* portraying diverse saints displayed on the walls amid shelves of myriad jars and canisters containing enigmatic and fragrant substances. Plato, the dog, lay sleeping under the table.

"I still do, in a manner of speaking. I have been appointed by Commissioner Trowbridge to investigate certain matters."

"Such as?"

"I would rather discuss this at another time, Doctor, if you are amenable."

"Call me Joseph, if you will." He held up his hands, somewhat disfigured by arthritis. "I must remind you, I have not practiced dentistry for many years. As you may recall, my impediment led me to join the army and ultimately to New Mexico Territory."

Swallowing a final forkful of stew, Collins said, "And

it appears you have done well for yourself. Do you and Santana remain on cordial terms?"

"The chief has died," Almer interjected rashly. "Smallpox."

"Well... not exactly smallpox," Blazer said, looking askance at his son. "It was pneumonia following small-pox. He was on the mend, but I was called away by business and when I returned, he had died. Nautzilli is probably considered the head man now. Caballero had joined Victorio."

Demetrio refilled their cups and Collins studied Blaz-er a moment. His hair and scrupulously manicured beard had become almost entirely white, but the man still appeared youthful of face and figure. There was striking resemblance between father and son, Almer be-ing a handsome lad with intelligent and regular features.

"And other head men?" C.W. asked, nodding thanks to the cook.

"Each chief has followers. You must remember how it was."

"Yes. I remember." His friend, Cadete, had been the Mescalero leader most able to negotiate with and skill-fully hoodwink soldiers and settlers alike. He had com-manded a large following due to his capabilities, but not among those who did not wish to treat with white men.

The boy yawned surreptitiously.

"Off to bed, son," Blazer said. "And take Plato with you."

Reluctantly removing himself from the table, Almer called his dog and departed. They could hear his heavy steps on the stairs to the second story.

"Nice youngster," Collins said.

Blazer smiled. "We get along. He could use the firm hand of a mother, however."

"I certainly benefitted from such a firm hand," Collins told him. "I do not recall seeing the boy when last I was here."

"No. He and his sisters, Ellie and Emma, arrived in

'77. Almer had contracted a ruinous strain of consumption and was not expected to survive. I finally judged the territory secure enough for the children to join me and sent for them. The boy has fully recovered and is becoming a proficient hunter and prospector and assists me in my business."

"And your daughters?"

"Visiting friends in Mesilla."

Collins smiled, briefly wondering how young ladies from Iowa might acclimate to a remote reservation.

"Come," the doctor said, getting up from the table. "Let us betake ourselves to the parlor. Demetrio, *más café por favor?*

"*Sí señor.*"

"Unless you prefer whisky?" Blazer asked, as they strolled through to an agreeable room on the other end of the house, passing beyond a dining area occupied by a massive Spanish colonial table surrounded by heavy, leather-covered chairs.

"No, I am content."

The parlor was modestly decorated. The rough plank flooring was mostly obscured by a plain rug, the walls were covered in wallpaper of a simple pattern and the furniture, consisting of two oak rocking chairs, a well worn day bed, a wall clock and two large bookcases, was serviceable more than ornate. Several framed chromos of diverse landscapes adorned the walls, an oblong table, covered in books, inhabited the center of the room and a tall wrought iron wood stove squatted in a corner. Collins sat in a rocking chair beside a window. Blazer lit the oil lamp on the table and seated himself in the other chair. Demetrio arrived with a chipped ironstone coffee pot and cups. He placed them on the table, shoving aside a mound of books.

"Have the men eaten?" the doctor asked.

"*Sí*, all of them."

"*Gracias*."

"*De nada*."

Blazer poured coffee and handed C.W. a cup. "Demetrio may be elderly, but the man works like a mule."

"And makes excellent coffee. May I smoke?"

"Of course. I have some fine cigars."

"I prefer my pipe." Collins removed his briar, match safe and tobacco pouch from an inner pocket of his jacket.

"Never could manage a pipe, myself."

They sat in genial stillness for a while, smoke from Collins' pipe curling toward the low ceiling.

"I had heard that Commissioner Trowbridge is ill," Blazer said after a prolonged interval.

"I am unaware. I suspect, having been employed by him before, that Secretary Schurz is behind my directive."

"And may I finally inquire as to the nature of this directive?"

"Certainly. I am particularly desirous of your account of the events in question, if you are agreeable."

The doctor considered him an instant. "I do not mind... as long as I do not betray a confidence."

"I do not believe this will present a difficulty. But firstly, I wanted to discover whether you have had dealings with Pat Coghlan of Tularosa."

Sitting back in his chair, Blazer produced a guttural and contemptuous sound, then said, "He is a malefactor and sharper of the first sort."

"No surprise there. Am I correct in my assumption he is also a stock thief?"

Reaching into a wooden humidor perched upon the overcrowded table, the doctor took out a figurado and snipped the end with a pen knife. Collins offered him his match safe and waited patiently as Blazer lit the cigar and puffed delicately in order to attain an even burn.

When, at last, the cigar appeared to content him and he had extracted a brass ashtray from under another stack of books, Blazer said, "Coghlan does not engage in such activities, but hires persons of debatable character to do so, not the least of whom is a fellow named Morris Wohlgemuth. He also purchases cattle herds of dubious provenance to fulfill his contract to supply beef for Stanton."

"And horses as well?"

"Horses, cattle... I would not be astonished if he traded in goats, sheep and dogs. No doubt if slavery were still lawful, he would barter for human flesh." Blazer tapped an ash from the end of his cigar and examined its glowing foot. "I have also heard that Coghlan, his chum James West and some others also profit from the sale of whisky to the Indians. Why do you ask?"

Collins heaved a sigh. "I lost an associate recently, not far from Tularosa. His horse was stolen and he was callously slain."

"Sheriff Padilla is a reliable man and he is categorically *not* an ally of Coghlan."

"My companion was a young Mescalero man. His name was *Gah'tsu.* Jackrabbit. Did you know him?"

Blazer frowned, visibly searching his memory. "There was a boy named *Gah'tsu,* but they called him another name when he grew older. Oh yes, I remember. They called him *Guzéé' gútsa',* in the denotation of someone talking too much. The boy was always telling stories. I know he was impatient to be a warrior and believe he went off with some of Victorio's band."

"He saved my life." C.W. reached to knock ashes from his pipe into the ashtray. He blew a puff of air through the stem and returned it to his jacket pocket.

"How did that come about?" asked the doctor, appearing perplexed. "How did the boy... forgive me, but I endeavor to honor the Apache tradition of not speaking the names of the dead... how did the boy come to be in your acquaintance?"

"I do not desire this to be general knowledge, but I was captured on the Pecos River by Apache warriors. Victorio's warriors."

"I can hardly countenance this. You survived?"

"The boy saved my life. But that is a narrative for another occasion."

"And I certainly wish to hear it," Blazer said, stubbing out his cigar. "Do continue."

"I encountered the Mesilla Scouts on San Augustín Pass two days ago. One of the assembly was mounted on the boy's stolen pony. Later, I found the young man's remains on the desert east of the old army road."

"But that is Albert Fountain's militia," Blazer said incredulously. "He is a trustworthy friend."

"I am fairly certain he was entirely ignorant of the circumstances. His colleague, however, appeared to be unsavory."

"And you imagine that Coghlan was somehow involved?"

"It is possible. But impossible to prove."

"Sadly, I agree." The doctor rose from his chair. "Would you care to accompany me in a stroll out of doors? The moon is waning, but offers sufficient brilliance with which to see."

Coming to his feet, C.W. answered in the affirmative and they exited the dwelling into a tranquil, clement night. They rambled along a path that skirted the base of the hills above them.

"Do you happen to know the boy's family?" Collins asked.

"Let me think... I believe the mother's name is Otottie. You must inform the agent."

They walked along in quietude for several minutes. The quarter moon cast eerie shadows across their pathway. An owl hooted from a tree across the river.

"I knew Victorio," Blazer said matter-of-factly, breaking the silence.

"You did?"

"I first met him when Chief San Juan introduced him to me back in '79. Agent Russell, the old fumbler, had given the Ojo Caliente band a few paltry items and insufficient food. San Juan brought them and I supplied Victorio with a weighty steer, some sugar and flour and as much coffee as I could spare. The Indians requested to be allowed to bring their families from San Carlos and I believe Russell was seeking approval for this. But the agent persisted in his miserly approach to allocating rations to the band and there was some tension between the Mescalero people and the Ojo Caliente group." He climbed a fence that paralleled their footpath and sat on the top rail.

Joining the doctor, C.W. asked, "Did you trust his sincerity regarding an intention to remain peaceful?"

"I did. But there had been loose talk about an indictment sworn against Victorio for horse theft or murder or some such. I do not know the truth of it, but when Albert Fountain came from Mesilla with a hunting party made up of a judge and some other practitioners of the law, general suspicion was aroused."

"Is Mr. Fountain an attorney?"

"And is known as such to many of the people here. Word reached Victorio that these men were passing through the reservation and he became convinced they were coming to arrest him. When next the band came into the agency for rations, there seemed to be some delay and the chief thought Russell was fabricating an excuse to betray him. I heard he became enraged and pulled the agent's lengthy beard and slapped him. Russell panicked and sent for soldiers. Later, Victorio's followers were warned that the troopers were coming and abandoned their camp. Astoundingly, the chief delayed long enough to seek me out and bid me farewell, shaking my hand in white man fashion and expressing gratitude for my assistance."

"That is remarkable indeed. And yet I found him to be an honorable and principled man."

In the murky light, Collins could see the doctor suddenly turn to look at him. "You met Victorio?"

"In the San Mateo Mountains. I was his prisoner."

"He did not kill you?"

"On the contrary, he gave me his protection and sent me on my way."

26

The next morning, having dispatched his son to milk the cow, feed the chickens and attend to numerous other chores, Blazer requested Collins accompany him on his rounds that included overseeing the sawmill operation, inspecting the progress in construction of a grist mill, examining hay fields and checking the pairs of mother cows and calves in a lengthy pasture along the north side of the river. As they walked, Collins recounted his tale of capture by, and subsequent ventures among, the Apache warriors, concluding with his separation from Jackrabbit.

"The boy did, indeed, save your life," the doctor said, whilst they made their way back across the field.

"He did. I am sorely aggrieved by his brutal death."

"I heard Victorio suffered losses at the Palomas."

"As did I." He paused to watch a flock of mallards pass over their heads.

Blazer turned to face him. "And the reason you were directed to the Mescalero Agency by the Indian Bureau?"

"Agent Russell has been corresponding with Commissioner Trowbridge in regard to the cruel and untoward treatment of the Mescalero people during the disarming on the 16th of April. I have been charged with gathering pertinent information and transmitting such back to the Indian Bureau or, more precisely I presume, to the Secretary of the Interior."

"Interesting." The doctor directed his steps toward a

foot bridge back across the Río Tularosa.

As they proceeded, Collins said, "Understandably, given our past association, I was keen to obtain your rendering of events."

"I did not witness what transpired, as I was absent on that particular Friday, but we were aware the soldiers were coming. Later, I spoke with Agent Russell and Chief Nautzilli. George Maxwell, one of the interpreters who had been present, came to see me as well. I visited the Indians who were held prisoner in the stock pens for a week after and attempted to give them food, but the soldiers prevented this." Blazer shook his head in dismay. "They were forced to stand in a thick layer of bovine excrement. Dr. Carter did his best for them, but a child perished and Nautzilli implied some of the women were violated by soldiers assigned to guard them."

"I had heard Chief Nautzilli escaped during the disarming."

"He returned about a week ago."

They paused in the middle of the bridge to gaze down at fingerling trout gathered in a backwater of the swiftly moving stream. "The army seems incapable of dealing fairly with the Indians," C.W. said quietly.

"I only know about my little corner of the world, but I can tell you these Indians want peace. For two years they have rested under the suspicion of being accomplices of Victorio. In truth, I have failed to find one single person in the vicinity of this reservation who now believes it so." Blazer stared at the river's currents reflectively. "I am aware that Colonel Hatch accuses them of not only harboring Victorio's Indians, but of sending them clothing, ammunition and food. Thusly does he excuse himself for his outrageous treatment of these poor people."

On the other side of the river, Collins said, "Will I need your assistance in meeting with Chief Nautzilli? I did not encounter him in '72."

"He was not on the reservation back then. I am willing to assist, but the agent should be able to arrange an introduction. Be warned, however, that the people remain prisoners and are guarded by detachments of cavalry and infantry."

The two men walked toward the house. "I passed a mail carrier on my way up from Tularosa," C.W. said. "Does he come from Fort Stanton?"

"He does. Daniels is my employee, as I have the mail contract, and makes three runs a week between Stanton and Tularosa. It is not particularly lucrative." The doctor ushered Collins into the house. "Demetrio should have the noon meal prepared."

Several men were seated at the expansive table in the dining area. Blazer pulled out a chair for Collins and sat beside him. Almer arrived shortly afterward, his dog Plato on his heels.

"Put the dog out," his father told him.

Demetrio made several forays between the kitchen and table with platters of food. Dishes of meat, potatoes, bread pudding and a stew of green chile and corn made their rounds. Pitchers of water and an enormous granite wear coffee pot were also passed from man to man. There was much talk among the men about Indian raids and the possible location of Victorio. One man spoke of the killing of two Mescaleros down near the village of La Luz.

"Some say the Indians was drunk and some say them Mexicans what shot them was," the fellow said.

To Collins, it seemed to be another poignant tragedy that played out over and over in a land where Indian people were not only disposable but worthy of target practice. The discussion turned to conjecture as to the whereabouts of William Bonney, a subject that was singularly uninteresting to Collins. He was of the opinion that the murderous young man deserved to be beaten and hanged and forgotten.

"Almer, Mr. Collins will be going to the agency this afternoon. Would you please accompany him?"

"Yes sir."

When the meal was concluded, Blazer apportioned assorted tasks to his employees and the men departed.

"I apologize, Charles," he told Collins. "But I must see to some pending duties. Almer knows the lay of the land."

"I am most pleased to have him as guide."

"Is there a horse available, father?"

"They are all in use."

"If he would like, Almer may ride my mule," Collins said.

The boy nodded. "That would be fine."

Blazer stood up from the table. "Very well. Almer, be certain to return as soon as possible so as to attend to your regular chores. Charles, I will see you this evening."

The three of them walked together to the barn, where the doctor left them and headed toward the sawmill.

"Do you have your own saddle?" C.W. asked the young man.

"Yes."

"I have never tried a saddle on Molly, but let us attempt it. She is even tempered."

While Collins caught the horse and mule and tethered them to a rail of the pen, Almer fetched his saddle and a blanket. Molly stood patiently as the boy saddled her and tightened the cinch.

"You should mount up in the corral," Collins told him.

"Okay." Almer placed a foot in the stirrup and gingerly swung aboard. The mule exhibited no objections, so C.W. opened the gate and the boy rode out. Mounting up, Collins followed him and they rode east along the river. Plato appeared and trailed along, keeping his distance from Molly's hind legs. The afternoon was clear and quite oppressive. Soon the dog changed his mind and retreated for home. The valley widened, but was vacant of Indian lodges or other signs of habitation and there was no evidence of horse herds, a customary sight on a reservation.

"There are no camps along the river?" Collins asked.

"The Indians remain under armed guard. They are forced to camp around the agency buildings while soldiers loiter about, at times conducting themselves as tyrants. It does not seem to me the commanding officers favor curbing their behavior."

"The agent is incapable of rectifying the situation?"

"He has been writing letters."

"Yes, I am aware," Collins said, smiling. "It is the reason I have come here."

Almer turned in the saddle to look at him. "You are here because Agent Russell has been writing letters?"

"Indeed. More I cannot say."

"Oh."

The bottoms of the Río Tularosa were home to several varieties of birds. Game animals seemed to be absent and Collins surmised this was due to sustained hunting by both whites and Apache people. The Indians probably hunted out of necessity, resulting from short rations and because it was their reservation. Soldiers, whites from embryonic settlements, and prospectors were scandalously profligate in their harvesting of wildlife for sport or meat.

"There is the south fork of the Tularosa," Almer told him, tipping his head toward a break in the ridgeline to their right. "Sometimes they call this the South Fork agency."

"Are those the agency buildings over there?"

"Yes."

They angled toward the cluster of buildings. Collins could see that the base of the hills and slopes behind the agency were scattered with assemblages of lodges and brush shelters. Tendrils of smoke rose from cooking fires among the dwellings. A regimented line of canvas army shelter tents extended along the perimeter between the agency and the Indian camps. The entire area was denuded of trees and soldiers were evident in detachments around the agency buildings and on horseback nearer to the Indian encampments. All appeared to be heavily armed.

Riding into the agency headquarters, Almer and Collins dismounted, eased cinches and tethered Ulysses and Molly to the rails of a nearby fence. Collins scanned the surroundings, taking note of several wood rail enclosures, one occupied by a team of draft horses, slaughter pens, an alleyway and shed for weighing cattle, a storage barn for supplies and issuing rations and a few other sundry outbuildings. A couple of men were evident, going about their labors. To the north and east lay farm fields of immature cornstalks, alfalfa and oats. A small herd of cattle grazed along the river bottom below.

A tall bearded man emerged from a substantial pine slab building and walked toward them. "Hello Almer," he said as he approached.

It appeared to Collins that the gentleman was in his later years and he momentarily pondered the anxieties of holding a post such as Indian agent. Certainly the position would take a daunting toll.

"Hello Mr. Russell. This is Mr. Collins. He has come to speak with you."

"Very well. Would you care to come into my office, Mr. Collins?"

"I would, thank you."

The boy hesitated. "If you do not mind, I will walk back home. I do not trust that the mule will care to leave the horse."

"Probably not," C.W. agreed. "Thank you for your assistance."

"Certainly. Until this evening." Almer gave a small parting wave and walked briskly away to the west.

Collins followed Agent Russell into the building. The office was sparsely furnished, with a desk, bookshelf, and three spindle back chairs. The walls were undecorated. A cross breeze blew through open windows and the room was pleasantly cool.

"Please be seated," the agent said. He gestured toward one of the chairs and established himself behind the desk.

Removing his hat and taking a seat, Collins ran a hand through his hair, damp with perspiration. "I have come at the bidding of Commissioner Trowbridge," he said.

The man raised his hoary eyebrows. "Truly? Commissioner Trowbridge?"

"Yes and Secretary Schurz, for whom I have performed other circumspect assignments in the past."

The agent stroked his long beard almost peevishly then trained his shrewd grey eyes on Collins. "And about what matter do Trowbridge and Schurz wish to chide me?"

"You mistake me, sir. I am not here to chide you. I am here to discover and report the truth regarding incidents of April 16. I have come to verify your version of those and subsequent proceedings."

AMBUSH

27

"When Colonel Hatch requested all the Indians come into the agency within a four-mile perimeter and bring all their stock, I was concerned," Agent Russell told Collins.

They were comfortably seated in the room that served as a parlor. The agent perched upon a tattered rosewood settee, seemingly out of place in the rustic chamber. Collins sat in a faded Morris chair. A rotund Mexican cook named Nestor had served them coffee and diminutive turnovers filled with raisins, placing the laden tray upon a ponderous and much abused library table.

"I acted in accordance with the request, however," the agent continued. "The Indians cheerfully complied by that Saturday evening, that is April 10th, with very few exceptions. All came in, that had not gone with Victorio or were in other ways improperly off the reservation, and numbered about four hundred."

"And they brought their horses?"

"Yes, I had designated a locality within four miles of the agency where their horses could be gathered."

"And they had no suspicions that the request may have been untoward?"

"It did not seem so." Russell took a sip of coffee and fastidiously ate a pastry. "At least not until Colonel Hatch arrived on the 12th with about one thousand soldiers, including more than one hundred Apache scouts that hailed from San Carlos and were ill-disposed toward their Mescalero cousins. Although the Indians had been told of their coming, meaning the soldiers, they did not expect so many and became very alarmed. Probably no one of them had ever seen as many soldiers at one time. In consequence of this fright, most of them moved their camps farther back in the mountains, more inaccessible but not farther from the agency.”

“ ‘Come not between the dragon and his wrath.’ ”

“You know Shakespeare. As a devout Presbyterian, I prefer the Bible. ‘The wise are cautious and avoid danger.’ Proverbs.”

“I would venture to say that the Indians were wise in that they removed themselves from the vicinity.”

“Alas, it did no good. And I admit to being astonished when the colonel expressed an intention to disarm them and take their stock. I told him that if the Indians had known this, they would not have come in. That they had relied upon me as their friend and had willingly and promptly come in and I did not like to betray them. I told him I would not be party to any deception of that kind.”

“I can see that you were placed in a problematic disposition. You are enjoined with retaining the trust and cooperation of the Apaches in your charge and could easily be perceived as having deceived them.”

“Yes... yes indeed,” Russell said ardently. “You can see the dilemma with which I was contending.”

“It is manifest. How did Colonel Hatch respond?”

“In a most reprehensible manner.” The man was becoming more animated in his recounting of the events. “He said, ‘I will turn my Indians loose on them.’ He said this jubilantly.”

“I am aware he was under orders from General Pope,” Collins said judiciously. “I do not doubt he was adamant about carrying them out.”

Stroking his beard again, Russell said, “Perhaps. Ensuing actions certainly proved the colonel to be determined and it resulted in the total and complete violation of each and every pledge given by him." He paused, then added, "We spoke further and I proposed that the Indians would be more willing to surrender their arms to me with the promise of being returned to them after the present troubles were over. To this, the colonel unequivocally assented in regard to both arms and horses." The agent picked nervously at a patch of worn upholstery on the sofa.

"Pardon my interposing, but may I smoke?" C.W. asked, taking out his briar.

"Please no. The construction of this building is such that fire could quickly and easily envelop it," Russell said, waving a hand distractedly at the ceiling. "I have requested the funds to erect new structures, but have been overwhelmingly disregarded."

Collins placed his pipe back in a pocket. "Then, of course, I will not indulge. Pray, continue. Did Colonel Hatch then acquiesce fully to your better judgement?"

"He did not. I have written several letters to Commissioner Trowbridge in this regard. I wonder that he requested you investigate." The man searched Collins' face as if seeking answers there.

"Perhaps he requires substantiation from an impartial emissary."

Russell considered this a moment, appearing to study a knee of his somber black trousers. "Certainly that must be the explanation," he finally said, seemingly reassured. He looked up and continued, "Let us see... oh yes, I directed the Indians to move nearer the agency. Over the 13th and 14th they located themselves within one fourth of a mile, where they were in full view. They abided by my demands in spite of dreadful tempests. This, however, was not satisfactory to the colonel and he had them remove to another location and bring in all their horses, being assured that they would be given into my charge. With a great display of forbearance, they obeyed."

"It undoubtedly seems they were in earnest."

"They were. All remained tranquil until, in the darkness of Friday morning, Colonel Hatch let loose the Apache scouts. They were under the command of Lieutenant Gatewood and a fellow named Maney. They killed two Indians who were merely bringing in more horses in compliance with my request. One of those killed was Chief Nautzilli's father. Later they killed several more of the Mescaleros. By this time, some of the Indians were scattering, especially the young men. I attempted to reassure them and Nautzilli endeavored to get all back, but then Captain Steelhammer opened fire on them. The Indians did not return fire, but kept going. Nautzilli went with them. It was not until a few days ago that he returned with some other Indians and a child."

"How did Colonel Hatch react to these exigencies?"

"He commanded the soldiers to escort the remaining Indians here to the agency. Their horses were instantly herded into a corral. The colonel informed me they were to be sent to Fort Stanton and I protested against such a course, reminding him of our agreement that the stock was to be turned over to me and restored to the Mescaleros after the conflicts were over."

"How did he respond?"

"With disdain. He then ordered a search of their belongings for contraband articles. The soldiers found a few pistols. I have reason to believe they plundered the Indians of much that was valuable to them."

"Is it true the women were violated?"

Russell fidgeted in dismay. "I am unaware of such incidents. I am unaware." He again plucked at the fraying fabric of the settee. "The soldiers surrounded the Indians that night. The next morning, after all the horses had been driven out and sent to Fort Stanton, they were placed under guard in the same corral, no more than a fourth of an acre in size. There were over two hundred and forty men, women and children huddled together in the hot sun. They were forced to remain there in a foul depth of excrement, supplemented by their own effluvium. Occasionally, one of the women would be allowed to remove herself for necessities, but only if escorted by a soldier. After five days and the death of a child, my friend Dr. Carter, the agency physician, demanded the Indians be removed from the corral and Captain Steelhammer finally acquiesced with the understanding that the Indians remain as you see now."

"How many horses were commandeered?"

"Almost two hundred."

"And all of them had been stolen from white settlers?"

"That was Colonel Hatch's contention. But he took some of the Indian horses for pack animals and Dr. Blazer reported having one of his horses taken by the San Carlos scouts as well as three belonging to his mail carrier. I am credibly informed that while the horses were en route to Fort Stanton, from ten to twenty of them were shot down because they were too poor to travel as rapidly as desired. I was also told that about one hundred and twenty-five Indian horses and mules were taken in a different direction by the army in leaving here."

"You do not maintain that most of the horses were stolen?"

"The Mescaleros engage in some horse stealing, but so do the Anglos and Mexicans. In truth, nearly everything of the kind that occurs in all this country is charged upon these Indians."

"That, I assure you, is not uncommon within my experience. I see that troops remain here."

"Around seventy of the 15th Infantry and two companies of the 9th Cavalry. The soldiers do as they please and I am unable to intercede. What is worse, the Indians no longer trust me, believing that I either did not do enough to thwart the actions and deaths or that I colluded."

"That is truly unfortunate."

"Colonel Hatch claimed that the Indians broke faith with him by leaving their camp, and thus justified his course afterwards. It is true that a part of them did leave through fear. Did that justify the harsh treatment given those who remained faithful, relying upon the pledges that had been given them? A few of the Indians that left at the time voluntarily returned, including Chief Nautzilli. Regardless, all of the Indians are still held as prisoners. Almost two months have passed since they were placed under guard. They often ask why they are held as prisoners. How long are they to be confined because others did wrong. They want to know if they will be paid for their horses."

Nestor came into the room to inquire whether they desired more coffee.

"I must return to the mill," Collins said, coming to his feet. "I am Dr. Blazer's guest. If I return on the morrow, will I be able to speak with Chief Nautzilli?"

"Yes, of course." The agent stood up and accompanied Collins to the door. "I will expect you."

28

Blazer and Collins walked down to the river where Almer was fishing with a bamboo bait rod. The water was swift with snow melt.

"I take it you were not as affected by drought as other portions of the territory," C.W. said.

"No. In fact, we had a significant storm in early April."

"Agent Russell mentioned severe rains just previous to the 16th."

"Yes, so I heard. As I said, I was absent during that week."

They watched as Almer reeled in a sizable trout, gutted it and placed the fish in a wicker creel. His dog sat and watched with interest.

"That makes four," he hollered over the sound of the rushing water.

"See if you can catch a few more. Demetrio will thank you," his father shouted back.

The young man nodded and studiously impaled another worm on his hook. He slung the creel on his shoulder and wandered out of sight along the riverbank, with Plato following after. The doctor and Collins ambled leisurely toward a downed cottonwood tree and sat together. The sun was descending and Collins found the shadows of early evening to be a refreshing reprieve from the heat of the day.

"Is it true that residents of surrounding communities have been known to come to the reservation to fallaciously claim horses?" Collins asked.

"Who told you this?"

"Victorio said something. And Agent Russell implied this to be so."

Blazer sighed. "Yes, it is true. I have known men to come from Lincoln, Tularosa, Mesilla, and even as far as the Pecos and Las Vegas, to prowl the reservation and look for distinctive brands. The next day, they either confront the agent or find a law man or army officer to enforce their claim that the animal belongs to them and was stolen by the Indians."

"Is proof required?"

"Not usually. Not when the word of a white man rivals that of an Indian. I have attempted to intervene in a few instances, but as a respected businessman, and one that wishes to remain solvent, I cannot afford to weigh in too heavily. Most of the time, the horses are taken and the injustice of it is maddening. And it is well known that Chisum occasionally hires men to raid Indian camps for horses."

"Of course he does," Collins said dryly, shaking his head. " 'Hell is empty and all the devils are here.' "

"Oh yes, you are fond of Shakespeare. I had forgotten." The doctor became pensive a moment then said, "I will tell you a thing, but you must never repeat it."

"Agreed."

"Three months ago or so, an Anglo by the name of William Smith took a horse from a Mescalero warrior, called Cata, who was camped not far from here. Smith was brazen in his manner and threatened the Indian's family, consisting of two wives and several young children. I happened to be passing the camp on my way back from Stanton. I knew the fellow to be a ruffian and occasional employee of Pat Coghlan, so I paused to witness what transpired. The man simply mounted his horse and ponied the Indian's animal behind, heading downstream, no doubt aiming for town. Cata sprinted after him, staying close to the brush along the river. I rode behind, keeping them both within sight. When Smith was almost to my boundary, the warrior knelt, raised a Spencer repeating rifle and dropped the man from his horse. It was a stupendous shot."

"What did you do then?"

"I rode by, nodded to the Indian and never spoke a word about it until now. An agency employee found him the next day and raised the alarm, but there was no way to discover who the culprit may have been." Blazer looked at Collins. "Do you find my actions scandalous?"

"On the contrary."

"Excellent," the doctor said, standing. "I remembered you as a judicious individual. Come, let us discover the extent of Almer's success."

As they walked, they discussed the dismissal of Indian Commissioner Hayt the previous year, President Hayes' refusal to run for another term, the recent purchase of Collins' ranch in Montana and Blazer's lumber business. Back at the house, a balconied affair constructed of adobe bricks, they found Almer with the cook, Demetrio. The boy proudly waved a hand, in the manner of a circus ringmaster, at eight enormous trout filling a large tin basin upon a dry sink.

"*Los cocinaré afuera, porque hace calor,*" Demetrio said, clearly unimpressed. "I will cook *allá,*" he added, nodding toward the back of the building and taking the basin of fish outside.

"He is going to cook in the outside kitchen," Almer told Collins. "He says it is too hot."

They sat at the table and the doctor poured glasses of water from a pitcher.

"You speak Spanish then?" Collins asked.

"Almer has learned the language very quickly and is becoming proficient in Apache as well," the doctor said. "I do not have his aptitude for languages."

"*'Aithiu cech delg is ou,*" Collins said. "The youngest thorn is the sharpest."

"That is not a language I have heard," Almer said.

"It is the Irish."

"Charles also knows Shakespeare," Blazer said.

"I had a wonderful volume," the boy said, "but I lost it when I attended school in Santa Fe."

"I always carry a volume of his complete works. You may borrow it."

"Perhaps you will read from it after supper?"

"With delight."

Plato came bounding into the room and threw himself upon Almer.

"That canine is a menace," Blazer said patiently and without a hint of annoyance.

The boy forced the dog to the floor and told the animal to stay. Plato crawled under the table and lay panting.

"Are you very hungry?" the doctor asked. "I prefer to eat in relative solitude in the evenings and I usually have Demetrio feed the men in their quarters before we dine."

"No. I am contented to wait."

"How was your visit with Agent Russell?"

"Informative. I will return in the morrow to converse with him further and meet with Chief Nautzilli, if he is agreeable."

"What is your opinion of the man himself?"

Collins smiled. "He seems an ounce too excitable, but he also seems considerate of the Indians under his guardianship."

"Too excitable by far. As to caring for them, I am a tad dubious. He once told me he thought these Indians are very low down in the scale of humanity and that they are a troublesome people to deal with."

"Such statements imply the theories of Sir Galton."

"Who is he?" Almer asked with interest.

"A cousin of Charles Darwin," C.W. told him. "He is developing speculations regarding the innate superiority of certain races. I find his notions distasteful."

"As you may recall, I am a Quaker," the doctor said. "We espouse the equality of all persons."

"I am in agreement. My experience has shown me that western European societies and philosophies can be distinctly inferior to others I have encountered. I recently befriended a Chinese man of exceptional character and principles."

"My connections with the Apache people here have taught me of their superior perception and pragmatism."

Demetrio entered the room carrying a serving platter laden with two trout and said, "*Los hombres estan comiendo...* the men eat." He set the dish in the center of the table. "*Uno momento,*" he said and went out again, quickly returning with a bowl of greens and a dish of pinto beans.

"Demetrio has been learning about native foods from the Indians," Almer told Collins. "He has gathered some and I think you will find them acceptable."

They served themselves and began to eat. Collins found the meal to be splendid. The trout had been coated in corn meal and red chile powder and the greens were savory with wild onion.

"The food is excellent," he said.

"Yes," said Blazer. "Demetrio's cooking is the reason our hired men tend to stay on."

"And your generous wages," his son added.

"I am obliged to pay well, considering this remote location."

"*Muy bien,*" Collins told the cook when he came to pour coffee for them.

Laughing, Almer said, "If you are attempting to compliment the food, you should say, *la comida es muy buena.*"

"We do not mock our guests," the doctor told him placidly.

"I am not offended," C.W. said and repeated the phrase to the best of his ability.

Demetrio smiled and gave a slight bow. "I am happy."

The cook departed and they ate in silence for the rest of the meal. The doctor finished a last bite of food and scooted his chair away from the table in order to stretch his long legs.

"I have to deliver a load of lumber to Mesilla and purchase supplies," he said. "I will be leaving tomorrow and Almer will accompany me so that he may assist. Then we will remain in the village to visit his sisters and Mr. Fountain's family. You are welcome to stay on here."

"That will not be requisite, but thank you. I will meet with the agent again and then take the road for Fort Stanton. I have vital telegrams to dispatch and a few more inquiries to make."

"If you are in need of provisions, my store has quite a few items."

"I believe I am amply stocked for the present."

"By what route will you return to Montana?"

"I plan to follow the Río Hondo to the old Goodnight Loving Trail along the Pecos and thence north to the railhead in Las Vegas."

"I am certain you are aware of the recent violence in Lincoln County. Chisum's iron grip on the Pecos country even now promotes enduring hostility among numerous factions."

"I do not plan to seek conflict."

Blazer smiled tolerantly. "You did not seek a confrontation with Coghlan's men."

"True enough."

━━━❧✦❦━━━

29

"I hear that Murphy is dead," Collins said.

After an extended and spirited reading from Act II of *The Tempest*, Almer had gone to bed and the two men sat on an old wagon bed outside the house. A soft radiance of lamplight shone from the windows, illuminating their immediate surroundings. Blazer smoked a cigar.

"Stomach cancer. I hope it was excruciating."

Collins laughed. "Ah yes, as I recall you were none too fond."

"The man was a scoundrel."

"I have always suspected him of being involved with Cadete's murder."

"It is probable. The chief was in complete opposition to whisky and, god only knows, Murphy supplied potent spirits to the Indians by the gallon."

"How long did he maintain his despotism as post trader?"

The doctor drew on his cigar. The end glowed in the dark and cast a ruddy tinge over the man's face.

"He was finally dislodged in '73. The military and Indian Bureau finally realized that Murphy was corrupt and had been taking advantage for years. The building then served as agency headquarters at the fort. Emil Fritz, Murphy's associate, had become ill and departed for Germany, where he died. Murphy had hired a young clerk named Dolan, who served with the army and had been discharged at Stanton. After Fritz was gone, he took

Dolan as a partner. Following the eviction from Stanton, they established a variety of enterprises in Lincoln, monopolized the local trade and continued to maintain underhanded dealings in supplying rations to the fort and the Mescalero Agency. By spring of '77, Murphy was already succumbing to alcohol and abdominal pains. He later went to Santa Fe and died there. Dolan then ran the Murphy-Dolan concerns that included a saloon, hotel, billiard room, bank and dry goods store, acquiring a new partner by the name of Riley. Dolan remains in Lincoln, despite all the recent disturbance. I have heard, however, that his business ventures are in difficulties."

After preparing his pipe and lighting it, Collins and the doctor smoked for a while without speaking. Coyotes yipped in the distant hills.

"There was much talk about closing Stanton in '74," Blazer finally said, snubbing out his cigar on the wagon bed. "General Sheridan wanted to move all the Apaches to a forsaken spot in the Tularosa Mountains, about two hundred miles west of the fort. The plan failed due to untenable conditions at the site and so Stanton remains worthwhile."

"I recall that the fort was sparingly manned in '72."

"Truly. Some of the time there was only one commissioned officer at the post, and he the post-surgeon with only a corporal's guard at his command."

"And the agency was relocated here a few years ago?"

"Yes. At first, I was not overjoyed to have the agency in such close proximity. I attempted to convince the Indian Bureau to purchase my property, to no avail. Instead, I rented rooms to several agents and some of my neighbors sold a few derelict cabins for use as storerooms. In '78, the agency moved to its present location, after leasing buildings from John Ryan, a trader who operated a store near there until recently and was an associate of Dolan. He died last February and, to my astonishment, bequeathed the buildings to the current agent and Dr. Carter, the agency physician."

"When was the reservation definitively established?

"In '73, according to an executive order by President Grant."

"Has the reservation afforded more security for the Mescalero people?"

"There have been conflicts. The boundaries were not entirely demarcated until '76, when a Lieutenant Walker of the 15th Infantry completed a survey and submitted field notes, a report and a map to the Indian Bureau. With the formation of the reservation, however, there has been no cessation of harassment. Not long after the reservation was sanctioned, a group of white marauders surrounded a Mescalero camp and opened fire upon it."

"For what reason?"

"Mostly to steal their horses. But they killed women and children in the raid and three Indians were scalped. The Mescaleros were never able to recover their animals. Then, a few months later, another Anglo crew attacked, plundering almost all of the Indians' belongings and all of their horses and mules. When rumors circulated that white raiders were about to strike once more, the Mescaleros panicked and disappeared into the mountains. The agent sent out two elderly Mescalero women to try to entice the Indians back. Their bodies were found near the fort, shot more than once and scalped. The scalps were later reported as being on display in Murphy and Dolan's saloon.

"Publilius Syrus wrote, 'The wickedness of a few is the calamity of all.' "

"I applaud the sentiment," the doctor said. "The people of this territory are all tarred by the same brush. I wonder how history will remember us."

"Did the military seek the perpetrators?"

"Yes, but they were unsuccessful. Ironically, a detachment of soldiers was subsequently dispatched to bring the Indians in and when the soldiers came upon Chief Roman's encampment, they opened fire. The Indians ran for their lives and left all their possessions behind. The army had not been able to assist the Indians when they were assaulted and robbed by white men, but the troopers felt justified in shooting at them where they had sought refuge for their own safety. It seems a few of the local citizens had expressed fear that the Indians were about to go on the warpath.'"

"Did the soldiers finally bring the Indians back in?"

Blazer laughed sardonically. "No. Instead, the captain in command, and the very same officer who had been unable to locate any of the white assailants or the stolen horses, burned the entire Mescalero camp, then took their few remaining horses and sold them. The agent at the time, a man named Crothers, sent out some agency employees to find the survivors. When they finally brought Roman's band into the agency, many of them were naked. All of them were malnourished and completely destitute. The other missing bands escaped into Mexico or the Staked Plains. They did not return for another year. But, nevertheless, the raiding continued. So, as you can see, when the agency was finally relocated down here, the situation improved some, but not entirely."

"I should venture to say not."

"And there are the miners, of course."

"Miners?"

"For several years, prospectors have been skulking around the Sierra Blanca and Capitan Mountains. The Indians killed a few, but this has not deterred the persistent search for mineral wealth on the reservation.

Early this year, there was a significant discovery. In consequence, miners are currently and adamantly contesting the reservation boundaries. Now that gold has been found, the Mescaleros will again be the losers."

" 'How quickly nature falls into revolt, when gold becomes her object.' I only recently have witnessed profound injustice in the shadows of avarice."

The waning moon presented itself above the mountains to the east and the evening star shone brightly in the west. The scent of fruit tree blossoms was carried in on a gentle breeze, mingling with the fragrance of conifers above them and freshly cut lumber from the sawmill. A calf bawled for its mother in the pasture beyond. It occurred to Collins that a tableau such as this belonged to all creatures without exclusion. Not a one should be set apart.

"Did not Dickens write that injustice breeds injustice?" Blazer asked.

"Yes. In *Bleak House* perhaps... I do not recall." Collins' pipe was out and he tucked it away. "And what of the whisky peddling? Does it endure?"

"Indeed. Especially since the new road was established over the divide between here and Dowlin's Mill in '74. The army found it to be advantageous, but civilian wagons from Mesilla and El Paso that are bound for Fort Sumner or the rail terminus in Las Vegas are passing through the reservation at an alarming rate. The teamsters sell whisky on the side to the Indians and when this is reported by them or the agent, no one takes them at their word. As I said before, the Indian's word means nothing when contesting that of an Anglo."

"Yes, it is regrettable."

"Regrettable and criminal. In addition, there are other legitimate settlers, like myself, on the reservation. Some of these ranchers also distribute liquor to the Mescaleros or allow others to do so. The Indian agents have no authority to address these matters on private land. One of the earlier agents, Frederick Godfroy, made recommendations to the Indian Bureau that agency goods be distinctively marked and if found in the possession of whites, they be charged with illegally trading with the Indians. It seemed an effective deterrent, but the bureau did not respond."

"It was no different in '72, when I reported my findings," Collins said. "I had discovered that Murphy was selling whisky to the Indians from his own distillery, but they were likewise acquiring it from neighboring villages, some of the soldiers at Stanton and even Comancheros. I had been hired to investigate, but my reports were buried in bureaucratic mire and, even though Commissioner Walker was sympathetic to the Indian cause and recognized that unlawful intrusion on reservation lands was profoundly detrimental to Indian welfare, he resigned at the end of the year. He was succeeded by Edward Smith, a sanctimonious gentleman who was intensely interested in the plight of black men. While undeniably laudable, this did little to amend the predicament of the Indian."

"If the Mescaleros could police themselves in regard to whisky, the problem would be alleviated. But, as you know, there are conflicting loyalties among the bands as well as limited cohesion. Your friend, Chief Cadete, was a strong influence, but his light was snuffed out too soon."

"*Armad ard in crand is móide co mór benaid na gaetha fris.*"

"And what would that mean, pray tell?"

"The higher the tree is, the greater the winds beat upon it."

30

They parted in the early morning. Joseph Blazer and son waved farewell from a heavily loaded freight wagon, piled high with freshly cut lumber. Collins made his way east along the Río Tularosa. The dawn was clear and calm and filled with bird song. Ulysses was sprightly in the chilly air, his neck arched, periodically blowing explosively through his lips. Even Molly seemed effervescent. Certainly C.W.'s mood was buoyant, given the untrammeled loveliness of the morning.

A short way down the trail, he espied a great flock of sheep spread out along the slopes across the river. Not having been aware that the Apache people possessed any affinity for the raising of livestock, Collins was mystified by their presence. The mile between Blazer's property and the agency headquarters passed quickly and he rode up to the main building, securing his animals to the same fence as the day before. He saw Agent Russell on his knees inside a small enclosure to the east of the structure and walked over. The man was delicately plucking weeds from among a miscellany of herbs, beans, spinach and carrots.

"Good morning," Collins said.

Russell leapt to his feet, patently disconcerted. "My goodness!"

"My heartfelt apology for startling you."

"Quite all right, quite all right," the man said, brushing soil from his knees. He came through a gate and put out a hand in greeting. "Mr. Collins."

They shook hands and C.W. said, "You have a fine plot of greenery there."

"Oh yes. Thank you. I always attempt to maintain a modest kitchen garden for my own use. Very healthful."

"Indeed."

"Well then," Russell said, brushing at his knees again. "Let us have some coffee and see if Nestor has baked."

They entered the building and once again ensconced themselves in the parlor. Collins removed his Stetson and placed it on a wooden chair beside him. The cook appeared almost instantaneously with a coffeepot and cups.

"*Tenemos conchas*," he said. Nestor poured the coffee and departed.

"Excellent. Most excellent," Russell said, rubbing his hands together gleefully. "Have you tasted *conchas*, Mr. Collins?"

"No, I have not."

"They are sweet buns traditional in Mexico."

Nestor returned carrying a plate stacked with rounded pastries. He was accompanied by a middle-aged man wearing a crisp shirt with a high collar and morning coat. The cook placed the dish on the library table alongside the coffeepot and the other fellow sat beside Russell on the sofa, crossing his legs in an easy and confident manner.

"Ah good morning Nathan," Russell said, filling an extra cup with coffee.

"Good morning." He accepted the cup that Russell handed to him and studied Collins a moment.

"This is Mr. Collins, dispatched by Commissioner Trowbridge to verify certain events of last April," the agent told him.

"Of course, Samuel. You mentioned him at supper."

"Mr. Collins, this is my friend, Dr. Nathan Carter. He is able to enlighten you on supplementary details regarding the occurrences about which you are inquiring."

Collins nodded at Carter, who did not offer his hand or noticeably respond. Here, thought C.W., was an overweening gentleman quite taken with himself.

The doctor and Russell each took a bun. Collins, none too fond of sweets, did not.

"Will you not try one of these?" the agent inquired, after he had consumed one of the pastries expeditiously.

"I have already breakfasted, but thank you. I will, however, have more coffee." He replenished his cup.

"Are you a government operative, then, Mr. Collins?" Carter asked, scrutinizing him as before.

"I am an independent operative."

"I see. Hired by Trowbridge?"

Collins returned the man's gaze for a protracted moment, his patience wearing with the doctor's patronizing deportment. "I am here at the behest of Commissioner Trowbridge and Secretary Schurz. The terms of the association are my own." He turned to address Agent Russell. "As I stated yesterday, I would much appreciate an interview with Chief Nautzilli. I would also value further information from you about the aforementioned incidents and ensuing consequences."

Visibly flustered by the predominantly wordless contretemps that had just occurred between Collins and his friend, Russell consumed another bun with startling haste. "Of course, Mr. Collins," he said, after taking a gulp of coffee to wash down the pastry. "I am at your service."

"Please pardon a slight digression, but I could not help but descry a considerable flock of sheep on my way here this morning. Are the Mescaleros engaging in wool production?"

Dr. Carter laughed derisively. "Good god, man, do you actually believe these Indians would abide raising sheep?"

"I did not suppose so, but there are sheep grazing on reservation lands."

Agent Russell stroked his beard in dismay. "It is that fellow Will Dowlin. He drove over four thousand sheep here to graze in early spring, offering the excuse that he could not hire men as herders over on his ranch for fear of Victorio. He refuses to leave."

"You have no recourse?"

"When Colonel Hatch originally acquiesced to my proposal that the Indians relinquish their weapons to me instead of the soldiers, we also agreed upon a scheme that provided for a selected number of Mescaleros who would retain their arms as a sort of Indian police detail. After the entire affair disintegrated into pandemonium, the remainder of warriors were forcibly disarmed and Hatch turned a deaf ear to my entreaties. The Indians are, even now, under military arrest, as it were. Therefore, I have neither constabulary nor recourse."

"Samuel and I differ. I, personally, would run the sheep off the reservation by force," Dr. Carter said.

"I do not desire enemies, Nathan. All my predecessors endured calumny from neighboring citizens." Russell turned to address Collins. "It has also been necessary to hire local men for farming. The Mescaleros promised to plant a number of fields this spring, but have been unable to do so because of their confinement. Anticipating that they may be released soon, I have taken on more employees to plant all the tillable land near the agency. I intend to turn the tracts over to the Indians when they are liberated."

"Your employees accomplished most of the farming last year as well," Carter said.

"Perhaps, but one must be patient. These Indians are childlike and primitive. Time and persevering effort may overcome this."

"I was in the vicinity of Fort Stanton when Andrew Curtis was the agent," C.W. interjected, made ill at ease by Russell's appraisal of the Mescalero people. "I found him to be earnest and industrious, but he was accused of fraud and of being a tool of the L.G. Murphy concerns. He was forced to contend with the absence of a circumscribed reservation and a much-reduced military presence at Stanton that coincided with the constriction of the military reserve by over a hundred square miles, opening the land up for settlement. And the whisky trade with the Indians, at the time, knew no bounds. The man was undone."

"Most unfortunate," Russell said, shaking his head. "Most unfortunate."

There was a pause in the conversation. Agent Russell consumed the last bun and Dr. Carter appeared to be deep in thought. Collins took out his pipe, remembered the agent's prohibition on smoking in the building, and put it away.

"I must report a deplorable occurrence," he said, breaking the stillness.

"Oh yes?" Carter asked. "They seem to be extraordinarily common in these parts."

Whether intended or not, C.W. found the doctor's comportment to be persistently acerbic, while Russell was mild and somewhat abstracted. The two friends were so at odds in mannerisms and demeanor, he was perplexed by their apparent ease in each other's company.

"Please say what you must, Mr. Collins. We are, indeed, accustomed to unhappy incidents of late."

"In '72, I met a young Apache boy. He was exceedingly bright and personable and he followed me about quite like a puppy and I became very fond of him. His name was Jackrabbit... *Gah'tsu* in his own language."

"I do not recall a young man of that name," Russell said.

"That was his earliest name. I believe they called him *Guzéé' gútsa'* later on, according to Dr. Blazer. I was told that it means someone who talks too much."

"Oh of course," the agent said. "The story teller. I called him Bernard. He spoke very good English, but had learned some ruinous terminology from the soldiers at the fort." He smiled fleetingly. "The boy was rather friendly to me when I first arrived, but later was undesirably influenced by Victorio's band while they were here on the reservation." Russell gazed out a window over Collins' shoulder. "Come to think of it, I have not seen him since the debacle of April 16."

"Just so," Collins said. "I met the boy again a few days ago near the post at Ojo Caliente. He was on his way back to the reservation and we traveled together through the *Jornada del Muerto.* We parted near old Fort Selden."

"Had he been fighting alongside Victorio?" Carter asked.

"I do not know," Collins said, unwilling to advance upon any part of the truth. "I did not inquire."

"If he has returned to the agency, I have not encountered him," Russell said.

"No. That is the point at issue. I found the boy on the desert near the road over San Augustín Pass. He had been cruelly executed and his horse stolen."

Russell frowned and gnawed upon a thumb, appearing genuinely distressed. "Poor boy. I must inform his family."

"Dr. Blazer thought his mother may be known by the name of Otottie."

"That may be. The woman is a widow. She had a son, a niece and a daughter, the last I was cognizant. There is also a brother, but I do not recall his name."

"She is without very many relatives and keeps herself apart," Carter said. "When smallpox came through in '75, Otottie's family suffered terrible losses."

"But you will tell her?" Collins asked. "You will tell her about Jackrabbit? About Bernard?"

"Nathan is skilled at consoling families. He will take our interpreter José and tell her of the loss."

"I will speak to her and learn whether he was her son," Carter said. "It seems you are in grief over his death, Mr. Collins."

"He was a fine young man. He did not deserve to be brutishly murdered for a horse."

"There was no skirmish? No signs of a pitched battle?" Russell asked.

"Come now, Samuel, you know very well that many of the local citizens require no reason to shoot an Apache," Carter said. "You surely recall the incident in late March near Tularosa? Perhaps a certain amount of whisky was involved, but those Mexicans had no call to kill three Indians just for the devil of it."

Russell nodded. "Of course you are accurate in this." He turned to look at Collins. "I apologize. I am confident your friend did not deserve to be killed." He refilled all their empty cups and toyed with a spoon.

"Thank you." Perhaps, C.W. thought, Carter possessed other qualities beyond conceit and vainglorious temerity. It seemed he was the dominant personality of the two, but conceivably Agent Russell was in need of robust shepherding. Thinking he ought direct the discussion elsewhere, he asked, "What is your view of Victorio? I presume you had much interaction with him while he was on the reservation. Is he the ruthless savage the newspapers proclaim him to be?"

"That is a vexed question," the doctor said. "I had almost no dealings with the old reprobate, but Samuel here had considerable interaction."

"Victorio may have been a disruptive influence and

enticed many of these Mescaleros away to their deaths, but I remain convinced of his sincerity regarding the desire for peace. He told me he wanted an end to conflict and pledged to obey my wishes in everything and only asked they not be sent back to San Carlos." Russell took a sip of coffee. "In truth, only last March two of Victorio's men, Thomas and Sabanon, came to Chief San Juan's camp. They had been instructed to inform me that Victorio was willing to talk peace and desired to speak with the commanding officer at Stanton." He paused and played with the spoon again. "It came to naught. All the army seeks is his absolute annihilation."

31

Agent Russell, Dr. Carter and Collins stepped from the building into bright sunlight. The day was already stifling.

"Those are my animals," he told Russell, indicating his horse and mule tied to the fence. "They require shade and water."

"If they are not obstreperous, you may put them in with my team."

The three of them settled C.W.'s stock in with a pair of Percheron draft horses. He left the saddles on for expediency, but removed the gelding's bridle and Molly's halter and some of the packs. The men stood in the shadow of a small tack shed and perused the scene a while, so as to hinder any likely equine disputes.

"You mentioned a smallpox epidemic," Collins said to the doctor. "I was curious about the types of diseases to which the Mescalero people are susceptible."

Carter was leaning against a rough lumber wall, smiling at the antics of Ulysses and one of the Percherons. His show of good humor evaporated. "Since the calamity of last April, I have seen several cases of syphilis in some of the older girls," he said angrily. "Samuel does not countenance the notion that several of the soldiers outraged these young women while they were incarcerated in the cow pen, but it is the only explanation."

The agent peered at the ground in silence.

" 'Blunt not the heart, enrage it,' " C.W. said, quoting

a line from *Macbeth.*

The doctor looked at him. "Apt," was all he said.

The animals appeared to be in accord, so they left the corral and walked toward the line of army tents that served as a periphery to the Indian camps nestled against and among the hills beyond.

"I am also detecting neuralgia, dysentery, a few tubercular cases, measles and rheumatism," Carter continued. "It is decidedly interesting, as all my predecessors reported general good health among the Indians here." He removed his straw hat to wave away a bee. "I, of course, must contend with medicine men. The Indians prefer a little white and red treatment mixed."

An unkempt, brawny man, wearing blue jean trousers and soiled cotton flannel shirt, overtook them. "Newman is here with the cows," he said loudly, then turned to walk away.

"Oh, I must attend to this, Mr. Collins," Agent Russell said breathlessly. "Nathan will serve as an ideal guide." He trotted back toward the agency headquarters in the wake of the other man.

"Maxwell is the agency farmer," Carter told Collins. "A bit of a brute, but worthy I suppose. He is not shy of hard labor."

A colored soldier, mounted on a handsome chestnut gelding, rode toward them. "Good morning, Dr. Carter," the private said, reining in the horse just ahead.

"Good morning, Private Hopkins."

"You are going to the camps?"

Carter adopted a defiant stance. "You know very well, private, that I have ready access to the Indian encampment and do not require the army's approval."

"Who is this gentleman here?" The trooper asked impertinently.

"My identity can be of no significance to you," Collins

told him. "My understanding is that your purpose is to stand sentry to the Indians and no more."

The soldier glared at them both in impotent antagonism, then wheeled his horse and cantered away.

"I despise the soldiers' presence here. The Mescaleros are in a constant state of uneasiness and apprehension," the doctor said.

The man was swiftly becoming less objectionable, thought Collins. "If you are amenable, please tell me of your experience in regard to their incarceration."

They angled to the east in order to circumnavigate the row of military tents and groups of soldiers scattered among them. The ground grew steeper and the trenchant sun bore down upon them. Collins felt his back prickle.

"After the disarming of the warriors and the entire disgraceful affair, captives numbering over two hundred and forty men, women and children were herded together into a cow pen covered to a depth of from two to five inches of half rotted manure and other debris, the decomposition of which, following rainstorms and subsequent blistering heat of the previous days, was producing an atmosphere. After a day, in connection with the body excrements related to the crowding together of so many little children, the circumstances became very injurious to health. In five days, the conditions were beyond description. I approached Captain Steelhammer, the officer in command at the time, and prevailed upon him to remove the captives to a more healthful location. He reluctantly conformed to my entreaties." Carter gave a back handed wave at the Indian camps ahead. "They remain as you see now and the confinement is a punishment in itself."

Removing his hat and mopping his forehead with a sleeve, Collins asked, "What is your general opinion of the Mescalero people?"

Carter ceased walking and stood gazing out over the valley. "A more quiet, peaceably inclined people I have never seen. If they had fire and spirit in their natures, the confinement has taken it all out of them. They beg and petition to be let alone. They do not want to be removed. They want liberty... that is to be permitted to hunt and trade and they want their arms and horses back, and ought to have them. The Indians have endured wrongs that would make white men grit their teeth and tear their hair, and yet if they show any of the fire in their savage natures, they must be disarmed and their property appropriated and, together with their women and children, thrown into prison. Will we never get ready to deal honestly and justly with the Indians and see that their wrongs are properly righted?"

Collins now completely recanted his prior estimation of Dr. Carter, seeing he had misjudged the man. As they approached the first collection of lodges and brush shelters, a tiny girl approached the doctor and stood shyly before him. She was clothed in a scrap of blanket. He knelt and stroked her hair, speaking nonsense to her in a low voice. Reaching inside his jacket, he drew forth a packet of Gibralters. The little girl accepted it gravely and retreated to a snug dwelling, constructed of bundles of willow shoots and covered with a piece of white canvas.

"You have a friend," Collins observed.

"I am unable to pronounce her name in the Apache language," Carter said. "I call her Daisy."

A fetchingly graceful woman sat upon the ground beside a proximate lodge. She held a cradleboard across her lap and this was the hub of her attention, behaving as if two white men were not passing through the camp.

"As you know, I planned to meet with Chief Nautzilli. Does he speak English?"

"Well enough. Samuel told me José, the interpreter,

would be joining us, but I am certain he has forgotten. We will make do."

Climbing higher up the slopes of ridges that girded the northern side of the valley, they came to another encampment. Two imposing lodges dominated the site and smoke from several fires eddied in the breeze and sent forth the pleasing fragrance of smoldering pine boughs.

"This is Nautzilli's camp. Caballo absconded to fight with Victorio and this chief is now considered the head man."

"What of Chief San Juan?"

"He was given permission in March to search for Caballo and persuade him to return. We have not seen him since."

A tall and robust man, of around sixty years of age, emerged from one of the lodges. He was dressed in buckskin shirt and leggings and wore a colorful Navajo blanket wrapped around his waist. His long hair was loose and unbound by a headband.

"*Da'anzho,*" Dr. Carter said. "How are you, Chief?"

"We are prisoners," the warrior said pragmatically.

"This man is Charles Collins," the doctor said, gesturing at C.W. "He was sent by Washington to find out about your troubles."

"Good. I will tell him. Sit and my women will bring food. No whisky."

"I do not drink whisky," Collins said, sitting on the ground by the lodge. Carter joined him.

"Good."

The chief spoke to a mature woman who was coming into camp with a bundle of firewood. She placed her load near a hearth ring and went into the lodge, quickly reappearing, accompanied by a younger woman. The two of them became occupied with tending to the fire, making coffee and roasting meat.

"I will tell you," Nautzilli said, lowering himself into a seated position across from Carter and Collins. "If Victorio comes round and kills people, we ought not to be held responsible for it. We cannot help it. My people will promise to be good. We do not want the Army to call upon us to go and hunt Victorio. We want to stay at home in peace with everybody. We want, for gods sake, to stay on this reservation, without anybody to molest us. We do not want to be bothered any more by the army."

Collins surmised there would be no need for an interpreter. The chief spoke proficient and eloquent English. "You say there was no provocation for taking your weapons and your horses?" he asked.

The chief became indignant. "We do not know why the Apache scouts came in here and killed our women and children. They killed my old father. We were good Indians and did no harm to anyone. We do not know why the army came in here and took our guns and horses and took us all prisoners after firing into our camp. We do not want any scouts, or any one else, to come on the reservation to kill or shoot at our people. *Duu 'ákáda!*"

Nautzilli took a small pipe from the folds of his blanket. Collins offered him his tobacco pouch.

"Good tobacco?"

"Yes. May I smoke with you?" Collins pulled the briar from his pocket.

"Yes."

The two men prepared their pipes and C.W struck a match and offered the chief a light.

"Do you blame Agent Russell for having the soldiers come here?" Carter asked.

Nautzilli gave a derisive rumble. "It is an old army officer that is to blame for that. His name is Hatch. The people were afraid when the many soldiers came here and that was the reason they run off to the mountains and scattered like goats. Hatch gave me a commission as chief and two days after he fired into my camp of women and children."

"You no longer trust Colonel Hatch?" Collins asked the chief.

"I do not like any man who will promise me freedom and then put a person in a corral for many days after and then put a guard around us." Nautzilli puffed firmly on his pipe. "I think this tobacco is good quality."

Removing the pouch from his pocket, Collins held it out. "Please allow me to give you this."

"But then you will have no tobacco."

"I have some in my packs."

"*'Ixéhe.*"

"*'Au.*"

Nautzilli looked at him and accepted the pouch, but said nothing.

"May I ask an impolite question?" C.W. asked.

"*'Au.*" The chief smiled faintly.

"Did the soldiers debauch your women? Violate them?"

There was a brief, uneasy silence during which Nautzilli studied C.W. At last he spoke. "We were under guard and if man or woman wanted to go to the bush, we had to ask permission and a soldier was sent with us. The agent knows this."

One of the women approached with a tin coffeepot and three blue enamel cups. She solemnly distributed the cups and deftly filled them, placing the pot close at hand and retreating to the cooking fire from which arose the enticing scent of roasting meat.

After blowing on his coffee and taking a sip, the chief said, "Cannot say what passed when our women went out. Our women had to have a soldier over them when they went to the bush. Some of them said things were done.”

“Some of the young women have diseases that suggest they were debauched,” the doctor said.

“You know these white man diseases,” Nautzilli said. “You are a doctor.”

“Yes.”

“The women are sick. Then I say these things were done,” the chief told Collins. He tugged a tight roll of paper from the top of a moccasin and waved it in front of him. “Here is a paper that shows I am head chief. It was given by Hatch and the agent. I do not want this paper with that man Hatch’s name on it. I want you to take this away and get me another one.”

“I will try, but you should keep this one,” Collins told him. “It will take some time.”

“We want our horses given back to us.”

“I will tell Washington.”

“Tell them at Stanton. They took the horses there.” Nautzilli finished his pipe and placed it back in the folds of his blanket along with the tobacco pouch.

“Only Washington can send the horses back.”

“Then we want you to explain to Washington all these things that I have told you.”

“I will explain what has happened here.”

“Good.”

Dr. Carter got to his feet and wandered into the backdrop of trees beyond the campsite. The chief refilled Collins’ cup and his own. “I saw you in Victorio’s camp,” he said. “I came back here after that. I did not want to go to Mexico and Caballo and San Juan would not come with me.”

“Yes, I was there. Will you tell the agent and the soldiers?”

“If you do not want this, I will not tell.”

Collins grinned. “I do not want you to tell.” He put

his pipe back in a pocket and drank some coffee.

"What of our horses?" the chief asked. "Will we get our horses back?"

"I do not believe so. White men will claim them."

"And what of our belongings? The soldiers took more than guns that day."

"I heard this. I do not know. It is difficult when Colonel Hatch thinks the Mescalero people are guilty of helping Victorio."

Nautzilli's mouth became frozen in a thin line. "It is the white men who are guilty. The soldiers are guilty. We are happy. We are pleased with the sun, moon and stars. We know our place and promise to be good so we can be left alone. But Indians are made prisoners and women and children are killed."

BUFFALO SOLDIER

32

Dr. Carter and Collins leisurely descended the hill below Nautzilli's camp, having shared roast venison with the chief and spoken further with him regarding diverse subjects, such as the new school Agent Russell was building, the government's policies toward Indians, the future of the Mescalero reservation and the enduring presence of the soldiers. The afternoon was advancing and erratic clouds cast transitory shadows across the landscape before them, offering periodic respite from the blazing sun. They were passing by the soldier camp, engaged in a discussion regarding the challenges of obtaining medicines in the remoteness of New Mexico Territory, when the sounds of a struggle caught their attention. They went to investigate.

Skirting one of the shelter tents, Collins stumbled upon a strapping red-haired private vigorously shaking an elderly Indian man, shouting at him.

"Give it over," the soldier kept yelling. "Give it over."

"What goes?" Carter demanded loudly, coming onto the scene.

"Son-of-a-bitch has a pair of field glasses. He ain't got no right."

The trooper continued to abuse the old man, who doggedly resisted the assault, his arms rigidly shielding the binoculars against his chest. Collins stepped in and wrestled the soldier away. The private turned on him, attempting to punch him in the face. Collins ducked and cuffed him alongside the head then brought a fist up under his chin and the soldier collapsed on the ground. The Indian dodged away, disappearing among the tents and reappearing upslope as he careened toward the tree line, hunched over, still protecting his treasured possession.

An infantry sergeant trotted over. "What the hell is going on here?" he asked the two men standing over the private, now on his knees and shaking his head like a dog.

"Your soldier was mistreating and attempting to steal from an old Indian," the doctor told him. "Is this how you conduct yourselves, Sergeant Phillips?"

"You struck him?" the sergeant asked, assisting the trooper to his feet.

"I struck him," Collins said.

"Goddamn," the private said. "I oughta shoot you," he told Collins.

"That will be sufficient, Casey. Get to your tent. I will find you later."

The soldier glared maliciously at C.W. and sauntered away. It seemed to Collins that discipline was rather desultory, if Private Casey's conduct was any indication.

"I will not have civilians striking my men," Sergeant Phillips said.

"Your men are molesting the people here," Collins observed. "I will be reporting this episode to your superiors during my forthcoming sojourn at Fort Stanton."

Agent Russell arrived, slightly winded. "Mr. Collins. I am heartily repentant at having abandoned you for so long an interval." He glanced around at the sergeant and the doctor. "Is something amiss?"

"One of the soldiers was endeavoring to rob *Tzozhonne*," Carter told him.

"You know this man?" the sergeant asked Russell, nodding toward Collins.

"Why yes, Sergeant Phillips. He works for Commissioner Trowbridge of the Indian Bureau."

The sergeant appeared to vaguely diminish in stature. "Well worst come to worstest. I will surely be busted back down to private."

Chapter 32

"Chin up, Sergeant," Carter said. "Truthfully, Mr. Collins, Phillips here is a decent man."

"I swear I will place Casey on report and have him removed from the agency," the sergeant said eagerly, evidently seeing a light at the end of a grim tunnel.

Collins saw no profit in besmirching the man's military career, even though he remained infuriated at the maltreatment of the Apache elder. "See to it and I will not recount this episode at the fort. But you must give me your word of honor that you will vigilantly thwart further incidents of this nature."

"My word of honor."

Shaking his head in uncertainty, C.W. watched as the sergeant passed from sight along the line of tents. "Is this a common occurrence?" he asked Agent Russell.

"Sadly, the soldiers tend to browbeat the Indians," the agent said. "As I told you yesterday, the soldiers do as they please. I cannot stop them."

" 'Who all sense of others' ills escapes, is but a brute in human shape,' " Carter said.

"Is that not Juvenal? Admirable sentiment, Doctor," Collins told him.

"By way of a classical education prior to medical school."

The three of them proceeded back to the agency buildings. "Will you dine with us?" Russell asked as they approached his headquarters.

"I am most obliged, but it is incumbent upon me to travel some distance while light remains." It was midafternoon and Collins was keen to make camp before nightfall, ideally at a distance from the army and Indian encampments.

The agent was perceptibly disappointed. "I had hoped we might discuss matters further in regard to the circumstances here."

"Be assured I have attained what I believe is a comprehensive understanding of the situation."

"Our meeting with Nautzilli was quite instructive,"

Carter said. "Even though the interpreter never arrived."

"Oh yes, he was inopportunely called away. So sorry."

"You need not worry."

"Well then, Mr. Collins, allow us to assist you with your livestock."

Presently, Ulysses and Molly were standing outside the corral prepared for travel. The men shook hands all around, then Collins swung into the saddle.

"It has been pleasant, Mr. Collins," the doctor said. "I hope we may be friends."

"I echo the sentiment and will pen a missive at my earliest convenience."

Giving an informal salute, Collins turned his horse and rode southeast toward the Río Tularosa and came upon the road to Fort Stanton. Above the confluence with the south fork, the river was sluggish and mosquitoes rose from its marshy banks to afflict both man and beasts. Ulysses exhibited his displeasure with half-hearted crow hops and even stoic Molly made throaty whimpering sounds in distress. Soon, however, the road departed from the dwindling water course, climbing into the timber where C.W. and his animals found relief in a freshening breeze soughing through the pines.

The road showed heavy use by wagons and before long, Collins shifted to the side of the trail to make way for two rack bed wagons and one newly built Schuttler wagon, its green paint bright and emblazoned with the cartwright's celebrated name. Each wagon had a four-up hitch of mules and was laden high above the box. The man on the Schuttler wagon was perched upon the spring seat, while the other teamsters rode the left wheel mules. Collins observed that the animals looked exhausted, galled and undernourished. He scarcely acknowledged salutations from the men.

The waning daylight was casting golden rays through the trees when Collins happened upon a middling rivulet that emanated from the mountains to the northwest of the road. He followed it a little distance into a narrow canyon and found a small glade in which to make camp. He was just unbuckling the flank cinch billet on Ulysses when he heard someone cough gently. On his guard, he whirled around and found a slim young Apache man. He wore a short bone and turtle shell breastplate over a red and white checked shirt and half of his long hair was braided and wrapped while the other half was loose.

The youth beckoned with a hand. "Come. *Dákugu.... k'adi, k'adi.*"

"Where? *Dónde? No comprendo.*" Collins knew that many Apache people spoke at least some Spanish.

"*Hanya' yuu.* Nautzilli." The boy pointed with his lower lip in the direction of the agency and beckoned again, gesturing he should mount up and follow.

Curious but wary, Collins nodded in consent, refastened the billet on his saddle, tightened the front cinch and checked the rigging on Molly's packs. He climbed in the saddle, took a dally with the mule's halter rope and nodded again at the Indian, who jogged back toward the agency headquarters. Reckoning that he had ridden around two hours since taking his leave of Dr. Carter and Agent Russell, it would be nigh on sundown by the time he retraced his route. His journey had certainly been replete with detours, he mused. *Cam ialla na conaire.* Crooked are the turns of the path.

Arbuckles'
Ariosa Coffee.
NORTH AMERICA
SOUTH AMERICA
OCEANICA
ATLANTIC OCEAN
PACIFIC OCEAN
INDIAN OCEAN
AUSTRALIA
ANTARCTIC OCEAN
North Frigid Zone
South Frigid Zone
EQUATOR

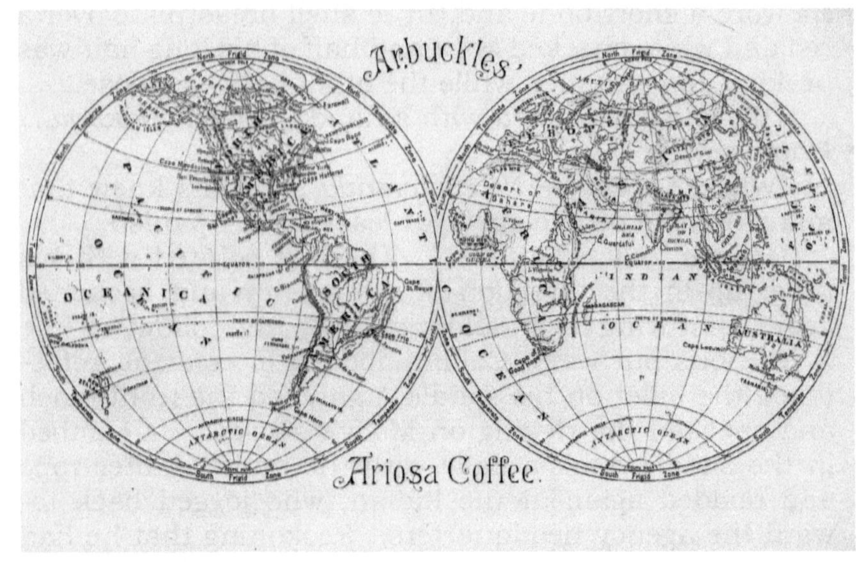

COFFEE

33

The fire crackled merrily, sending sparks, like tiny shards of shooting stars, into the surrounding darkness. There were several Indians gathered around, their indomitable faces resembling polished bronze in the roseate radiance of dancing flames. Collins sat quietly smoking his pipe while his hosts spoke amongst themselves, visibly in high dudgeon. His guide, who had identified himself as *Askissay*, sat beside him in affable camaraderie, even though they could not adequately converse. Collins was back in Nautzilli's camp, summoned by him for a further discussion of the tragedies of April 16. Apparently, Dr. Carter had already spoken to Jackrabbit's mother, for she was present somewhere in the campsite. He had not gotten the opportunity to speak with her, but one of Nautzilli's wives, who spoke some English, had told him she had come.

"*Gaxee'?*" Askissay asked. "Coffee?"

Not certain whether he was requesting coffee or offering, Collins shrugged helplessly.

"Do you have coffee?" Nautzilli asked from across the fire. "Can you make coffee?"

"Yes," He told the chief, then turned to look at his new friend and said, "'*Au.*"

Getting to his feet, he went over to a rope enclosure intertwined around an assembly of stout yellow pines. His horse and mule stood within, nose to tail, deep in slumber. He knelt beside one of his panniers, next to the mound of saddles and belongings at the base of one of the trees, and dug out the coffeepot, his grinder and the last sack of Arbuckles' beans. He also unearthed a half bag of sugar.

Back at the fire, Collins opened the sack of coffee and took out the peppermint stick with a twinge of guilt, remembering that Jackrabbit had delighted in the candy from a previous bag. He noticed a young boy, peering at him with large eyes from behind one of the women. C.W. held the treat out to him, nodding in encouragement. The child tentatively circled behind the adults and earnestly accepted the offering. Soon, the pot was resting upon the edge of the fire and when Collins reclaimed his place by the hearth, Askissay patted his shoulder by way of expressing gratitude.

There was a lull in the discussion among the Apache men and Collins looked up to see a woman of middle age coming toward him accompanied by Nautzilli's wife. He came to his feet again. The woman was attired in a faded cotton blouse worn over a darker grass cloth skirt and bounded by a heavy leather belt. She held her head with a rigid affect, half-hidden by a drab shawl draped over her hair.

"*Otottie*," Nautzilli's wife said, gesturing loosely at the woman. "Tell about her son." Her tone was imperious.

Nautzilli appeared by her side. "I will help with the talk," he said and spoke to his wife in his own language.

"The truth," his wife told Collins forcefully, then retired into the gloom of the camp.

"*Bééskantsu* is a good woman but she frightens me," Nautzilli said with humor.

Otottie bashfully peered at the ground in front of her. The chief spoke to her gently. They moved away from the fire into the outer halo of light.

"Tell me of her son's death and I will pass this on,"

Nautzilli said.

There was an uproar by the fire. Askissay had apparently poured hot coffee on another man's hand by accident. The chief shouted a single word at the group and the raised voices subdued.

"I am so terribly sorry I did not protect her son," Collins said. "I want her to know this."

"I will tell her. Give me the whole story. Let us sit here and talk."

The three of them sat together in the soft duff beneath a pine tree. Otottie had yet to look at C.W., but continued to keep her eyes cast down. He began to speak, recounting the tale of how Jackrabbit had saved his life and mindful not to say the boy's name in deference to the prohibition as explained by Blazer. He told how they had travelled together and decided to separate and about discovering the place of his murder in the desert. Nautzilli translated while Collins spoke. As the narrative came to its end, drops of moisture fell upon Otottie's folded hands and Collins saw she was weeping. Impulsively, he reached to comfort her, but restrained himself, remembering that physical touch was mostly unwelcome and probably unsuitable between a strange white man and an Apache widow.

"I am so sorry," he said again, profoundly conscious of the inadequacy of the expression. "So, so sorry."

Otottie raised her moist eyes briefly to gaze at him in resonating grief, her lower lip held firmly between her teeth. Momentarily, Collins thought dire remorse might unman him. The anguished mother spoke to the chief in a quiet and timid voice.

"This woman wants me to tell you she is happy someone remembers her son fondly," Nautzilli told Collins.

"*'Ixéhe*," he said.

She glanced at him briefly. "*Washindun'*," she said

almost inaudibly.

"Yes," Collins said, mildly astonished. "*'Au.*"

Otottie gave a very slight and enigmatic smile through her tears and, shifting as lightly and swiftly as a doe, departed their company for the surrounding darkness. The chief gestured for Collins to accompany him back to the fire, where Askissay handed him a mug of steaming coffee.

"You do not know who committed this act of killing the boy?" Nautzilli asked after speaking with some of the other men.

"No. There was no sign to show me who it was. If I knew, I would track and kill him."

The chief said something to the assembly. There was a murmur of approval around the fire.

"There is a feast tomorrow. It is for *Tahdasto's* daughter. You should remain with us and eat with us."

"I am honored, but I am required to report to Washington about the bad deeds that happened here. I must ride to the fort tomorrow."

"Will you get our horses back?" one of the other men asked.

"I will try. I cannot promise and there is small hope the soldiers will give them back."

"Even so, you are always welcome among us. We will call you *Haastį' ndeesń dzat'i*," Nautzilli told him. "I have told the people about seeing you in Victorio's camp."

"He did not kill you," the man who asked about the horses said. "Why?"

"I helped steal guns from some white people. I shot one. I think this is why he did not kill me."

There was a round of animated conversation in the Apache language. Several of the men nodded at Collins in approbation.

"You will speak well of us to the soldiers at the fort

and to Washington?" Nautzilli asked. "We are tired of trouble and do not want anyone to come and kill us anymore. We want peace."

"I will speak well of you. I was sent here to report about what happened. To report to the Indian Bureau. You should know that Agent Russell has been writing letters telling the truth and that is why I was sent here."

The chief translated his statement and this inspired a great deal of discussion. "The agent is a shaky old man and sometimes worthless, but I do not think he is bad," Nautzilli said. "It is good he told the truth, but he could not stand up to Hatch. He should have stopped the killing."

Collins thought a moment. "The soldiers and the Indian agents do not agree," he finally explained. "Both sides are trying to be in charge of the Indians everywhere. There is always fighting in Washington. Agent Russell could not stop Hatch and the soldiers."

The chief considered this. "White men are greedy, they lie, they steal, they make us as children when we are strong and wise," he said. "They cannot even agree about who must be the head man." Nautzilli sighed. "I do not see why we are pushed around and killed and kept as prisoners by people who have no honor."

"It is wrong and should not happen," C.W. told him. "But there are so many whites that their flood simply washes over every place and everyone and this makes it difficult for anything to survive."

Nautzilli regarded Collins for a long minute. "How do you know this?"

"It happened to my people too."

JOHN CHARLES FRÉMONT

34

The road to Fort Stanton wound through coniferous forest and open parks. Game was sparse, but Collin's spied the occasional deer and wild turkey. He had departed the Indian camp at daybreak, planning to camp along the Río Bonito before nightfall. Several freight wagons and mule trains had passed, sure signs that the population of New Mexico Territory was growing in leaps and bounds, in spite of Victorio's aggression and enduring confrontations between the Santa Fe Ring and powerful cattlemen. As he rode, he thought about his previous sojourn in the area over eight years before and the stories related to him by his friend, Chief Cadete. He had told Collins how the Mescaleros had fought General Carleton's troops back in '62 until gun powder and ammunition ran out and they were forced onto a reservation with their enemies, the Navajo. Even with that, the chief had stated proudly that the white soldiers could never steal their dignity nor their strength of belonging within the sacred mountains under their own sky.

Despite Carleton's best efforts, the Mescalero people had survived incarceration at Bosque Redondo, the ill-famed prison camp at Fort Sumner, as well as the loss of pivotal leaders, many subsequent assaults on life and limb and this latest transgression perpetrated by Colonel Hatch and Grierson's troops out of Texas. How many more ignominies and offensives would be leveled at these people in coming decades was uncertain, but it seemed to him they would probably prevail, or at the very least, survive all efforts to wipe them out. He sadly pondered the probable fate of Victorio and his followers and the audacious threat purportedly made by the recalcitrant woman on the Las Palomas. His people would eat him up rather than have his body fall into the hands of the enemy.

He recalled a letter, written by John Quincy Adams, during the negotiations at Ghent, Belgium to end the War of 1812. Authored in response to the British demand that an Indian barrier state be created, it had confirmed unequivocally that the U.S. government would not "avow a system of arresting their natural growth within their own territories, for the sake of preserving a perpetual desert for savages." Thusly, American expansionism and manifest destiny had been openly declared. A British negotiator had later written that, prior to the negotiations, he had not grasped the full extent of American resolve in regards to the annihilation of Indian populations and the acquisition of Indian lands.

Steadily gaining altitude, the road finally reached the apex of a small pass and Collins roused himself from his musings to admire the summit of Sierra Blanca rising above the far landscape before him. Vestiges of snow still adorned its massive heights and regalia of verdant green graced its wide slopes. It was an arresting sight and C.W. reined in his gelding to pause and view the scenery and let his animals blow. The jangling of trace chains and the sound of tramping hooves alerted Collins to an approaching wagon train. He glanced down to see an enormous freight wagon, loaded almost ten feet high with bales of goods, sacks of grain, items of furniture and other unidentifiable bundles and boxes. As it advanced toward him, he saw that the wagon was drawn by a sturdy ten-up mule team and was hitched to a second wagon also loaded to implausible dimensions. The animals labored to the top of the northern grade and the teamster, walking beside the wagons, gave a command for them to halt. Collins was forced to admit to himself that the mules appeared to be in excellent condition.

"Mornin'," the fellow called out. He was a lanky man with wide shoulders and a muscular frame, dressed in plain work clothes. His face was shaded by a wide, flat-brimmed hat.

"Good morning. Headed for Mesilla?"

"Shore."

"All the way from the railhead in Las Vegas?"

"Shore." The teamster spit a stream of tobacco juice at the left wheeler mule's hind foot.

It was apparent the man was no great raconteur, so Collins, not particularly interested in a prolonged conversation anyway, took his leave. As he passed, he heard the teamster say, "Nice mule."

Unable to resist, C.W. answered with, "Shore," and made his way down the road.

By noon, he was skirting a grist mill, driven by an elevated water flume that channeled water from the Ruidoso River, and situated against a long narrow adobe structure next to a single-story residence and store. The mill was nestled among several buildings at the base of a conical hill, towered over by the Sierra Blanca, and a few other adobe houses were scattered about the vicinity, forming a small community. A couple of saddle horses were ground-tied nearby. Collins rode past, following the road up a steep draw, girded by tall pine trees. The trail began again to gain altitude, swiftly becoming monotonous with thick conifers creating a barrier of dense boughs, obscuring any and all extensive vistas. The uniformity of the backdrop was only occasionally broken by passing wagons. Individual travelers were rare, probably due to fear of Indian attacks, but he encountered a small troop of colored cavalry soldiers a few miles along. They overtook him at a canter and moved past with complete disregard, obliging him to calm a startled Ulysses.

After a good while, the road leveled and the route was not as constricted. Collins was able to see the occasional far ridge or mountain peak. Then, climbing again, he was riding through open undulating grasslands. Cattle grazed the slopes and signs of throughgoing timber harvesting could be seen everywhere. The trail eventually and abruptly descended to follow a river and he knew this to be the Río Bonito, leading directly to Fort Stanton. He watered his animals in a bend of the stream and stretched his legs.

The river bottom was thick with deciduous undergrowth and trees. Songbirds, turkeys and deer were numerous inhabitants and a few cow elk were bedded down in sheltered coulees above. The multiplicity of wildlife, he thought, must result from the area's isolation from the fort and civilian settlements. As he had in the past, Collins experienced envy of those, such as William Clark and Meriwether Lewis, who had witnessed the untrammeled beauty of remote wilderness regions prior to white encroachment. Thusly inspired, he resumed his erudite introspection regarding the advance of European civilization upon Indian peoples of western territories.

Collins had studied the writings of Senator Thomas Hart Benton, not incidentally a great supporter of his son-in-law, John Charles Frémont, the explorer, invader and erstwhile bosom friend of Christopher "Kit" Carson. Benton had remained in the U.S. senate for thirty years and been a vigorous proponent of aggressive expansionism and an enthusiastic disciple of Andrew Jackson and his Indian removal policies. As a steadfast promoter of the subjugation of Indian tribes, he championed the annexation of Texas, was pivotal in acquiring funding and congressional provision for Frémont's three expeditions to explore and survey uncharted western regions and had been the author of the first Homestead Act. C.W. deemed the man, excepting "Old Hickory," to be one of the most catastrophic American politicians regarding the encroachment on and violent acquisition of Indian lands since the inception of the United States.

Benton's pretentious autobiography exalted the American character and the need for "giving lands, in parcels suitable to their wants, to meritorious cultivators," without apportioning any consideration to the original occupants of said lands. His son-in-law, with the tacit approval of President Polk and absolute sponsorship of Benton, had behaved abominably toward the Spanish and Indian populations of California throughout 1845 and '46, going so far as to establish a murderous volunteer militia that engaged in the massacre of countless inhabitants albeit prior to any declaration of war with Mexico. Even after Frémont was charged with mutiny, illegal assumption of powers and other offenses, Benton rose to his defense and he was pardoned, with Frémont later becoming a presidential candidate in 1856. As always, Collins thought, nothing was to stand in the way of American empire building.

By late afternoon, Collins had come upon a congenial glade among some cottonwood trees along the riverbank. There was an abundance of palatable green grasses among the trees for his stock, so he decided to make camp, markedly fatigued after the previous evening with very little sleep. Nautzilli had generously supplied him with an antelope steak and, after graining and hobbling Ulysses and Molly and arranging a comfortable situation, he gathered dry wood and built a hearth ring, intent on having a leisurely meal. Resulting from his plan of resupplying at Stanton, the meat was meagerly supplemented by hard tack and coffee, but Collins found the supper to be more than adequate. Afterward, he leaned back against his bedroll, smoking his pipe and further deliberating upon the arrogance and self-congratulatory aspects of Benton's book, *Thirty Years' View*.

The senator had been unyielding in the belief that the U.S. government had established fixed policies to "cherish and protect" Indians and to improve their condition by adapting them to "the habits of civilized life." None of this could be said to correspond with actual events of the past or current decades. Collins could not comprehend how herding women and children into a putrid stock pen could be perceived as cherishing, but justification of any vile act seemed to be the unique purview of colonial powers and Benton had been a true zealot. He recalled what Secretary Schurz had once told him. He had said, "We are creatures of the times." Surely, he thought, this should not be cause for brandishing a patriotic sophistry. He wondered whether the wrongs committed against Indians would be vindicated and cleansed by passing years. Ben Jonson had written, "Let them call it mischief. When it is past and prosper'd, 'twill be virtue." Benton's book would survive to be read by future generations, no doubt, and his malversations resound with devotion to country and beneficial progress. The stories passed along by Nautzilli's descendants would be poignantly dissimilar, but principally ignored by historians.

35

The path of Río Bonito opened up into a wider plain rimmed on the north side by steep knolls bedecked with sporadic juniper trees. Ahead, as the screen of thick cottonwood foliage gave way to open fields where all trees had been cleared, Collins could see the dark rim of the Capitan Mountains. He rode into the western end of the fort, passing the rather substantial building that housed the old L.G. Murphy sutler's store and had been the headquarters of the Indian agency when C.W. had last been at Stanton.

It was early and the aroma of fresh bread, arising from the post bakery, was carried upon the soft breeze. Reveille must have already been sounded, as he could see troops were lined up on the parade grounds for roll call and C.W. heard the bugle call for stable duty, no doubt meant for cavalry soldiers. Bearing to the south side of the grounds, he made his way to the adjutant's office, dismounted, eased cinches and secured his mule and horse to a hitching rail beside the building. Stepping into the interior, a mature man bearing second lieutenant insignia was seated behind a substantial oak desk. The man's head was framed by a large map of New Mexico Territory affixed to the wall behind him. The officer trained steely grey eyes upon Collins.

"Good morning, Lieutenant," Collins said, removing his Stetson. "My name is Charles Collins. I was hoping to speak with the commanding officer."

"Major Mauck is out surveying the morning's assembly. He should be present before long," the captain told him with no particular effort at cordiality.

"I was also looking to speak with Captain Steelhammer. Might he be at hand?"

"Captain Steelhammer has been unwell and is about to depart on the morrow for a leave of absence. You will, no doubt, find him in his quarters or within the hospital in the company of the post surgeon."

"Are you willing to direct me to his quarters?"

The lieutenant gave the impression that he considered Collins to be creating a nuisance of the first order. "The row on the northeast quadrant of the parade grounds.," he said and nodded in the general direction.

"Thank you," Collins responded brusquely, donned his hat and departed the man's company with pleasure. "I shall return to speak with Major Mauck."

Loosing the halter rope and reins, he led his animals toward the row of junior officers' quarters as indicated by the adjutant. Unsure where to find Steelhammer's quarters in the four units that made up the building, he secured his stock to a nearby tree and endeavored to listen for some indication of occupancy. A young woman appeared in one of the doorways leading a small boy by the hand.

"Pardon me," Collins said.

"Oh! Oh my goodness!" the woman exclaimed, demonstrably flustered. She pulled the door to, as if barring him from entry.

"Pardon me," he said again. "But I am looking for Captain Steelhammer."

"He is just there," she told him, waving a hand at the adjoining domicile, and walked briskly away, dragging the child behind and almost lifting him from his feet in her haste.

Not believing himself to be remarkably frightening, Collins was baffled by the woman's apparent alarm, but he supposed he was rather rough in appearance, not having shaved for two days. He made his way to the neighboring door and knocked. The door promptly opened and he found himself face to face with an exceptionally tall man in undershirt and suspenders. He had kindly blue eyes circled by grey shadows, a sallow complexion and a rigorously trained cavalry moustache.

"How may I be of service?" he asked formally. His pronunciation revealed a hint of foreign origins.

"My name is Charles Collins. You are Captain Steelhammer?"

The man nodded.

"I have been commissioned by the Indian Bureau to investigate the events of last April on the Mescalero Agency. I was hoping to speak with you."

"I am all at sixes and sevens at the moment, preparing to leave for the states in the early morning. I have not been well, you see. Pleurisy."

"I am quite repentant at causing vexation," C.W. told him. "But it is imperative I speak with you."

Steelhammer stepped back and gestured for Collins to enter his quarters. The front room was sparsely furnished, with a worn bearskin rug on the floor, a table, two spindle back chairs, a handmade wooden bench below the single window, two stacked crates for bookshelves and a small fireplace with a narrow mantle displaying a few arrowheads, two oil lamps and an old daguerreotype of a young woman. Stacks of items piled haphazardly upon the table spoke of hurried organizing and packing.

Having noted Collins' perusal of the room, Steelhammer said, "As you see... I am in disarray." Of a sudden, he was afflicted by a prolonged episode of coughing. When it was over, the captain looked at Collins through eyes bleary with tears. "I was sent here for medical treatment in early March," he said with irony. "The assistant surgeon at this post, a man who specializes in diseases of the lungs, had already been transferred. Please sit." He removed a heap of clothing from a chair.

Accepting the invitation, C.W. took a seat and Steelhammer situated himself upon the other chair across the table from him.

"Again," Collins said, "I must express my apology for disturbing you. But I am most anxious to hear your version of events surrounding the disarming of the Mescalero people last April."

The man bowed his head, closed his eyes and rubbed his forehead in consternation. "I am pleased to be quitting this post and New Mexico Territory," he said softly. "I am surfeited with the wrangling of superiors, obeying orders that are manifestly unjust and hunting down and killing Indians as if they were beasts afflicted with rabies." He glanced up at Collins and held his eyes. "I was an unwilling participant that day." The captain's accent seemed to have intensified with his fervency.

"Please just recount your recollections at your own pace."

"Very well." Steelhammer gazed down at his hands, resting upon the tabletop. "I was ordered to report to the South Fork Agency on April 10 with Company G of the 15th Infantry. We had heard that Colonel Grierson was due to arrive at the agency and there were rumors that General Pope had ordered the confiscation of all Mescalero horses and weapons. My misgivings began when word arrived that a company of the 10th Cavalry under Captain Lebo had struck an Apache encampment in the Guadalupe Mountains at Shake Hand Spring, killed their head man, destroyed all their belongings, took possession of around twenty-five head of horses and mules and took captive four women and one child. One of the women gave birth during or just after the skirmish and was forced to ride thirty miles the same day." He paused in thought. "My deteriorating health had already overcast my general mood and a perception of impending misfortune began to be a plague upon me."

"Was Colonel Hatch already at the agency?"

"The colonel had arrived on the 12th with such a colossal force, I could not see how I was required, especially as I had been made temporary commanding officer here at Stanton in March after Lieutenant Colonel Peter Swain was placed on leave of absence due to illness. Colonel Grierson arrived shortly after. Would you care for coffee? I think there is some in the cook shack from earlier."

"My thanks, but let us continue your narrative for now. I do not wish to keep you from your packing." Collins dearly longed for his pipe, but given the man's ailment, he forbore the pleasure.

"Well then, I will carry on. Hatch directed Grierson to place his command in camp and await further orders. This did not appear to sit well with him and I overheard him tell Colonel Hatch that because the Indians were encamped across the Río Tularosa, with a half mile of boggy ground between them and the soldiers, they were well outside the control of the military. To this, Hatch was strikingly dismissive. There seemed to be some share of acrimony between them."

"Please tell me of your experience of the disarming."

"On the morning of the 16th, we heard that some of Hatch's Apache scouts had killed Chief Nautzilli's father and some others. The Indians were frightened so Agent Russell, Colonel Hatch and I agreed that I should approach with my company of infantry. A few of the bucks gave us their guns, but many began to move off. Nautzilli made a few attempts at bringing them back, but Hatch sent orders for me to warn them that if they did not come in, I would open fire." Steelhammer shook his head gloomily. "I am a soldier. I obeyed orders and opened fire even though the chief was still doing his best to coax his people back. That is when Grierson's troops began to shoot as well. There was a general rout but none of the Indians returned fire."

"How many were killed?"

"I believe it was around fifteen, including a woman. Colonel Hatch's troops and Mr. Russell addressed the disposition of casualties and I was not included."

"Nautzilli also escaped?"

Steelhammer succumbed to another painful bout of coughing. When he had recovered sufficiently, he said, "Yes, but he has returned with a handful of his people. I am certain more will come in once they find it is safe to do so."

"And what of the cow corral?"

The captain became more outwardly despondent. "It was shameful what was done. Only about twenty revolvers and rifles were taken, good, bad and indifferent. Most of the warriors had escaped. All the horses and mules were then driven off and herded here to Stanton or seized by the Apache scouts. Those Indians painted themselves and behaved as if they had captured the ponies in battle with the Mescaleros. I heard later they stole some cattle and horses from local residents. Hatch departed with his troops and only my company and the Texas detachments remained. The following day, Grierson took all of his men and left the reservation in order to scout the territory."

"And the cow pen?" Collins prodded.

"The Indians were first merely held under guard, then we were ordered to drive them into a stock pen near the agency. I was ordered to hold them there indefinitely, but after a period of five days and many discussions with the agent and Dr. Carter, and after a child had perished, I allowed the group, mostly women and children, to remove themselves."

"How long are they to remain prisoners in their encampments?"

"I do not know. I was released from duty at the agency on April 29 and was pleased to be so. It was heartrending to hear them pleading with the agent to give them answers. How long would they be prisoners? Where were their horses?"

"And there is no plan for returning the animals?"

"They are all gone, either given to white claimants in this locality or from Texas." He paused and wiped his forehead with a handkerchief. "Or gone with Hatch and the scouts," he added.

The bugle call for fatigue duty sounded.

Collins came to his feet. "I thank you for your forthrightness, Captain. Where do you plan to convalesce?"

Steelhammer rose from his chair and stretched his long limbs. "To my family in Karlskrona, Sweden. It is my home."

"And then you will return to New Mexico Territory?"

"*För i helvete*, I hope not. But I have a year's leave of absence. After that, we shall see."

"I thank you again, Captain. I will leave you to your labors."

"Will you pass along my report to the Indian Bureau?"

"I will."

"That is acceptable. I regret my involvement utterly," he said and held out a hand to shake.

"May your journey be safe from harm," Collins said, accepting the gesture.

"And yours, Mr. Collins," Captain Steelhammer said and yet again began to convulse with a deplorable cough.

⎯⎯⎯⎯⎯⎯◦•◦⎯⎯⎯⎯⎯⎯

FORT

36

"Did you find the Swede?" the adjutant asked when Collins returned to the office.

"I found Captain Steelhammer," he answered coldly. "Has the major returned?"

"He is apt to be at the post commander's quarters straight across the parade grounds there."

"Very well. Are you aware of any telegrams that may have arrived for Charles Wolfe Collins? I was, perhaps, to have received communications."

"There are no telegrams."

"You are certain?"

"Quite certain."

"Thank you," Collins said, unsure whether to be relieved or uneasy.

"What, pray, is your business here?"

About to exit the building, Collins paused. "Pardon me?"

"I inquired as to your business here."

He turned to look at the lieutenant. "I will discuss the matter with your commanding officer."

The man laughed unpleasantly. "He is my commanding officer at present. Not for long I will warrant."

Collins hesitated, then asked, "What do you imply?"

"Major Mauck is a 'lunger.' " The lieutenant appeared to regard the poor health of his superior officer as a matter for satisfaction.

"You are a disagreeable fellow," Collins told him. "*Ualach sé chapall de chré na h-úire ort.*"

"What?"

Collins quitted the office, slamming the door behind him. Having billeted his horse and mule in the stables with an accommodating private of the 9th Cavalry, he strode across the parade grounds toward a freestanding white washed house, evading miscellaneous soldiers going about their duties and noting that the colored cavalry troopers seemed to maintain distance from any of the white infantry soldiers. He stepped onto the portico that sheltered the front door and knocked. A handsome older woman answered the door. She wore a fashionable blue and white striped dress.

"Yes?"

Removing his hat, Collins gave a shallow bow. "Good morning. I am here to see Major Mauck."

"Come in."

The woman stood back in the entry to allow Collins to move past into a hallway. "Step through to the parlor there," she said, directing him with an understated but elegant motion of her hand.

The room was well-appointed with agreeably simple furnishings. He seated himself in a walnut rocking chair to wait. In a few minutes, a crisply uniformed man entered briskly. Collins stood.

"You requested to see me," the major said matter-of-factly.

"I did. My name is Charles Collins. I have been authorized to investigate certain allegations regarding the confiscation of weapons and horses from the Mescalero Apache."

The officer was scrutinizing Collins in a most overt manner. "Charles Collins... Captain Collins, as was," he said.

"Many years ago, I was Captain Collins."

Mauck's face broke into a delighted grin. "Captain Collins, of course. We briefly served in the Freedman's

Bureau together."

Despite the man's graying hair and wan complexion, C.W. was suddenly transported back to his days in Atlanta after the war. "Clarence. Clarence Mauck. They sent you to Texas."

"And I have served in remote regions since."

He called to his wife, who summarily appeared in the doorway. "Helen, this is an old friend, Mr. Collins."

The woman gave a slight curtsy. "Pleased to meet you."

"And you."

"Would you be so kind as to fetch some coffee and a portion of your excellent corn bread?"

"Surely," she said and went out.

"Sit down, Captain," the officer said, taking a seat on a small divan near the fireplace.

"Not captain, merely Charles," Collins said, reclaiming the rocking chair.

"No matter... it is quite remarkable to see you again. You said you were authorized to investigate Hatch's blunders of the past April? By whom are you mandated?"

"By Commissioner Trowbridge of the Indian Bureau."

"I see," Mauck said pensively.

It seemed to Collins that his friend had aged considerably and appeared to be indisposed. Perhaps the irksome adjutant had been accurate in his spiteful diagnosis of the major.

"Are you well?" he asked.

"I have been decidedly fatigued of late and am afflicted with circumscribed breathing. I was set to consult with a specialist when the army saw fit to propel me into this temporary station of duty." Mauck shrugged. "I am not overly concerned, but Helen does worry so."

"When did you arrive?"

"Early May. So, in point of fact, I was not here when the disarming took place."

"No matter. I believe I have gathered sufficient intelligence."

Helen arrived bearing a tray of cups, coffeepot and a plate of cornbread cakes. She set the burden upon a round table in the middle of the room. "You may help yourselves," she said. "I am obliged to visit Lieutenant Clark's wife." She departed the room and they heard the front door open and close.

The major served Collins, then poured coffee for himself. "Am I able to assist you in some manner?" he asked after a moment.

"I must send telegrams. Who is your signal officer?"

"The post adjutant, Lieutenant Garst."

"That is unlucky." Collins finished his cornbread and brushed crumbs from his moustache with a napkin.

Mauck contemplated him sardonically. "You have met him, then, I take it?"

"I have."

"If it meets with your approval, you may write out your messages and I will beard Lieutenant Garst."

"It is most appreciated."

"I am not astonished that great men in Washington continue to engage your particular skills, Charles, but why is the Indian Bureau gathering further information about a routine military operation, even if it went amiss?"

"The agent and some other civilians have been expressing concern in sustained correspondence. You no doubt are aware of the schism between the War Department and the Department of the Interior?"

"Yes, it is common knowledge."

"I believe that Secretary Schurz may use the information to strengthen his case for retaining control over Indian policy. General Sheridan's previous miscalculations have worked to the secretary's advantage."

"This specific instance belongs to General Pope and

Colonel Hatch."

"That may be, but unquestionably taints Sheridan and Sherman into the bargain."

Mauck nodded. "You are, of course, correct."

Collins poured himself more coffee and took a sip. Replacing the cup on its saucer, he resolved to advance the topic for which he had come to see the major in the first place. "What do you know of the horses?"

The major looked at him in puzzlement. "Horses?"

"The Mescalero horses. Do any of the animals remain at the post?"

"To my knowledge, there are no Indian horses here," Mauck said, shaking his head. "I assumed they had all been returned to their rightful owners."

"Their rightful owners were the Indians."

"Certainly not according to Lieutenant Garst. He apprised me of the events and concomitant circumstances upon my arrival."

Collins groaned in perturbation. "Lieutenant Garst is an unmitigated ass."

"You are saying the animals truly belonged to the Apaches?"

"Most of them. Over two hundred were driven here."

"I did not know. According to Garst, the horses and mules were taken in raids and were therefore ill-gotten. As for the remainder, I am credibly informed that, while these horses were en route to Fort Stanton, from ten to twenty of them were disposed of due to their debilitated condition."

"And none remain on the post?"

"None." Mauck sighed shallowly, the inhalation and exhalation seemingly labored.

"It is unjust," C.W. said in supreme annoyance. " 'My heart suspects more than mine eye can see.' "

"My least favorite of the bard's plays, but a laudable

quote." The major raised his hands in a conciliatory gesture. "I can only say I am sorry, old friend. As I said, I was not present at the time."

Collins smiled at the officer. "Of course, Clarence. You are not blameworthy in this."

After a prolonged interval, during which Collins exchanged pleasantries and reminiscences with the major and composed his telegraphic communiqués to Trowbridge and to Secretary Schurz, especially regarding Victorio's last attempt at surrender as related by Agent Russell, he took his leave. Mauck had sincerely urged him to remain as his guest, but Collins was desirous of resupplying at the sutler's and proceeding upon his route back to Las Vegas.

After retrieving Ulysses and Molly from the stables and slipping a Morgan dollar to the kindhearted private who had cared for them, Collins walked back across the parade grounds headed for the post trader's store. Situated at a fair distance from the fort, the single story adobe building was wide and long, divided into sections, and had a porch shading the entire anterior, two front doors and several windows. *Canales* protruded from the wall above the porch to allow rainwater to drain from the flat roof. They were painted white, as were the window shutters, porch columns and doors, in sharp contrast with the mud brown of the building.

He tied his animals to a hitching rail set perpendicular to the store and entered the structure through the middle door, thereby jingling a brass spring doorbell. Inside, the spacious room was chockablock with items and equipment ranging from blankets, tonics, galvanized buckets, oil lamps, and copper kettles to playing cards, confectionaries, cartridges, toothbrushes, tobacco, clothing and a variety of other dry goods. Smoked hams were suspended from the round ceiling rafters alongside saddles and other tack. No doubt ardent spirits were also available, albeit clandestinely.

A young man emerged from a back room and moved behind the extensive wooden counter that occupied the entire west wall. The clerk wore a smudged white shirt, vest and equally soiled apron.

"Good morning," he said.

Unsure whether it was, in fact, still morning, Collins responded in kind.

"Are you in need of supplies?" the clerk queried.

"I am. Quite an amount as it happens. I am curious, though, who is the proprietor of this establishment?"

"Mr. George W. Maxwell. He is over in Santa Fe at the moment."

"I see."

Strolling around and perusing the shelves, barrels, baskets and boxes, C.W. began to gather items and place them in an open space upon the sprawling countertop, crowded by boxes of cigars, tins of biscuits, granite wear pots and wax coated wheels of cheese. When requested, the clerk removed assorted commodities and provisions from shelves behind him and added them to the growing collection. Most especially, Collins augmented his procurements with a goodly supply of tobacco, coffee and ammunition.

When he had paid for the supplies, the clerk voluntarily aided Collins in transporting and loading his purchases. The young man was adept at packing and securing a top load and they rapidly completed their task. After expressing sincere gratitude for his assistance, Collins tightened his cinches and swung into the saddle. He passed back through the military post, nodding to a few of the soldiers, then made his way toward the northeast along the military road that followed the course of the Río Bonito. He hummed a lilting Irish tune as he rode, his heart gladdened by contemplation of finally going home.

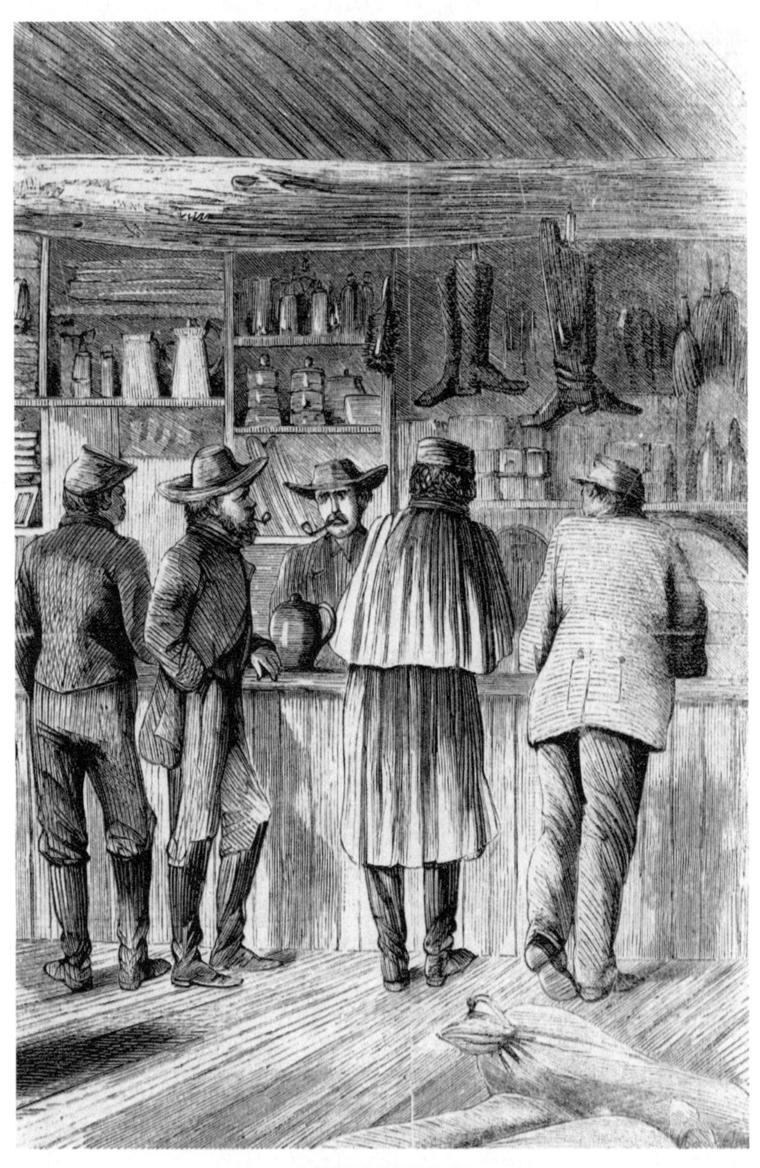

MERCANTILE

37

It was a premeditated risk, but Collins departed the last water source at Patos Spring and angled across open plains, using his compass to guide him. If he kept to a persistent northeastern course, he would inevitably reach the Pecos River. The more practical route would have taken him along the Río Hondo to the Pecos, but that would have meant journeying through regions prowled by rustlers and other sundry outlaws. Dr. Blazer had duly warned him of the danger. Supplied with full water bags, including two additional receptacles purchased at the sutler's, he planned to ride during the morning and evening and rest during the heat of the day, gauging the distance at around seventy-five miles of desolate country.

After perusing the map the night before in his camp at the spring, he had decided to take the gamble. He set out at daybreak and, as the Sacramento and Capitan mountains retreated into the horizon, Collins once more traversed flat, tedious land without trees or remarkable features. His mind was swiftly beleaguered by the torpidity of boredom and he began to ruminate upon the early colonization of *Nuevo Mexico*. He had read W.W.H. Davis' estimable book, The *Spanish Conquest of New Mexico* and reviewed in his mind such information as he was able to recall. He remembered the tale of Stephen, a colored slave and trusted envoy of the Franciscan friar, Marcos de Niza. During Niza's expedition to find *Cibola*, one of the mythical cities of gold assiduously sought by avaricious Spanish adventurers, Stephen had come to the vicinity of a great pueblo of the Zuñi people. After he had sent a gourd talisman ahead as a token of amity, his overture had been precipitously spurned by the Zuñi. The head man had supposedly delivered a message back that they knew what kind of people the Spanish were and if any of them came to the village, they would be put to death.

Undeterred, Stephen and an entourage of around three hundred Indian slaves proceeded to the pueblo and he was straightaway made prisoner. Stripped of all possessions and interrogated as to his purposes, Stephen had spoken of the might and erudition of the Spanish king. Certain he was a spy for a country that sought to conquer them and appalled by his arrogant deportment and unabashed demands for riches and women, the head men kept him imprisoned. Following a period of a few days, the Zuñi ordered his execution, but the plan somehow disintegrated into the massacre of all of the negro's followers, except for three of the Indian slaves. The author Davis claimed he had gleaned the particulars of Stephen's story from the journals of the friar, who never made it to the village. According to Niza's writings, however, upon learning of Stephen's death, he had surveyed the pueblo from a neighboring mountain. The imaginative Franciscan had reported seeing people of light complexion who were adorned with an abundance of jewels, possessed many vessels of gold and silver, and resided in great houses built of stone.

Niza's fictions, as related to Don Francisco Coronado and many others, inspired the viceroy of New Spain to sanction an expedition to conquer Cibola, appointing Coronado as captain-general. Coronado's excursion led to a succession of lamentable incursions, slaughter, thievery and abuse. Collins was less captivated by the causal sequence that inspired these dire consequences for the Native peoples of the region than he was by the implied knowledge of Spanish intentions and motives as expressed in the suspicion and wrath of the Zuñi leaders. Through miscellaneous sources, he had become aware that European trade goods had come into the possession of tribes in North America long before colonizers made contact with them, attesting to extensive and established channels of exchange throughout the Indian domains. Tragically, the same was true for diseases that traversed vast territories. Would it be so improbable then, he pondered, to infer that the Zuñi knew of Spanish purposes through barter with southern Indian bands, especially those who had been preyed upon and enslaved by Spanish conquerors?

By late morning, he came across an old wagon road not indicated on his map. It headed in a northeasterly direction and provided smoother footing for his animals, so C.W. began to follow its track. Just to the west, he noticed a small range of hills, darkened by stands of juniper trees. The sun blazed down upon them more intensely as the day wore on. When it was nearing its zenith, he arrived at a wide and steep arroyo that bisected the road and decided to use it for shelter. Riding along its perimeter, he found an animal trail down into the wash and chose a sandy dogleg in which to rest until the cooler hours of the afternoon. The opposite margin of the wash provided some nominal grazing for his horse and mule, despite the tenacious drought. After unloading and unsaddling Molly and Ulysses, he watered them, fed them some oats and turned them loose to forage for whatever palatable vegetation they could find.

Having cut and peeled two willow rods the day before, he shoved them into the soft sand and used them to construct a lean-to, stretching a piggin' string between the poles to support the canvas of his shelter tent and securing the back edge with rocks. Unrolling his bedroll for a couch, Collins removed his holster and hat and stretched out in the shade. Although not particularly apprehensive about interlopers, having seen no horse or human tracks along the trail, he kept his revolver and Winchester handy, not inclined to forget his recent capture by Apache warriors.

When he awoke from a peaceable nap, Collins found Molly dozing with her head in the shade of the elevated periphery of the shelter. Ulysses, unable to wedge in beside her, stood perpendicular, his eyes closed and his lower lip slack. Shooing off the animals, he scrambled out of his shelter and was assailed by the glare of blanched sunlight. Even though the day remained blistering, it was somewhat tempered by an escalating breeze, so he ate a quick meal of hard tack, jerky and tepid coffee from a canteen, packed up his primitive camp and prepared to resume his journey.

Back in the saddle, he reckoned it would take a good nine hours or so to reach the Pecos River, barring unforeseen occurrences, which meant that by traveling until he could no longer make out the trail, he would come to the river by the following midday. There would be only a bare sliver of moon, providing inadequate illumination for riding much past sundown. Nudging Ulysses out of the bottom of the wash, he scanned the dreary, parched countryside stretching interminably before him. Sighing in resignation, C.W. located the old road and submitted unwillingly to the cadence of horse hooves upon the sun baked and wind-scoured terrain. Swirls of sand danced across the desert like wraiths, occasionally lifting bits of dried brush and carrying them far overhead. Perspiration trickled down his cheeks from beneath his Stetson, evaporating almost instantly.

As a means to stay awake, he once more returned to his reflections upon William W. H. Davis' book of history. For several years after the expedition of Coronado, assemblages of clerics and mercenaries, aflame with greed for mineral wealth or missionary fervor, blundered through much of the same territory. They persisted in offending and pillaging the Indian populations of the region. Then, in the spring of 1598, Don Juan de Oñate made a monumental foray north along the Río Grande, accompanied by four hundred soldiers, one hundred and thirty families of colonists, ten Franciscan friars and hundreds of goats, sheep, cattle, oxen, horses, mules and pigs. He established a camp at the confluence of the Chama river and Río Grande beside a Tegua village and the multitude settled down to build houses, farm crops and raise livestock. The outpost allegedly flourished, but in spite of this, numerous soldiers deserted.

Not long after the colony was begun, many of the Spaniards embarked upon a quest for precious metals, forsaking their agricultural labors. Meanwhile, Oñate set out to explore the eastern plains and other Indian villages. Davis' history described Oñate's subjugation of native inhabitants along the way as well as the undaunted zeal of the Franciscan missionaries. Although not included in Davis' account, Collins had read elsewhere that one of the pueblos had resisted, killing several Spaniards. In retaliation, Oñate attacked and burned the village, killing over six hundred Indians. In the aftermath, he ordered that every male Indian of the pueblo have his right foot hacked off. Many of the women and children were pressed into slavery. Resulting from the barbarity of these reprisals, Oñate was eventually banished from New Mexico by King Philip of Spain. Collins considered this a small enough price to pay, given the heinous nature of his crimes.

Even though the wagon road was barely visible along segments of the route, it kept an invariable course to the northeast and permitted Collins' woolgathering more than if he had had to navigate the unremarkable landscape. As the afternoon dragged on, Collins stopped frequently to water the animals, drink from his canteen of coffee, stretch his legs and moisten the scarf around his neck. Thoughts of Oñate's offenses reminded him of Davis' account of the Indian revolt that took place in 1680. The Spaniards, it seemed, did not prove to be kindly or generous overlords. They proscribed native religious practices, destroyed sacred icons, exploited the Indians as slaves, demanded tithes of food and goods, compelled conversion to Christianity and executed or publicly scourged Indian men accused of witchcraft.

By means of a cleverly planned and coordinated assault, many pueblos rose up simultaneously, killing around four hundred Spanish settlers and many Franciscan missionaries. Churches and Christian imagery were demolished. Surviving colonists were driven south to the northern border of Mexico and, until Spanish conquerors returned in 1692, the Indians had a reprieve from foreign subjugation and tyranny. Even after the reconquest, the uprising led to greater autonomy of religious beliefs and provincial sovereignty for the pueblo Indians.

His thoughts turned from the Spanish conquest of New Mexico to the invasion of Anglos that ironically began with another Stephen, General Stephen Watts Kearny, who had arrived at the head of the Army of the West back in '46 and claimed the area for the United States. Later, as forts were constructed and the Indians were continually beleaguered and rounded up by military troops, more and more white settlers moved into the newly established New Mexico Territory. Many men, such as Martin at Alemán and John Sullivan at Cañada Alamosa, stayed to seek economic opportunities after they were discharged from the army. Others, like Chisum, came from Texas to build empires on country purloined from the Indians. For over two hundred and fifty years, the original inhabitants of the land had been displaced and otherwise killed, oppressed and maligned, with no end in sight.

With the approach of evening, Collins knew he was probably about ten miles shy of the Pecos River. He had been conserving water and Molly and Ulysses would soon require a greater quantity, so he pushed on, even though he and his animals were weary. Dismounting, he led them for a couple of miles to spare his gelding. A near encounter with a rattlesnake inspired him to climb back into the saddle, especially as Ulysses almost pulled free of his grip on the reins in panic. Twilight was almost upon them and Collins was somnolent with fatigue when a high-pitched and unmistakable sound, one that provoked a fierce reaction of instinct, splintered the incessant howling of the wind.

Hunkering down upon the horse's neck and wrapping the mule's rope tightly around the saddle horn, Collins urged the animals into a dead run, keeping to the road, predominantly unimpeded by cactus and vegetation. There was another sharp report from a big bore rifle and he experienced searing pain in his left shoulder. Ulysses sprang forward with renewed vigor and Molly pressed him from behind. There was no shelter but distance and nightfall. Switching the reins to his right hand, Collins gritted his teeth against the agony of his wound and remained firm in the saddle as yards, then miles, sped beneath them. Finally, he knew he could no longer ask his horse and mule to bear up under the arduous pace and he reined in, drawing his Colt and bending his horse to study the country behind him.

The darkening skyline was vacant. C.W. could spy neither human form nor dust trail. In spite of this, he felt utterly exposed. Molly and Ulysses stood with heads hanging, sides heaving and white with lather from their exertions. Blood dripped from the fingers of his left hand and sweat nearly blinded him. Allowing his animals to catch their wind, he kicked his feet free of the stirrups and slid down from the horse, retrieved the canvas bucket and filled it from the last water bag. While Molly and Ulysses drank, Collins took a long gulp from a canteen, his gun close at hand on the seat of the saddle. Reaching the Pecos was now imperative and, attentive to any movement in his periphery, he checked cinches and swung awkwardly into the saddle, determined to keep riding, whether he could see clearly or not. When they had found a redoubt along the river, there would be time to rest and tend to injuries.

He set out again at a fast walk, cradling his left arm. The sun glided beneath the stark margin of horizon, leaving in its wake a golden band of radiance that faded into the blue black of impending obscurity. Taking a last reading of his compass by the lingering light, Collins aimed his horse and endeavored to keep to the road, ever vigilant for sounds of pursuit. He began to sense encroaching weakness from blood loss, but with a greater measure of safety in the shroud of night, he refused to halt for any reason. They plodded onward and once the stars came out, he located Polaris, using it to orient himself. As the hours wore on, it became difficult to concentrate and his horse faltered more often.

Without any comprehension of passing time, adrift within exhaustion and the dreadful throbbing of his shoulder, he was suddenly revived by the scent of riverine vegetation and moist earth. He could just make out duskier shadows before him that he thought must be a riparian tree line. Near to swooning, Collins swung down and guided his exhausted animals into a bower of dense cottonwoods, stumbling more than once over deadwood and underbrush. With barely enough strength remaining, he clumsily undid ropes and cinches and heaved Molly's packsaddle to the ground along with its entire load. Then, having managed to unsaddle Ulysses, he turned them loose. With his last dogged groping, he drank the residual water from a canteen, unrolled his bedding, wrapped his right hand around the Winchester and surrendered to a blackness more profound than that of the night.

OUTLAWS

38

Sunlight, filtering through lush foliage of branches above him, roused Collins from insentience. His first thought was of his horse and mule and he came slowly to his feet, wincing at the pull of his shirt sleeve bonded to the dried blood of the wound. Surveying the surroundings, he caught sight of his animals beneath an antiquated cottonwood tree, swishing flies and grazing upon grasses interspersed among undergrowth along the riverbank. He filled a canteen from a pool and sat back down on the bedroll to minister to his wound. By soaking the caked blood of his sleeve, he was able to pull the fabric loose and used his Green River knife to gingerly cut away the cloth to expose the injury.

Upon examination, he could see that the bullet had dug a furrow through his flesh, but no trace of the projectile remained. Although it had bled a good amount and caused a substantial degree of pain, the ragged graze was far from lethal, as long as he could avoid suppuration. Whoever shot him might be tracking him and Collins was loath to start a fire in order to sear the wound, so he washed the gash thoroughly then worked a slug loose from a cartridge with his knife and sprinkled gunpowder into the bloody trough. When he struck a match to ignite it, he muffled an involuntary outcry in the crook of his other arm.

After he had awkwardly bandaged his shoulder with strips from the ruined shirt, donned a clean set of clothes and eaten some dried meat and hard tack, Collins grained and picketed the horse and mule. He backtracked along his trail from the night before, crouching low and using brush for cover. Climbing the embankment of the flood-plain and lying flat, he scrutinized the landscape with his field glasses. Aside from a herd of antelope, he could see nothing. Favoring his shoulder, C.W. scrambled back down to the protection of the river bottom and set about packing up.

It was nearly the middle of the day when Collins was ready to depart his sanctuary. His wound hampered preparations, but his animals were patient and he, at last, was able to accomplish the now arduous tasks of breaking his meager camp. He clambered to the rim of the bank one last time to survey his trail and, reassured he was not being tracked, he mounted up and headed north beside the river. When the undergrowth became too thick, he was periodically forced onto higher ground, but retreated back down to concealment along the riparian area whenever possible.

Certainly, Collins thought as he rode, the occasion of being a recipient of gunfire was not novel for him, but the attempt to dry-gulch him was bothersome. He could think of no one who had cause to pursue him. The encounter with Coghlan and his men made him suspect his attack-ers were of a similar ilk, ever on the lookout for opportune victims and unguarded prey. Outlaws had been drawn to New Mexico Territory since its inception, roaming the inhospitable countryside and defying rudimentary laws enforced by inconsistent and often corrupt local authori-ties. It was not uncommon for lawmen, and even military men, to become engaged in questionable dealings outside civilized parameters. In the end, he surmised, there was small doubt that he had nearly suffered the same fate as his young Apache friend.

Coming upon the head gate of an irrigation ditch, an indication of proximate farming, he abandoned the river bottom and rodc out toward the west, intent on evading the town that was once the location of Fort Sumner and reservation for the Navajo and Apache people. While a member of the secret service during the war, Collins had had the misfortune of being dispatched by General Grant to reconnoiter conditions there and it was at this time he had met Cadete, the Mescalero chief, and they had become friends. His detailed report about the abysmal circumstances at the reservation had supported further investigations by a congressional committee and the subsequent decision to close the fort.

Not long ago, Collins had learned that a man named Lucien Maxwell purchased the old buildings in 1870 before he died. Maxwell had been, in Collins' estimation, a rogue, an opportunist and a land speculator of the first magnitude, coming into possession of a colossal Spanish land grant through marriage and providential acquisition. A boon companion of both John Frémont and Christopher Carson, he had been a member of the '42 expedition into the Rocky Mountains that explored the uncharted interior of the west. The man had been yet another vanguard of American expansionism willing to exploit Indians and Spanish colonists alike.

By keeping to the west bank of the Pecos, he was able to circumvent the town and reunite with the old Goodnight Loving cattle trail. Collins made an early camp in a secluded canyon and awoke much refreshed. His injury was less troublesome and the indulgences of hot food and coffee improved his spirits. He was pleased to find Molly and Ulysses were recovering from their ordeal. Neither had thrown a shoe and a thorough inspection reassured him they had not been chafed nor suffered any lasting harm from their desperate flight.

Three uneventful days of travel, during which he eluded villages and fellow humans, brought him back to the town of Las Vegas. Collins settled his animals, saddles and packs in the J.S. Duncan stables and ambled the dusty streets in earnest hope of finding Santiago Duran. At the railroad depot, he queried a Mexican man as to his whereabouts, but the fellow merely shrugged. He purchased accommodations for his animals and himself aboard a north bound train departing on the following day. Then, toting his carpetbag and rifle, Collins walked across the bridge over the Gallinas River and to the plaza, where he booked lodging in the Exchange Hotel.

Immediately after depositing his possessions in the hotel room, he availed himself of the tonsorial services and bathing amenities in Judd's Barber Shop, situated off the lobby. When he was once more suitable for civilized company, Collins climbed the stairs to the office of Dr. Skipwith, situated above the Herbert and Company Druggists on the plaza.

"This is an ugly laceration. Gunshot?" the doctor inquired.

"From a rifle, I believe," Collins answered, presuming the man hailed from Boston by his accent. "I never had the pleasure of confronting my assailant."

The elderly gentleman's eyeglasses recurrently slipped down the bridge of his nose, forcing him to wrinkle his muzzle in a comical fashion in order to thrust them back into position. "I have had many such injuries of late," he said, prodding the wound with an instrument and causing C.W. to wince. "It appears to be healing soundly. It is well up on your shoulder and exhibits no sign of infection. It has been cauterized. Did you do it?"

"With gunpowder."

Dr. Skipwith studied him momentarily, once more gimbling the eyeglasses back up his nose. "How did you know to do this?"

"I was in the war."

"Ah yes, that would explain it. I will stitch the wound so that it closes more efficiently. Do you require laudanum?"

"No."

Upon leaving the doctor's office, he espied a passing cart below, pulled by two burros. The animals were escorted by a small boy and Collins thought he remembered the youngster from before. Descending the steps two at a time, C.W. caught up with the lad.

"Pardon me," he said, "Do you speak English? *Hablas inglés?*"

The young man smiled. "Yes. I speak very well."

"Do you know *Señor* Santiago Duran? I am looking for him."

The smile faded from the boy's countenance and he removed his tattered straw hat. "*Señor* Duran he died a week ago. *Lo siento, señor.* I am very sorry. *Asi le toco.*"

"*Gracias*," Collins said and touched the boy's shoulder lightly.

Walking back toward the hotel, he experienced genuine sorrow at the death of a man he had known only briefly. Santiago had offered friendship and advice and had inspired a sense of camaraderie in return. It was the final pathos of his inauspicious and harrowing foray into New Mexico Territory and the weight of it was stultifying.

HON. CARL SCHURZ

39

The railway carriage offered few comforts and a surplus of passengers.   Collins claimed an unoccupied
bench seat, arranging himself by the window, and placed
his valise beside him as a barrier to anyone drawn to
sharing accommodations with him.   It was early afternoon and, as a veteran of train travel, both opulent and
humble, he had packed his carpetbag with a canteen
of coffee, apples, a wedge of cheese, jerked beef, a tin
of Huntley and Palmers biscuits, writing paper and stylographic pen.   There were a series of jerks and thuds,
after which the car began to move.

Having purchased an April copy of Harper's Weekly,
noting that the cover satirized anti-Chinese sentiment
as espoused by one Denis Kearney, he made use of the
journal as a support for composing a letter to Secretary
Schurz.

Atchison, Topeka and Santa Fe Railway
New Mexico Territory
June 12th, 1880

Department of the Interior
Honorable Carl Schurz
Washington D.C.

    Sir;

In compliance with requests made by you and Commissioner Trowbridge, I journeyed by rail to New Mexico Territory, arriving 16th ultimo, and proceeded south by horse.

I met with Victorio in San Mateo Mountains and beg to inform you that this chief refuses to accept aught but permanent residence at Ojo Caliente. Until such is granted, the band of Apaches will not submit. I learned from a citizen of Cañada Alamosa and Agent Russell at South Fork that Victorio was persisting in offers of surrender as recently as January and March.

I have telegraphed a dispatch to Commissioner Trowbridge reporting I have ascertained that Agent Russell has, in my judgement, been very unjustly censured. I believe him to be an honest man, who has conscientiously endeavoured to discharge the difficult and important duties assigned him to the very best of his ability. I also am of the opinion that acts of unnecessary cruelty were perpetrated upon the Indians at the Mescalero agency and many were killed unnecessarily. I have come to this conclusion through discussions with Dr. Joseph Blazer, Colonel Edward Hatch, Agent Samuel Russell, Dr. Carter, M.D., and Mescalero Apache Indians.

I anticipate return to Montana Territory no later than 17th instant and will compose and submit final record and accounting for settlement at that time. Additional correspondence will be pending.

Your Obedient Servant,
Charles Wolfe Collins

In anticipation of the opportunity to post his missive in Denver, C.W. folded the letter and slipped it into an envelope. After penning Schurz' address on the exterior, he placed it in an inside pocket. Removing his Stetson and resting it upon its crown on the valise, he smoothed down his hair, took off his jacket and pivoted to gaze out the window. Miles of dreary, drought-stricken countryside slid by as Collins meditated upon the preceding days, barely able to credit that a mere month had transpired since he had come to New Mexico. He was listless and downcast and thoughts of Jackrabbit, Santiago and the plight of the Apache peoples beleaguered his spirit. So as to curtail this lugubrious proclivity, he opened the periodical.

Within its pages, he found illustrations of artifacts on display in the new Metropolitan Museum of Art in New York City. Vases, sarcophagi and jewelry from different periods and regions of the world were featured. Collins could not help but think of Prince Albert's Great Exhibition of 1851 and wondered whether the museum would also be a self-congratulatory salute to Anglo superiority and ingenuity. He skimmed past an installment of facile fiction and began to peruse advertisements in the back by way of distraction. He marveled at the breadth and variety of products, manufactured goods, commodities, services, tonics and implements competing for the American dollar. Even a cure for a morphine habit was being offered by a certain Dr. Stephens in Lebanon, Ohio.

"Where are you bound?" a proximate voice inquired. Mildly startled, Collins glanced around to find a pretty woman, seated behind him and leaning forward. She appeared to be in her thirties and bore an air of confidence. Her clothing was practical and sturdy and her hat was sensible.

"Forgive me," she said, "but I am mortally jaded with observing the landscape and none of our fellow passengers interest me. You interest me."

Turning on the seat and resting his arm across the back of the bench in order to face the woman, Collins said, "That is quite all right. I do not, however, wish to disappoint your expectations."

She smiled. "I have no expectations. My name is Olivia Cooper."

"Charles Collins."

"Good afternoon, Mr. Collins. I must state that I am wealthy, independent and lacking in most admirable female traits."

Collins grinned in spite of himself. "I am no great enthusiast of admirable female traits."

"Most excellent. Now, tell me where you are bound."

Intrigued and contentedly sidetracked from his own doleful turn of mind, he speculated upon the quantity of information he should share with this impertinent but appealing woman. "I am bound for Montana Territory and an unpretentious ranch near Deer Lodge."

"And where have you been? I really must insist you submit to my interrogations. It is the only method by which I will not perish from tedium."

"I am newly returned from a perilous journey into the wilderness of New Mexico."

"There is a small amount of blood staining your shirt. Just there," she said, pointing to his left shoulder.

"It is a gunshot wound. It continues to seep. I beg your pardon."

"No need. I knew you were decidedly interesting, Mr. Collins. Who shot you?"

"I cannot say. I was shot at a distance and was obliged to run for it."

"Indians?"

"Outlaws, I suspect. They probably coveted my horse and mule and the rest of my outfit."

"And for what reason were you on a perilous journey into the wilderness?"

"Oh come now," Collins said chidingly. "May I not ask a few questions?"

Olivia stood, and leaving her portmanteau and overcoat upon her seat, came around to perch on the end of Collins' bench. Taking the hint, he placed his valise on the floor at his feet and put on his hat. She moved closer and he could smell perfumed soap. Her brown hair was haphazardly bunched up under her hat, her skin was more sun kissed than was fashionable and tiny lines graced her eyes and mouth. He found her beguiling.

"You may ask a single question," the woman said.

"Why are you on this train?"

"I thought perhaps I would have a notable experience in Las Vegas. I had heard it was a wicked town and full of bandits."

"You are capricious then."

She cut her eyes at him with a spark of defiance. "I know what I want. Does that make me capricious?"

Perhaps, he thought with disenchantment, this woman was a flighty and willful dilettante.

She scowled, as if reading his thoughts. "No, Mr. Collins, I am not a risible adventuress. I am a journalist and write for the Rocky Mountain News... under a gentleman's name of course."

"Oliver, I would expect."

"Clever," she said, giving him a wry look.

"And is not the current owner of the News a gentleman named Cooper?"

"Too clever by far."

"And did you, indeed, have a notable experience in Las Vegas?"

"You have now asked several questions," Olivia observed. "I suppose it was a tad notable. Not, it seems, as notable as yours." She leaned in closer to him. "Now enlighten me. What undertaking took you to such dangerous climes?"

Collins examined the woman a moment. He thought he could possibly describe something of his recent ventures. Perhaps, if he related details of crimes against the Apaches and the murder of his friend, she may pen a narrative for the newspaper, thereby counterbalancing

the relentless vitriol widely circulated about Indians, especially Apaches.

"Very well," he said, and began to tell her as much of
his latest undertaking as he saw fit.

40

When Miss Cooper disembarked in Denver, her indomitable levity seemed to have diminished and she appeared somewhat chastened. Although unrepentant that his ingenuous portrayal of events in New Mexico had disabused the woman of certain opinions, he had found her to be pleasant company and was sorry their association could not have been prolonged. They exchanged their goodbyes and made promises to correspond, which Collins knew would soon be abandoned.

The remainder of his journey consisted of deadening ennui, stalwart evasion of contact with fellow travelers, scrupulous care of his animals, composition of detailed reports for Commissioner Trowbridge and Secretary Schurz and the perusal of assorted newspapers purchased along the route. When, at last, he rode out of the forlorn and disorderly hamlet of Terminus, Collins experienced a sensation of buoyancy and the persistent dull ache between his temples vanished felicitously.

Molly and Ulysses, having benefitted from the ministrations of an obliging blacksmith and their prolonged indolence, gave the impression of sharing C.W.'s renewed spirit. The gelding, in particular, tossed his head and blew air through his lips raucously and repeatedly. The miles passed by congenially while Collins admired the mountainous landscape and abundant vegetation, and he was amply grateful for a respite from imminent danger. Although eager for a reunion with Peng and his cherished animals, he carefully chose campgrounds graced by vibrant beauty as balm for his much-abated fortitude and abounding in lush grasses and bordered by pristine streams for his stock.

As his habitual equipoise began to slowly reassert itself, Collins urged his gelding into a faster pace and he rode into Deer Lodge by midafternoon of the third day. After retrieving his post and purchasing a few more supplies, he headed out of town, chafing now at the distance yet to travel and concerned for the welfare of his Chinese friend after so long an absence. When the buildings of his ranch finally came into view and he found they appeared as he had left them, Collins' anxiety was greatly assuaged. At the first gate, he dismounted, loosened cinches and led his gelding and mule into confines of his very own sanctuary.

He crossed to the next pasture, scattered with pairs of cows and their maturing calves, and was pleased at the apparent health of the small herd. He could see Joey, Felix and Mona grazing in the next field and his heart eased. As he neared the corrals, frantic yipping pierced the air and a delirious canine threw herself against his legs. Kneeling down, Collins joyfully embraced his little dog as she wriggled and squirmed and licked with enthusiasm. As soon as Gal had calmed a bit, he took his animals into the cool of the barn and began to undo the lash ropes on Molly's packs.

There was a slight noise behind him and he heard a quiet voice say, "*Huángjīn wàn liǎng róngyì dé, yí gè zhīxīn zuì nán xún.* Gold is easy to get; a close friend is harder to find. I am exceedingly glad you have returned."

Turning to see Wú Peng in the doorway, C.W. stepped over and took the man's hand in both of his. "It is good to see you, my friend," he said with genuine emotion. "Are you well?"

"I am very well and all here is exceptionally correct and superbly decorous."

"That is splendid," Collins said, grinning broadly.

Peng assisted him with unloading and unsaddling Ulysses and Molly. They turned them loose in the pasture with the other mules and Mona. The animals engaged in the customary equine rituals of renewed acquaintance and Peng and Collins leaned on the rail fence and watched, with Gal sitting close by.

"A person has come," the Chinese man said after a while.

"Who is it?" Collins asked, vaguely alarmed.

"A person who is, at this instance, hunting in the mountains."

Drawing breath and summoning patience, Collins said, "And you will not reveal the identity of this person?"

"Not yet," Peng said enigmatically.

Incapable of being truly annoyed with the man and finding no particular reason for concern, C.W. gathered his valise and other belongings from the packs on the barn floor. "There are some supplies in the panniers," he told Peng.

Walking together to the house, Wú Peng related details of stewarding the ranch, narrated comical tales about various animals and reassured Collins that there had been no recurrence of attempted interference or violence from intruders.

"I have become very proficient in the use of my magnificent little weapon," Peng said.

"I am pleased. And, it seems, you have taken excellent care of my dog."

"It is my belief she has taken excellent care of me. We have been most delighted in each other's company."

They went into the house and Collins stowed his gear in a corner. He was taken aback by the methodical tidiness of the interior. "I give you my heartfelt gratitude for the care you have given our home," he told Peng.

Bowing slightly, the Chinese man beamed and said, "You have used the designation of 'our home.' I am most indebted."

Collins sat at the table and gratefully accepted the cup of coffee placed before him. "It is I who am indebted, Wú Peng."

Gal leaned against his leg and he rubbed an ear. He packed his pipe and and smoked, watching as the Chinese man arranged the new provisions and began to prepare food. Without prompting, he abruptly began to unburden himself to Peng, relating all his travails and tales of near demise on more than one occasion. His voice choked with grief in the retelling of his discovery of the Apache boy's dead body.

"To be alive is to endure hardship," Peng finally said after listening to the narrative with acute concentration and empathetic silence. "It seems that the people who desire wealth and ascendancy must always abolish true prosperity. There is a saying... to draw a snake and add legs. When a person cannot perceive what is already correct, they endeavor to improve only to become more dispossessed."

"You are a wise man, Peng. Shakespeare wrote, 'So that in venturing ill we leave to be the things we are for that which we expect; and this ambitious foul infirmity, in having much, torments us with defect of that we have: so then we do neglect the thing we have; and, all for want of wit, make something nothing by augmenting it.' I believe you expressed the very same sentiment."

The dog barked and the door opened unexpectedly. Collins was dumbfounded to see his esteemed friend, Wakalyapi, framed in the entryway. The Indian woman was burdened by a deer carcass, already skinned and eviscerated. Her crooked mouth, drawn down on one side by an old scar, broke into a sincere and wholehearted smile of affection and she slung her kill onto the floor as Collins stood to clasp her shoulders and pull her into an embrace.

"A person has come," Peng said.

"Jesus, Mary and Joseph... you are truly here," Collins exclaimed, stepping back and studying the woman. "How are you here?"

Wú Peng gently ushered Arbuckles to a chair and poured her a cup of coffee. "This celebrated person has been here for many days. She has provided superb assistance and protection."

Sitting back down, as yet unable to give credence to her presence, Collins shook his head. "This is truly an auspicious homecoming. I am delighted you are here."

"Your letter found me," Wakalyapi told him.

He smiled at her wearily, gently stroking his dog.

"How is it, Charles?"

" 'None can cure their harms by wailing them,' " he said, telling her much with his eyes. "Suffice it to say, I fulfilled my duty as mandated. And, as ever, the rampant iniquities therein have riven my loyalties and trodden upon my moral compass." He took out his tobacco pouch and handed it to her. "How is it with you?"

PERSONAE NON GRATAE

The End

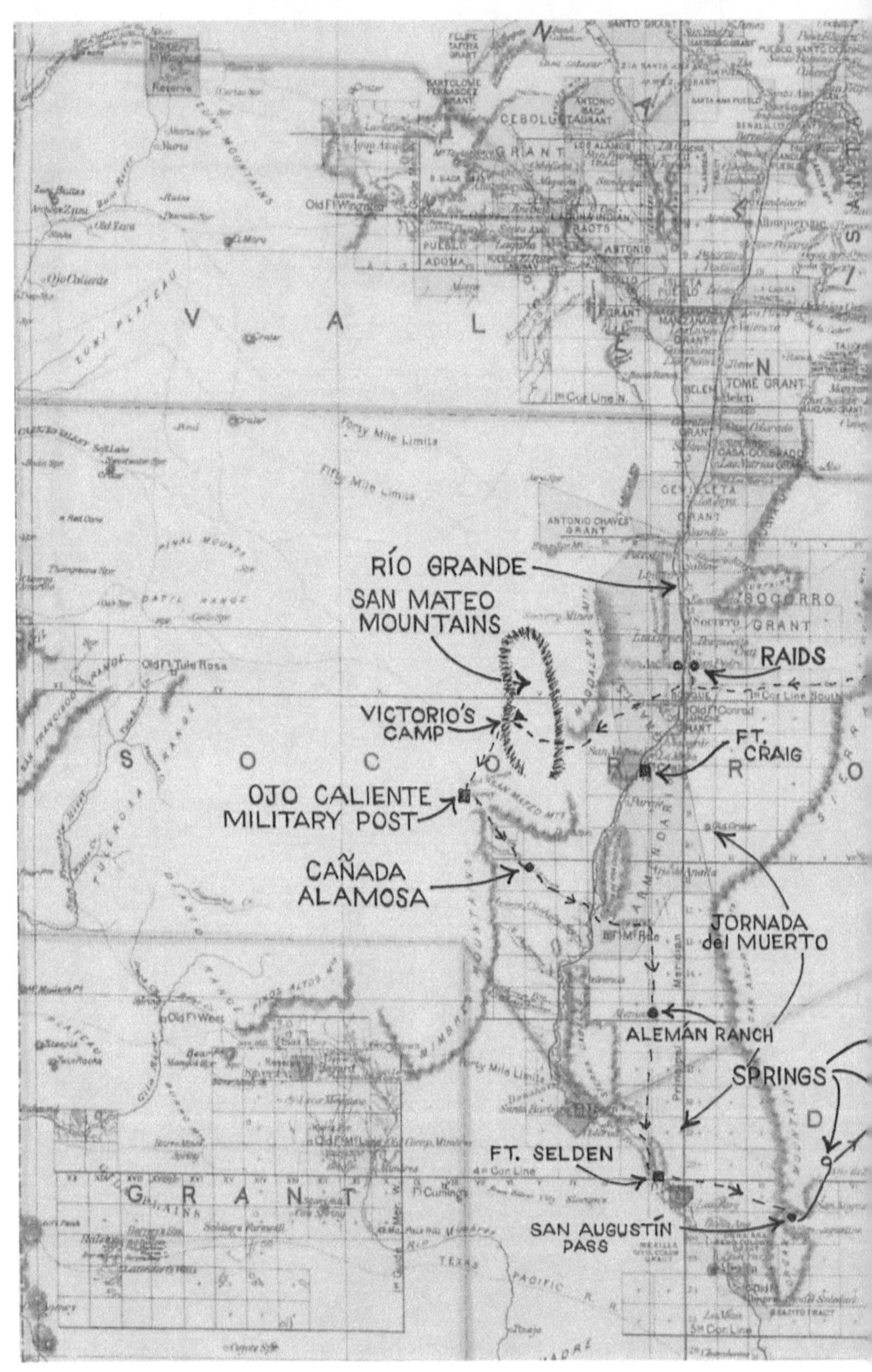

Thayer's Map of New Mexico 1880, Courtesy the Barry Lawrence Ruderman Map Collection,

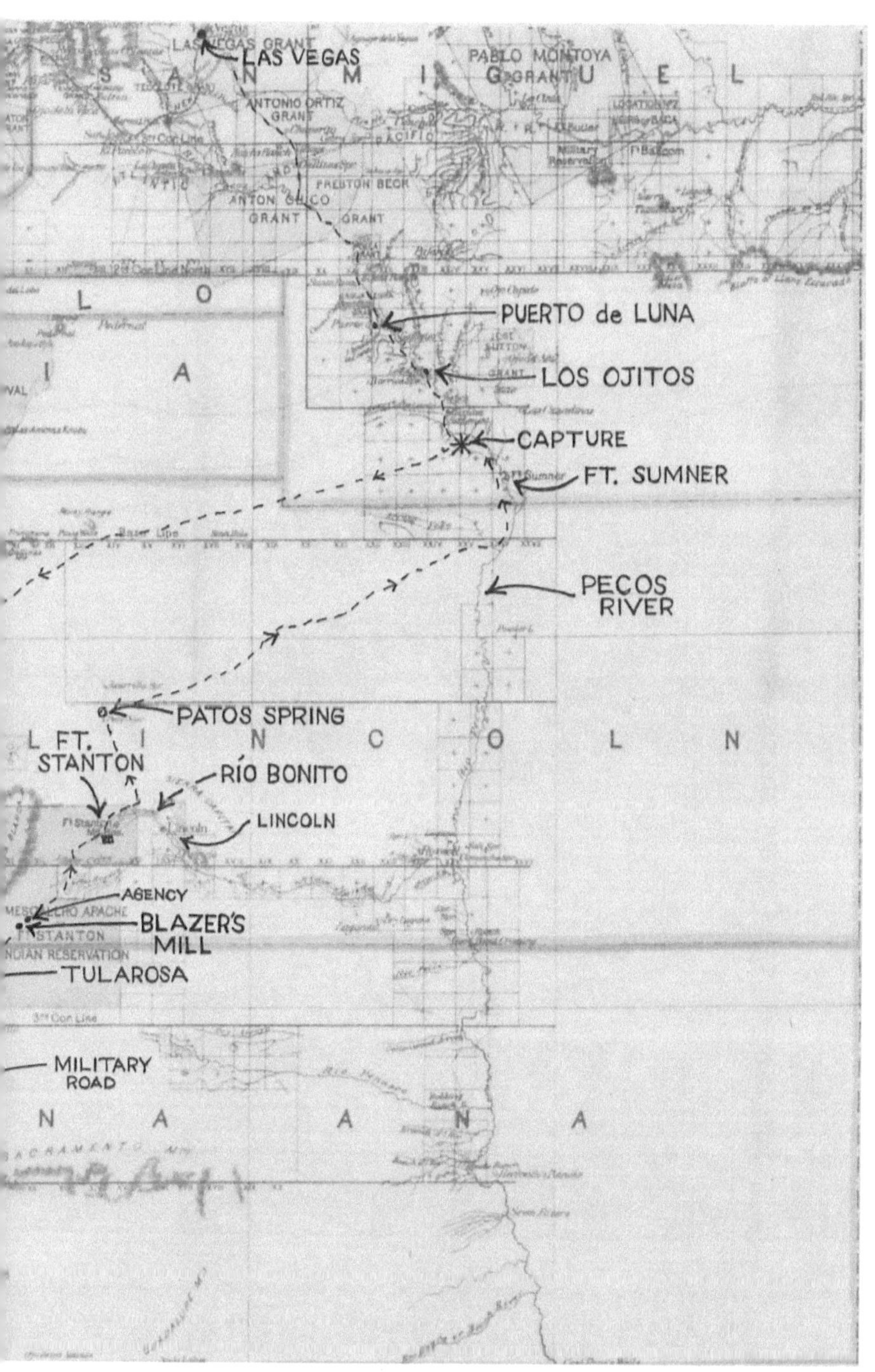

LAS VEGAS
PUERTO de LUNA
LOS OJITOS
CAPTURE
FT. SUMNER
PECOS RIVER
PATOS SPRING
FT. STANTON
RÍO BONITO
LINCOLN
AGENCY
BLAZER'S MILL
TULAROSA
MILITARY ROAD

WHEN MANIFEST DESTINY FAILS

Epilogue

Throughout the summer of 1880, Victorio and his warriors kept ahead of Colonel Hatch's 9th Cavalry and Colonel Grierson with the 10th Cavalry, raiding, depredating and fighting occasional skirmishes with the military. The soldiers ultimately chased him from New Mexico into Texas and, at one point, Grierson led his troopers on a forced march of 1,500 miles, exposing them to severe heat, lack of water and deleterious exhaustion. Victorio used his knowledge of west Texas and the Guadalupe, Carrizo and Quitman mountains to evade pursuit until Grierson cornered the Chíhenne at a place called Rattlesnake Springs. After a three hour pitched battle, the Apache retreated to the Carrizo Mountains and made their way south into Mexico. Almost immediately, Colonel Joaquín Terrazas, head of the Chihuahua volunteer militia, took up the chase after he commanded that pursuing U.S. troops to return to American territory. He eventually tracked the Chíhenne to the Candelaria Mountains, a well-known Apache refuge about sixty miles south of the border of Texas.

In October, Terrazas and the militia finally surrounded the Apache at Cerros Tres Castillos, killing Victorio and, after the Apache fought a prolonged and resolute battle of defense, slaughtering over sixty warriors and around twenty women and children. Sixty-eight prisoners were sold into slavery in Mexico. Some of the Mescalero and Chíhenne Apache who were in the battle managed to escape and several Chíhenne, including the respected chief Nana, were absent on a separate raid, thereby surviving to initiate a campaign of revenge. Rumors still circulate that Victorio committed suicide at Tres Castillos, but given cultural prohibitions for such an act and the man's proven courage in the face of dire circumstances, it is highly unlikely. A direct descendant of Victorio has adamantly refuted the possibility.

Willing to settle on a reservation situated on traditional lands surrounding sacred hot springs at the base of the San Mateo Mountains, the Chíhenne avoided conflict until the U.S. government repeatedly failed to honor agreements and sought to confine them away from their homelands. Victorio fought to protect the sovereign right of a free people to live as and where they chose, refusing to abide by the edicts of settler-colonists determined to exploit all the natural resources of New Mexico Territory and imprison its original inhabitants. He was a superb strategist, distinguished leader and resolute resistance fighter and remains one of America's most notable Native paragons.

Although I entertain strong convictions on the merits of the controversy which has resulted in this Indian war, I do not consider it my duty to express them in this report, but think it would be well for the Secretary of the Interior to ascertain what were the engagements entered into and the promises made by the agents of that department from the time of General Howard's mission to this band of Apaches down to the late outbreak. It is probable that much would be developed by such investigation to extenuate at least the feeling, if not the conduct of the tribe.

Meantime the military forces, under the present condition of affairs, have only to continue the pursuit and, if possible the capture of the band...It has been the hardship of pursuit... the breaking down of horses, and finally of men, and not success of the Indians in battle, which has protracted this pursuit of Victoria so long. The near refuge in Mexico, swiftly and easily attained... has still further embarrassed military operations, and will probably continue to do so.

The force of Indians with Victoria is certainly less than two hundred men. The last heard of them indicated that they were in the Candelaria Mountains of old Mexico, west of Fort Quitman.

(General John Pope, Commander Department of the Missouri. Taken from Report of the Secretary of War, 1880.)

The undersigned citizens of Southern New Mexico would most respectfully and urgently present to your Excellency the following statement. – That hostile Apaches under Victoria have been and are now being reinforced from the Apaches reservation and are becoming bolder and more aggressive and merciless in their raids on our settlements. That during the past two weeks some fifteen of our people have been murdered by these savages. Large herds have been scattered or wantonly shot down. Miners and farmers driven from their homes and their property destroyed and whole communities are terrorized and have suspended their usual avocations to watch and guard against hostile Indians. About eighty of our citizens have gone as volunteers to the rescue of settlements nearly a hundred miles distant. They were left unprotected by the troops and were attacked by these Indians. That the troops now in the field have been operating against Victoria for several months and have entirely failed either to subdue or punish him or to protect our people from his murderous raids. We do not believe that the true gravity and dangers of the situation have been correctly reported through military or official channels and we would therefore beg your Excellency to heed our statement and petition and cause to be sent to our aid a sufficient force to speedily conquer these Indians and restore peace to this afflicted portion of our territory.

(Letter written by citizens of New Mexico Territory to President Rutherford B. Hayes, spring 1880)

There have been some persons killed by the Indians and some stock taken in this long chase but most of the reports from that section are now, and always have been the grossest exaggerations.

(General John Pope, Commander Department of the Missouri, to Adjutant General of the Army, 1880)

The Mescalero Apache remained virtual prisoners for many months, under armed military guard. They continuously requested more freedom and inquired whether they would have their horses returned to them. In early September of 1880, they were finally allowed to venture short distances from the vicinity of the agency headquarters, which was later extended to an eight mile limit. The Mescalero were not, however, allowed to approach white ranches nor use any roads. By autumn, some of the people who had escaped the reservation during the incidents of April 16 began to drift back to the agency having heard rumors that weapons for hunting and, perhaps, some horses might be provided to them. It was not until January 17, 1881 that soldiers were eventually removed from the agency. The Mescalero Apache were never able to reclaim the horses or guns that had been taken from them.

By early winter of 1880, Agent Samuel Russell was considering resigning his post. Many of the Mescalero resented him for what they perceived as a betrayal following the guarantees he had made to them prior to the disarming and confiscation of their horses. Because Colonel Hatch had preempted Russell's promise to return their arms and livestock after the troubles with Victorio were resolved, the agent had lost credibility. In addition, Russell was still contending with interference from local settlers, trespass of gold prospectors on the reservation, whisky peddling, disintegrating infrastructure and an intractable Indian Bureau. In his mid-sixties, Agent Russell had already served as agent for the Utes at Abiquiu and was, apparently, prepared to return to civilization. He submitted his resignation on December 27, 1880. Due to delays, Russell was unable to depart until the new agent, William Llewellyn, assumed charge on June 23 of 1881.

On June 16, 1880, the Adjutant General of the United States Army forwarded correspondence to General Pope from Agent Russell and Commissioner Trowbridge "relative to the disarming and dismounting of Indians at the Mescalero Ind. agency" with an endorsement requesting that the Commander of the Department of the Missouri, General Pope, call on Colonel Hatch to report his version of "the facts attending the occupation by the military of the Mescalero agency, and whether unnecessary cruelty was perpetrated by any under his command on the persons of innocent Indians."

On December 7, 1880, instructions from the Secretary of War were transmitted to the General of the Army, W.T. Sherman, to investigate Agent Russell's and U.S. Indian Inspector J. L. Mahan's reports about "acts of unnecessary cruelty" during the military proceedings of April 16. U.S. Indian Inspector J.L. Mahan had submitted a report specifying that Colonel Hatch had no right to go onto the reservation and demand that the Indians "living quietly and peaceably upon lands they had been told belonged to them" to give up their weapons and horses, especially for the use of the army.

Sherman responded by citing Colonel Hatch's own reports concerning the events and asserting that no further action was required, adding, "unless specific charges and specifications are preferred by some responsible party and a General Court Martial ordered by the President." No further action was ever taken and the affair was permanently concluded.

White settlers, military officers and Indian agents made many attempts to have the Mescalero Apache removed from their traditional domain. Encroachment, lack of agricultural lands, lawlessness and the trespass of miners were some of the reasons this was seriously considered. The most compelling motives undoubtedly involved the beauty, natural resources and ideal location of the Mescalero Apache Reservation.

The agency occupies a central position in a very mountainous region, being situated between the White and Sacramento Mountains, which are mostly covered by cedar and a variety of pine, of all sizes, and in many places of large growth. The numerous ravines, gorges, and cañons afford excellent hiding places for Indians, and, everything considered, the reservation is, if civilization is the object, the most unsuitable place that could have been selected. The Mescalero-Apaches should, therefore, be removed, without delay, to another reservation, where they can be kept under proper control by the agent, or guarded, if necessary, until they settle down and become peaceable. So long as the present reservation is retained for them they will continue to be troublesome. The Indians, however, are not the only thieves who infest the country; there are many other persons in the vicinity of the Indian reservation who make a business of stealing stock alike from citizens and the Indians; and others who are always ready to purchase stolen stock or other stolen property from the Indians, giving them in exchange either whisky or guns, pistols, and ammunition. It 1s not surprising, therefore, that the Indians, with all their savage proclivities and propensity to steal, should, under such circumstances, continue to engage in the business.

(Colonel Benjamin Grierson, Commander Department of Texas. Report of the Secretary of War, 1880.)

This agency will not be a complete success until it is removed from the main road and comparatively out of the reach of the influence of designing and unscrupulous persons, both Americans and Mexicans, as has been recommended in my former annual reports, and to which I would respectfully call your attention. I am fully satisfied that these Indians are tractable and obedient, and by removing these outside influences their civilization could be advanced rapidly. The Indians of this agency have been so annoyed by raids, &c., that they are very suspicious, and will not place confidence in any stranger.

(F. C. Godfroy, United States Indian Agent. 1878 Report of the Commissioner of Indian Affairs)

This reservation is well suited to wild, roving Indians, but a more unfavorable locality for an Indian reservation could scarcely have been found in the whole country, if selected with reference to civilizing the Indians and encouraging them to become self-supporting by engaging in agriculture. The reservation is a large one for the number of Indians, being some 40 miles square (perhaps larger), and yet there is less than 600 acres of land (exclusive of that owned by white men) within the reservation that can be brought into cultivation. Of this some 300 acres would have to be under-drained at a heavy expense, and could then only be cultivated in small grain and the hardier vegetables on account of the elevation. This would be less than two acres for each family. There is now in cultivation about 80 acres. This can be increased at a comparatively small expense to 220 acres. This would give less than one acre to each family, while with the present aversion to work this is sufficient. It will be seen by this statement that if all were disposed to work there is not enough land for them. Is not this statement of facts the strongest possible argument in favor of their removal to the Indian Territory?

(S. A. Russell, United States Indian Agent, 1879 Report of the Commissioner of Indian Affairs)

If placed on that reservation it will be very difficult for them to enter Texas or Mexico upon raids, should they be so disposed, without passing in the vicinity of one of the military posts situated in Southern New Mexico. I there-fore recommend the advisability of considering the question of the removal of the Mescalero Indians to the Hot Springs Reservation, and that a council be held with representative members of the tribe, with the view of obtaining their consent to the proposed change.

(E. M. Marble, Acting Commissioner of Indian Affairs, 1880 Report of Commissioner of Indian Affairs.)

I wish to call attention to the fact that some Indians in Arizona and New Mexico have always been troublesome and difficult to manage, lawless Indians, belonging to no particular reservation, and desperate white men compose bands of marauders who commit depredations and when pursued fly to the mountains of Chihuahua and Sonora. My opinion is that the most effectual remedy for all this is to remove the Mescalero Apaches, and eventually all other Indians, north of the center line of New Mexico and Arizona, so as to keep them at a distance from Chihuahua and Sonora. The removal of the Mescaleros would not seem to be difficult of accomplishment, inasmuch as a special Indian agent, who was recently dispatched to their agency for the purpose of ascertaining their views upon the subject of removal, reports them as expressing a willingness to remove to the Jicarilla Reservation on the north line of New Mexico. For the past five years the office has been importuned to take measures for the removal of the Mescaleros from their present reservation and settle them permanently on some other reserve, where they can be more easily guarded and will be far less liable to commit depredations. The citizens of New Mexico and Texas have urged this, and the military authorities have regarded such a movement as indispensable to the protection of the citizens and the welfare and good conduct of the Indians. The county of Lincoln, in which this reservation is situated, has for a population the very worst elements that can be found in the Territory or upon the borders of Mexico Spanish and Mexican refugees from justice, outlaws from the States, &c. In brief, as stated by Inspector Watkins, who made a thorough investigation of affairs in that section and that reservation in 1878, "the whole county of Lincoln is under the control of cut-throats and thieves." He was also of the opinion, concurred in by many others who have been personally cognizant of affairs there, that a large share of the crimes committed by this class of settlers are charged to the Indians. There is abundant evidence before the office to show that these outlaws have for years been in the habit of enticing the Indians to go out upon their raids, &c., and are the recipients of their plunder. Indians under such circumstances and with such surroundings will not progress very far in civilization. The result has been that over one-half of these Indians within the past five years have been scattered and exterminated; depredations have been committed by them, and large sums of money have been expended by the government in military operations against them. If removed to the Jicarilla Reservation, one agent can take charge of the two bands, Mescaleros and Jicarillas (the former affiliate well with most of the latter and have intermarried), and the cost of removal will be less than the proposed expenditure for buildings and for troops to guard the Indians where they are. The agent of the Mescaleros and our special agent advised the office, when the removal to the Jicarilla Reservation was first contemplated, that the military at Fort Stanton and certain persons who have large contracts with that branch of the service would prevent such removal if possible and, as predicted, these influences are now busily at work to prolong the disastrous state of affairs which for the past ten years have existed in Southern New Mexico, to continue the large expenditures resulting therefrom, and to prevent the government from settling the question now and permanently. The Indian problem is at best difficult of solution; but by removing the Indians from unfavorable surroundings and bad men, as far as possible, a long step will have been taken in the direction of success.

(H. Price, Commissioner of Indian Affairs. 1881 Report of the Commissioner of Indian Affairs)

Commissioner Price was apparently cognizant that certain individuals in the area had a vested interest in keeping the Mescalero Apache where they were, due to lucrative military contracts; a great boon to local settlers, cattlemen and rustlers. Considering some of them had political connections within the Santa Fe Ring, the fact that the reservation was never moved may be owing to their influence.

Gold and silver deposits were discovered within the boundaries of the Mescalero Apache Reservation in 1879. Civilians and military men alike had been illegally prospecting and soon several mining camps were established on reservation lands, later becoming towns such as Nogal, White Oaks and Bonito City. The correct boundaries of the reservation were challenged and if soldiers were dispatched to remove the trespasser, the miners would simply return after the troopers had left. In December of 1880, a petition signed by 160 men was sent to President Hayes requesting the abolishment of the Mescalero Reservation or, if this was not possible, that mineral rich portions be returned to public domain. Prior to his departure in 1881, Agent Russell informed the Indian Bureau that flocks of miners were swarming into the reservation.

William Llewellyn, Russell's replacement, reported that Nogal Cañon was occupied by a blacksmith shop, forty houses and a supply store. Subsequent efforts to expel the Mescalero people from their reservation came to naught, but in May of 1882, President Chester Arthur issued an executive order that redefined reservation boundaries in order to legitimately open up the mining districts to white settlement. On March 24, 1883, President Arthur officially established the reservation boundaries that remain intact today, embracing 463,000 acres.

The southwestern region of North America, encompassing what is now Texas, Arizona, northern Mexico and New Mexico, was home to the Mescalero Apache for hundreds of years. Hunters and gatherers, the Spanish colonists named them Mescalero after their staple food prepared from the root of the mescal plant. The four sacred mountains, Three Sisters Mountain, Oscura Mountain, Sierra Blanca and the Guadalupe Mountains formed the center of Mescalero traditional lands.

In the 1881 Report of the Commissioner of Indian Affairs, Agent William Llewellyn wrote the following:

> Within the boundary lines of this reservation is included what is called the " garden spot" of New Mexico. The Sierra Blanca range of mountains extend from the north line of the reservation south to the Rio Tularosa, and the Sacramento Mountains extend south from the Rio Tularosa to and beyond the southern line of the reservation. Fine grass lands, excellent water, forests of grand timber, small, fertile, well-watered valleys and lofty mountain peaks constitute the general physical features of the reservation... Bear, elk, and deer abound. In considering these facts, together with the well-known healthfullness of the country, is it to be wondered at that these Indians love the mountains and are loth to surrender to the whites this their home?

WILLIAM TECUMSEH SHERMAN
COMMANDING GENERAL OF US ARMY

Author's Note

Native American, Chinese, African-American and Hispanic readers will hopefully understand that any denigrating or otherwise objectionable terminology in this text is used to illustrate prejudices and attitudes of the historical period within which this story occurs and were endemic to the writing of the time. It should be noted that all documentation and newspaper references during the period of this book used the term "Mexican" for residents of Spanish descent in the American Southwest.

Almost without exception, the name "Victoria" was written in the reports of the commissioner of Indian affairs and secretary of war, military correspondence and newspaper articles, therefore in direct quotes this is not misspelling on the part of the author.

According to at least one direct descendant of the great chief, the famous photo that is supposedly of Victorio is actually not his image. According to this reliable source, the Apache leader would never allow his photo to be taken, much the same as Crazy Horse of the Oglala nation and Santana, a principal chief of the Mescalero Apache.

Although not every white inhabitant of the 19th century American West was literate, it must be said that perusal of popular literature, magazines and newspapers of the period reveals the average reader must have certainly been capable of comprehending a sophisticated style of writing that incorporated somewhat erudite vocabulary. The two most popular books in the West were the collected works of William Shakespeare and the Bible. Harpers Weekly and many newspapers, favored by residents of dusty towns and ranches scattered across the frontier, offered serialized stories written by authors such as Charles Dickens, Thomas Hardy and Lord Lytton and poetry by Alfred Tennyson. Also, education was highly valued in the West of the 1800s, as evidenced by the Salina, Kansas Eighth-Grade Final Exam from 1895. https://www.grc.nasa.gov/WWW/K-12/p_test/1895_Eightgr_test.htm

Following a visit to America in 1831, Alexis de Tocqueville wrote, "There is hardly a pioneer's hut which does not contain a few odd volumes of Shakspere. I remember that I read the feudal play of Henry V for the first time in a log house."

Apache nations and languages are diverse and should not be considered homogenized. Although Chiricahua, Lipan and Mescalero Apache people are all members of the Mescalero Apache Tribe, they retain their own cultural identities. *Chihende* is the Mescalero word for the Red Paint (*Chihenne*) people.

All versions of the events of April 16, 1880 that took place on the Mescalero Reservation are taken from actual testimony recorded in documentation preserved by the National Archives and Family Search and the annual reports of the secretary of war and commissioner of Indian affairs.

The Río Tularosa runs through the Mescalero Apache Reservation. The Tularosa River is located near the western border of New Mexico.

The Spanish language dialogue included in this book is unique to northern New Mexico. It is known as "Cervantes Spanish," after the author Miguel de Cervantes, because the language spoken by Spanish colonists remained isolated and virtually unchanged for hundreds of years and still does not include words for modern items and concepts. For example, it is not unusual to hear words such as *carro* for a car, *trõcka* for pickup truck and *lõnché* for lunch throughout northern areas of the state.

In this book, the dialogue that freely mixes English with dialectic Spanish is indicative of common linguistic patterns that have existed in New Mexico for centuries. The reader will notice that the speaker will often clarify in English what he has previously just said in Spanish.

Although the Apache consultant and direct descendant of Victorio, who was of such great assistance in language, history and culture, wishes to remain anonymous, the author extends sincere gratitude to this individual.

Many, many thanks to Mr. Arthur Blazer, former president of the Mescalero Apache Tribe, for his assistance and support. Mr. Blazer's great-great grandfather was Dr. Joseph Blazer, a pivotal figure in this history.

Thank you to Roberto Chavez and Juana Hernandez for clarifying and providing dialectic Spanish.

Thank you to Teddy Moreno, Library Specialist at New Mexico State University and Heather McClure of the Fray Angélico Chávez History Library in the New Mexico History Museum for digitized documentation and creative research.

Heartfelt thanks to Dr. Bruce Johansen for his precise editing, consistent support and advice.

Much gratitude to Dr. Jeffrey M. Sanders for years of generous friendship and the incredible assembly of valuable resource materials.

Thank you to Lynda A. Sánchez for her interest and kind words.

Of course, abiding and unreserved gratitude to my husband for his encouragement and artistic talent.

And last but not least, credit must be given to the small army of patient dogs who encircle my desk and provide creative inspiration.

Additional Reading

NOTE: The combined post-contact history of Apache cultural groups in the American Southwest, spanning hundreds of years, is extremely complex and a comprehensive overview is difficult to achieve. It is the author's opinion that the Geronimo resistance period has received disproportionate attention, thereby marginalizing other history that is equally compelling and that highlights the valiant struggle of all Apache nations to resist absolute subjugation.

Victorio and the Mimbres Apaches by Dan L. Thrapp

Conquest of Apacheria by Dan L. Thrapp

Indeh, an Apache Odyssey by Eve Ball, with Nora Henn and Lynda A. Sánchez

Apache Legends and Lore of Southern New Mexico, From the Sacred Mountain by Lynda A. Sánchez

Victorio, Recollections of a Warm Springs Apache, By Eve Ball

"Victorio's Military and Political Leadership of the Warm Springs Apaches" by Robert N. Watt, *War in History*, vol. 18, no. 4, 2011, pp. 457–94. JSTOR, http://www.jstor.org/stable/26098284.

Santana, War Chief of the Mescalero Apache by Almer Blazer, edited by A.R. Pruit

The Mescalero Apaches by C.L. Sonnichsen

Tularosa by C.L. Sonnichsen

From Cochise to Geronimo, The Chiricahua Apaches 1874-

1886 by Edwin R. Sweeney

The Official Website of the Mescalero Apache Tribe
https://mescaleroapachetribe.com

NOTE: For an exploration of dominant prejudices of the historical period and defective notions held by early writers about the Apache, read:

History of Arizona and New Mexico, 1530-1888 by Hubert Howe Bancroft

Apache Days and After by Thomas Cruse

Life among the Apaches by John C. Cremony

The Spanish Conquest of New Mexico by W.W.H. David

Also investigate the following:
https://digitalrepository.unm.edu/nm_newspapers/
and https://www.coloradohistoricnewspapers.org/

The Discretion Series

The Series is an accumulation of engaging stories intended to challenge pre-existing cultural and historical generalizations, especially regarding American Indian peoples. While intended to educate as well as entertain, these novels are eminently provocative, comprehensively researched and woven into the fabric of the 19th century West, populated by noteworthy historical figures, compelling events and vivid landscapes. The reader becomes immersed in the language, daily existence and predominant societal perspectives of the waning days of the American West. Most importantly, Native American cultures and languages are respectfully portrayed throughout the series via the author's own indigenous worldview, personal experience, accurate research and consultation with mentors from specific tribal nations.

Two books in the Discretion series were finalists in the High Plains Book Awards for 2022 and 2023. The series was a finalist in the Next Generation Indie Book Awards for 2024 and includes *Commendable Discretion*, With *Great Discretion* and *Small Light of Discretion*. *Discretion is Valor* is the fourth book to date.

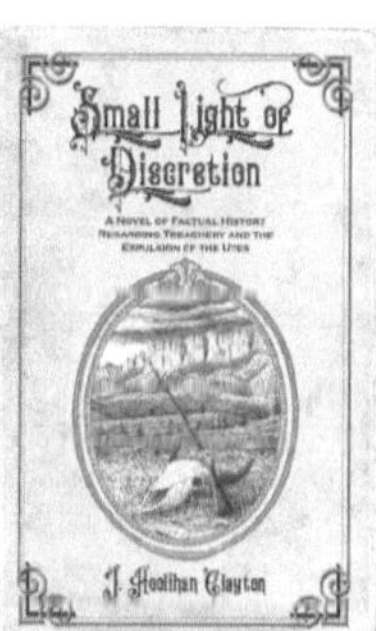

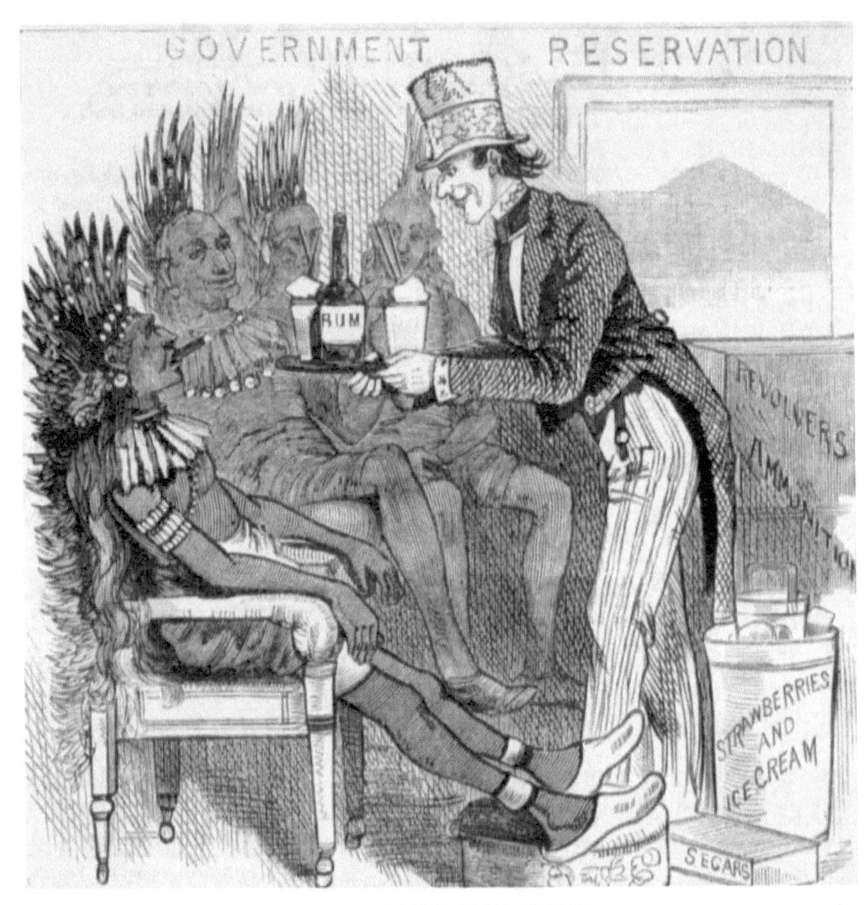

DECEPTIVE RENDERING

About the Author

Juliana "Hoolihan" Clayton

J. Hoolihan Clayton is First Nations Plains Cree. Adopted by a white family and raised on a cattle ranch in Wyoming, she has lived a diverse and authentic life in the American West as a cowboy and wildland firefighter. With a degree from the University of Montana, she taught history and Native American studies for several years. Hoolihan now works full time as an author and research consultant.

POISON

List of Illustrations

PAGE 326: DECEPTIVE RENDERING, *Frank Leslie's Illustrated Newspaper*

PAGE 328: POISON, *Frank Leslie's Illustrated Newspaper*

Illustrations from *Harpers Weekly* are used with explicit permission, and are available through the Library of Congress (LOC) Prints & Photographs Reading Room, Prints and Photographs Division, Prints & Photographs Online Catalogue.

Readers Comments

From the first sentence, J. Hoolihan Clayton grabs the reader's imagination, telling this story with rare beauty. Hoolihan is a steadfast historian and, with a singular talent, creates a compelling narrative, weaving lessons of history from which readers may derive instruction from America's searing past as well as anticipate a precarious future. Read and enjoy, but never surrender the book's implications.

> Dr. Bruce E. Johansen, Research Professor, emeritus
> Communication, Environmental, and Native American
> Studies
> University of Nebraska, Omaha

With a specific writing style that takes the reader, and sometimes with compelling force, into the minds of her characters, J. Hoolihan Clayton helps you feel the anguish and understand the courage of the Apache people as they scattered across New Mexico, running, fighting and hoping to survive to do battle another day.

> Lynda A. Sánchez, author, historian and educator
> True West Preservation Project in the Nation, 2007
> L. Bradford Prince Historic Preservation Award, 2008
> Lincoln, New Mexico

J. Hoolihan Clayton incorporates historical research and unique and effective writing in depicting the disturbing offenses endured by the Chíhenne and Mescalero Apache Peoples. The narrative clearly illustrates the unwarranted violence inflicted upon the Chíhenne and Mescalero Apache that tribal leaders were trying to prevent in their fight for survival. Fascinating reading that brings a historical perspective not previously portrayed nor felt.

Arthur "Butch" Blazer, Former President,
    Mescalero Apache Tribe
New Mexico State Forester Jan. 2003 - Dec. 2010
First Native American New Mexico State Forester
USDA Deputy Undersecretary Oct. 2011 - June 2016
    Supervisor - US Forest Service
Santa Fe, New Mexico

Through painstaking and accurate research, the reader becomes completely engrossed in the 19th century American West. J. Hoolihan Clayton uses the vernacular of the era to create a tableau that brings the reader into every scene through exquisite descriptions of sights, smells and sounds. Intertwined in the many twists and turns in the action is rock solid history, cultural competence and suspense.

Jeffrey M. Sanders, Professor Emeritus
Social Sciences and Cultural Studies
Montana State University - Billings

www.ingramcontent.com/pod-product-compliance
Lightning Source LLC
Chambersburg PA
CBHW022007310726
48972CB00006B/1553